ROADKILL

The Dan Warden Series in Chronological Order

Roadkill

Jenny Cay

Digger

The Rogue

The Rampart Alert

Also by Larry Quillen

Snowbound

The Lost People

ROADKILL

**A Dan Warden Novel
By**

Larry Quillen

BookLocker
Trenton, Georgia

Published by BookLocker.com, Inc., Trenton, Georgia.

Printed on acid-free paper.

The characters and events in this book are fictitious. Any similarity to real persons, living or dead, is coincidental and not intended by the author.

BookLocker.com, Inc.
2023

First Edition

For King

ROADKILL

1

Day 1
Wednesday, November 25, 1998

JIM AND MARTHA WORKMAN had spent a cool, overcast day in Pulaski, Tennessee, visiting relatives and buying sorghum molasses. On their way home, they had done some last-minute grocery shopping in preparation for their kids and grandkids showing up for Thanksgiving dinner tomorrow. The store was crowded, so they had gotten back to their small farm west of Bailey Springs, Tennessee, just before sundown. After helping Martha bring in the groceries, Jim built a fire in the fireplace. When he went outside for an armload of firewood it was already dark, and misty rain was getting him wet.

As he headed back inside, Jim saw the distant headlights of a vehicle coming from the north down the two-lane county road. When it was a couple of hundred yards away, it stopped momentarily, then turned into his neighbor's driveway. Jim watched the headlights flickering through the bare trees on his neighbor's property until the vehicle reached the house. The vehicle's lights remained motionless for a moment, then the vehicle vanished in the darkness.

That puzzled Jim. Hal and Bernice weren't home, as far as he knew. Bernice had called Martha yesterday and said they were leaving early this morning to drive down to Mobile to spend Thanksgiving with their oldest boy and his family and wouldn't be back until sometime Sunday. Jim continued to look down the road to his neighbor's house for a couple of minutes, expecting to see the vehicle leave. It didn't. Frowning, he went inside with his load of wood, wondering if he should do something about the vehicle. He had seen robberies on television and in the movies many times, but the idea that he might be witnessing a real robbery and should do something about it was difficult for him to accept.

* * * *

When no one in the darkened house responded to the doorbell chiming and the sound of someone banging on the door several times, Randy Royel and Donny Channel hurried around to the back of the house, then up the steps to an open porch big enough for two cane-bottom rocking chairs and a swing suspended from chains attached to the ceiling. Randy knocked on the kitchen door, waited, and then banged harder. Hearing no sound from within, the two teenagers nodded to each other. Randy tried the knob and felt it turn, but when he pushed on the door it didn't move. The deadbolt was locked.

"You need this?" Donny asked, holding up a pry bar. They had found an unlocked utility shed at their first site. Inside the shed they had found the fifteen-inch tool made of forged steel and had used it to open the back door of the house. It had been with them since. They had learned that most people spent a great deal of money on a substantial front door, but any safety and security that a backdoor offered could usually be defeated with their pry bar.

"Not yet," Randy said, smiling. The door was made of solid wood, but the upper half was composed of six small glass panels that provided some sunlight into an otherwise dark kitchen. One panel was less than six inches from the deadbolt lock. "Piece of cake," he said as he took a roll of masking tape out of his jacket pocket, pulled a strip off, and applied it diagonally to the glass nearest the lock.

"What're you doing?" Donny asked.

"I read about it," Randy explained. "I cut myself last time. The guy in the story put tape on the glass before he busted it. It came out all in one piece for him."

"No shit?"

"I'm about to find out," Randy said as he continued to apply masking tape to the small glass panel, forming a large asterisk. When he was done, he tossed the roll of tape out into the yard and turned to his buddy. "I'll take that pry bar now."

"Let's do it," Donny said, as he handed Randy the tool.

"Number five," Randy said, grinning.

"Number five, man. Go for it!"

Randy paused for an instant, then hit the center of the tape star with the curved end of the pry bar. The safety glass shattered into hundreds of tiny chunks, but, although it was dented inward, it remained in the frame, supported by the tape.

"How about that?" Randy said in amazement as he gently pushed the shattered glass with the pry bar. The entire panel of glass fell inward, leaving only a few crumbs of glass around the edges.

"How about that?" Randy repeated. He gave the tool back to Donny then reached inside the opening, turned the thumb latch on the deadbolt, then opened the door and stepped inside. Donny, right behind him, found the light switch and turned it on. The sudden brightness of the kitchen lights startled them for a moment, but they had agreed to go for the lights this time. They had used flashlights before and were sure they had missed out on some good stuff in the darkness, while at the same time both had banged their shins in the unknown territory of a strange house.

They hurried into the master bedroom and jerked the pillowcases off the king-size pillows. With their loot bags ready, Randy opened the dresser drawers and dumped the contents onto the floor while Donny searched the walk-in closet, pulling everything down from the shelves and allowing it to tumble onto the floor. Donny was admiring a Konica 35mm camera when he heard Randy yell as he opened the drawer of a nightstand.

"All right!"

"What?" Donny asked as he turned to look.

"Paydirt," Randy said, holding up a Colt Cobra .38 Special revolver with a 2" barrel.

"Is it loaded?"

Randy flipped the cylinder open. "Sure as hell is."

Randy shoved the gun into his jacket pocket, then the two boys hurried from the master bedroom in search of other prizes. In the living room, Donny unplugged a VHS videocassette recorder he found next to the television set and put it near the front door. In the second bathroom, he found a box of jewelry in a cabinet drawer. In another bedroom, Randy found an IBM ThinkPad laptop computer with a printer attached. He didn't have a computer and didn't know how to use one, but he closed the computer, unplugged the cables and cords, and added it to his loot bag. The printer was too bulky and heavy for his loot bag so he left it.

Donny grinned when he found a Sony camcorder in a bedroom closet. He'd heard that the new Sony camcorders could, unintentionally, see through thin clothing. "I just might hang on to this," he said.

As Randy ran down the stairs to the den, Donny went to the kitchen and opened cabinets and, using the pry bar, began to pull everything off the shelves onto the floor. He knew there was nothing he wanted on the shelves, but it was a rush to hear the noise and see the destruction. When he was done, the kitchen floor was littered with pots, pans, cans, broken dishes and glass. As he walked back into the living room, Randy came up from the basement. "Find anything?" Donny asked.

"Found a Kodak slide projector," Randy said, holding up his bulging pillowcase. "The old TV down there ain't worth nothing."

Donny picked up the videocassette recorder and slid it down inside his pillowcase along with the pry bar and his other loot. "Let's go. I think we've got everything worth taking, unless you want to go for the big Sony TV over there. It's got to be at least 35 inches, so it's worth a few bucks to the man, but it'll take both of us to carry it out. It's got to weigh a hundred pounds at least."

"Let's do it."

* * * *

Jim Workman was watching television while waiting for supper, but he couldn't concentrate on the program, thinking about the vehicle he had seen pulling into his neighbor's drive. He mentioned it to his wife as she passed through the living room. She offered to call Bernice and he agreed. She waited for the four rings, let the recorder play its message, then said, "Hi, Bernice, it's Martha. Give me a call when you get back." She hung up the phone, then went to a window and looked toward her neighbor's house. Through the misty fog she could see lights on in the house. "I can see some lights, but Bernice didn't answer the phone. She always answers the phone after two rings if she's home," she said and turned to her husband, frowning. "Maybe you ought to call nine-one-one."

"I don't want to look like some snooping fool, sending the sheriff out on some wild goose chase."

"I'd want Bernice to call the sheriff if somebody was in our house when we weren't home."

Jim thought about it for a minute, then said, "I guess I'll call. Hal is going to give me a hard time about it, though, if it ain't nothing."

* * * *

The ringing phone startled the two teenagers. They stood still, frozen in fear while they listened to the voice of the woman on the other end. When the recording ended, they glanced at one another, then grabbed their loot bags and carried them out to the pickup. They hurried back into the house and carried the heavy 35" TV set to the truck as well. Randy leaned on the edge of the truck bed, grinned at Donny and said, "That's about it, except for the starter."

"I'll go check the garage."

"There's a kerosene heater down in the den," Randy said.

"Do you think it's got any kerosene in it?"

"In November? In Tennessee? You want to bet your share of weed against mine it doesn't?" Randy asked, grinning.

"No bet," Donny said.

* * * *

Sergeant Dan Warden of the Creek County Tennessee Sheriff's Department had finished with a nasty accident. A Toyota Corolla, hurrying home over the speed limit on the two-lane county road, had come over the crest of a hill to find a John Deere tractor directly in front of him slowly pulling a trailer with an oversized load of hay bales. In the other lane, a Dodge Ram pickup truck was rapidly approaching both of them. When it was over, the Toyota's nose was tangled with the trailer under bales of hay, the Dodge Ram and more hay were in a ditch, and the farmer was on his way to the Bailey Springs hospital after being ejected backwards onto the road when the Corolla smashed into his trailer.

As the first deputy on the scene, it had been his job to try to sort out what had happened, issue citations, and clear the vehicles and hay from the scene. He was on his way back to the sheriff's station when he got a call from the dispatcher on his two-way radio, asking him to check out a call they had received about possible prowlers at a vacant home on Murphy Road. The dispatcher knew Dan was already on the county road where the call had come from and was within a couple of miles of the location.

As Dan slowly approached the rural mailbox with the right name and number on it in his Chevy Caprice patrol car, he glanced into the foggy mist in his rearview mirror. Seeing no headlights in either direction, he stopped on the roadway in front of the rural mailbox and looked down the one-lane driveway from his side window. The driveway was at least a hundred feet long with a thick growth of trees on both sides. The lights were on in the house, the front door was open, and a small pickup truck was parked near the front door.

As he watched, two young men came out of the house, carrying a large television set. They loaded it in the bed of the pickup truck, paused for a moment, then hurried back inside. Dan turned off his lights, turned into the driveway, then called the dispatcher. He told her a possible burglary was in progress, gave her his location, and requested backup. He grabbed his flashlight, stepped outside his vehicle, closed the door, freed his weapon, and waited.

Dan knew there might be a legitimate reason for their actions. On the other hand, he also knew there was the possibility that these men might be the arsonists and burglars who had destroyed four vacant homes in the rural area of Creek County, Tennessee, within the past year. They had all been suspicious fires, but not much had been made of them until the third one. The volunteer fire department had gotten to it in time to save much of the structure and most of the contents. When the owner discovered he had been burglarized before the fire started, the first two fires were revisited, and a pattern was discovered that was confirmed with the fourth fire a month ago north of Bailey Springs. Someone was burglarizing houses while the occupants were away, then setting them on fire to cover their tracks. The sheriff's department was now taking any reports of prowlers around vacant homes seriously and responding to them quicker than before.

* * * *

The two teenagers hurried down to the den. The kerosene heater was full of fuel. Randy opened the filler cap and tilted the heater. He poured kerosene onto the shag carpet of the den as he carried the heater across it, then continued pouring as he went up the stairs to the master bedroom. He dribbled kerosene on the bed and the clothing he had dumped from the dresser drawers, then carried the heater down the hallway, trailing kerosene, into the other two bedrooms. In the living room, he dumped the remaining kerosene onto the carpet, then tossed the heater aside.

"Your turn to light it," Donny said.

"Get your ass out of here," Randy said as he pulled a small box of matches out of his pocket. "I'm going to do it right now." As Donny waited outside the front door, Randy grabbed several small matches out of the box, lit them and threw them toward the kerosene stain on the living room carpet. As he turned to run, he heard a low thump and felt the hot air of the burning fuel as he ran out the door. Yelling and laughing in exhilaration, both teenagers ran toward the pickup.

"Freeze!" Dan yelled, turning on his flashlight and holding it and his gun side by side in his hands. As he flicked the light from one teenager to the other, he yelled, "Sheriff's Department! Stay right where you are! Down on your knees!"

The two teenagers stopped short of the pickup and looked into the brightness of the deputy's flashlight for about two seconds, then looked at each other, and then both turned and bolted into the woods, in opposite directions.

"Oh, shoot," Dan muttered under his breath. He picked the taller one, simply because he had run into the woods on his side of the driveway. Soon, Dan knew he had lost the boy in the darkness, so he stopped, turned off his flashlight, and listened. Nothing. But it didn't mean the boy had stopped as well. It had been raining off and on all day and the new layer of leaves was soaking wet. The boy could still be running and he wouldn't hear him.

When he heard sirens approaching, Dan decided that, instead of going deeper into the woods, he would move a few yards to one side and wait for reinforcements. He had their truck blocked. The boys wouldn't go far without it. At the same instant Dan moved, he saw the bright muzzle flash of a gun. Simultaneously, he heard the loud report of a handgun and felt flying bark from the tree behind him stinging his neck and the back of his head.

"Sweet Jesus," Dan whispered as he dropped to one knee and aimed his gun toward the muzzle flash. In that instant, Dan knew he was as close to death as he ever had been or ever hoped to be and, at the moment, there wasn't a lot he could do about it. As the high-pitched wail of sirens grew louder, Dan yelled, "You hear that? The whole department is coming to track you down. If you don't give up right now, you won't get out of these woods alive!"

There a pause, then Dan heard a voice call out, "Don't shoot. I give up."

"Walk back toward the house, your hands in the air," Dan demanded. Shortly, he heard the muted rustle of leaves nearby and soon the boy appeared, then continued walking past him toward the house, apparently unaware he had passed close to the deputy. As Dan rose to follow him, he realized why the boy had come so close to shooting him in the darkness. He had been between the boy and the house. The light of the burning house had backlit his silhouette, offering the boy a target in the dark woods.

"Stop right there," Dan growled as he turned on his flashlight and pointed it and his gun at the back of the teenager. The boy quickly complied. Dan made the teenager lie down on the wet leaves and spread his legs, with his hands behind him. With him in that position, Dan handcuffed him, searched him, found a revolver in his jacket pocket, then led him back toward the house, its interior now engulfed in smoke and flames. Another deputy had the other boy in custody. He was crying, cursing, and begging for mercy, all at the same time.

While keeping the two boys separated, first at the fire, then at the sheriff's station, Dan learned that the boys had found a pawnshop owner who would take stolen property in trade for marijuana. The boys smoked most of their profits. What they didn't smoke, they took to school and sold to their classmates for cash. They selected their burglary and arson targets by overhearing their parents, neighbors, and classmates gossiping about friends, neighbors, or family traveling somewhere for some reason. It didn't take much effort for the two boys to find out if the house would be vacant while the family was gone. In total, the two boys had caused over a half-million dollars in property damage for a few hundred dollars of marijuana.

The younger one, Donny Channel, was only fifteen and lived on a farm west of Bailey Springs. His mother was usually there, but his dad was doing time for marijuana dealing. The older one, Randy Royel, was seventeen. He was the leader of a gang of teenage boys that had caused headaches for the Bailey Springs police and the Creek County sheriff's department in the past. Randy's dad had a roofing business and could afford good attorneys who had kept Randy out of jail so far.

* * * *

After returning the patrol car to the sheriff's station and writing his report, Dan headed home in his brown and tan Chevy pickup truck. Once inside the quiet darkness of his rented single-wide mobile home, he performed his usual security checks, then turned on the lights and glanced at his answering machine. He had two messages. He punched the play button, then walked to the kitchen, wondering what there was to eat, if anything.

The first message was a hang-up. The second was a familiar woman's voice: his estranged wife. "Dan? This is May. Elaine called and asked me to bring the kids to your family's Thanksgiving dinner tomorrow. If you want to come over around eleven and drive down with us that would be fine with me."

Finding only dry breakfast cereal, Dan put the bowl, cereal, sugar, and milk on the breakfast bar and sat on a stool. As he poured the milk on the cereal, he watched the carton shake noticeably. He put the carton down, closed his eyes and put his hands to his face. He felt like crying. He knew he wouldn't, but he felt like it. He took his hands away, opened his eyes, and slowly shook his head.

Some punk teenage kid had almost killed him tonight. The muzzle flash in the darkness was etched in his memory. Even now, he thought he could see the bullet coming toward him in slow motion, the way they showed it in the movies sometimes. If he hadn't moved when he did, he would have been dead.

Five counts of burglary, five counts of arson, one count of attempted murder of a law enforcement officer, selling illegal drugs to minors, and a long list of other charges should put them away for a long time. Dan slowly shook his head. They would probably get away with it. The American justice system didn't know how to cope with children committing felonies.

Dan took a deep breath and slowly exhaled. What he needed was to have May and the kids with him. He could hug his boys and tell them how much he loved them, and they would tell him how much they loved him. May would hold him, and he would hold her. She would tell him it would be all right and, somehow, he knew it would be.

But it wasn't what he had. Not anymore. Five months ago, May had gotten fed up with his unwillingness, according to her, to communicate with her about anything that went on in his life, either good or bad. She always got upset when something happened to him on the job and she didn't hear about it until she got it second hand from some other deputy's wife. May didn't understand that being a law enforcement officer was what he did; it wasn't who he was. When he came home at night, he wanted to be a husband and father. Reliving the crap that happened on the job was the last thing he wanted to do in the warmth and safety of his own home.

Now, she and the kids were living in their Bailey Springs house, and he had moved into a rented mobile home across town. Neither had filed for divorce yet, and May let him come over and visit the kids sometimes, but not as often as he would have liked. The phone call was an invitation for him to drive her and the kids down to his uncle's house in Helleston, Alabama, tomorrow for the big Warden family Thanksgiving dinner.

Dan thought it was awfully nice of her to do that, to let his family see the kids on Thanksgiving. Her family lived up around Nashville. She could have driven up there with the kids and spent the day with her folks, but she hadn't. He would have to remember to tell her he appreciated what she was doing for his family. What he wouldn't tell her, or anyone else at the family gathering, was how close he had come to getting his head blown off tonight. Sitting around discussing and dissecting the grim event wasn't his idea of an enjoyable way to spend Thanksgiving with his family.

He sighed, got up, opened another cabinet door, and retrieved a bottle of Jack Daniel's whiskey. She had the house and the kids. He had Jack Daniel's. Jack Daniel's was a good friend to have around when your wife didn't want you around anymore. Ignoring the bowl of cereal, he got a plastic cup and took it and his friend to the couch and put his feet up on the coffee table. He poured a liberal amount of whiskey into the cup and drank it. The fiery liquid felt good as it burned his throat going down. You had to be alive to feel pain. Dan decided it felt wonderful to be alive. If only he didn't have to be alone.

Dan took another sip of whiskey and picked up the newspaper. The Iraqi disarmament crisis was heating up and President Bill Clinton's problems were still on the front page. He had been impeached by the House of Representatives last week for lying under oath to a federal grand jury about his affair with Monica Lewinsky, an unpaid intern with whom he had nearly a dozen sexual encounters in the White House in an area where there were no cameras. The President had already announced that he intended to finish his term.

He tossed the newspaper aside and took another drink. He thought about going down to Uncle Buck's Tavern for a couple of beers, but he knew he wasn't welcome down there, especially on a busy night like tonight. Junior wouldn't kick him out of the honky-tonk bar, but the presence of an off-duty deputy sheriff would put a damper on the evening's fun for everyone while he was there. He never wore his uniform and always drove his Chevy pickup truck when making a social call at the beer joint, but there was always someone there who recognized him and knew he was a deputy sheriff.

As the word got around the bar about the presence of an off-duty deputy, some of the customers would get up and quietly leave for reasons of their own. Dan had gone down to Uncle Buck's a few times since he'd moved out of the house, but he'd always gone with J.D. Montgomery or another deputy so he would have somebody to talk to, and they always picked a slow night so Junior wouldn't get too mad at them.

The noise of the ringing phone startled him. "Yeah?"

"Dan? J.D. The Square Deal Pawnshop down on Greenbrier is just outside the Bailey Springs city limits, which makes it our case. The owner lives above the store. We're heading down there. You want to come along?"

"You've got a warrant already?"

"We told the judge we needed to take a look tonight before the news about the kids hit the airwaves. He wasn't happy, but he signed it."

"When?"

"We're getting ready to roll right now."

"I'll meet you there. I'm going to stop and grab a hamburger."

"Ah, yes, the wonderful life of a bachelor, huh?"

"You can't beat it."

"It's still misty rain and it's starting to get a little foggy. How is it over there?"

"About the same. It wasn't too bad over on Murphy either, but it's usually worse on Greenbrier down toward the state line for some reason."

"You got that right! Man, I've been down there when the soup was so thick I couldn't see the double-stripes more than ten feet in front of my grill. I would drop down to thirty, hoping I could stop in time to keep from hitting someone going slower and praying some nut doing sixty wasn't coming up behind me."

"Been there; done that."

"The beer drinkers down at Uncle Buck's have tomorrow off, so there'll be a rowdy crowd down there tonight. Let's hope they stay between the ditches on their way home."

"They usually do. Lord knows how."

"Hey! I'm outta here."

"See you at the pawnshop."

2

Day 1
Wednesday, November 25

"HEY, JUNIOR! TWO MORE down here!" Jack Constone called out from the bar in a voice loud enough to be heard over the din of noise from the music and the other beer drinkers.

"Hold your horses," the big bartender growled.

Jack thought about making a smart-ass remark to Junior's back, then changed his mind. He knew Junior didn't take crap from anybody. Instead, he turned to Billy Blakeley, his eight-ball partner, and complained. "You'd think he'd hire some help on a busy night like tonight."

"Aw, man. He's as stingy as Uncle Buck ever was," Billy said, then pointed to a framed one-dollar bill behind the bar. "Hell, he's still got the first dollar he ever made."

"Come on, Junior, we're up next!" Jack yelled. He turned to Billy and said, "We're going to win tonight. I just know it. I'm hot, man. I'm making everything in sight. Just don't leave them a good shot. I'll take care of the rest."

"Think you're going to take it tonight, huh?" Junior asked as he set two cold long-neck beers in front of the men, then helped himself to the money on the bar.

"Damn right," Jack said. Then he and Billy grabbed their beers and turned to go.

"Big pot for the winners tonight," Junior called out.

"You hang onto that pot, man, it's ours!" Jack hollered over his shoulder as he and Billy headed back to the pool tables.

"Yeah, right," Junior called out. He watched the two regulars weave their way through the couples on the small parquet dance floor, then disappear into the crowd shooting pool and playing pinball and video games in the large room beyond.

* * * *

Organizing a Wednesday night pool tournament was the best idea Junior had since he bought the place. Like ABC's "Monday Night Football," it gave his customers a reason to drink his beer on an otherwise dull day of the week and low gross night for his bar. Tomorrow was Thanksgiving, though, and most of the men had the day off. It was still early, and he was already as busy as he usually was on a Friday or Saturday night. That was all right with him.

Junior had been a regular at Uncle Buck's Tavern after retiring from the Army as a Sergeant First Class. He had worn a Ranger patch while participating in Operations Desert Shield and Desert Storm. He had gotten married a couple of times over the years but neither of the women understood that they came second to the Army. Both were taking a bite out of his retirement pay now but he still had enough left over to do pretty much whatever he wanted.

He had gotten bored with civilian life and was looking around for something to do with his time and money when he heard that Uncle Buck was thinking about selling his place. By then, Junior knew the Tennessee honky-tonk bar was a friendly place where a country boy could have a few beers, shoot pool with his friends, dance with other men's wives, and forget his troubles for a few hours. Most of the regulars lived across the Tennessee state line, down in Helleston, Alabama, or one of the farming communities in Chickasaw County.

But Chickasaw County, Alabama, was dry; the sale of alcoholic beverages had been illegal since Prohibition. Uncle Buck's Tavern was in Creek County, Tennessee, about sixteen miles north of Helleston. That was why there was a constant stream of traffic northward across the Alabama state line, especially on Friday and Saturday nights, to the Tennessee honky-tonk bar. As long as he stayed out of trouble with Sheriff Johns and his Creek County deputies, and the do-gooders kept voting down the sale of alcohol in Chickasaw County, Junior knew he would do all right.

Fights broke out frequently, especially on weekends. Junior didn't mind his customers having a good fist fight, as long as they took it outside, but anyone using weapons had to deal with him. He knew a man could get beat up on Saturday night and still be able to show up for work on Monday morning. Bruises, black eyes, skinned knuckles, and loose teeth never stopped a man from punching a time clock, but if Sheriff Johns ever had to come and haul away someone's son or husband with a bullet hole in his head or a knife in his gut, he knew the holier-than-thou hypocrites in the county would try to pull his license. If that happened, everything he had worked for would be gone.

* * * *

Thirty minutes later, Jack and Billy came back to the bar, whooping and yelling at the tops of their lungs. When Junior verified that they had won, he threw a stack of bills down on the bar in front of them.

"Hot damn, look at that!" Jack yelled. "That's got to be the biggest pot we've ever won."

"We did it, partner, we did it!" Billy yelled as the two men slapped their palms together in a high-five.

"Come on over here," Jack called out to the two men they had defeated. "Drinks are on us."

"Sounds good to me," one said. "It's raining too hard to leave anyway."

"And the fog's getting so thick you can't see where you're going anyway," the other man said.

"Then we'll sit here and drink all night," Jack proclaimed.

"Damn right," Billy said. "Hey, Junior! Four cold ones, right here!"

"Man, oh man. Is this a great night or what?" Jack asked no one in particular. He lifted the bottle to his mouth, drank long and deep, then banged the bottle down on the bar. "Hey, Junior! Keep them coming!" he yelled, then turned to the three other men. "Hot damn! We're going to drink beer tonight until there's not a dime left on the bar!" Jack watched the big bartender set the beers down amid the clutter on the bar and help himself to some of the money. "Hey, Junior!" Jack cried out in joyful enthusiasm. "Is this a great country or what?"

Junior looked at Jack, then snorted in disgust. "It used to be," he said, then walked away.

*   *   *   *

"What the hell!" Jack cried out as he stabbed his foot toward the brake pedal, missed, then tried again. As the brakes grabbed, all four wheels locked and the worn tires on the pickup truck began to slide on the wet pavement. With a hand that seemed only vaguely connected to his brain, he tried to keep the truck on the two-lane roadway as the rear end slid back and forth across both lanes. When the vehicle came to a halt, he stared at the large red hexagonal STOP sign that had suddenly appeared in the misty rain and fog ahead of him. "What the hell is that thing doing there?" the confused drunk mumbled.

As his brain tried to process the weaving and wandering images in his truck's high beams, Jack looked at the four-lane highway beyond the stop sign and tried to figure out what it was doing there. He didn't remember an intersection like this on his way home to Helleston, Alabama. As he listened to the slap-slap of his wipers clearing away the drops of misty rain collecting on his windshield, he tried to understand what was happening. Forcing his eyelids wide open, he tried to focus on the double image of a rectangular road sign beneath the stop sign. Finally, he closed one eye and squinted. BAILEY SPRINGS 1 MILE.

"Bailey Springs? Why in hell am I going to Bailey Springs, Tennessee?" he mumbled as he looked at the vague shapes of buildings on either side of the road. He didn't recognize any of them. "Hell, I can't even remember leaving the goddamn bar!"

He squinted at the clock on the dashboard but couldn't focus well enough to tell the time.

"Goddamn it!" Jack yelled. He knew Bailey Springs was about eleven miles north of Uncle Buck's, which meant he had been driving in the wrong direction for ten miles. Now, he would have to turn around and drive ten miles back to Uncle Buck's. Once there, he would head down to the Alabama state line and then to Helleston, a fifteen-mile trip that he'd made a few dozen times before. Tonight, it was going to be a thirty-five-mile drive. He didn't need the hassle.

With his pickup heading south once more, Jack stomped on the accelerator. The worn tires spun uselessly on the wet pavement until he took his foot off the accelerator for a moment, then pressed down again, this time more gently. With his left eye closed to eliminate his double-vision, he tried to see the road ahead through the fog and rain. When he did, he saw a rectangular white sign: SPEED LIMIT 50.

Embarrassed at what he had done, he hurried to undo it. If anyone saw him up this way tonight, they might think he had gotten too drunk to know his way home. They wouldn't let him live it down at Uncle Buck's for a long time. Aggravated that he would have to drive an extra twenty miles tonight, and embarrassed that he had turned the wrong way when he had left Uncle Buck's, he pressed the accelerator down until he was doing sixty.

It never occurred to him to wonder how he had driven within a mile of Bailey Springs, Tennessee, tonight with no memory of how he had gotten there. After driving several miles on the winding, hilly, two-lane county road, he began to anticipate reaching Uncle Buck's again, fully intending to stop and have another beer or two while he tried to figure out what was going on tonight.

He could count on one hand the number of times he had been to Bailey Springs, Tennessee, with a couple of fingers left over. He tried to recall the last time and couldn't. He thought it might have been a year or so ago. He couldn't remember why he had been up this way, but his vague

18

recollection of the road was that it wasn't much different from the two-lane county roads in Alabama. Like Alabama, the road was posted at fifty, but most drivers drove at least sixty even though there were dozens of private home driveways, small businesses, and secondary roads intersecting with it.

The only section of the road that stuck in his mind was a curve down toward the Alabama state line. It was so sharp it had a guardrail on the outside of it to keep vehicles doing sixty from launching themselves off the road and down a steep embankment.

As Jack continued south for several minutes, he became aware that the fog was getting thicker. Without being aware of it, he slowed to fifty while trying to see through the fog. He tried switching from high beams to low beams and found he could see better. Then, while passing through a hilly section with trees on both sides of the road, a yellow diamond-shaped sign with an arrow bent to the left suddenly appeared out of the fog with a rectangular sign below it advising: SAFE SPEED 30 MPH. He had found the curve.

He glanced down at his speedometer and saw he was doing fifty. He was in trouble. If he went into the curve at fifty, he wouldn't make it. If he slammed on his brakes, his worn tires would probably hydroplane, and the truck would slide like it was on ice into the curve. He downshifted into second, hoping his transmission would slow him down, so he wouldn't have to use his brakes. As the roaring engine complained about the sudden increase in revolutions per minute, the truck's speed dropped to forty-five as the guardrail on the right shoulder suddenly appeared in his headlights.

Breathing rapidly and gripping the steering wheel with both hands, he squinted to keep his left eye closed as he gently touched the brake pedal. Forty. So far; so good. As he entered the curve with his left-side tires riding the double yellow line, he applied more braking. Bad idea. He felt his rear tires lose traction and slide toward the guardrail. In response, he turned his steering wheel to the right to compensate, then quickly steered back to the left again when it felt like the rear of his truck was heading in the same direction as the front again. By then the right-side tires were riding the white stripe on the outer edge of the road surface and the side of the truck was inches away from the guardrail.

He came out of the curve with his tires still riding the right-hand edge of the pavement. Suddenly, his low-beam headlights lit the dark form of someone standing on the narrow right-side shoulder of the roadway with his arm extended and his thumb up. Jack's panic reaction was to slam on his brakes.

With detached curiosity, as if watching a scene in a movie, he felt his hydroplaning tires sliding uselessly on the wet road as the truck bore down on the man. Jack heard a loud thump and felt the truck shudder momentarily as it slammed into the man. As the truck continued, the body became airborne then hit the side of the cab before it bounced away into the darkness.

"Jesus Christ Almighty! What the hell was that?" Jack continued to brake hard and had to fight his truck to keep it on the road until it stopped. He got out and peered into the foggy haze behind him. "Hey, anybody back there? Anybody hurt?" When he heard nothing, he walked unsteadily around to the front of his truck and immediately noticed his right-side headlight was out. On closer inspection, he saw that the clear plastic covering both the headlight and side light was broken and some of the pieces were missing. Some of the yellow plastic for his turn signal was missing as well. The rectangular chrome frame around the light group was damaged and the sheet metal around it was dented. He had hit something, that was for sure.

Jack found his flashlight in the glove box. When he turned it on, he discovered the batteries still gave him a weak beam of light for a few feet. He lurched and stumbled along the road back toward the curve, his flashlight alternately sweeping across the foggy road and then shining down into the darkness of a steep embankment that became much higher as he approached the guardrail. "Damn, I'm drunk," he mumbled. "If a deputy comes along now, I'm in real trouble."

He had walked almost back to the guard rail before he found what he had hoped he wouldn't find. A man wearing jeans, sneakers, a blue jacket, and a blue backpack was lying on his left side against the brush and dead weeds at the bottom of a steep ten-foot embankment. "Hey! Hey down there! You all right?" There was no answer.

With his flashlight in his right hand, Jack stepped off the narrow shoulder in his high-top work shoes onto a layer of damp leaves and wet clay with his right foot and felt it move down the steep slope several inches before it came to a stop. He aimed the dim light of his flashlight down toward the man. The arms and legs looked unnatural, bent at awkward angles to the body. Trying to see the face in the weak light, Jack cautiously stepped off the shoulder and onto the slippery slope with his left foot. With both feet on the steep slope, he reached out and touched the slope with his fingers to balance himself as he took another step downward with his right foot.

"God damn it!" he cried out as both feet slid down the steep embankment, pushing clay mud and leaves along with them. His feet, and the mound of mud and leaves underneath them, came to a stop against the man's legs and feet.

Bracing himself against the steep bank with his left hand, he pointed the flashlight at the man's head. It was turned away from him, but he could see blood. Trying to get closer to his head, he moved cautiously, one slow step at a time, on the steep slope above the body. However, each time he took a step, the loose soil and leaves gave way, pushing more clay mud and leaves against the body.

When he was near the head, Jack turned the flashlight beam onto the face. "Jesus," he whispered. It might have once been the face of a man, it was hard to tell, it was so mangled and bloody. He took a few more steps until he was closer to the man's head. Then, switching the flashlight from his right hand to his left, Jack reached down and pressed his fingers against the sticky wetness on the side of the man's bloody neck to check for a pulse. There was none. "Oh, my god, what have I done," he said, looking down at the body. Then he looked up at the steep slope. "I'm as drunk as I've ever been. I'm going to jail tonight if I don't get out of here."

He switched the clay-smeared flashlight from his left hand back to his right and looked up at the steep slope of wet clay.

He shook his head, knowing he wouldn't be able to climb up the slippery surface. He pointed his flashlight toward his truck, saw that the bank wasn't nearly as high in that direction, and headed that way. He worked his way through and around brush and dead weeds until the slope was no more than waist high. Holding the flashlight in his right hand, he grabbed a bush with his left and pulled himself up and onto the shoulder of the road.

He stomped and scraped his feet on the road, trying to clear the clay from his high-top work shoes, then he walked back toward the body. He was surprised at what he saw in the dim light of his flashlight, or rather, didn't see. By walking on the steep slope of soft clay above the body, he had pushed a thick ridge of mud and leaves against the body so that it was now almost hidden from view from the road. The only thing he could see was some of the blue backpack and the bare hillside where his shoes had dug holes in the bank above the body.

He looked up at the oak trees above him. In a few days the rest of those leaves would be on the ground, covering the slope again. It would look as though nothing or no one was down there. He frowned as he turned and looked across the road. Above a five-foot clay bank was a steep slope covered with hardwood trees that disappeared in the fog. He wondered if there might be houses up on top of the ridge. Then he smiled. It didn't matter. If someone was up there, they couldn't see him down here any better than he could see them up there.

Jack opened the door to his truck, tossed the sticky flashlight onto the floor, then paused for a moment, wiping the mud, leaf particles, and blood from his hands onto his shirt and pants. Then he got in and drove away. Staring into the rain and fog with only one headlight to show him the way, he shook his head in a moment of remorse. "I gotta tell somebody he's down there. I can't just leave him there! That's a human being. It's not like I hit a stray dog or coon or something," he cried out in frustration, then frowned as the reality of killing a man while driving drunk came to him. "But, if I do call somebody, I'll go to jail." He stared into the fog for several seconds before shaking his head. "I sure as hell don't want to go to jail."

Maybe it was somebody who was passing through and wouldn't be missed. Even if it wasn't, it was probably some Tennessee hick from around Bailey Springs. Nobody he knew would be walking along that road this time of night. The body could lie there for weeks, months . . . maybe forever. After a few days, new leaves would cover his tracks down there. Anybody walking past wouldn't see anything but that backpack, maybe not even that.

Jack nodded He knew one thing for sure, he was as deep in it as he could get right now. It couldn't get any worse if he kept his mouth shut. If he reported it tonight, he would spend the rest of the night in jail and who knows how many more. If he didn't report it, as long as no one found the body, he was clear. He might go to jail eventually, but by then maybe he could come up with a good story.

Having decided not to report the body, Jack slowly nodded his head. "Until somebody finds the body, it never happened. I can live with that." Then he smiled as another thought came to him. There was an alternative. He'd wait a few days until he got his story straight about what happened to his truck, then he would make an anonymous call to the Creek County Sheriff and tell them about the body at the curve. There was nothing down there that could connect him to the man, no one saw him doing it, and by the time he called he would have a good explanation as to what happened to his truck.

Jack smiled as he pulled into Uncle Buck's parking lot. Getting the man's body out of the woods within the next few days appealed to him. He hadn't meant to kill him, so it was almost as if he was doing the man a favor, helping to get him out of the woods before the meat-eating birds and animals found him. Jack nodded, feeling good. Beer would taste good right now.

Then, he looked down at himself. His shoes and clothes were wet and covered with mud and bits of leaves. Someone would want to know where he had been and what he had been doing. They might remember later that he had left the bar, then came back looking like he'd been wallowing in a hog pen. Going in for another beer might not be a good idea. Jack started the engine, shifted in reverse, then glanced at his outside rearview mirrors out of habit.

"Damn!" The right-hand mirror was missing. He hadn't seen it on the road. It had to be down the embankment. He would have to go back and try to find it in the dim light of his weak flashlight. "No!" he whispered. The last thing he wanted to do was to go down that bank again tonight. "Goddamn it!" he cursed as he slammed his fist onto the seat beside him, knowing his plan to call the sheriff about the body wouldn't work. They might find his mirror down there. If they did, they might be able to match it with where it had been broken off his truck. "Damn!" As much as he wished the man didn't have to stay down there in the woods, he knew he couldn't call anyone. It might get them looking for the truck with the missing mirror that had hit him.

As he headed south at a moderate speed, the fog seemed to dissipate a bit, giving him a much better view of the road ahead. As he neared the Alabama state line, with the anonymous call no longer an option, Jack reminded himself that nothing had happened, no one had been hurt, and no one was dead until someone found the body, which might never happen. As long as no one had seen him there, he was never there; he wasn't the one who did it.

Then he remembered his broken headlight and glanced at the space where the right-hand mirror should have been. How would he explain it? Someone would notice in the next few days, Cathy probably, Billy for sure the next time they rode together to work. How could he explain the damage? He was in a little accident. Yeah. A little fender bender. Where? When? Was anybody else involved? Jack shook his head as all the unanswered questions came pounding on his head.

At a time when he desperately needed to be sober, Jack knew he was still very drunk. As he neared the Alabama state line, driving around a familiar curve, at a speed he knew would take him safely around, he saw a big oak tree a few yards off to the right. "That's it!" The big oak was the answer. This would be where he had his accident.

If he could sideswipe the tree just enough to obliterate the damage that had already been done, then no one would ever know he had driven north instead of south when he had left Uncle Buck's tonight. If he did it right, he could get the lights and fender fixed next week, the insurance company would pay for it, and the Creek County sheriff would have to go looking somewhere else for the hit-and-run vehicle.

Jack pulled into a farmhouse driveway, turned around, drove a hundred yards past the curve and turned around once more. The 1993 F-150 didn't have an airbag and Jack never wore his seatbelt, but now he snapped the buckle in place, then tugged on the loose shoulder strap, wondering if it would work like it was supposed to when the time came. Wishing desperately for a crash helmet, he knew it was too late to wish for anything. He would have to be good enough to barely sideswipe the tree instead of ramming it head-on. "Just peel the paint, buddy," Jack muttered. "Just peel the paint."

As Jack approached the curve, he tried to guess how fast he should be going. Fast enough to get the job done without killing himself at the same time, he decided. Jack almost changed his mind, but at the last second, he jerked the truck to the right, aiming it at the left edge of the big tree. However, as the truck pitched over the low embankment, the front end slid to the right and headed toward the center of the tree. Jack screamed and jerked the steering wheel to the left just before impact.

3

CATHY CONSTONE HEARD a groan and looked up to see her husband, his wrists attached to the hospital bed railings, thrashing about in a fitful sleep.

"Are you all right?"

"Get out of the way! Get out of the way!" Jack cried out in a raspy voice. His throat was irritated, and his words were made almost unintelligible by the tube leading down from his nose to his stomach.

"I'm not in your way. What's wrong with you?"

"Get out of the way," Jack pleaded as he made a feeble effort to pull his hands free of their restraints. He mumbled something unintelligible and was soon calm once again.

Cathy rose from her chair and stretched her arms high above her head as she looked out of the tall slender window. It was already dark. Thanksgiving Day was over. "What a hell of a mess," she muttered. She didn't want to be here; she had to be here. In North Alabama, a wife was expected to be near her husband when he was in the hospital. She hated hospitals. She hated North Alabama even more. Cathy was barely eighteen and already pregnant when she married this man and left her parents' home in San Diego, California, to move into a two-bedroom rented house in Helleston, Alabama. That had been over five years ago.

Cathy turned and gazed at her bruised and bandaged husband with mixed feelings. On one hand, she felt empathy for any human being who was suffering as he was.

On the other hand, maybe God was getting even with him for all the physical and mental pain he had caused her.

Cathy had been spanked, whipped, and slapped by both her parents as she grew up. One of her fondest teenage dreams was to escape the repressive atmosphere of her parents' home by marrying a loving man who wouldn't mistreat her. It hadn't turned out that way.

4

Day 3
Friday, November 27

THE FOLLOWING EVENING, Cathy looked up when she heard her husband moaning in obvious pain. "How're you doing?"

"Oh, oh," Jack moaned. "It hurts."

"You want me to get the nurse to give you some more pain medicine?"

"It hurts," Jack wailed.

"I've got to go to the Barn and cash a check. I'm about broke, and I need to buy a few things. Are you going to be all right for a while?"

"It hurts," Jack moaned.

Cathy rose from her chair, gathered her purse and coat, then gazed down at the man in pain. "Tell me about it. It didn't feel so great when I was in here giving birth either."

As Cathy drove toward Bart's Bargain Barn where she had check-cashing privileges, she decided she was too hungry to eat in the hospital cafeteria again. A view of something besides four beige concrete walls would be nice, too. As she considered her limited evening dining options in Helleston, it suddenly dawned on her that she was making a decision all by herself, for herself alone. For the first time in twenty-three years there was no one to make the decision for her, and there was no one else to consider in the decision. She was on her own tonight, for the first time in her life. She smiled as a pleasant feeling of euphoria came over her. Like a caged bird that had been released into the open air, her spirit soared.

For the first time in her life, she was in charge of her life. For a few hours, she could go anywhere she wanted to go and do almost anything she wanted to do. Cathy opened her mouth, and her eyes grew wide as a thought came to her. With her husband lying in a hospital bed, she was on her own. She didn't even have to go home tonight if she didn't want to. She could spend the night anywhere she wanted, with anyone she wanted.

She smiled as an erotic fantasy came to mind; then, just as quickly, she chastised herself for even thinking it. When she pulled into the parking lot at Bart's Bargain Barn, she still felt a joyful sense of freedom, like a schoolgirl on the first day of summer vacation.

Cathy presented her check, driver's license, and check-cashing privilege card to the woman behind the service counter at Bart's Bargain Barn. While waiting for her money, Cathy gazed idly at the pictures of the owner, the manager, and the assistant managers displayed on the wall behind the service counter. The night assistant manager looked like a frail teenage boy right out of high school. Later, as she waited in the checkout line to pay for a few items she needed, her stomach rumbled. She decided a burger and fries would taste good, and there was a fast-food restaurant nearby.

As Cathy walked into the restaurant, the harsh glare of the bright fluorescent lights was painful to her eyes. She pulled her jacket closer around her as she shivered in the cool temperature of the sparsely populated restaurant. She ordered a plastic burger, plastic fries, and a plastic cup of coffee. She took her plastic tray to a plastic booth and tried to eat with music blaring much too loud from the overhead speakers. She sighed. The artificial world of plastic, chrome, and glass wasn't much different from the hospital cafeteria, but at least it had windows through which she could watch the outside world.

As Cathy watched the traffic passing by, the feeling of euphoria wouldn't leave her. It was exciting, and a little scary, knowing she was alone. She could sit here as long as she wanted or leave whenever she wished. She could go back to the hospital from here, but only if she wanted to. There was no one to give her orders or directions. It felt wonderful.

Cathy looked up as another customer entered the restaurant. He looked like a scrawny high school kid wearing an ill-fitting suit, white shirt, and tie. Why would a high school kid be wearing a suit this time of night, this time of year? He wasn't much taller than she was and probably weighed less. He looked almost emaciated, like a man who needed a woman to feed him something more nutritious than plastic burgers and fries.

She watched as he chose the next booth, facing her. Once seated, he clasped his hands in prayer, bowed his head and closed his eyes. After a few seconds, he raised his head, opened his eyes and began unwrapping his meal. As she watched him squeeze a package of catsup on his hamburger, she thought she recognized him.

He looked up from his preparations, saw her staring at him, and smiled. "How're you tonight?"

The young man's comment startled Cathy. "Oh, I'm sorry. I guess I was staring at you. I just came from the Bargain Barn. I think I saw your picture while I was cashing my check."

He nodded. "That's me. I'm Peter Torrey, the evening assistant manager. Just call me, Pete."

"Hi, Pete," Cathy said with a little wave. "I'm Cathy."

"Cathy as in Catherine, or Kathy as in Kathleen?"

"Just Cathy, with a C."

Pete smiled and wrinkled his forehead. "Do I hear a California accent?"

Cathy nodded her head. "I was born and raised in California, but it's been years since I've been back. I'm surprised you can still tell."

"I'm from California myself. It's nice to hear someone pronouncing words like they do out there."

Cathy brightened. "You're from California, too? Where?"

"My mom and dad live in La Jolla."

"Oh, yeah? I was born and raised in San Diego. We were almost neighbors, weren't we?"

"Just about. As they say around here, I lived just up the road from you."

Cathy told Pete her husband was in the hospital, and why. Pete seemed genuinely concerned about him. With gently prodding questions, Cathy learned Pete was single and lived in a nearby apartment building.

"I guess your kids are excited about Christmas," Pete said.

"We don't have any kids."

"Oh, I'm sorry. I just . . . " Pete stammered, his cheeks red with embarrassment.

"That's all right. We did have one for a little while," Cathy said, a sad look on her face. "He was a little boy, we named him Thomas Lee."

"I'm sorry."

"He was so cute," Cathy said quietly as she stared off into the distance.

As they continued to talk, they discovered each was homesick for California. The conversation ended when Pete glanced at his watch. "Well, back to the salt mine. They're probably out looking for me right now."

"Oh, it was so nice to talk to someone from back home. I wish we had more time," Cathy said sadly.

"I know what you mean. I wish I could stay a few more minutes, but I've really got to get back."

Cathy bit her lower lip as she looked at Pete. She wanted very badly to invite him to join her here again tomorrow night, but it would be almost like asking him for a date. Would it be such a big sin, she wondered, if they shared a booth while eating their greasy hamburgers instead of eating them in separate booths? It would be wonderful to have another conversation with this cute-looking guy, but she didn't have the nerve to come right out and ask him to meet her here. It would be so embarrassing if he turned her down. Maybe there was a middle ground. She took a deep breath. "Do you come in here often this time of night?"

"More often than I should. I know the sodium and fat content in this stuff isn't doing my body any good. But it's warm, I don't have to make it, and it gets me out of that crazy place for a few minutes."

"Uh, I was thinking about eating here again tomorrow night. If you happen to be here, too, maybe we could talk some more."

Pete gazed silently at her for a moment, then said, "Uh, sure, if I can make it. That would be great. I like talking to you, too. I'll try really hard to make it, but now that Thanksgiving is over, the Christmas rush is keeping me as busy as I can get."

"I'll probably be here around seven o'clock."

"I'll try my best to be here. It's been fun, talking about the old days. But if something comes up, I won't be able to leave in the middle of it."

"That's all right, I'll probably hang around here for a while, even if you don't show. There's nothing going on at the hospital the nurses can't handle anyway."

"I hope I don't have to go to the hospital. I don't have any family around here to look after me. I'll bet your husband really appreciates what you're doing."

"Oh, he's the most grateful man in North Alabama," Cathy said sarcastically.

5

JACK BLINKED HIS EYES several times, then tried to pry them open long enough to look about him. He wasn't dead. He was in a hospital room. He hoped he wasn't dead anyway. Spending eternity in a hospital room would be Hell for sure. He tried to turn his head sideways and discovered he was wearing a surgical collar that prevented much movement. He tried to move his arms and found his wrists were attached to the bed. He saw Cathy out of the corner of his eye, reading a magazine.

"Hey," he whispered from a dry throat through parched lips. "Water."

"Oh, you're awake," Cathy said, then got his water glass and held the straw close to his parched lips.

Jack took the straw in his mouth and drank half the glass before spitting out the straw. "I guess so," he said in a raspy voice, a look of pain and discomfort on his face. "Am I all right?"

"Don't you remember?"

Jack tried to shake his head. "Ow! Damn! That hurts."

"The doctor put the collar on you. He thinks you might have a whiplash injury."

"It hurts like hell, that's for damn sure. What else did he do?"

"Me and you and the doctor have talked three or four times since Thursday morning. Don't you remember?"

"The last thing I remember, there was a tree coming at me."

"You did that Wednesday night. This is Saturday night."

"Is there anything bad wrong with me?"

"You look pretty beat up right now. I don't think you want to see yourself in a mirror. Your two black eyes make you look like a raccoon and you've got several stitches along the top of your forehead. Your pickup truck doesn't have an airbag, so the doctor thinks you hit the steering wheel with your head. He also said your sternum, pelvis, and kidneys are bruised from the seatbelt and shoulder strap." Cathy paused and looked up at Jack, frowning. "I didn't know you ever wore your seatbelt."

"Only when I get ready to hit a tree."

"Yeah, right. Good idea," Cathy said in reply to what she assumed was a lame attempt at humor on his part. "The doctor said you probably would have gone through the windshield if you hadn't been wearing your seatbelt."

"Lucky me," Jack muttered as he looked down at his arms. "Why are my wrists tied to the bed?"

"You've been having some nightmares. The nurses think you might jerk your IVs out of your arms if they aren't restrained. Would you like me to ask the nurse to cut the bands off?"

"No, not right now. What else is wrong with me?"

Cathy looked down at the tablet with her notes. "Let's see. You've got blood in your urine . . . the doctor calls it hematuria . . . your face and your chest look like you've been in a fight . . . the doctor says you have a concussion . . . your left kneecap is cracked, and your left ankle is swollen. You lost some blood from the cut on your forehead, but not enough for you to need a transfusion. The doctor says there's no displacement, so the kneecap should heal the way it is, and the ankle doesn't show any broken bones." Cathy paused and looked up at her husband. "So, the doctor wants to keep you here while there's blood in your urine and he wants to make sure your concussion is better; other than that, he thinks you're going to be fine in a few days."

Jack closed his eyes, trying to recall what had happened. "Where did it happen?"

"On Greenbrier Road, just north of the state line. You were coming back from Uncle Buck's. I guess you'd had too many to keep it on the road."

"How's my truck look?"

"It's in worse shape than you. They towed it to Art's Auto up in Bailey Springs. Your dad went up and took a look at it. He says it looks like it's totaled. Art let him get your tools out of your lockbox and the stuff out of the glove box after he paid for the tow."

"Was anybody else in the wreck?"

"Not that I know. Why, was there somebody with you?"

Jack grimaced as he unconsciously tried to shake his head. No, he didn't remember anybody else in the truck. But he had been having dreams about hitting somebody standing on the side of the road. It was always the same dream, always the same young man with a surprised look on his face. Thank goodness. It was only a dream. Maybe it would go away as soon as he got all the drugs out of his system.

"Oh, my throat is so sore," Jack complained.

"They stuck a tube in your nose down to your stomach to suck the beer out when you first came in," Cathy explained. "You want some more water?"

Jack nodded his head.

"A lot of people have been in to see you . . . some of the men you work with . . . Billy's been in a couple of times . . . a lot of your parents' friends have stopped by . . . they signed that pad of paper over there. I thought it would be nice to keep track of who came by."

"How long have you been here?"

"They called me around midnight Wednesday. I've been here most of the time since then."

"You've been here since Wednesday night?"

Cathy nodded. "Most of the time. Your mom and dad have been here, too, during the day."

"Why?"

"In case you needed us for something," Cathy said defensively.

Jack looked at Cathy. It had been a long time since either one had expressed a need, or love, for the other. They had burned a lot of bridges between them since they had left California. Maybe this was a chance to start building a new one. "You must be getting tired of this place by now."

"I'm exhausted. This chair has given me a backache. I'll be glad when I can go home and get a good night's rest."

"Go on home now, if you want to."

Cathy glanced at her watch. "It's almost seven. I guess I could go get something to eat somewhere. You want me to come back afterwards?"

Jack growled in a hoarse voice, "Go on, get out of here! There's plenty of nurses around." Jack frowned as soon as he said it. It hadn't sounded the way he had meant it, but he had never apologized to this woman for anything he had said to her in five years. He wasn't about to start now.

Cathy's shoulders slumped as she bowed her head and closed her eyes. It was Saturday night. For three days she had maintained a bedside vigil. This was the thanks she got. Nothing. She silently gathered her things, walked to the door, then paused. "Your parents said they were coming sometime tomorrow morning. I guess I'll go to Mass and then come later in the afternoon."

"Whatever."

Cathy left the room, tears welling up in her eyes. But, as she walked down the hall, she sniffed, then smiled as she recalled her brief conversation with Pete last night. What a cute, sweet guy he was. It would really be great if he was there again tonight. As she drove away from the hospital, she was aware of her trembling hands. She knew why they were trembling. Once again, the thrill of freedom to do whatever she wanted in the darkness of this winter evening was exhilarating.

It was almost like the thrill she had felt the night she told her parents she was driving to a San Diego skating rink to join friends, but instead she had driven to the Navy base and picked up a sailor. It was the first time in her life she had done something she knew her father had absolutely forbidden. She had paid for that night of forbidden pleasure with five years of torment.

Cathy sighed as she waited for the traffic signal to change. She was on her way to meet a man. Granted, it would be a perfectly innocent meeting in a very public place; still, she had never done anything like this as a married woman. All she wanted to do was talk to him about the old days in California. What was wrong with that? What would be so different tonight than the chance meeting between two strangers last night? It would be the same, wouldn't it?

There wouldn't really be any difference as far as she was concerned. Still, she knew that if Jack ever found out she had met a man for supper while he was in the hospital, no matter how innocent it had been at the time, she might regret it. When he was in a bad mood, sometimes the least little thing she said or did would cause him to slap or spank her.

* * * *

Cathy sipped coffee she didn't want as she glanced first at her watch and then at the door. At seven-thirty she walked to the counter and ordered her burger and fries. She had scarcely returned to her booth when Pete came in and waved to her. She smiled and waved back, then glanced around at the sparse crowd to see if anyone had noticed. As she watched Pete wait for his order, she was amazed at how young he looked. His pink baby face was so cute, with a body that was so thin she was sure he would blow away in a strong wind. He looked more like a frail little boy who needed someone to mother him than the assistant manager of a large discount department store.

"Hi, sorry I'm late," Pete said as he joined her in the booth. "I couldn't get away."

"That's all right, I don't mind," Cathy said, and meant it.

"I wasn't sure you'd still be here," Pete admitted. "Thanks for waiting."

As Cathy watched him prepare his hamburger and fries on the plastic tray, she said quietly, "I wasn't sure you'd come."

Pete frowned. "Why not? I said I'd come if I could."

Cathy leaned her head forward and, in a soft voice, said, "It feels almost like a date to me. I wasn't sure how you felt about dating a married woman." To her surprise, she saw Pete's face turn a deep red. He was blushing! How sweet.

"Uh, well, this isn't really a date," he stammered. "I mean, you know, we're only sitting here talking."

"I know," Cathy said sweetly. "It's just that I've never met a man like this before, to do anything. I know it's all innocent, but I still feel a little guilty about it."

Pete, his mouth full of hamburger, nodded. "To be honest with you, I did wonder if I was doing the right thing."

"Well, I'm glad you decided it was."

"I guess I decided that meeting you in a place like this couldn't count for much either way. But I will admit that I've been looking forward to seeing you again. Talking with you last night was the only bright spot in my day."

"Mine, too," Cathy admitted. "I mean, talking to someone who's almost from my hometown is so wonderful. Every time you mentioned something, I remembered something I hadn't thought about for years."

Pete nodded, his mouth full of food.

"Sunset Cliffs . . . the beach," Cathy murmured, gazing off into the distance.

" . . . Balboa Park . . . the zoo . . . " Pete offered.

Cathy groaned. "Oh, my goodness, does that bring back memories! That's where I met Jack. I thought he looked so cute in his sailor's uniform. I was there with two other girls when we met up with Jack and two other sailors. After a while we divided up into pairs if you know what I mean."

"Like the animals in the zoo, huh?"

"You can say that again, in more ways than one," Cathy said with bitterness in her voice. Then she turned her head and gazed out the window. "My daddy told me I wasn't allowed to date sailors or Marines. Gosh, I sure wish I'd listened to him."

"I wish I'd listened to some things my dad told me, too. Now that I'm older, I appreciate what he was trying to tell me."

"Tell me about it," Cathy murmured, nodding her head. With more probing questions, Cathy learned Pete had graduated from San Diego State, then worked as an aerospace engineer in Huntsville for a couple of years before he had gotten laid off. The other Huntsville aerospace companies were laying off engineers as well, so he accepted the position of night assistant manager at Bart's Bargain Barn a year ago, working twice as many hours for half what he had been paid as an engineer. Cathy was amazed. This man could pass as an eighteen-year-old but was at least twenty-five. That meant he was older than she was!

"Did you ever . . . ?" Pete started, then glanced at his watch. "Wow, where did the time go?"

"I really enjoy talking to you, Pete."

"Me, too. It's great to talk to someone who grew up out there," he said, then stuffed the last piece of hamburger into his mouth.

"By the way, you forgot to say grace tonight," Cathy said, then smiled at Pete.

"Oh, yeah, I guess I did," Pete said, his cheeks turning red. "I usually do. It's a habit I've gotten into lately. I was afraid I might embarrass you if I did it tonight."

"It wouldn't have embarrassed me. I go to church pretty often myself. I'm not sure thanking The Lord for plastic burgers is worth the effort, though."

"Where do you go to church?"

"Our Savior."

"Oh!" Pete said with a start. "You're Catholic."

"Sure, what's wrong with that?"

"Uh, nothing," Pete stammered. "It's unusual to meet a Catholic here in Helleston, that's all."

"Tell me about it. If there are two dozen people at Sunday Mass, it's a crowd."

"I go to Central Methodist. We usually have about three hundred show up for Sunday worship," Pete said, then glanced at his watch again. "I've really got to get out of here."

Cathy tilted her head and smiled as she watched the cute guy sitting across from her gathering wrappers and napkins onto his tray. He seemed to be so kind and gentle, like a cuddly little puppy dog. She wondered if he had a girlfriend. A girl could do a lot worse. He really was a sweet guy. If she were single, she might be interested. Then, she remembered she wasn't expected back at the hospital. Her husband had ordered her to leave and not return. There was no one waiting at home. She could spend the night anywhere she wanted with anyone she chose.

She trembled as she realized that she was considering adultery. No, not really. Not seriously. She knew she didn't have the nerve to go that far with this man, or any man. Jack would kill her if she did. Still, the erotic thought was exciting. "Are you working tomorrow?"

Pete nodded. "I'm afraid so."

"I'll probably eat here again tomorrow night. It's not great, but it's better than anything they've got at the hospital at night," Cathy said, then swept her arm toward the evening traffic outside the window. "And the view is fantastic!"

Pete smiled and nodded. "I'll try to be here. But if I get tied up with the boss, I can't walk out on him."

"That's all right. I don't mind. I'd rather be sitting here than in an uncomfortable chair in a cramped hospital room, listening to Jack moaning and groaning about everything."

"I'd much rather be here with you than back at the Barn," Pete admitted.

"That's awfully sweet of you to say so."

6

Day 5
Sunday, November 29

JACK AWOKE AND LOOKED frantically about him. It was almost dawn, and forms and features were beginning to emerge from the darkness outside his window. The recurring nightmare had returned, this time with a clarity he hadn't experienced before. Then, in the steel-gray predawn light, Jack's world came crashing down on him. It wasn't a nightmare. It had really happened.

Most of the pieces he would ever remember about that night tumbled into place. He had been so drunk when leaving Uncle Buck's, he had driven north instead of south, killed a man on the way back, left him in a ditch, then almost killed himself trying to hide the damage to his truck. "No! No!" he yelled into the night, his sober brain unwilling to accept the reality of the decisions he had made while he was drunk.

"Are you all right, Mr. Constone?" the nurse asked as she hurried into the room.

Jack stared at her, a puzzled look on his face. He wanted to tell her he had killed a man. He didn't, but he wanted to very badly. "I guess so."

The nurse walked over and put her fingers on his wrist and looked down at her watch. Fifteen seconds later, she grabbed a blood pressure cuff and began to attach it to Jack's arm. "Did you have another nightmare?"

Jack nodded. "Have I been having nightmares?"

"Every night. Days, too, sometimes," she said as she pressurized the cuff. "Do you remember what they're about?"

"Not really," he lied. "Bits and pieces, that's all. Nothing that makes any sense."

The nurse nodded her head. "The pain medicine you've been taking might be doing it." When she was done, she asked if there was anything he needed.

"Could you cut these bands off my wrists so I can move my arms?"

"Sure, I can do that for you," she said, found some scissors, and cut the bands.

"Thanks," Jack said as he gently massaged his wrists.

"Just press the button if you need anything. It works better than yelling loud enough to wake the other patients."

"Sorry about that."

"That's all right, Mr. Constone. Good night."

By dawn, Jack had gone through the same decision process he had on Wednesday night and had come up with the same conclusion. He felt bad about killing the man, but he hadn't meant to do it, so he didn't feel all that guilty about doing it. Going to jail for doing something he hadn't meant to do didn't seem right to him. In any case, the body might never be found. There was no reason for anyone else to be walking on that curve anytime soon, and even if they did, there would be nothing to see down there but a big pile of leaves.

Jack nodded. Until the body was found, it hadn't happened. There was no need to tell anyone anything until he had to. The only thing that really bothered him was his missing mirror. He knew it was there and he knew he had to get it. But if he ever went back down that bank again, as surely as God made little green apples, a deputy sheriff would come along and want to know what he was doing down there with a dead body. Once again, he repeated his mantra: The body might never be found. Until then, it had never happened.

As dawn broke on a sunny winter day in Alabama, Jack stared up at the ceiling, then closed his eyes and whispered, "Oh, Elaine. I really screwed up this time."

* * * *

Jack Constone and his siblings had been raised on a small farm that was mostly hardwood trees. There wasn't enough acreage to justify growing cash crops, but there was space for peanuts, pumpkins, watermelons, and a big garden. Although he was a bit more than five-ten, when he was asked, Jack always told people he was six foot. Although he enjoyed playing sports, he wasn't tall enough for varsity basketball, didn't have the hand-eye coordination for the baseball team, didn't weigh enough to be a football lineman, and wasn't fast enough to play in the backfield. He wasn't movie-star handsome, but he had the rugged good looks and an insolent attitude that some teenage girls found appealing, especially one of the cheerleaders, Elaine Warden. During their senior year at Double Head High, their relationship had blossomed into serious discussions about marriage.

However, shortly after graduation, with no plans to attend college and no job, Jack enlisted in the Navy for four years of active duty. When he told Elaine he had enlisted in the Navy, he also told her he didn't want to get married until he got out. She was disappointed but said she would wait for him.

After boot camp at the Great Lakes Naval Training Center north of Chicago, he was sent to NAS Pensacola to be trained as an aircraft mechanic. Once he graduated from the school, he was assigned to one of the A-4 Skyhawk squadrons based at NAS Pensacola. It was better than either he or Elaine could have hoped for. Once he started getting paychecks of almost eight hundred dollars a month, he bought a used car and used it to drive back and forth from Pensacola, Florida, to Helleston, Alabama, on many occasions.

Then, with only five months remaining on his four-year enlistment, his squadron was transferred to NAS San Diego in January 1993. The scuttlebutt was that the squadron was going to be loaded onto the USS Nimitz in February for a six-month cruise. Believing he would spend the rest of his enlistment at sea, Jack left his car with Elaine in Alabama and hitched a ride to San Diego with a sailor from California. Shortly after they arrived, Jack learned that the scuttlebutt was wrong, which was fine with him. Although he was a sailor, he had never been assigned to sea duty, nor did he want to be.

On a warm Saturday in late March, with a new tattoo of a naked woman on his forearm and nothing else to do, Jack and two of his buddies decided to visit the famous San Diego Zoo. At the monkey cage, they encountered three teenage girls and struck up a conversation with them. A half-hour later, he had a date with the one who said her name was Cathy. He didn't have a car, but it turned out she did. He talked her into picking him up outside the Navy base's Main Gate that night. To his surprise, she showed up only a few minutes late.

They ate at a restaurant she was familiar with, then they drove to the coast for a view of the ocean from a parking area she was also familiar with. He soon learned the naive girl had never dated a sailor nor anyone else that was four years older than she was. He also discovered it was possible for two adults to have sex in a 1990 Honda Civic hatchback. Back at the gate, she agreed to come and get him at the same time the following Saturday. He gave her the number of the pay phone in his barracks, but she wouldn't give him her telephone number or tell him where she lived.

As he watched her drive away, it occurred to him that he knew what she said her name was, that she said she was eighteen, that she was an only child, that she was Catholic, that she lived in San Diego, that she planned to attend San Diego State in the fall, and that she was a fine little piece of ass, but he didn't have the slightest idea about how he could contact her. He thought that was a little strange.

She did show up the following Saturday, as well as every other Saturday for the next four weekends. On that Saturday, while still sitting in the car after she had delivered him back to the main gate again, he asked, "So, when am I going to meet your parents?"

"Probably never."

"Why is that?"

"My dad is a police officer. He hates sailors. It wouldn't be healthy for either of us if he knew I was dating one."

"One of those, huh?"

"He's spent his career in law enforcement dealing with drunken sailors and the damage they do to the property and citizens of San Diego."

Jack smiled. "We're not all drunks, well, not all the time anyway."

Cathy smiled and shook her head. "That's why I haven't given you my phone number or address . . . or tried to get a gate pass. It would be best for everyone if you go back to Alabama without my dad finding out we even met."

Jack frowned. He knew from day one that his relationship with the teenage girl was going to end when his enlistment ended. No way in hell was he going to take her back to Alabama with Elaine waiting for him back there, but he wanted her to want to go with him. He was a little peeved that she didn't. "You wouldn't like to go back to Alabama, huh?"

"Is that a proposal?" she asked smiling.

"Hell no. Just a question."

"I'm a California girl. I like it here."

"Well, I'm an Alabama boy. I don't like it here. Too many people and too many palm trees."

"I heard that everybody in Alabama is a redneck," she said, smiling.

Jack frowned, snorted, then grabbed the door handle and opened the door.

"Same time next Saturday?"

"Nope. Going to be busy. As a matter of fact, I'm going to be busy until I leave for Alabama."

"I'm sorry I made you mad. I was just joking."

Jack got out of the car, then leaned forward to look at her again. "I'm not mad. I just think we ought to stop seeing each other before your old man finds out you've been dating one of his drunken sailors. I've heard stories about what some of these San Diego cops do to sailors who've had one too many," he said, then slammed the door and walked away.

With less than a month to go before his four years of active duty was up, Jack heard someone call down the hall to tell him he had a phone call. He assumed it was either his parents or Elaine, but when he answered it, it was Cathy. She was crying. When she stopped crying, she told him she was pregnant. Jack turned and looked around him. When he saw no one nearby, he asked quietly, "Are you sure it's mine?"

"Yes. I haven't done it with anybody except you for months."

"I think we need to talk about it."

"When?"

"Saturday. Same time. Same place."

"Thank you. I'll be there."

"See you then," Jack said and hung up the phone with his trembling hand, and then he headed for the NCO Club and the first of several beers. By Saturday, he had spent many hours considering his options. Option one was to not be there when she showed up. He had no way to contact her, but it was true the other way around as well. She had no way to contact him except the pay phone in the day room. Problem solved.

But Jack was pretty sure the kid was his. He had used the same brand of condom that night that he had used since he was a teenager—without a single failure—until that night. To leave a girl in California with his boy—he knew it would be a boy—as a bastard without a name bothered him. If his dad ever found out he had a grandson in California without a name, he wouldn't like it either. He was pretty sure his dad would remind him that, "Sometimes a man's gotta do what a man's gotta do."

Option two was to talk her into getting an abortion, but she had told him that she was Catholic. He was pretty sure she wouldn't go along with it and he wasn't so sure that it was a good idea either. He wasn't against abortions in general, but the idea of killing his own boy wasn't something he felt good about.

That left option three. Get a Justic of the Peace to marry him and the little California slut and take her back to Alabama with him. After the kid was born, he would kick her ass all the way back to California, marry Elaine, and get on with his life.

* * * *

"Ah, shit," Jack muttered in disgust as he watched the sunlight become brighter outside his hospital room. That had been his plan. But it hadn't worked out that way. Elaine had told him to never speak to her again, the kid had died, and five years later he was still married to the little California bitch.

Cathy hadn't been all that bad to come home to. He had to get a little rough with her sometimes to remind her who was the boss, but what man didn't have to give his wife a little physical education every once in a while? Wives were no different than kids in that respect; you had to let them know what the rules were and what the consequences would be for breaking them. He'd sure found that out while he was growing up. The sting of a small tree branch or belt being applied to his rear and bare legs was often the punishment for breaking the rules when a spanking wouldn't have been adequate.

Knowing her rear would suffer if she got too nosy kept Cathy from asking too many questions about where he had been and who he had been with when he came home late at night. On the other hand, she knew what would happen to her if he found out she was running around on him. He had told her two or three times in ways he was sure she would remember.

It never occurred to Jack that there was anything wrong with his double standard. That was just the way it was. It was the same reason he had never taken Cathy to Uncle Buck's. In North Alabama, a man's wife wasn't supposed to be seen in rowdy bars like Uncle Buck's. It was all right for a married man to go stag to Uncle Buck's and spend the evening drinking beer and shooting pool with his friends. He might even buy a drink for the lonely wife of a long-distance trucker and dance with her a few times, but bringing your own wife to a honky-tonk bar would put a damper on the whole evening.

It didn't matter to Jack that, while he was drinking beer and having fun with the rowdy crowd of working men and women, his young wife was forced to spend another miserable evening alone with television as her only company. She was where she was supposed to be, doing what a North Alabama housewife was supposed to be doing.

* * * *

A few hours later, the Sunday morning atmosphere at the hospital had become quiet and Jack was bored. His parents had dropped by for a few minutes, then had left in time to go to church. Cathy hadn't been around all morning. It was the first time he had been alone since he had been here. It wasn't all that much fun. There wasn't anything on television but religious services and he had finished the Sunday newspaper. Except for the comics and University of Alabama football news, there hadn't been anything interesting.

Jack heard a knock on the open door and looked up in stunned silence at the beautiful woman standing in the doorway holding a potted plant with a big red ribbon tied in a bow around some green foil.

"Hi, there, stranger, mind if I come in?"

Jack's eyes widened as he stared at a woman he hadn't seen in five years. Her hair was shorter and she had gained a few pounds, but she still looked stunning in an outfit that she had probably worn to church. "Elaine! My god, what a surprise! Come in! Come on in!"

"We heard at work Friday that you'd been hurt in a car wreck. I bought you a plant from some of us. How're you doing?"

"I'm doing great now that you're here," Jack said as the scent of her perfume reached his nose. It smelled like honeysuckles . . . springtime. For the first time since the accident, he was glad he was alive.

Elaine set the plant on the windowsill, then turned back to Jack. "You don't look so great."

Jack unconsciously touched the surgical collar around his neck. "They tell me I look better now than I did when they brought me in here Wednesday night."

"What happened?"

Jack paused and clenched his teeth. More than anyone else, he wanted to tell this woman what he had done. She would understand. No, she wouldn't. No one would. "Well, as best as I can remember, I was on my way back from

Uncle Buck's when I ran off the road at that curve just north of the state line. I hit a tree pretty hard. They say my truck is totaled."

"Oh, Jack, I'm so sorry. Are you going to be all right?"

"I think so. My neck hurts when I try to move it, I've got stitches on my forehead where I hit the steering wheel, my ankle is sore, and I've got a lot of bumps and bruises, but they'll go away. I'll be all right in a few days."

"I'm glad it wasn't any worse. Was anybody with you?"

Jack grimaced as he tried to shake his head, "No, thank goodness," he said as he breathed Elaine's scent, then smiled. "You're the last person I expected to walk in here this morning, but I'm sure glad you came."

"I'm glad I came, too," Elaine said softly.

"Last time I saw you, you told me you never wanted to talk to me again. That was five years ago."

"I know. That was terrible of me. When I heard about your accident, I realized you might be dead right now if it wasn't for the grace of God. I would have never forgiven myself if those were the last words spoken between us. I decided I should act like a good Christian and forgive and forget a little while you're still alive," she said, paused, then smiled and added, "So, here I am."

"I heard you got married three or four years ago."

Elaine nodded. "I married Russ Gerhart. It didn't work out. He's a regional sales manager for the company. He makes good money, so I guess he's good at what he does, but he was gone more than he was at home. I got awfully lonely while he was gone, but I found out he wasn't nearly as lonely on the road as I was at home. I've been divorced for over a year."

"Any kids?"

Elaine shook her head. "No, thank goodness."

"I was a daddy for a while, but something happened to him. He didn't make it."

"I heard about that. That's so sad."

"Anyway, that's why I married her. It was sort of a shotgun wedding if you know what I mean."

Elaine frowned as she looked down at Jack for a moment. "Jack, I'm not so naive that I believe you were faithful to me all those years you were in the Navy. I don't know if you know it or not, but I had a few dates with other men, so I can understand why you dated other girls. But, if you really loved me and wanted to marry me, why didn't you use something to prevent that from happening?"

"I did. It was, you know, defective."

"Oh," Elaine said, then stared at Jack for a moment, a perplexed look on her face. "I never considered that."

"Sometimes life surprises you."

"It surely does. I was making wedding plans when I got this half-page note from you telling me you were already married. You have no idea what that did to me."

"I wanted to explain it to you, but I wanted to do it in person. You know what a lousy letter writer I am. There was no way I could explain on a piece of paper why I married her like that. I knew that. I was hoping I would have a chance to explain it to you in person. But the first day I saw you at work, you told me to get lost. I don't blame you. I guess I still feel responsible."

"That's a step in the right direction."

"I still think about you a lot."

"I think about you, too," Elaine said.

"We had some great times."

"We surely did. Especially when I rode back down to Pensacola with you just before you had to leave for San Diego. We spent three glorious days . . . and three wonderful nights . . . together in that beachside motel before I drove back home by myself in your car. Oh, that was so wonderful!" She paused and snickered. "My mother almost had a fit when I called and told her where I was."

"You were twenty-one," Jack pointed out.

"I know," Elaine said, "But, I was still her little girl. I guess I always will be. It was a shock to her, knowing her little girl was sleeping with a man while I was still single. Anyway, she didn't stay mad at me too long, knowing I was with you."

Jack pointed to the tattoo on the underside of his right forearm, a naked woman surrounded by tiny flowers and tall grass. "And you've been with me ever since."

Elaine walked over for a closer look at Jack's arm. "Is that supposed to be me?"

"Sure. Can't you see the resemblance?"

"Uh, I'm not sure my measurements measure up to her measurements."

"That's how I remembered you when I was two thousand miles away. See how the grass spells 'EW' if you look at it the right way?"

"Oh, yeah. Now I see. What does your wife have to say about a tattoo that's supposed to be me on your arm?"

"I told her it's no specific woman, that the 'EW' stands for Every Woman."

"Every woman, or just the women you've slept with?" Elaine asked with raised eyebrows.

Jack smiled. "Sometimes, when I'm making it with her, I look at your tattoo and imagine it's you I'm making it with."

"Oh, you're so bad!"

"Yeah, but when I'm bad, I'm good."

Elaine looked at him and slowly shook her head. "I've heard that before."

Jack shrugged his shoulders. "So, how was your Thanksgiving? Better than mine, I hope."

"Oh, it was great! Just about all the family was at Mom and Dad's house. Mom cooked a big turkey with all the trimmings, with a little help from me. Uncle Fred and Aunt Ellen were there. Mom's sister and her family came over from Huntsville. Dan, May, and the kids came down from Bailey Springs. Oh, did you hear about Dan's promotion?"

"Old Deputy Dawg got promoted?" Jack asked in an exaggerated drawl, then grinned at his subtle jab. He had met Elaine's cousin at several Warden family gatherings when they were dating. When Dan had joined the Creek County Sheriff's office, Jack had kidded him about it, likening him to the slow talking, slow walking, slow-witted cartoon character, Deputy Dawg. Jack was the only one who thought the comparison was funny.

"Uh-huh, about a year ago. He's a sergeant now."

"Oh, yeah?"

"We're all very proud of him."

"I'll bet you are," Jack said, nodding his head. Things couldn't be better. If and when they ever found the body, Dan might be in charge of the investigation. As far as Jack was concerned, Dan didn't have the brains to find a man's asshole if the man dropped his pants, bent over, and spread his cheeks for him.

"He and May are separated," Elaine said quietly.

"Oh, I didn't know that."

"We're trying to get them back together again. That job of his is hard on both of them sometimes. He gets called out at all hours of the day and night. She told me that the worst times were when she would wake up at night and find herself alone in their bed. She didn't know if he had gotten up to go to the bathroom, or if he'd gotten a call and was in danger somewhere. She told me she had become a basket case, not knowing where he was or what was happening to him. Now, she's upset with him more than ever for not telling her about what happened to him last Wednesday. She didn't find out about it until she read the newspaper."

"What happened? Did he wreck his truck, too?"

Elaine smiled and shook her head. "He caught those two kids who've been robbing people and setting their houses on fire. One of them took a shot at Dan. I almost lost both of you guys on the same night."

"I didn't know that," Jack admitted. "I haven't felt like reading a newspaper until today."

"Anyway," Elaine continued, "we had a big houseful this Thanksgiving. Everybody was there except Jake. Oh, did you know he's going to Middle Tennessee State up in Murfreesboro now?"

"No, I didn't. Jesus! How time flies. Last time I saw him, he wasn't old enough to shave."

"He's all grown up now. We're so proud of him. He wants to be a doctor."

"Good for him."

"We were sort of hoping he could make it down for the weekend, too, but he called Mom last Sunday and told her the transmission in his old car went out on him a couple of weeks ago, whatever that means."

"It probably means a few hundred dollars in repair bills."

"Oh," Elaine said quietly. "I guess that's why he hasn't had it fixed. He doesn't have a lot of extra money. He said he'd come if he could get a ride with someone heading in this direction, but I guess he didn't. It'll be Christmas before we see him now."

"That's only another month. That's not so bad."

"I still wish he could have made it down for Thanksgiving. We've become really close. He's one of the nicest guys I know."

"What about me?"

"You're nice, too . . . sometimes. Sometimes, you're not so nice."

"Would you mind explaining that?"

"Sometimes your temper has a short fuse."

"That was back in the old days. It's not so bad now. At least, I don't think it is."

"Your temper almost got you kicked out of school."

"He started it," Jack stated loudly.

"But you were the one who used the baseball bat."

Jack grinned and snickered. "He sure did look funny after that, didn't he? Every time he smiled, you could see those cheap false teeth of his."

With a look of resignation, Elaine shook her head, then walked over to Jack, leaned over, and kissed him on his forehead below the stitches. "I'd better go. Take care of yourself."

"I hope the nurse doesn't take my temperature now, she'll think I've got a fever."

"It's nice to know my kisses still have an effect on you."

"Lady, you don't know the half of it," Jack declared.

Elaine glanced down at the sheet covering Jack's thighs, biting her lower lip as she smiled, then turned to go.

"Elaine, wait," Jack called out as she reached the door. "Uh, you bit my head off the last time I asked, but I'll try again. Can I call you sometime?"

Elaine tilted her head to one side and gazed at Jack.

"Well, can I?" he pressed. "You know, just to talk about the old days."

Elaine nodded. "My number's in the phone book."

"Thanks for coming by. You've really brightened my day."

"It was nice talking to you, Jack. Get well, soon . . . and don't forget to water the plant."

* * * *

"Hi," Cathy said with a smile as she walked into the hospital room.

"Hey," Jack said without emotion.

"You're looking better. Had many visitors?"

"A couple," Jack admitted, wondering if Elaine's perfume was still in the air. "Mom and Dad were here earlier."

"Oh, you got a plant. Who from?" Cathy asked as she examined the label.

"Some people at work took up a collection. One of the secretaries brought it over."

"It looks nice."

"Yeah, I guess."

"I brought you the Sunday paper."

"Mom and Dad brought their copy. I've already read it."

Cathy shrugged her shoulders and tossed the paper into the trash can. The professional football games were already on. Cathy sat in the recliner and opened a magazine. The two rarely said much to each other at home unless it was in a heated argument. At the moment, neither had anything to say and the silence was appreciated by both. As long as the football game was on, she knew he would be glued to the television set until he fell asleep.

She felt like taking a nap herself. She had found it difficult to sleep last night. Alone in the house, she had heard noises she couldn't identify while cowering in the lonely bed, afraid to stay where she was, even more afraid to get up and investigate, afraid of what she might find. Twice, she had answered the phone only to hear silence for a few seconds before it was disconnected. That bothered her, too.

Then, in the quiet darkness, her thoughts had turned to fantasies with Pete. She hadn't gone to confession in years. It was probably just as well. She wasn't interested in telling anyone, including a priest, about her nighttime erotic fantasies with a man who wasn't her husband.

Cathy glanced over at her sleeping husband, then closed the magazine, leaned her head back against the chair and closed her eyes.

* * * *

At five, Jack changed channels to watch the local news. When it was over, he turned to Cathy. "Where's my clothes?"

"I took everything home. They cut your pants to get them off, so I threw them away. I tried to wash your shirt, but the clay mud and blood wouldn't come out. I cleaned as much mud off your work shoes as I could. What were you doing to get that much mud all over you and your shoes?"

"I slipped and fell in a big mud puddle in Uncle Buck's parking lot."

Cathy stared at him, frowning, then said, "There was a lot of blood on your shirt. That'll never come out. You want me to throw it away?"

"Might as well. It's an old shirt."

"Maybe I can use it as a cleaning rag," Cathy said, then added, "I brought you some more clothes and shoes and put them in the closet. The doctor said you might be getting out of here in a day or so if your tests show everything is clear."

"I'm ready right now," Jack said, then shifted his attention back to the television set, ending the conversation.

Shortly before seven, Cathy glanced up at the clock once more, then turned to Jack. "I'm going back to work tomorrow. Your mom said she would be here during the day. I'll be back after I get off work."

"You and Mom don't need to do that. I don't mind if you visit for a few minutes, but you don't have to live here."

Cathy stared at Jack. "It wouldn't hurt you to let people be nice to you for a change."

"It would be a change, that's for damn sure."

"Well, be that way then," Cathy said, then grabbed her coat and bag and stormed out.

Jack watched the open door for a minute or so. She didn't come back. Why did they do this to each other, he wondered? It could have been different. If their boy had lived, it might have been different. Jack shivered. Some other mother's son was dead, too. There was a man's body in a ditch because of him. He tried not to think about it. Whenever he did, he felt a painful compression against his injured chest.

* * * *

Pete was late again, but he eventually made it. Cathy had already started eating, but when he joined her, then bowed his head in prayer, she paused and bowed her head as well. When he finished, Cathy crossed herself, then continued eating. Pete hurriedly unwrapped his burger, squirted a liberal amount of catsup on it, then stuffed a large bite into his mouth. No mention, not even jokingly, was made about this being an illicit encounter. Tonight, each was comfortable sharing a meal with a new friend who happened to be of the opposite sex. They both hated Alabama and missed California.

Suddenly, there was an electronic warble. "Uh, excuse me for a minute," Pete said as he reached inside his jacket, retrieved his cell phone, and flipped it open.

Cathy sat silently, listening to one side of the conversation. Clearly, there was a problem at the Barn and Pete was supposed to be there to solve it.

Pete ended the conversation and put the phone back in his pocket. "Sorry about that."

"Those cell phones must be nice. I wish I had one."

Pete shook his head. "Their signal isn't like radio or television. You have to be pretty close to a cell phone tower to get any kind of reception. There aren't many towers yet. From what I've read, the only reception you can count on is in cities and on major highways. Helleston has a few towers but reception is spotty anywhere around it until you get close to Huntsville."

"Oh, I didn't know that."

"The biggest mistake I made with it was giving the number to the people at the Barn. Now, I can't get away from that place even when I'm not there."

As they talked, they both agreed the conversation was much better than the food. They also agreed eating burgers and fries four nights in a row would be too much to expect their stomachs to digest without protest.

Cathy bit her lower lip and paused. "Uh, how about some barbecue tomorrow night?"

"Sounds good, but I can't leave long enough to go to a real restaurant," Pete said, then paused. "Besides, I'm not sure it would be a good idea."

"I know. This is an awfully small town with a lot of small-minded people. They would get the wrong idea, for sure. I was thinking about getting a couple of takeout boxes from Big Daddy's."

"Where would we eat? They might frown on us eating here."

Cathy tilted her head to one side as an embarrassed smile formed. "Now, don't get the wrong idea, but I thought maybe we could eat at your place."

"My place?"

"You said you lived at the Cross Winds, right?"

Pete nodded.

"That's as close to the Barn as this place is. I could meet you there if you think you'd like to do that. It may be the last chance we'll have for a little conversation. The doctor says he'll probably release my husband on Tuesday."

They stared silently at each other for several seconds. Maybe what she had proposed wasn't an illicit rendezvous, but it sounded very close to one.

"Two . . . one . . . two," Pete said slowly. "First building on the left, second floor, facing the pool."

"Same time?"

"I'll try my best," he promised.

"Is that your blue car out there?"

Pete nodded. "The Mustang."

"It's pretty, looks new."

Pete shook his head. "Nah, I bought it in California right after I accepted the job here. Driving cross-country in that

Mustang GT with a supercharged V8 engine was a blast. Didn't get a single speeding ticket . . . although I should have," he said, smiling. "Yours is the little gray one?"

Cathy nodded. "Yeah, the Honda Civic hatchback. Jack and I drove back from California in it. We didn't enjoy our cross-country trip as much as you did yours."

Pete silently nodded.

"If I see your blue Mustang, I'll come on up. Otherwise, I'll wait for you."

"I'll try to be there a little early."

Cathy smiled. Pete seemed so timid, so immature. She was fairly certain he didn't have very much experience with women. But there was something about him, a benign sexuality, that pleased her. "Don't worry," she said. "I'll wait for you if you're a little late."

7

ON HIS MONDAY MORNING rounds, the doctor told Jack he would discharge him the following morning if everything still looked good. Cathy had stopped by the hospital on her way to work and was still there when the doctor gave them the news. Both she and Jack were elated. They had long since grown tired of the hospital. At six-thirty that evening, Cathy told Jack she was thinking of eating out again.

"Hell, yes, get out of here. I'd go with you if I could."

Cathy gathered her things and was on her way out when Jack called out to her. "Hey!"

"Yeah?"

"I'm going to need some reading material when I get home. Get me some magazines."

"What do you want?"

"I don't know. Anything I haven't read, sports, hunting, cars, whatever you can find. Something with some naked women would be good. I may need something to jumpstart my battery after being in here."

Cathy nodded. "Chek Mart has a magazine section. I'll see what they have tomorrow."

Cathy walked down the hospital corridor, a frown on her face. *What about me? Is my body so sexually boring to my own husband that he has to look at pictures of other naked women to get aroused? Sometimes I see him looking at his tattoo of Every Woman while he's in me. Do other men need to look at a tattoo of a naked woman while they're having sex, or is it just him when he's with me?*

The wall opposite the elevators consisted of several narrow vertical mirror panels. While waiting for the elevator, she faced the mirrors and appraised herself, then turned sideways and did the same before turning her back to it and looking back over her shoulder. All she saw, from any angle, was a pretty young woman with all the right curves in all the right places. Not too much; not too little. She boarded the elevator, wondering why any man would need nude pictures of other women to get turned-on to her.

* * * *

Five minutes after Cathy had left, Jack picked up the bedside phone and entered a number he thought he would never be allowed to call again. His hand was noticeably shaking as he punched in the number.

"Hello?"

"Elaine? This is Jack. How're you doing tonight?"

"Oh, hi, Jack. I'm sorry. I was expecting a call from someone else."

"If this is a bad time, I'll call back some other time. Cathy ran out and left me in here all by myself, so I thought I'd call, you know, to see if you really meant it when you said it was all right to call."

"I don't mind you calling, but something's come up that's got the whole family worried."

"Oh? I hope it's nothing too serious."

"We can't find Jake."

"What?"

"That's what's got everyone worried. We don't know where Jake is. His roommate at Middle Tennessee called Mom today. He told her he hasn't seen Jake since last Wednesday. We thought he was still in Murfreesboro, but his roommate said Jake left a note saying he had found a ride heading this way last Wednesday. No one has seen or heard from him since. I've left a message with his girlfriend's parents in Chattanooga. I'm waiting for them to call me back."

A knot clenched Jack's stomach as a thought came to him. Then he shook his head. No way would that be possible. "Then I'd better get off the line. I hope everything turns out all right."

"It probably will, but it's been five days now since anybody's seen or heard from him. We just can't imagine why he hasn't called somebody by now."

"I'll let you go. I'm getting out tomorrow. I'll check with you in a few days."

"Do that. I'll talk to you then. Bye."

"Bye, Elaine."

* * * *

Cathy saw Pete's blue Mustang in the parking lot near the first building. She pulled into a parking space near the Mustang and climbed the stairs on trembling legs while trying not to drop the warm Styrofoam containers of barbecue. She was scared more than she had been in a long time. It had seemed such a simple idea last night, eating barbecue instead of hamburgers and eating it at his place instead of a restaurant. She hadn't considered all the ramifications then. Since then, she had.

Suppose someone had seen her buying two barbecue dinners? How would she have explained that? Suppose someone recognized her at the Cross Winds tonight? She would never be able to explain it to Jack. Somehow, a chance meeting at a fast-food restaurant had quickly evolved into something much more serious, and Cathy wasn't sure how it had gotten that way.

She didn't know anything about Pete, either. Not really. What was going to happen once she was alone with him in his apartment? She was here for barbecue and conversation; what were his plans once she was inside? No one knew she was here. Could she handle him if he decided to attack her? No, she decided; he wouldn't attack her. Pete was too sweet to do anything like that. Well, maybe. If he was so sweet, why did he invite a married woman to his apartment? She found Pete's apartment and, with a quick glance both ways down the walkway, knocked on the door. It opened immediately.

"Hi, there."

"Hi, Cathy, come on in."

"Thanks," she said as she walked into the room. Then she saw Pete do an odd thing. He stuck his head out the door and looked both ways down the walkway before he closed the door. Why did he do that? She was the one who would have some explaining to do if anyone saw her here. What was he worried about? Was he married, too?

"Are you, uh, expecting anyone else?" Cathy asked and giggled nervously.

"Uh, no," he said lamely. "Come on in."

"Thanks," Cathy said as she looked about the sparsely furnished one-bedroom apartment. The carpet, the Naugahyde and fake wood furniture, and the paint on the walls were all variations of brown. "Nice place you have," Cathy offered.

"Yeah, well, it came furnished. The only thing that's mine is the television set, the audio equipment underneath it, and the little tree."

Cathy smiled. The only color in the room other than brown was a tiny green plastic Christmas tree, about two feet tall, sitting on an end table with tiny silver balls hanging from its plastic branches. "What a cute little Christmas tree."

"I thought I'd do something to brighten the place up."

"Let's eat. I'm hungry and this is great barbecue."

Cathy opened the bag and spread the food out on the counter that divided the kitchen area from the living area as Pete prepared soft drinks. Pete set the drinks on the counter then came around and joined Cathy on one of the bar stools. "Looks delicious, Cathy. Thanks."

"Dig in," Cathy said as she stabbed the pile of barbecue.

"Do you mind if we say grace first?" Pete asked quietly.

With her fork suspended in midair between her plate and her mouth, Cathy said, "Uh, sure. I'm sorry. I forgot." She put her fork back down and listened to Pete say a short prayer of thanks. The little slip in her social graces was embarrassing to her, but the only times she had heard thanks given for a meal in the last five years were at Jack's parents' home during holiday family gatherings.

The food was good and the conversation pleasant. They found things to laugh about, things that made them feel good about themselves and each other. Cathy asked about the pictures on the wall in the living area. Pete introduced her to his mother, father and three older sisters, two of whom were identical twins.

"So, you're the baby, huh?"

He nodded and smiled.

"I'm an only child," Cathy offered, then asked, "What's it like to be bossed around by four women?"

"It got really boring after a while."

"I'll bet your dad was the only one on your side."

Pete grinned. "Mom bosses him, too. He wasn't much help."

"It's a wonder they didn't turn you against women."

"I guess they tried. Mom didn't like the girls I dated. None of them were good enough for her little baby boy."

"She probably wouldn't like it if she knew you had a married woman in your apartment."

"That's for sure," Pete said. "That's why I took the engineering job in Huntsville rather than something on the West Coast, to get away from everybody telling me how to live my life."

"I hope it's worked out better for you than it has for me," Cathy said bitterly. "Living with Jack is at least as tough as it was living with my dad."

When they had finished, Cathy helped him gather the trash, then she excused herself and went to the bathroom. After flushing the commode, she approached the small window and pulled her fingertip along the top of a blind slat, plowing a groove in the layer of accumulated dust. She quietly opened the medicine cabinet, closed it, then opened the drawers on either side of the sink and looked inside. She was satisfied. No other woman had been here in months, not even a cleaning lady.

Cathy looked at her reflection in the mirror. She was alone with a man in his apartment, yet nothing had happened. She had entered this man's apartment, concerned that he might attempt to sexually assault her. Not only had he not attacked her, he hadn't touched her. She found it a little disappointing. Her husband wanted to look at pictures of other naked women and this guy had treated her like she was his sister. Was she really so unattractive that all men had lost interest in her?

She moved her hands to her blouse, opened another button and pulled the edges aside, revealing a few more centimeters of skin and a tiny bit of her bra. Satisfied with the result, she walked out of the bathroom, anxious to see if Pete would notice the change. Instead, she saw him standing in the middle of the living area, clearly impatient to leave. Cathy's shoulders slumped as her spirits sank. Their little rendezvous was over.

"Well, I've got to get back," Pete said, then paused. "I guess I won't be seeing you again, unless I see you in the Barn."

"Uh, yeah, that's right. I guess this is good-bye, huh?" Cathy said, then paused as she looked at Pete, biting her lip. "I really enjoy being with you, Pete."

"I enjoy being with you, too, Cathy," Pete said softly, paused, then blurted out, "I swear, Cathy, sometimes I find it awfully hard to remember you're married."

"I know, so do I," Cathy said, then added, "I mean, I have so much fun talking with you about the good old days in California, it makes me wish I was single again."

Pete paused, his cheeks turning red, then said, "I know I shouldn't say this, I mean, I wouldn't do anything, you know, to jeopardize your marriage, but I wish we could get together again sometime. You know, just to talk."

Cathy tilted her head to one side and looked at Pete. They could no longer pretend. Pete had asked her for a date and they both knew it. "I wish we could, too. But Jack is getting out tomorrow morning. With him at home, I don't know when I'll be able to get away again in the evening."

Pete slowly shook his head. "I go to work at four, sometimes earlier, six or seven days a week."

"I don't work on the weekends, but I don't get off work during the week until five."

"Two ships passing in the night, huh?" Pete said, an unhappy look on his face.

"Well, we could have a little rendezvous in one of the aisles at the Barn."

Pete laughed. "I'm not sure about that. Some of those women shoppers have radar ears that can pick up a conversation from fifty feet away."

Cathy's eyes lit up. "I know! We could get together here before you go to work, you know, maybe for lunch or something on the weekend. I'm off on Saturday and Sunday and I can get out a lot easier in the daytime than I can at night."

"We could, couldn't we?" Pete exclaimed. "It'd be nice to be able to relax, without having to worry about rushing back to work . . . if I'm not working that day."

Cathy nodded. "I could come around noon on Saturday. We could have something to eat and then sit around and, you know, get to know each other without you being in a rush to get back to work."

"That would be great. I'm good at making ham and cheese sandwiches."

"Is your number in the phone book?"

"Yes, it is, but let me give you my cell phone number, too." Pete found a piece of notepaper and wrote both numbers for her. "Here you are. You should be able to get me at one or the other."

"Great. I'll call you sometime Saturday morning if I can get away. It might be on short notice."

"That's okay. Just give me time to pick up my dirty clothes and straighten up the place."

Cathy laughed. That was probably why he was here early tonight. "I'll be sure to give you time to do that."

"Thanks for the barbecue. It was great. I'll be waiting to hear from you," Pete said as he opened the door.

Cathy reached up and touched Pete's cheek with her fingers as she smiled at him. "See you Saturday . . . around noon . . . maybe," she said, then hurried out the door. Once back in the car, she started the engine, then paused, staring out the windshield. What a strange, sweet guy. Then it dawned on her: she had just made a date with a man who was not her husband. Was this thing getting out of hand or what? Eating burgers with Pete had been innocent enough, but going to his apartment while her husband was confined to a hospital bed had been a big step forward. Now, it was about to get much more serious. Next Saturday, Jack would be home. She would have to invent some excuse to get out of the house, then lie about what she had done, where she had been, and who she had been with. She had never done that before.

Cathy closed her eyes and shook her head. At the moment, a few more minutes of casual conversation didn't seem to be worth the complications the conversation would cause, and she was sure she wasn't ready to take the next step and go to bed with him. Between now and Saturday she had to decide whether or not another conversation with Pete was really worth the pain if her husband found out where she had been.

8

Day 7
Tuesday, December 1

CATHY WAS AT THE HOSPITAL before seven on Tuesday morning, anticipating Jack's release. She had hoped to get him settled at home in time for her to be at work on time. It didn't happen. The doctor took one last look at him, removed the stitches on his forehead, and declared him healthy. After the doctor left, they waited in the room while the paperwork was completed and signed by Jack, then he was delivered to the front door in a wheelchair by an orderly.

After Jack cautiously climbed into the passenger's seat of the Honda Civic, they headed home. By then it was after nine o'clock. When they got home, Jack took some pain pills, went to bed, and promptly fell asleep. Cathy hurried to work, praying her boss wouldn't fire her for being late again.

In mid-afternoon, Jack awoke and decided he was hungry. Using his new crutch, he hobbled his way to the kitchen. As he opened and closed kitchen cabinets in an unsuccessful attempt to find instant coffee and something to eat, the phone rang.

"Hey, get the phone!" Jack yelled before he realized he was the only one home. "Damn," he muttered as he hobbled over to the phone. "Yeah?" he growled. There was silence for an instant, then he heard a high-pitched nasal voice. It sounded like someone talking while pinching their nose, like children sometimes do to tease their siblings or irritate their parents.

"I saw what you did, asshole."

"What?"

"You heard me. I saw what you did at that curve on Greenbrier. "

Chills ran down Jack's spine and his hand holding the telephone began to tremble. "What the hell are you talking about?"

"Don't act like a dumb ass, you dumb ass! I saw what you did, I know who you are, and I've got your telephone number."

There was a long silence. "Why're you calling me?" Jack asked.

"I want a hundred dollars."

"A hundred dollars!"

"That's right, a hundred dollars . . . every week."

"I can't afford that kind of money."

"That's a lot of bull! I know where you work. You can afford it. It's either that or spend the next twenty years doing hard time. Can you afford that?"

"I'm in a bind right now. I've had a lot of expenses lately."

"Hey, don't tell me your problems. I ain't interested. We all got problems. All I want to know from you is whether or not it's worth a hundred dollars a week to stay out of jail? Yes or no, that's all I want to hear."

Jack took a deep breath. "I'll get it somehow. Where do you want to meet?"

"We ain't never going to meet, hoss. Letting you see my face would take all the fun out of it. No, here's how we're going to do it. I want you to stick a hundred dollars down in a beer bottle. Make sure it's dry. I'll get pissed if you get beer on my beer money."

Jack heard a cackling nasal laugh on the other end of the phone. Apparently, the bastard thought his comment was funny. "What do you want me to do with your damn beer money?" Jack snarled, knowing very well what he'd like to do with it.

"Listen real good, hoss. About two miles north of that curve is an old run-down house right off the road. Nobody lives there anymore. Just past the culvert there's a chain with a 'POSTED' sign on it. You know the one I'm talking about?"

"I'll find it."

"You damn well better. It's on the right-hand side as you're going toward Bailey Springs. What I want you to do every Friday, sometime before eight o'clock, is throw that beer bottle down in the weeds at the old mailbox next to the culvert, then get your ass out of there."

"You live around there?"

"Why don't you try to find out sometime? I've got a thirty-ought-six; maybe I'll have you in my crosshairs when you pull up to that mailbox. Don't get smart with me. Don't ever get smart with me, hoss. I can knock a tick off a dog's ear at two hundred yards. Hunting accidents happen all the time, hoss."

"You sound like a real bad ass."

"You got that right, hoss! You learn to be a bad ass real fast when you do hard time. But I'm going to be real nice to you. I'm going to keep my mouth shut about what I saw you do. All you have to do is keep throwing beer bottles in them weeds every Friday. You got that?"

"Yeah, I got it. Are you going to tell somebody about the body?"

"Not me. Ain't none of my kin."

"Who is he?"

"Don't know. Don't care, as long as I keep getting paid. Every Friday night, I want a hundred dollars right there at that mailbox. You got that, hoss?"

"I got it," Jack growled.

"If the money's not there by eight, I'm calling the sheriff. You hear me?"

"I hear you."

"Well, that's good. I sure am glad we had this little conversation. I'll be watching for you every Friday, but if I ever catch you watching for me, you're a dead man. You hear me, asshole? I ain't going to worry about you hiding in some bushes somewhere waiting for me. If I ever find out you know who I am, or if I ever catch you hanging around waiting for me up there, I'm going to blow your goddamn head off, right then and there. You hear me? If you ever find out who I am, you'd better have a gun handy if you want to stay alive."

Jack slammed the phone down. "God damn you! God damn you to Hell!" Jack looked at his hands. They were trembling. He needed a drink in the worst way. He had hoped the body might never be found. Instead, not only did someone know where the body was, they also knew he was the one who was responsible for putting it there.

Jack was devastated. Less than a week after it happened, his plans to pretend it had never happened were worthless. Now what was he going to do? He didn't want to go to jail, that was for sure. They put drunken hit-and-run drivers away for a long time if they killed somebody.

"Damn!" he exclaimed in frustration. He had no choice. He had to keep the man from calling the sheriff until he could figure out something else to do. "Jesus! Four hundred dollars a month!" he muttered. Cathy's job was a minimum wage job. His union job didn't pay much more than minimum wage. After the tax man took his cut, he banked less than two thousand a month. Four hundred was going to take a big bite out of that. Rent, groceries, and beer were going to take most of the rest. "What next? Goddamn it, what next?"

9

THREE DAYS LATER, Jack hobbled on his crutch into the kitchen where Cathy was washing the Friday night supper dishes. His bruises were beginning to heal, but he still ached all over, especially his neck whenever he tried to turn it from side to side. He didn't want to go out tonight. He had to. "Where're your car keys?" he demanded.

"Where're you going this time of night?"

"None of your goddamn business! Where're the goddamn keys?"

Cathy glared at Jack. "You're going up to that beer joint, aren't you?"

"I might."

"Jesus Christ! You've only been out of the hospital for three days. You know you're not supposed to drink alcohol while you're taking those pills."

"I'm not going to stand here and listen to you tell me what I can and can't do!" Jack stumbled over to her and raised his hand as if to slap her. "Are you going to give me the damn keys or am I going to have to remind you who's the boss around here?"

Cathy glared at him, then stalked off to their bedroom, found the keys in her purse, returned to the kitchen and threw them at Jack. He made a grab for them and missed. They hit his chest and fell noisily to the kitchen floor.

Propped up on his crutch, Jack glared at Cathy. "Pick them up. Pick them up or I'll brain you with this," he said as he raised the crutch in his hand.

Cathy glared at him silently for a moment, then picked up the keys and slapped them in his hand. "There! You're going to wreck mine just like you wrecked yours, then where will we be?"

"Go to Hell!" Jack snarled.

"You go to Hell!" Cathy said as she turned to go.

"Hey! Get back here! Right now!" Jack demanded.

Cathy paused in the hallway, then walked back to him.

Jack pointed his finger. "Do you know what happens when you talk to me like that?" he asked, glaring at her. "Do you?"

"I'm sorry," Cathy whispered softly.

"Not half as sorry as you're going to be. It's been a while, but you're due, lady. If you keep acting like that, you are definitely due."

* * * *

"Goddamn California bitch," Jack muttered to himself as he hobbled out the door, then slammed it hard behind him.

Out in the carport, Jack rummaged around in the garbage can, found an empty beer bottle, rolled five twenties and pushed them down into the bottle. With some effort and more cursing, he was able to fit himself into the cramped driver's seat of the small Honda Civic hatchback.

Jack was beyond Uncle Buck's and halfway through the curve before he realized it was the right curve. That meant he had already passed the body. A couple of miles farther north, the bright beams of his headlights illuminated a little shack near the right-hand side of the road. As Jack slowly approached it, he could see the rough-sawn unpainted wood siding, weathered gray from many years of exposure to the heat of summer and dampness of winter. Its corrugated metal roof was rusted, and the windows had been boarded up.

Beyond the culvert spanning the roadside ditch, amid knee-high weeds and tulip poplar saplings, were two thick posts on either side of the overgrown driveway. Attached to a heavy log chain suspended between the posts was a metal 'POSTED' sign with several bullet holes in it. On the north side of the culvert was a rusted mailbox mounted on an equally rusted metal post.

Deciding it was the right house, Jack turned into the culvert and stopped beside the mailbox. He rolled down his window, looked about in the darkness, then tossed the bottle out the window into the darkness beside the mailbox. He looked up at the shack for a moment, trying to see if he could spot the reflection of a rifle scope pointed at him. Realizing he might be in big trouble if he did, Jack quickly backed out of the driveway and headed south once more, the little car's ninety-two horsepower engine straining as he pushed the accelerator down hard. This time, he carefully rounded the curve at a safe speed. When Uncle Buck's parking lot came into view, he grinned. "Hell, if she's going to accuse me, I might as well."

Seated on his favorite stool, with no one seated on either side of him, Jack stared at his beer bottle as he absentmindedly scraped the label away with his thumbnail. He had killed a man, then had almost killed himself; now, to stay out of jail, he had to pay a man a hundred dollars a week with money he was going to need when he went looking for another truck.

The only good thing that had come out of the whole mess was Elaine's hospital visit. If he hadn't hit that tree, Elaine wouldn't have forgiven him. He thought he had lost her forever; now she was interested in being friendly with him again.

If Elaine ever told him she would like to get back together with him, he would pack his clothes and move out the same day. A marriage that had begun with a busted rubber was doomed to fail sooner or later. His life with Elaine would be perfect. All he had to do was to get rid of the blackmailer and hope somebody would find Jake somewhere else. It couldn't be Jake in that ditch. It just couldn't be! "God wouldn't hand me a pile of shit like that."

"What's that?" Junior asked.

Jack replied by holding up his finger to Junior.

"You look like shit," the big bartender growled as he placed the beer on the bar.

"I feel like shit," Jack admitted as he slowly massaged his aching neck.

"I heard you wrapped your truck around a tree."

Pain shot down Jack's back as he nodded his head. "It's a wonder I didn't kill myself."

"It's a wonder somebody else didn't kill you."

"What're you talking about?"

Junior snorted in disgust. "You were trying to start a fight with everybody in the place. If Billy hadn't got you out the door, I was about ready to knock some sense into you."

"Jesus Christ Almighty," Jack said, shaking his head in wonder as he stared at his beer. He still had no memory of leaving the bar and driving almost to Bailey Springs that night. He had heard that concussions had that effect on short-term memory but he didn't remember driving up to Bailey Springs before he had his wreck either. That bothered him. Then he glanced up at Black Billy hanging on the wall behind the bar and nodded with a wry smile on his face. He would have been better off in the long run if Junior had used it on him.

Black Billy was a policeman's baton that Junior had carried in the Army while temporarily assigned to a military police detachment for a few months. There were five tiny hash marks cut into the side of the club. When anyone asked him about them, Junior's standard reply was, "Private joke."

Junior didn't have a bouncer. He didn't need one. All the regulars knew that Junior and Black Billy were a combination you didn't want to mess with. The sight of Junior reaching for Black Billy was usually enough to end a shoving match between two potential combatants. The last time Jack had seen Junior use it, a drunken customer had threatened another man with a hunting knife. Without a word, Junior had grabbed Black Billy and hit the man a glancing blow from behind, peeling a two-inch section of scalp down to his ear. Jack had been sitting at the bar a week later when the man had returned, subdued and sober, displaying a large irregular curve of black surgical stitches on one side of his shaved scalp. When the man tried to extort a free beer from Junior in payment for the pain he had suffered, Junior reached for Black Billy and, instead of giving the man a free beer, offered to peel the other side of his scalp to match.

Jack had heard that Junior also had a gun stashed somewhere behind the bar. He didn't know anyone who had seen it, but all the regulars assumed he had one around somewhere. Junior had never confirmed or denied that he had a gun behind the bar, but anytime anyone asked him about it, he restated his position on firearms. "Anybody showing a weapon in here deals with me."

Jack took another drink and looked around. There was a gap in his life for which he had no memory. That was bad enough, but he didn't know how long that gap was either. Half an hour? An hour? Two hours? He wanted to ask Junior what had happened last Wednesday night, but the usual Friday night crowd was beginning to fill the place. The music was loud, the cue balls were clicking, and Junior was down at the other end of the bar, tending to other customers. Jack sighed, lifted the bottle to his mouth and drank once more.

Soon afterwards, he realized Cathy and the doctor were right. He was getting high, and his first bottle of beer was still half-full. He usually didn't feel like this until after four or five bottles. It occurred to Jack that he might wrap the little hatchback around a tree somewhere tonight if he stayed much longer.

Jack retrieved his change from the bar, grabbed his crutch, and dismounted the bar stool. He would come home with beer on his breath, which was all he needed to make his point to Cathy that she couldn't tell him what to do or where to go. He paused, wondering if he should call Elaine. What the hell, why not? He walked over to the pay phone, dropped a quarter, entered her number, and got a recording informing him he was attempting to dial a long-distance number. "Damn," he muttered as he stared at the phone. A mile down the road, on the other side of the Tennessee state line, it was a local call. Disgusted with the phone company's rate scheme, he walked back to the bar, grabbed more quarters and returned to the phone.

"Hello?"

"Hi, Elaine. Jack."

"Oh, hi, Jack."

"Have you heard anything about Jake?"

"Nothing so far. We're still hoping and praying we will soon."

"Uh, would you like to have some company? Maybe we could sit around and talk about something else, you know, just to get your mind off of it."

"Oh, that would be nice. I've tried watching television, but I can't concentrate on it."

"I'll be there in about thirty minutes."

"You know how to get to my house?"

"Is your address in the phone book?"

"Yes, it is, but you'll know you're on the right street when you see a big sign about Oakwood Estates."

"I'll find it, if Cathy's little piece of crap stays on the road long enough for me to get there."

"You need to think about getting another truck."

"That's about all I do think about whenever I'm driving that thing, but the insurance company hasn't paid me for my old one yet. The agent says any day now."

"Let's hope so."

* * * *

Elaine's address was in an upscale neighborhood of brick homes. Like most of them, hers was a two-story brick home with an attached two-car garage and professionally designed and maintained landscaping. When Elaine met Jack at her door, she was smiling, seemingly happy that he was there. Once inside, he reached for her and they hugged each other for a brief moment. Then Elaine led him into the living room.

Jack looked about the living room that looked as professionally designed as the exterior. "Nice place you've got here."

Smiling, with her eyes raised, she said, "The house is mine, but Russ is paying the mortgage."

Jack smiled and nodded as he recalled one of his buddies at work declaring, "A married man will find out in divorce court the true cost of a piece of ass from another woman." Jack chose the couch, and she sat in a chair across from him.

"Mom called a few minutes ago. We have a little news about Jake," she said.

"Oh, yeah? Where is he? Panama City?"

"I wish." Elaine bit her lip and sadly shook her head. "We still don't know where he is, but the Murfreesboro police talked to the student who gave Jake a ride. He said Jake rode with him to Pulaski."

"Pulaski?" Jack asked. "That's less than fifty miles away."

"I know," Elaine said quietly. "I guess that means he didn't go to Panama City. But we don't know which road he might have taken from there."

In an outburst of aggravation, Jack cried out, "Jesus! Why didn't he take the frigging bus? A bus ticket from Murfreesboro, Tennessee, to Helleston, Alabama, can't cost that much. If those Warden family dinners are half as good as they used to be, it would have been worth the price of a bus ticket to get here."

"Oh, you don't know Jake. He's at least as tight with his money now as our dad ever was. He watches every dime he spends. I can't blame him, though. He's trying to get through college without getting loaded down with a big student loan. He's working part-time, waiting on tables, to help pay expenses. I offered to lend him enough money to fix his car, but he said it would be another temptation to keep him from studying right now. He said he might take me up on it if he passes his finals," Elaine said, then smiled. "Besides, these are the nineties. When he has a date, his girlfriend picks him up."

Jack laughed. "That's a great idea! Would you have done that for me?"

Elaine tilted her head to one side and pursed her lips. "I might have."

Jack paused, gazing at the gorgeous woman sitting across from him. "So, are your mosquito bites all gone?"

Elaine knitted her brow. "Mosquito bites?"

"Yeah, you know, the mosquito bites we got the night of the senior party out at the lake."

Elaine's hand flew to her mouth. "Oh, that was so embarrassing. The next day I was itching in places I didn't dare rub, much less scratch."

Jack laughed. "We had a lot of fun back in those days."

"We surely did," Elaine nodded. "You remember the picture of us in the yearbook?"

"Yeah, I do. It's been a while since I've seen it, though."

"Would you like to see it again?"

"You still got your copy?"

"Sure," Elaine said as she arose. "I'll be right back. Oh, you want anything to drink?"

"Got any cold beer?"

"Nope, sorry. Nothing alcoholic, just some soft drinks and iced tea. I'll make some coffee if you'd like some."

"I'll pass."

When Elaine returned with the yearbook, she joined Jack on the sofa. "Our ten-year reunion is coming up next June. Are you coming?"

Jack inhaled the aroma of the woman's perfume. It smelled wonderful. "I don't know, I haven't really thought about it." Jack frowned. "Ten years? Jesus, has it really been that long?"

"Just about," Elaine said, as she opened the yearbook. First, they reread all the comments her classmates had written to her inside the front and back covers. Many of them referred to her special relationship with Jack. Then they turned to the senior pictures and tried to recall something about each of their classmates. Elaine pointed out several of their classmates who had graduated from college, mostly at Auburn or the University of Alabama. "I wish now I'd gone to college."

"Why didn't you?"

Elaine stared silently at Jack for a few seconds, then said quietly, "I thought I was going to have a career as the wife of Jack Constone and the mother of his children."

"Oh," Jack said softly and nodded his head.

They found pictures of Elaine in her cheerleader's uniform. Toward the back, there was a candid shot of the two of them standing under a tree, holding hands and smiling at one another. Jack had written next to it, "I hope we will always be together like this."

"Oh, gosh," Elaine said, then sniffed. "I get weepy every time I read that."

"I know how you feel."

Elaine turned and looked into Jack's eyes. "Do you, Jack? Do you really?"

"Yes, I do," Jack said as he reached out for her.

They held each other, just to feel the other's body. They kissed. Initially a tentative touch of their lips, but soon hungry mouths opened and pressed hard against the other for a long time. As the kiss continued, Jack placed his hand on her cheek, then moved it slowly down her neck and then onto her breast. Elaine allowed the hand to remain for a few seconds, then broke the kiss and removed his hand. "It's been a long time since we've kissed like that," she said.

"Much too long. You're a very sexy woman."

"It's nice to know someone still thinks so."

"I'd like to show you how sexy I think you are."

Elaine paused, then said softly, "I'd be lying if I said I wasn't tempted, but you're married now. I've met Cathy."

"You know her?"

"Not really, but I see her sometimes when I go through her line at Chek Mart. She seems like a very, uh, interesting woman."

"Not nearly as interesting as you are," Jack said as he reached for Elaine.

Elaine held Jack at arm's length and smiled. "Are you sure you don't want some coffee?"

"That's not the stimulant I'm after right now."

"Sorry, that's all I can offer tonight."

Jack paused, then asked, "What about some other night?"

"We'll just have to wait and see about that."

"I'll be waiting, that's for sure."

With a puzzled look on her face, Elaine pointed to his forehead. "That's going to be a nasty-looking scar."

"I know," Jack said, grinning. "I think it will add to my nasty character. What do you think?"

Elaine smiled as she shook her head. "Goodnight, Jack. Drive carefully. Don't hit any more trees for a while."

"I'll try not to. If I hit a little sapling with this piece of crap I'm driving tonight I'll never make it out alive. I'm going to look around for another pickup this weekend."

"I'd feel better if you'd find something with an airbag."

"My ninety-three was the last Ford pickup without a driver's side airbag, so that shouldn't be a problem."

"Thank goodness."

10

Day 11
Saturday, December 5

SHORTLY AFTER ELEVEN o'clock the next morning, Cathy asked, "Have you answered any hang-up phone calls lately?"

Jack frowned. "What're you talking about?"

"Ever since Thanksgiving, sometimes when the phone rings I answer it and there's no one there. I think I hear someone breathing but no one says anything, then they hang up. Has that happened to you?"

"No, it hasn't," Jack said, knowing who was calling and why.

"It's weird."

"Probably some nut getting his jollies doing shit like that. Don't worry about it."

"I'll try not to," she said. "Meanwhile, I'm going to do some Christmas shopping while it's not so crowded. I fixed you a sandwich and put it in the refrigerator."

"You're going shopping again?" Jack asked as Cathy slipped on her coat at the door.

"I thought I'd buy your mom and dad a little something. I might even find something for you if you'd stop acting grumpy for five minutes."

Jack glared at her snide remark. "Make sure you don't go overboard. The checking account is running low these days."

"How much is in it?"

"Not as much as there should be," Jack declared.

"I wrote a check for twenty dollars on Friday so I could have enough money to buy a hamburger. Was that all right with you?" Cathy asked sarcastically.

"Don't get smart with me," Jack warned, then added, "What the hell's the matter with you this morning? You've been acting nervous and jumpy ever since you got up."

"Nothing's the matter with me. I need to get out of this damn place for a while, that's all."

"Then get out of here while you can still sit down," Jack snarled.

She put on her coat and grabbed her purse. "I'll be back around two, maybe three, depending on how crowded it is," Cathy called out.

"Hey!"

"What?"

"Make it two. I want to go take a look at my truck and then I'm going to look around for something to drive."

"I'll try."

"You damn well better. You know what's waiting for you if you don't."

Jack listened to the little hatchback pull out of the driveway. He had gotten the check from the insurance company in today's mail. It wasn't anywhere near what he thought the '93 F-150 was worth, but he knew he had no choice but to take it. It was time to do something with it as soon as the bitch got back with that little piece of shit so he could go looking for a decent vehicle to drive.

As the door slammed behind her, Jack heard the phone ring.

"Damn," Jack said as he hobbled over to pick up the receiver. "Hello?"

"It's a pleasure doing business with you, asshole," the nasal voice said. "Keep up the good work." An abrupt click was followed by the hum of the dial tone.

Jack stared at the telephone, a rage boiling inside of him. Maybe he would sign up for Caller ID. Jack snorted. What the hell would he do with the bastard's phone number if he had it? He sure wasn't planning on calling it anytime soon.

* * * *

Cathy pulled up beside a pay phone booth at a gas station and called Pete. The grubby phone booth, the grubby phone, the trash, the demolished phone book, and the filthy writing created an appropriate venue to call a man who was not her husband.

"Hello."

"Hi, Pete. It's me."

"I've been waiting for your call. Is everything all right?"

"Everything's fine. I'm on my way."

"Great."

"See you soon."

Cathy pulled into an unreserved parking space at the Cross Winds and looked nervously about. The self-confidence she had felt while her husband had been confined to a hospital bed was gone. Her brief moments of independence in the dark of night that had encouraged her dangerous flirtations with Pete were over. Now, at midday on a sunny Saturday, her illicit rendezvous felt very different. The people she saw entering and leaving the apartment buildings were going about their normal, everyday lives, unaware that the married woman sitting in the little gray hatchback was contemplating a very private encounter with a man who was not her husband. It seemed unreal to Cathy as well. In the movies, married women met their secret lovers at night, in some secret hideaway, not out in the open, in the middle of the day.

She didn't have to do this. She could leave and go shopping. This man had no control or claim on her. If she never saw him again, it would be her choice. "But I want to see him," Cathy whispered to herself. "He's the only decent man I've met in a long time." Cathy sighed, got out of her car, and slowly walked to the stairs leading up to Pete's apartment. She kept her head lowered, afraid to make eye contact with anyone she might meet on her way, afraid they might recognize her or see in her eyes that she was a married woman on her way to a man's apartment. A dozen times since their last meeting she had vowed not to come here today. There was very little to gain and a great deal to lose if Jack ever found out she had been here today. As she approached Pete's door, her discomfort almost caused her to turn and hurry away. With some trepidation, she knocked softly on Pete's door, at the same time, vowing never to allow herself to get into this predicament again.

Pete opened it immediately and allowed her to quickly step inside. "How's your husband?" he asked as they walked to the kitchen area.

"He's okay, I guess. He's been having nightmares a lot since his accident. Sometimes he wakes me up tossing and turning and talking in his sleep. The past ten days have been exhausting."

"I'll bet," Pete said. "Come on. I've got everything ready, I think. I've never had lunch with another person in here."

"I'm sure it's fine, Pete." Cathy climbed onto a barstool and spread her napkin on her lap. "The only time I get to relax these days is when I'm with you."

Pete put sandwiches, chips, and drinks on the bar, then walked around and joined Cathy on a barstool next to her. "I know how you feel. I've been going nonstop since before Halloween."

As Pete bowed his head, Cathy clasped her hands, bowed her head, closed her eyes, and remained silent as Pete said grace. When he finished, she quickly crossed herself, then helped herself to the food. As they ate, they talked mostly about their jobs. She complained about her job at Chek Mart, and he told stories about how screwed-up things were at the Barn. Then they moved on to how wonderful things had been in California. With fondness, they recalled things they had done and places they had gone in the carefree world of their childhood. With the food gone, the counter cleared, and the dishes in the dishwasher, they stood at the doorway once more.

"I really enjoy being with you, Pete. You're good for me," Cathy said as she gazed up at Pete. She reached out, touched Pete's face, then quickly drew her hand away.

"I'm glad you came," Pete said as he reached out and touched her shoulder. "I really enjoy being with you."

"I feel the same way about you, Pete," Cathy said, then paused. "But I almost didn't come today. I've never done anything like this before. I mean, I know it all started out as innocent conversation, but I think we both know it's gone beyond that. Meeting you in your apartment like this is pretty serious stuff, even though all we did was talk about old times. Married women aren't supposed to do this sort of thing and we both know it."

Pete silently nodded his head. "I know what you mean. We haven't sinned, but it sort of feels like we have, doesn't it?"

Cathy nodded with her head lowered; then she raised her head and gazed into Pete's eyes. "Oh, Pete, you're such a great guy. You're so different from my husband. I have really enjoyed the few minutes I've shared with you. I enjoy being around a man who doesn't treat me like a dog or slave or something."

"Does that mean we're on for next Saturday?" Pete asked.

Cathy bit her lower lip and slowly shook her head. "I can't, Pete. I wish I could, really I do. But I'm not cut out to run around on my husband like this. You can't imagine how scary it was for me to come here today. I could get into an awful lot of trouble with Jack if he ever found out. He would never believe I came here and did nothing but talk with you. I don't want to take the risk again. If he's in a bad mood, he might spank me. I might not be able to sit down for days if he finds out I was here."

"He spanks you?" Pete asked, frowning in disbelief.

She nodded. "It's not so bad when he uses his hand, but sometimes he uses other things. Once he used his belt. That hurt."

"Jesus! Why do you put up with that? Why don't you report him to the police?"

Cathy gazed at him for several seconds, frowning. "I honestly don't know. My mom and dad whipped and spanked me while I was growing up, so I guess I got used to being treated like that. I read somewhere that thirty percent of women suffer some sort of abuse in their relationship with a man. I guess I'm in that thirty percent. I try really hard to do the things he wants me to do, the way he wants me to do them, but sometimes he gets upset with me anyway. Most of the time he just threatens to do something, but every once in a while, when he's really mad at me, he'll do something that hurts me." She shrugged. "He's always nice to me the next day. He never comes right out and says he's sorry for hurting me, but I sort of think he is."

"Incredible," Pete said, shaking his head, amazed that the low esteem of this woman would allow her to be subjected to such physical abuse.

"Didn't you get spanked while you were growing up?"

Pete shook his head. "Never. They didn't believe in corporal punishment."

Cathy frowned. "How did they control a house with you and all those girls?"

"Denial of privileges. We knew what the rules were and knew they would enforce them fairly if we broke them."

"And that kept you on the straight and narrow, huh?"

"Most of the time," Pete said, then smiled. "Sometimes breaking a rule was worth the consequences of breaking it."

"What do you think the consequences might be for dating a married woman?"

"I don't know, but I do know this," Pete said softly. Then he gazed at Cathy for several seconds. "I like you an awful lot, but I would never ask you to do anything you weren't comfortable doing, and I wouldn't want to be responsible for you getting mistreated," Pete said, then paused as a smile curled the corners of his mouth. "I guess this means we'll have to settle for meeting in one of the aisles at the Barn, huh?"

"Women's underwear, right?" Cathy asked, then sniffed, trying to smile.

"Ah, no. I feel sort of uncomfortable wandering around in that section. How about auto supplies?"

Blinking rapidly to clear the tears from her eyes, Cathy sniffed, then smiled and nodded her head. "Auto supplies it is."

"It was nice talking to you, Cathy," Pete said earnestly. "I don't think I've ever met a woman I enjoy being with as much as I do you."

Cathy reached up and touched Pete's cheek. It felt soft. She wondered if he shaved. "You're so sweet. I'd better leave before I change my mind."

Pete nodded and opened the door. "Bye, Cathy."

"Bye, Pete," Cathy said, then lunged toward him, kissed his cheek, and hurried out the door. "Don't work too hard."

* * * *

Jack watched the local news at noon. When the sports came on, he relaxed. He had heard nothing that interested him. No one had found a body in a roadside ditch. No one was looking for a body in a roadside ditch. So far, so good. He picked up the phone and entered a number from memory.

"Hello?"

"Hi, Elaine . . . Jack. I thought I'd call to see if you've heard from Jake yet."

"Oh, Jack. We're awfully worried about Jake. We can't find anyone who's seen or heard from him since he was dropped off in Pulaski. That was eleven days ago. His girlfriend hasn't seen him either. We've checked all the hospitals and have reported him missing to every police and sheriff's department between Helleston and Nashville and from Florence to Huntsville. We printed some flyers with his picture, description, and a couple of phone numbers. We're offering a five-hundred-dollar reward, too. A bunch of us are getting together after church tomorrow to post the flyers in the windows of businesses. We're awfully afraid he's lying in a ditch somewhere."

An overwhelming sense of sadness swept over Jack as he saw once again the surprised look on the man's face as his pickup slammed into him. Jake really was lying in a ditch. Jack knew where. He was the one who had put him there. "Oh, my God! No!"

"That's what we're afraid of," Elaine said.

"No, it can't be, not him," Jack cried out, wanting desperately to reject the thought that he might be responsible for killing the younger brother of the woman he loved.

"We're all praying, hoping to hear something. I guess we're expecting it to be bad news at this point. It's so frustrating, not knowing one way or the other."

"Oh, Elaine, I don't want to even think about it."

"Would you like to help us distribute the flyers tomorrow?"

Jack closed his eyes and gritted his teeth. He wanted very badly to help Elaine, but he knew he wouldn't be able to look at a picture of Jake's face in her presence without going nuts. "I want to, Elaine. I really wish I could. But my knee hurts a lot when I sit for a long time, and my ankle hurts if I stand up too long. I wouldn't be able to ride around in a car for long. I'm sorry."

"I'm sorry, too, Jack. I hope you start feeling better soon."

"I feel a little better each day. I'm going back to work on Monday."

"So soon? Are you going to be able to work on your sore ankle?"

"Yeah, I called them yesterday and told them to find something for me to do. I'm about to go nuts sitting around here all day. They've got me a desk job out in the shop scheduling the numerical controlled machines."

"Well, it will be great to have you back at work, Jack."

"It'll be great to have a truck again. I've found one I like. I'm going to take one more look at it this afternoon and make them an offer. Meanwhile, I don't pray much, but I'm praying you hear from Jake soon."

"We're all praying, Jack. But I appreciate your prayers, too."

11

Day 12
Sunday, December 6

ON HER WAY HOME from Sunday Mass, Cathy stared up at the sky while waiting for the signal light to change from red. It had been a cold, frosty morning when she got up, but now the temperature was well above freezing on a beautiful, bright, sunny December day. Going home and listening to her husband moan, gripe, bitch, and complain was the last thing she wanted to do on a day like this. Spending the day with Pete would be a lot more enjoyable.

She sighed. She had thought a lot about Pete since she left his apartment yesterday. He was so cute, especially when he blushed at something she said. Last night she lay awake, wishing she could somehow continue her friendship with Pete, knowing it was impossible. One secret rendezvous with another man was hard enough on her nerves. She knew she couldn't live a life of lies and deceit for very long before it would drive her crazy or Jack would find out.

Eventually she fell asleep, resigned to the reality that she had neither the strength to stand up to Jack nor the will to leave him. Pete, with his little-boy, bashful grin, was a casual friend who would soon fade from her memory.

Then she remembered the announcement the priest had made from the pulpit. The Warden family from Central Methodist was looking for volunteers today to help post flyers about Jake Warden, a Middle Tennessee college student who hadn't been seen since the day before Thanksgiving. She didn't know anyone in the Warden family, but it didn't matter. It would be a good excuse to get out of the house and drive around the countryside.

As she and Jack were eating lunch, Cathy said, "Your truck looks nice. I like that color green. What year is it?"

"It's a ninety-five."

"Does it have an airbag in it?"

"Yeah. Let's hope I never have to use it."

"Let's hope you never hit a tree with it."

"No shit."

After a couple of minutes of silence, Cathy asked, "Have you heard about that guy that's missing . . . Jake Warden?"

Jack's fork fell from his hand. He picked it up and stared at Cathy, frowning. "What? What did you say?"

"At Mass this morning, the priest said the Warden family is looking for someone in their family who is a student at Middle Tennessee. He hasn't been seen since the day before Thanksgiving. Have you heard anything about it?"

"Uh, yeah, some guys at work mentioned it."

"I guess they're getting worried about him. They're looking for volunteers to drive around and post flyers this afternoon. Would you like to go?"

Jack stared at Cathy for a long time, then shook his head. "Nah. My neck and ankle still hurt, and my knee gets stiff if I don't flex it every couple of minutes. Besides, I didn't get much sleep last night."

"I know. You woke me up again last night, yelling something."

"It's these damn pills," Jack muttered, then said, "If you want to go, go ahead, I don't care. You'd better ride with somebody else, though. Your car is a piece of junk."

"I really don't want to go by myself, but it's such a nice day outside, maybe I will. Are you sure you don't want to come?"

"Not today."

"Well, maybe I'll find somebody else I can ride with."

"Whatever."

* * * *

Cathy walked through a small crowd standing around outside the Methodist church. It was much larger than the church she attended. She wasn't surprised. In Helleston, the majority of people were Protestants, mostly Baptists and Methodists. Those of the Jewish and Catholic faiths were a very small minority within the town. Helleston was in the middle of the Bible Belt, an area of the country where the church is the center of social life.

Over the years, she had learned how difficult it was for a young woman who pronounced words differently, attended a Catholic church, had no children, knew nothing about farming, and was married to a man who refused to attend a church of any faith, to form friendships with other women in the community. She simply had nothing in common with them. Perhaps today would be different.

Once inside the main door, she saw a young woman sitting at a folding table and decided to start with her. "Hi."

"Hi, I'm Elaine Warden. Thanks for coming."

"I'm Cathy Constone. I go to Our Savior. Our priest said you needed volunteers to pass out flyers today."

"We sure do. Uh, are you Jack Constone's wife?"

Cathy nodded. "You know him?"

"Oh, not really. We went to high school together."

"I think I've seen you somewhere."

"I go through your line at the grocery store sometimes."

"Oh, yeah," Cathy said, then smiled. "Now, I remember."

"I'm a secretary out at the plant."

"Jack works there, too . . . out in the factory."

"That's what I heard."

"I tried to get him to come with me, but he said he was still too sore from the wreck."

"Oh, that's too bad. I heard about his wreck," Elaine said, then paused. "I'm trying to get the carpools together right now. My cousin, Dan, is over there with Dad assigning routes to people once I get them sorted out. Do you want to drive or ride?"

"I'd rather ride. My car is kind of small and it's got lots of miles on it."

"That's all right. We'll find somebody for you to ride with."

"She can ride with me."

"Oh, hi, Pete," Elaine said as she looked past Cathy to the man standing behind her.

Cathy turned around and her mouth dropped open. "Oh, hi," was all she could manage.

"Cathy, do you know Pete Torrey?"

"Uh, no, not really. I've seen him at the Barn a few times."

"He's one of the good guys. He's the leader of our Bible study group." Elaine looked up at Pete. "We missed you this morning."

"I had to stop by the Barn for a few minutes."

Elaine pursed her lips and shook her head. "You work too hard at that place."

"Tell me about it."

"Well, do you two want to be a team of two, or do you want me to find someone to go along with you?"

"Just the two of us would be fine with me," Cathy said, hoping the anxiety in her voice did not show too much. She wanted very badly to be alone with this man. The thought of taking a long drive with Pete on a beautiful Sunday afternoon thrilled her.

"Okay with you, Pete?" Elaine asked, her eyebrows raised. "You know what some of these people are going to think when they see you and another man's wife leaving together without a chaperone. Your reputation might be in trouble."

"I'll take that chance."

Elaine looked at Pete, then at Cathy, then back at Pete and grinned. "Great! Have a nice afternoon, you two. Thanks for coming. Oh, everyone is invited back to Mom and Dad's house after you get back. We'll have snacks, coffee, and iced tea. Can you make it, Pete?"

"I've got to be at work by four, but I'll try to drop by for a few minutes if we get back in time," Pete promised.

"Cathy?"

Cathy nodded. "Maybe, for a few minutes. I'll need the address."

Elaine jotted down an address and gave it to Cathy. "Hope to see you there."

Cathy smiled. It was nice to feel wanted, to be needed, to be part of a team doing something good for someone else.

"Nice meeting you, Cathy."

"Nice meeting you, Elaine. I hope this is, you know, wasted effort."

"Thanks, Cathy. We can only hope and pray at this point."

Pete and Cathy walked over to the other table where two men were preoccupied with colored pens and road maps spread out before them. Pete recognized the older man as Elaine's father, greeted him, and shook his hand. As the younger man at the table rose, smiled, and extended his hand to Pete, Elaine's father introduced him as his brother's son, Dan Warden. With noticeable pride, he announced that Dan was a sergeant in the Creek County Tennessee sheriff's office. Pete then introduced Cathy to the two men, and they shook her hand as well. When Dan learned that Pete had to be back at work by four o'clock, the two were assigned US 72 between Helleston and Athens.

"I don't believe this," Cathy said as she walked with Pete to his car. "Yesterday, I broke off our friendship because I was afraid of what people would say if they saw us together again. Now, twenty-four hours later, we're going to spend the entire afternoon together and it's all right with everybody! It's weird. I mean, it's really weird, isn't it?"

"It's pretty amazing," Pete admitted.

"It's more than that. It's eerie. It's almost like God is telling us it's all right for us to be together. I mean, it's His day, right? I don't think it was purely accidental that you walked up when you did. I believe things are fated to happen sometimes, don't you?"

"I'd like to think so," Pete admitted.

"We'd better leave before I forget I'm a married woman and do something that God would definitely frown on."

"We'd better go before you do something to embarrass me."

"Excellent suggestion," Cathy said, then added, "Oh, this is going to be so great! I was afraid I was going to get stuck in the back seat of a car all afternoon, riding around with people I never met before. Now, if Jack ever finds out I spent the afternoon with you, I'll just tell him to call his old high school classmate, Elaine Warden, and complain to her about it."

Intermixed with farms, churches, cemeteries, and dozens of private homes, there were several small family-owned businesses along the road between Helleston and Athens. Both had driven this road many times, yet neither was aware of the number of gas stations, markets and small shops along the way.

Between stops, Cathy gave Pete more details about her life in California. "I was a pretty good kid, at least I think I was. I had my share of fun with guys, if you know what I mean, but I got good grades and I stayed out of trouble most of the time. I had already been accepted at San Diego State when I met Jack at the zoo that day. I wanted to go to UCLA, but my parents told me I had to stay at home and commute. My dad kept me on a short leash while I was growing up. He wouldn't let me go out with a boy by myself until I was sixteen. Even then, he told me I wasn't allowed to date a sailor or a Marine. Dating Jack was the only time I really disobeyed my father. Jesus! I wished I had listened to him. Something happened the first night we went parking. A month or so later, I knew I was in big trouble. I told Jack I wasn't willing to get an abortion, knowing my Catholic parents would disown me if they ever found out. So, he took me to a JP and married me.

"You know where I spent my wedding night? Alone in my room, in my parents' house. I dropped him off at the gate to the Navy base, like I always did, like it was another date or something. I didn't even bring Jack home to meet my parents until we were packed and ready to leave for Alabama. My parents were so mad at us when I told them I was pregnant, married to an ex-sailor, and heading to Alabama to live; if it hadn't been for my mom, my dad would have killed both of us."

Pete shook his head.

"What a shock this place was. I grew up in a city where I could roller skate on the sidewalks and walk to school. I'd never been on a farm before. I'd never known anyone who had grown up on a farm until I met Jack. After we came back here, we were out at his parents' house for a family gathering when I asked if peanuts grew on trees or bushes. I didn't know! I was just trying to act like I was interested in things. The whole family thought it was the funniest thing they'd ever heard. I mean, how was I to know the damn things come out of the ground? For five years now, every time we're at a family gathering, somebody throws it up to me!"

Pete smiled and said, "It is pretty funny."

"Oh, you," Cathy said, then gave him a playful punch on his shoulder. Then she giggled. "I guess it is now. It sure was embarrassing then."

"I'll bet."

"Now, tell me about you."

"There's not much to tell that you don't already know. All I do is eat, sleep, and work. Mostly work."

"Good lord! How many hours did you work this week?"

"I don't know. Assistant managers are paid a salary. We don't get paid overtime, so they don't keep any record of it. At least sixty, probably more. Maybe seventy or eighty."

"Eighty! My god, when do you get any sleep?"

"Assistant managers aren't allowed to sleep this time of the year."

"You're going to be ready for a break after the Christmas rush . . . if you don't have a breakdown before then."

"You could be right about that. I was supposed to get some time off after the first of the year. I'd already told Mom and Dad I was coming out to see them for a couple of weeks. But my boss changed his mind. He said I can go sometime in the spring."

"Well, let me see . . . " Cathy said sarcastically. "He's not going to let you leave during the January sales, or the Presidents' Day sales . . . then there's Valentine's Day . . . after that there's Easter . . . Mothers' Day . . . Fathers' Day. Just when do you think you'll get a day off?"

"Maybe never."

"I've got a suggestion."

"What?"

"Why don't you take off for the rest of your life from that damn job?"

"You mean, quit?"

"Look, Pete, they're using you. They don't give a damn about you. You've got better things to do with your life than spend it at that place. Sooner or later, you're going to wish you had left anyway."

"You know, you're right. I could leave. I really could. There's nothing holding me here. They keep telling me how I can move up the corporate ladder if I work hard, but right now, I think you're right. They're going to keep making me work eighty-hour weeks until I can't take it anymore, then they'll fire me and hire somebody else. I know that's what happened to the last assistant manager."

"I haven't known you very long, but I do know you've got a lot of potential. You can do anything you want to if you set your mind to it. Don't they have engineering jobs in California?"

"Lots of them."

"I guess I don't understand why you didn't go back to California after you got laid off. I mean, the Barn doesn't sound like a good career move to me."

"I guess you've never been laid off from a job."

"No, I haven't."

"It's . . . demeaning . . . degrading. It robs you of your self-confidence. A few other engineers got laid off at the same time I did, but most everybody else kept their jobs. I never did get a good explanation as to why I was one of those chosen. I had good reviews, my boss seemed to like me, I thought I got along with the other engineers, but I still got laid off. All they said was, although I had shown a lot of potential, their budget had been cut, so they had no choice but to keep the experienced engineers and let the new guys go. I never understood that. I was doing twice the work of some of those old guys. Anyway, there I was, in a strange place with no job, no friends . . . nothing . . . except my rent and car payments. I filled out job applications at all the other aerospace companies in Huntsville, but they were laying off, too.

"When I didn't get any calls for interviews, I wasn't ready to return home with my tail between my legs and admit to everyone I failed, so I started looking at the want ads. I saw an ad for the assistant manager position at the Barn. Assistant Manager sounded like a big deal to me at the time. The way I make it sound in my letters and phone calls, my parents still think it's a big deal. I guess I know different, though."

Cathy stared at Pete. She wished she could grab this man and shake some sense into his head. Didn't he see what was happening to him? Didn't he see where he was heading? "Well, if you know differently now, why do you let these people kick you around? Get up off the floor and kick some ass yourself!"

Pete grinned and slowly shook his head. "It's been a long time since I've talked to somebody like you. You really believe I should tell Big Bad Bart to shove this job, don't you?"

"First thing tomorrow."

"I swear, Cathy, a man could go far in this world with a woman like you behind him. Your husband is a lucky man."

"My husband doesn't know I exist," Cathy said.

"I know you exist. In the few hours we've had together, you've changed me. I want to thank you for that."

"You've changed me, too. I thought I was a worthless piece of trash who deserved to be kicked around by my husband. Now, I know that all men aren't like him. Some men are like you."

Pete stared out the windshield and shook his head. "I can't believe I'm driving down US 72 with a woman I've only known a few days, making life-changing plans." He turned, glanced at Cathy, then back at the road. "I feel like my life started the night I met you, Cathy."

"Sometimes a few days can be a lifetime, Pete," Cathy said as she gazed down at the picture on the flyers in her lap. She had never met Jake Warden and, somehow, she knew she never would. "Pete?"

"Yes, Cathy."

"Do you really think this guy, Jake Warden, is still alive somewhere?"

"I doubt it. It's been too long. Somebody would have heard something from him by now if he was still alive. Maybe that five-hundred-dollar reward will make somebody call. I'm afraid it's going to be bad news if they do."

"That's so sad," Cathy said as she continued to look down at the face of Jake Warden. "He's younger than we are. He had his whole life ahead of him." As she looked at the flyer, she realized Jake Warden had a message for her: live today; tomorrow you may die.

"Elaine told me he was planning to become a doctor," Pete said.

"He was going to save lives. Instead, someone took his."

"It sure looks that way."

There were several minutes of silence interrupted only by soft music from a CD. Cathy sniffed a couple of times and then said softly, "Pete?"

"Yes, Cathy?"

"If you still want to get together again next Saturday, it would be all right with me."

"Aren't you afraid he will hurt you if you do?"

Cathy bit her lower lip, smiled and shrugged. "Not if he doesn't find out. I can be pretty sneaky when I want to be."

"Same time, same place?" Pete asked, unable to suppress his astonishment.

"That would be fine."

12

"CREEK COUNTY SHERIFF'S Department!"

"Uh, yeah, I saw a picture of a young man in the hardware store window today. It said to call this number if I recognized him."

"What's your name, sir?"

"Jim Workman."

"Where do you live, Mr. Workman?"

"I've got a farm on Murphy Road, about a mile past the chert pit up here."

"Yes, sir, but what address is on your mail?"

"Uh, hang on a minute, let me make sure. Oh, yeah, it's, uh, Route Seven, Box three-seven-one, Bailey Springs, Tennessee."

"Thank you, sir. Now what young man's picture did you see? Are you talking about Jake Warden? Was that the name on the flyer?"

"Yeah, that's the one."

"Have you seen him?"

"Yes, sir, I believe I did. It was the day before Thanksgiving. That's the same day I called about the kids who burned down Hal and Bernice's house. They lost just about everything they had. I sure hope those kids get what's coming to them. Now, back in my day . . . "

"Excuse me, sir. We'll have to let the judge take care of those kids. You said you recognized the face on a flyer. Where did you see him?"

"Well, sir, me and Martha went over to Pulaski to get some of that good sorghum molasses they have over there. We were on our way back when I saw this young kid standing beside the road with a sign saying he wanted to go to Helleston. I don't usually pick up hitchhikers these days, but he had on a Middle Tennessee State ball cap. My boy went to Middle Tennessee, so I thought it would be all right. When he introduced himself, he said his name was Jake Something-or-Other. I remember his first name was Jake because I've got an uncle named Jake. You might know him. Jake Workman's his name. He lives over toward Waynesboro, got a nice farm . . . "

"Mr. Workman? Sorry to interrupt again, sir. When was the last time you saw the young man? Where did you drop him off?"

"Right after we got to Bailey Springs, I dropped him off right there at the McDonald's down by the high school. Poor old boy. When he got out, he offered to help with the gas, then he found out his billfold was gone. We looked around for it but didn't find it. He thought it might have dropped out of his blue jeans when he went to the crapper in Pulaski. I offered him a couple of bucks so he could buy a hamburger, but he turned me down. He said his mama would have something already cooked for him when he got home."

"About what time did you drop him off, sir?"

"I don't remember the time, but it was close to sundown. By the time I got home and did a few chores it was dark, that's why I noticed those kids down at Hal and Bernice's place. If it had been any earlier in the day . . . "

"Mr. Workman, excuse me again. Are you going to be home for a while?"

"I've got nothing to do and nowhere to go, so I'll be around all day."

"I'm going to send a deputy out to talk to you if you don't mind."

"Send him on out. I'll be here."

13

Day 17
Friday, December 11

MYRON "RED" BLACK had been squirrel hunting between rain showers in the hill country of southern Tennessee most of the chilly December afternoon. Over the years, the teenage boy had killed several squirrels with his daddy's old Marlin 60 .22 rifle in the wooded hills near the mobile home he shared with his mama. Fried squirrel tasted good with beans and rice when you couldn't afford hamburger meat.

Red usually found their nests, crafted from twigs, leaves, and grass, high up in big oak and hickory trees. If Red stealthily approached a nest, sometimes a squirrel showed itself long enough to give him a shot. There hadn't been anything to shoot today. Tired, cold, damp, and unhappy that he'd be eating nothing but rice and beans again tonight, he worked his way down the steep hillside through tall oak, ash, and hickory trees to a sharp drop-off above Greenbrier Road.

Red paused at the top of the five-foot clay slope, then slid down to the shoulder of the road on his feet. He stomped and scraped the wet clay off the bottoms of his shoes onto the pavement, then paused to get his bearings. There was nothing but trees and brush on both sides of the road for as far as he could see in either direction, but there was a familiar yellow diamond-shaped sign northbound with an arrow bent to the right and a 30 MPH speed limit sign below it. He knew where he was.

He crossed the roadway and headed north on the narrow left-hand shoulder toward the curve that had a guardrail on the outside edge to prevent speeding vehicles from launching themselves over the edge of the roadway and down a ten-foot embankment. As Red approached the guardrail, he looked down at the accumulation of wet leaves, brush, and discarded trash at the bottom of the steep slope. When he saw a large patch of blue nylon cloth among the orange, red, yellow, and brown leaves, he stopped.

As he stepped closer to the edge of the narrow shoulder, he thought it might be a backpack, the kind kids used to carry books to school. He didn't need it. He never carried books home. As soon as he turned sixteen, he was going to quit school, get a job, and start making some money so he wouldn't be hungry all the time.

He decided to retrieve the backpack anyway, thinking he might be able to sell it to some kid at school, or trade it for something worth something to him. Red propped the rifle on the guardrail, stepped off the edge of the shoulder, and began working his way down the soft clay embankment by carefully sidestepping on the layer of wet leaves covering the wet clay bank. The slope was so steep he could reach out and touch the wet leaves with his hand as he took another tentative step downward.

"Goddam it!" he cried out as his feet slipped out from under him, giving him no choice but to continue sliding down the slippery, leaf-covered clay bank on his backside. His progress was abruptly halted when his feet jammed against the backpack and a long mound of wet leaves on either side of it. With wet clay on his hands, shoes, and the bottom of his jeans, he kicked the backpack to roll it out of the way to give himself room to stand.

As the backpack rolled away from him onto the dried weeds and briars beyond, a human body emerged from the mass of leaves and clay. With a look of wide-eyed horror, Red stared in awe at the human head, defiled by weather, carrion-eating birds, and small animals. Larger animals had found access to the body cavity and fed on what they had found there. When he realized his feet were still in contact with the body, he turned and frantically kicked and clawed his way back up the sticky clay embankment.

On the roadway again, Red walked to the guardrail and scraped the clay off his shoes and hands before wiping his sticky hands on the sides of his jeans. As he looked down at the ravaged body, Red felt himself trembling. He had never seen a real dead person before. They looked different than they did in the movies, that was for sure.

When he heard a vehicle approaching from the south, he turned toward it. As a pickup truck neared, Red frantically waved with both arms. "Stop! Stop! Stop!" he screamed as the driver sounded his horn, gave him the finger, and continued on his way around the curve.

Red grabbed the rifle and headed north, knowing the gravel road where he lived was about a mile north of the curve. Just before he reached the guardrail, two vehicles came toward him around the curve. The first was a woman in a Toyota Corolla. Obviously terrified by the boy screaming and waving a rifle, she accelerated past him. The second was a Creek County Tennessee Sheriff's vehicle.

* * * *

As Sergeant Dan Warden drove around the blind curve in the department's old Chevy Caprice, he saw a teenage boy standing on the edge of the road just before the guardrail, yelling at him and pointing down the steep embankment. When he got close, he recognized the tall, skinny, redheaded boy as Red Black, one of the thorns in the side of Tennessee law enforcement from time to time. Dan nodded at Red, and then continued well beyond the curve before he pulled over onto what little shoulder was available and turned on his emergency flashers.

Dan glanced in the rearview mirror and saw the boy hurrying toward him carrying a rifle. He patted his gut. Assured he was wearing his vest underneath his uniform shirt, Dan freed his weapon in its holster, opened the door, and stepped out onto the road. "Stop right there, Red! Put the gun down!" Dan called out with his right hand resting on his pistol grip and his left arm out with its palm turned up. Dan suppressed a smile as he watched the boy quickly comply with his command and then raise his hands over his head without being requested to do so. The teenager had been through this drill before.

For over two weeks, the sheriff's departments of Creek County, Tennessee, and Chickasaw County, Alabama, had searched for a Middle Tennessee State University student who had told his family in Helleston, Alabama, he was hitchhiking home from Murfreesboro for Thanksgiving. He never arrived. He was last seen the day before Thanksgiving at a McDonald's in Bailey Springs, Tennessee, about twenty-five miles north of his destination in North Alabama. This was Greenbrier Road, the main highway between Bailey Springs and Helleston.

When Dan saw what Red had found at the bottom of the embankment, he thought they had finally gotten a break. After getting a report yesterday that a citizen had dropped off Jake at a McDonald's in Bailey Springs, he and the other deputies had driven past this curve several times without seeing a thing. He started making calls.

Shortly thereafter, the county medical examiner showed up and another deputy arrived to help direct traffic. After looking at the scene from the roadway, the medical examiner's team waited with everyone else until the volunteer fire department arrived and installed a ten-foot ladder against the steep embankment several yards away from the body.

Without touching or moving anything, the medical examiner's team, wearing gloves, took dozens of photos of the body, the embankment, and its immediate surroundings. Then they opened the backpack, put its contents into evidence bags, and passed them up to Dan on the roadway. Wearing gloves, Dan opened one of the bags containing a college textbook, opened the book, looked at the name written on the flyleaf, and felt sick.

* * * *

During Dan's interview with Red Black, he learned that the teenager and his mother lived by themselves about a mile north on Wolfe Road, a short gravel road off Greenbrier Road that ended farther along the ridge. Dan nodded when he made the connection with another Black. Red's daddy, Lloyd Black, was in Kilby prison outside Montgomery for the armed robbery of a convenience store just across the state line in Alabama.

When he was done with the interview, Dan offered to drive the boy home, but Red declined, saying he would rather walk. Dan nodded, understanding. Red Black was a member of the Randy Roycl gang that was well known to the Creek County Sheriff's Department for the criminal mischief they had gotten into over the years. Unlike Randy, who thought it would be a good idea to shoot a deputy sheriff, Red hadn't been as much trouble as some of the other members; still, riding in county vehicles was something they all tried to avoid. Dan thanked Red, gave him his card, and told him he was probably eligible for the five-hundred-dollar reward being offered by the family.

When the medical examiner discovered the body cavity was almost empty and that an animal had dragged a loop of the small intestines several yards away from the body, they called for portable floodlights so they could find and photograph all the damaged organs *in situ*. When told no lights were available, they decided to call it a night.

With a part-time deputy posted to guard the crime scene, Dan headed home. There was still more work to be done by him and the medical examiner, but it would be done better in the light of day.

* * * *

Jack lifted the beer bottle to his mouth and looked at the clock behind the bar. It was Friday night and almost eight o'clock. Time to throw another hundred dollars away, money he couldn't afford to throw away now that he had his own pickup truck again. It was a green 1995 F-150 with good rubber and low mileage, and it seemed to run good and handle fine. After some haggling with the used car salesman, he thought he had gotten a good deal. The price was right and his insurance money from the '93 took care of the down payment.

Now all he had to do was stay employed for the next five years to pay off the loan.

As the door to Uncle Buck's opened, Jack looked in the mirror behind the bar and saw two men enter dressed in camouflage clothes and orange hats. Hunters! Why hadn't he thought about that before? Hunters were all over the place this time of year. He had been worried about his missing truck mirror but had been afraid to go anywhere near the body, afraid someone might see him there. Now, he realized that all he had to do was to put on his camouflage clothes, grab his rifle, park somewhere close to the curve, get out, walk along the road, and act like he was hunting for something. In less than five minutes, he could be down that embankment, find his mirror, stick it in his jacket, and be back in his truck. As long as no one saw him down the embankment, he could be any hunter walking along the road. If a Tennessee game warden caught him without a Tennessee hunting license, he'd be in trouble, but it was a chance he was willing to take to solve a bigger problem.

Jack took another drink, smiled and nodded his head. He felt as though a big weight had been lifted from his shoulders. He had a plan to get his mirror and he knew it would work. By this time tomorrow night, he would have the mirror, the only thing that might connect him to the body. Maybe he would stop off at the oak tree on his way home and throw it out there. That would wrap things up in a neat little package.

Except for the bastard who had seen him do it. How did he know? Did he write down his license plate and trace him through that? Jack didn't think so. You probably had to know somebody in law enforcement to be able to get a name and phone number from a license plate. Somebody who'd spent time in prison probably didn't know the police or sheriff well enough to ask a favor like that. How did he know?

"He knows me," Jack whispered, banging his beer bottle down hard on the bar in frustration. "He's been in here. He knows my face!" He slowly turned and looked at the busy

Friday night crowd. The man was here, or would be, tonight or maybe tomorrow night. Who was he? It really galled him to realize that he probably knew the other man as well as the blackmailer knew him.

"That son of a bitch!" Jack hissed as he slammed his fist on the bar. He had been conned. There was no way anyone could have seen him down there well enough to know it was him that night; it had been too foggy for anyone to see much of anything. All the blackmailer might have seen was a red pickup stopped at the curve and he decided to play the odds.

"Damn," Jack said. The stranger had called him, accused him of killing the man, and demanded money without knowing if it was him or not. The man had been bluffing. Jack had fallen for it, acknowledging that he had been the driver. Now it didn't matter whether the man had seen him or not. The man had him by the balls and there wasn't anything he could do about it.

Jack glanced at the telephone. It was temporarily idle. Maybe Elaine had heard something from the flyers. Maybe they had heard from Jake. It was possible. Anything was possible. He grabbed his change and headed toward the pay telephone.

"Hello?"

"Hi, Elaine, Jack. I thought I'd call and see if you've heard anything yet."

"Oh, Jack! We might have some news about Jake. Dan called and told us a farmer outside of Bailey Springs recognized Jake's picture on one of the flyers. He said the farmer believes he gave Jake a ride from Pulaski over to Bailey Springs the day before Thanksgiving, so we're pretty sure he got that far. The Creek County sheriff and the Chickasaw County sheriff have been looking up and down every road between Bailey Springs and Helleston all day today but so far they've not come up with anything. I don't know if that's good news or bad."

"Well, let's keep our fingers crossed."

"Oh, Jack, if he got as far as Bailey Springs, I'm awfully afraid something really bad happened to him up there. I'm a nervous wreck right now, thinking about all the things that might have happened to him."

"You want some company?"

"Oh, that would be so wonderful. I've had a glass of wine, but it hasn't helped. I'm still as jittery and jumpy as I can be, my mind going in six different directions at the same time, thinking about what might have happened to him."

"I imagine it is," Jack said, then remembered something. "I thought you told me last week you didn't have anything alcoholic to drink."

"I have a friend at work who lives in Huntsville. I had her bring back a couple of bottles of wine for me the other day. I thought I'd have some in case you came over again."

Jack grinned. How about that? Not only did she want him to come again, she had some wine in case he did. On top of that, she had already had a glass of wine. He grinned as he recalled the effect that a glass of wine had on this woman's libido in a Pensacola motel. Things were looking up all over. "I've got to make a quick side trip first, but I'll be there in, oh, about thirty minutes."

"That would be great."

"See you then."

* * * *

From a quarter mile away, with the money in a beer bottle on the seat beside him, Jack saw the red and blue lights flashing through the bare trees as he approached the curve. Did someone else have a wreck at the same curve? Suddenly, chills coursed down his spine as he realized what was happening. They had found the body. He slammed his fist against the steering wheel. "No! God damn it! Not now."

Everything was going wrong. If they had found the body, they would find his mirror. They might trace it to him somehow. Now, if the blackmailer told them what he saw that night, he'd be in deep trouble. To stay out of jail, he would have to keep paying the man.

He slowed as he continued to approach the curve, then suddenly stopped. He couldn't drive past those deputies. They might stop him and start asking questions. What was an Alabama driver doing going north toward Bailey Springs tonight? Jack couldn't think of a good answer. They might think he was drunk. He'd only had a couple of beers, but they still might take him in for drunk driving. He couldn't afford that. There was no way he was going to make the drop tonight. He turned around and headed for Helleston and the only woman he had ever loved.

* * * *

Jack opened the glass storm door, then rang the doorbell. Elaine opened the front door, smiling at him. "Hi, there. Come on in." Jack walked inside, waited until she had closed the door, then opened his arms out to her. Quickly she rushed to him and wrapped her arms around him and pressed herself against him with an intensity that surprised him. She looked up at him, "Oh, I'm so glad you're here."

"So am I," Jack assured her. Smiling, she broke the embrace, took his hand, and led him into the living room.

Elaine pointed to the glass of red wine on the coffee table. "I'm afraid this is my second glass already. Would you like to have a glass?"

"Sure," Jack said. All wine tasted like rotten grapes to him, but he knew she didn't have any beer.

Elaine retold the events of the past two days to Jack as they sat on her couch, each holding a glass of wine. "Oh, Jack, I don't know what to think anymore!" Elaine cried out.

"I wish there was something I could do to help."

Elaine closed her eyes and slowly shook her head. Then she opened her eyes, sniffed and said, "Just hold me a few minutes."

"I think I can handle that," he said and moved over next to her.

They held each other tightly, then they kissed as they continued to hold each other as Jack found her breast once again. This time she allowed his hand to remain. Finally, she broke away, sniffed and smiled. "Oh, I'm so glad you're here."

"So am I," Jack said as he opened the buttons on her blouse. When he saw a sexy bra of mostly crimson lace, he smiled. Things were definitely looking up. Women didn't wear underwear like that unless they were planning for a man to see them in it. "My favorite color, University of Alabama crimson."

"I know. I remember," Elaine said, looking deep into Jack's eyes as he pulled the edges of her blouse aside, fully exposing her bra. "I've never stopped loving you, even when I was married to another man. Sometimes, I wish I could, but I can't."

"I love you more now than I ever did."

Elaine looked at Jack, perplexed. "If that's true, I guess I don't understand why you're still married. You told me why you got married, and I guess I can accept that. I'm sorry your son is dead, really I am, but I guess I don't understand. If that was the only reason you married her, why are you still married?"

Jack cocked his head and wrinkled his brow. He wasn't sure he could explain it in a way that a woman would understand it, especially this woman. He wasn't about to tell her that living with a woman, any woman, even one he didn't love, was a lot better than living without one. Never in his life had he heard either of his parents express love for the other. Still, after thirty-five years, they were still married, still slept in the same bed, and got along with each other most of the time. Cathy got on his nerves a lot, and sometimes he had to remind her who was the boss, but she was a good-looking woman, wasn't too bad in bed, cooked halfway decent meals, kept the house clean, washed his clothes, and didn't give him a bad time when he had a few beers up at Uncle Buck's.

Until Elaine walked into his hospital room, living with Cathy had been a better deal for him than not living with her. Now, maybe something better had come along. Jack smiled. "If I thought you'd be willing to forgive and forget, I'd be out of there in five minutes. I know I've screwed up my life, maybe yours, too. I swear to God, Elaine, if you'll give me another chance, I'll spend the rest of my life making it up to you."

"Will you, Jack? Will you really? Is that a promise?"

"It's a promise I'll keep until the day I die."

Elaine gazed at Jack, tears welling up in her eyes. She blinked her eyes, fighting the tears, but to no avail. She sniffed, smiled and said, "Excuse me for a minute. I'll be right back. Don't go away."

"I'll be right here."

After a few moments, Elaine returned wearing nothing but the crimson bra and matching panties. Instead of rejoining him on the couch, she stood facing him, her hands clasped in front of her. "Since the day I came to see you in the hospital, I've been wondering how I would feel afterwards if I had sex with you, knowing you're married to another woman."

"I sincerely hope you'd feel good."

"I'm not sure about that," Elaine said seriously. "We'd be breaking one of the Ten Commandments. That puts it right up there with killing somebody."

A cold chill crawled over Jack as he saw the bloody face in the ditch. He looked up at Elaine, a pained look on his face, and said softly, "I don't think so. I honestly don't think so."

"I kind of agree with you. I have reason to believe your wife is being unfaithful to you, so I don't think I would be doing any more harm to your marriage than she is already doing with another man," Elaine said, then smiled. "In any case, spending the evening with you would certainly get my mind off everything else for a while, but I'd better warn you."

"About what?" Jack asked, frowning.

"I haven't had a man since Russ moved out. That was over a year ago. I've had two glasses of wine, so I'm in a very loving mood. You might not survive the evening."

"Take me, Lord! I'm ready to go!" Jack cried out as he stood and flung his arms outward and upward as he looked up at the ceiling.

"I'm not ready for you to come or go," she said, grinning, then pointed toward the bedroom. "Uh, if you'll follow me, I'll show you what you've been missing."

"I can hardly wait," Jack said as he walked toward her.

"Neither can I," Elaine said, then turned and made a point of wiggling her rear.

"Very sexy underwear," Jack said, then smacked Elaine's rear hard enough for the sound to echo in the quiet of the room.

"Ouch!" Elaine cried out, then turned to Jack, frowning. "Naughty boy!"

Jack shrugged and smiled. "You used to like it when I was naughty."

"Sometimes . . . sometimes you're too rough."

"Sorry about that."

"I doubt it, but you're forgiven," she said, smiling. "Now, come with me and I'll let you decide if the real thing compares favorably with the tattoo on your arm."

Once in the bedroom, they grabbed each other and kissed with their mouths open for a long time. When they broke, she slowly dropped to her knees and looked up at him, smiling. "Now, let me see if I still remember how to do this."

"Well, at least you're not going to get mosquito bites on your ass this time."

Elaine looked up at Jack, frowning, then she burst out laughing. "Oh, you're so bad."

"Yeah. But when I'm bad, I'm good."

"I've heard that line before," she said as she reached for his belt buckle.

The phone rang. They both froze, looking first at the phone and then at each other. It rang again and then a third time. "I'd better answer it," she said quietly as she stood.

Jack nodded.

"Hello? Oh, Mom." After a moment, she said quietly, "I'll be right there." Then, in slow motion, she carefully replaced the handset onto the cradle. She turned to Jack, her face like stone. With a blank stare that looked through Jack to some point beyond, she said softly, "That was Mom. Dan called and said they've found a body down a bank in some roadside bushes near the Tennessee state line. Dan said there's no identification, but they found some books in a backpack with Jake's name in them."

"God, no," Jack moaned as he covered his face with his hands. He could no longer deny it. He had killed Jake. "No, no," he moaned over and over as he shook his head.

Elaine came to him and wrapped her arms around him and leaned her head against him. "I'm really going to miss that guy."

Jack raised his head and turned to Elaine. He watched as her chin began to vibrate and big tears ran down her face. "Let it go, Elaine. Let it go."

"Oh, dear God!" Elaine screamed in a high-pitched wail. "Why him? What did he ever do to deserve this?" she asked, then began to sob uncontrollably. Jack held her and let her cry. Five minutes later, she wiped the tears from her eyes once more, then said, "I'm sorry, I've got to go to Mom. She needs me."

"You need each other," Jack said, fighting back the tears in his own eyes.

Elaine gazed up at Jack. "It doesn't ever work out for us, does it?"

"Not yet," Jack said as he watched tears running down Elaine's face.

She came to him and hugged him for a long time, then she stepped back. "It's going to take me a few minutes to put myself back together again."

"I'll be on my way. I'll call you in a few days."

"Please do. Knowing you're around will be a big help."

"I'll do what I can. Goodnight, Elaine." Jack walked to the front door and opened it. As he reached for the handle on the glass storm door, he heard Elaine call, "Jack, wait!" He turned and waited as she hurried to him still dressed in her underwear. She glanced quickly out the door and into the darkness beyond, then wrapped her arms around him. "I'm really sorry it turned out like this tonight," she said, trying to smile.

"So am I," Jack said earnestly as he held her in his arms. "Christmas is coming. Maybe I'll get a chance to see you in that red underwear again before then."

"I hope so," Elaine said. "I've got so much love for you stored inside of me. I can't wait to give some of it to you."

With their arms around each other and their bodies pressed together, their lips met in a kiss that lasted a long time.

* * * *

"Hi, Pete, this is You-Know-Who. It's Friday night and I'm here all by myself again, as usual. I wanted to call and let you know I really enjoyed our little road trip last Sunday. It looks like you were right about Jake Warden. I saw on the ten o'clock news that they've found a body in a ditch just north of the state line that might be him. That's so sad. I still plan to see you tomorrow around noon. I'll call you on your home phone if I can get away."

14

Day 18
Saturday, December 12

THE COUNTY MEDICAL Examiner's team spent most of Saturday morning searching for, finding, and photographing various pieces of the human body scattered about the crime scene. Without saying anything about it to anyone, the team was silently thankful that it was a time of year when temperatures were below freezing much of the time. If this body had been lying exposed to the creatures of the forest for a couple of weeks in the summer, they would also have had to deal with flies, maggots, and the overwhelming, unforgettable odor of a decomposing human body. Once the team had finished, they gathered up everything into a body bag and left the scene for the sheriff's deputies.

Wearing their dark blue sheriff's department coveralls, caps, and heavy work shoes, Sheriff Johns and his deputies, including Dan, gathered at the crime scene and began their work. The air temperature had risen above freezing but there was still frost in the shady areas. Two men were assigned to inspect the road surface for fifty yards in either direction, looking for anything that wasn't part of the original road surface. When they finished the task, with small flags and evidence bags, they searched the shoulders and ditches for the same distance.

Within the crime scene tape, Dan, with other deputies, began picking up the leaves on the bank above, below, and near where the body was found, a few at a time, and depositing them in bags beside them. Any item they uncovered was photographed where it lay, then it was marked and removed, and a numbered peg inserted in the ground where the item was found. When they stopped for lunch, there was still much to be done.

* * * *

Shortly before noon, Cathy spent several minutes in the bathroom, applying new lipstick and brushing her hair; then she put on her coat and quietly left the house, not bothering to wake Jack as he lay on the couch, snoring lightly. She found a pay phone at a strip mall and entered Pete's home number. It had been less than a week since they had helped distribute the flyers, yet she found herself looking forward to their little Saturday lunch date with eager anticipation.

"Hello?"

"Hi, Pete! Ready or not, here I come," she said happily.

"Oh, Cathy, hi. I've been waiting for you to call. I've got bad news."

"What's the matter?"

"I've got to go to work. We can't get together today."

Cathy's shoulders slumped. "What happened?" she asked in a voice that clearly transmitted her disappointment with the news.

"The assistant manager during the day had a family emergency. I'm having to cover for him and then work my usual shift tonight."

"Damn!"

"Tell me about it. I'm sorry, Cathy, really, I am."

"So am I, Pete," she said and meant it. "Do we want to try again next Saturday?"

"Sure, but I might be able to get away for a few minutes to grab something to eat this evening. I know you told me it would be hard for you to get away during the evening, but if you can get away around seven, give me a call on my cell phone. I'd like to see you for a few minutes if we can arrange it."

"I'll do that," Cathy said, suddenly elated. "Oh, did you read about Jake Warden in the paper this morning?"

"I took a quick look at it before I came to work. The sheriff says it looks like he was killed by a hit-and-run driver a couple of weeks ago."

"Probably the day before Thanksgiving, while he was hitchhiking home."

"Looks that way."

Cathy nodded. "That's the same night Jack had his accident, on the same road."

"These narrow county roads can be awfully dangerous at night."

"Especially if the driver is too drunk to keep it on the road, like Jack was."

"At least he came out of it alive."

"If one of them had to die, it's too bad it wasn't Jack."

"You don't really mean that, Cathy."

"Don't I? I'm not so sure about that," Cathy said, then waited in silence for several seconds before she heard Pete clear his throat once, then again.

"Well, anyway, there was nothing in the paper about funeral arrangements and I doubt there will be for a while."

"Why not?"

"The body is part of a crime scene. The sheriff is going to want to do some tests with the body to try to find out who did it. It might be a week or so before they turn the body over to the family."

"Oh . . . well, let me know if you hear anything."

"I will."

* * * *

Jack let the phone ring for a long time, knowing who it might be. Finally, he picked it up and growled, "Yeah?"

"Where's my money?"

"I tried, damn it! There were cops all over the place up there last night. I'll be damned if I'm going to let the law catch me driving around up there at night."

"Yeah, I saw them lights myself."

"You did? How close do you live?"

"Wouldn't you like to know, smart ass? Tell you what, just because I'm a nice guy, I'm going to give you a chance to do it tonight."

"That's nice of you."

"Damn right it is. Only problem is, I charge interest."

"How much?"

"I want two hundred."

"Two hundred!"

"You heard me! Two hundred. If you give me a hard time about it, I know how I can make five hundred real quick. I saw a piece of paper the other day with a picture of a college kid that's been missing since Thanksgiving. They're offering five hundred for information about him. All I have to do is drop a dime and mention your name and I've made five hundred. Sounds like easy money to me."

"God damn you!"

"Hey, we're both going to Hell sooner or later. If you get there first, save me a seat. I wouldn't mind spending eternity holding hands with a good-looking man like you."

Jack slammed the phone down on the cradle so hard it bounced and landed on the floor. He left it there as he stalked off.

* * * *

By late Saturday afternoon, the Creek County deputies had cleared everything, down to the bare ground, from an area twenty feet wide, beginning at the road and extending into the brush beyond the young man's body. They stood on the roadway and appraised their work. There really wasn't much to see.

There was a spray-painted outline around the depression where it appeared the body had been lying before the kid kicked it. Most of the little numbered pegs in the ground identified areas where pieces of yellow and clear plastic had been found. They had also found three rusty beer cans . . . one Miller, two Budweiser . . . the remnants of a recent newspaper advertisement insert, an empty Jim Beam whiskey bottle, the rusted and bent handlebars from an old bicycle, a Middle Tennessee State baseball cap, and a right-side rearview mirror from a vehicle.

Last night, they examined the blue backpack and inventoried the items in it: books and binders with Jake Warden's name inside, and two sets of underwear. They had also bagged and tagged the clothes he had been wearing as well as the items in his pockets, including seven cents in change. There was no wallet. Based on what the farmer had told them, they didn't expect to find one.

Dan was holding several evidence bags that contained the only interesting things they had found all day, several pieces of thick plastic, some clear, some yellow, and an outside rearview mirror with a broken mounting post. One of the other deputies said it looked like the mirror on his 1993 Ford pickup. Dan knew it was possible someone could have discarded the mirror here after breaking it off somewhere else, but he didn't think so. He thought the odds were good that it came from the same vehicle that had hit Jake. It would be too much to expect that there would be fingerprints on it now, but it would be checked anyway. They might also be able to determine the vehicle make and model the plastic shards came from. One of the yellow chunks was a large corner piece. If both the mirror and plastic could have come from a Ford pickup, they would have a place to start. If the Ford dealer could tell them the year and model as well, they would have something to work with.

"What do I know . . . and what do I think I know?" Dan murmured.

He knew his nephew, Jake Warden, was dead. That was all he knew for certain. Dan looked up and down the road. Other than that, he would guess Jake was killed right here sometime after sundown on Wednesday before Thanksgiving by a hit-and-run driver traveling so fast the impact had thrown the body down the embankment. A vehicle hitting a human body that hard would have done damage to the vehicle as well, probably breaking the yellow plastic of the turn signal and the clear plastic covering the headlight and side light. It might also have bent the sheet metal of the fender and broken off the mirror.

Dan turned his head and looked back at the curve. Since the body was in the ditch on the west side of the curve, the driver would probably have been coming from the north, around the curve, driving too fast to see Jake in time to avoid hitting him. He had to have known he had hit something. Did he stop? Or did he keep on going to . . . where? Dan looked south. How far did he go down the road after he hit Jake? Did he stop? Was he coming from somewhere, or going somewhere? Did he live in Alabama or Tennessee, or was he just passing through from somewhere else?

Dan shook his head. There were too many questions and not enough answers at the moment. He could drive himself crazy trying to imagine all the possibilities. Meanwhile, until he came up with a scenario that worked better, he was going to assume Jake had been killed while hitchhiking on Wednesday night before Thanksgiving. He had probably been hit by someone in a Ford pickup, a '93 model or something close to it, coming south on this road from Bailey Springs.

* * * *

The discovery of Jake's body on Friday night was the lead story on the North Alabama TV channels at noon and again at five on Saturday. The story at noon included a video of Sheriff Johns describing how the body had been discovered and identified as Jacob Lee Warden of Helleston, Alabama. He went on to describe what had apparently happened and approximately when. The five o'clock news replayed the video of the sheriff, then showed Jake's graduation picture from his high school yearbook and included some sound bites from two neighbors of Jake's parents.

"That's so sad," Cathy said as she and Jack watched the news during supper.

"Yeah, it is."

"I can't imagine anyone doing something like that to another human being and leaving the body there to rot. He could have been lying there for years if that kid hadn't found him."

"You're right, he could have."

"I can't imagine how Elaine and her parents are feeling right now. This has got to be hard on them."

"I imagine it is." He picked up his jacket and headed toward the door.

"Going to that beer joint again?"

"Yes, I am. You got a problem with that?"

"You never take me anywhere on Saturday night. I'd like to get out and have some fun sometime, too."

"Uncle Buck's ain't your kind of place."

"But it's your kind of place, huh?"

"It's where men like me go to get away from women like you," Jack said, then grinned as he watched his wife scowl at him in silence. Soon he was out the door.

* * * *

"Hello?"

"Hi, Pete. It's me again. I'm calling you on your cell phone number. Are you home?"

"Yes, I am. It's been a long day. I decided to take a little break before I have to go back and close the place."

"I know you must be tired, but Jack has just left to go up to the line. He's got a truck again, so I've got my little Honda back. Would you like to have some company for a little while? He'll probably be gone for a couple of hours."

"That would be great, Cathy."

"Give me a few minutes to freshen up and I'll be there."

"I'll be waiting."

Cathy hurried into the bathroom, fixed her hair and face, then left a note for Jack on the kitchen counter that said she was going to take a look at some of the sales when there wouldn't be such a mob of Christmas shoppers.

* * * *

On his way to make his drop, with no headlights coming from either direction, Jack slowed and crossed over into the left lane as he approached the curve, knowing he wouldn't see anything. But, as he passed by, he saw a large area encircled with orange tape tied to stakes near the road and to bushes at the bottom of the slope. He was thankful that someone had found Jake's body, but now he was worried, and a little scared, wondering what was going to happen next. The sheriff would try to find out who had done it.

Maybe Dan wasn't so dumb after all. Jack would have to be careful what he said around him from now on. He was also committed to paying the blackmailer money he couldn't afford. How long would he be able to keep it up before Cathy started wondering where all their money was going? In his mind, there was a big whirlpool at the bottom of a deep, dark well and he was in the middle of it. Trying to figure out how to get out of the well was no longer his primary concern, trying to keep the vortex from pulling him under was all he could hope for right now.

He needed to think. From past experience, he had found that he did his best thinking while sitting on a barstool at Uncle Buck's with his hand wrapped around a cold beer.

* * * *

Two hours later, in the raucous noise of a Saturday night crowd, Junior put another beer in front of Jack and took the empty and enough money to pay for the fresh one. Jack lifted his beer and had a long drink. Two hundred dollars! Two hours ago, he had literally thrown away two hundred dollars. It was enough to make a preacher cuss. Jack looked around him. There was a big crowd, normal on a Saturday night. Was the man in here, right now, drinking beer with his blackmail money?

Then Jack heard him. The high nasal voice was unmistakable. He turned his head and saw a crowd down at the other end of the bar. One man was telling a joke with his nostrils pinched between his thumb and forefinger. When he got to the punch line, everyone around him laughed and so did he. Suddenly, the man jerked his head around and looked directly at Jack.

It was Bulldog. Jack might have known. He didn't know what the man's given name was or much about him, just that he started showing up here a few months ago. When he got into a fight with a bigger man and beat him senseless, someone called him a bulldog and the name stuck. No more than five-foot-six, he weighed close to two hundred pounds, all muscle. He had a bulldog's attitude, too. One of his pleasures, it seemed, was to pick on any man over six feet tall, prodding him with verbal insults until the man got fed up and took a swing. When Junior made them take the fight outside, Bulldog would beat the man senseless. He was the dirtiest fighter Jack had ever seen.

Jack and Bulldog stared at one another from a distance for a moment. Then Bulldog laughed out loud, said something to the men around him, and walked toward Jack. Standing next to Jack, Bulldog took a deep drag from his cigarette and exhaled it into Jack's face. "You remember what I told you would happen if you got too smart?"

"Yeah. Now let me tell you something," Jack said in a low voice, then glanced about him. Assured that no one was within hearing range in the noisy bar, he turned back to Bulldog. "I've heard about all the time you've spent in prison. Nobody's going to believe anything an ex-con says. Besides, it was so foggy that night, you couldn't have seen me or anybody else down there. I can make up any story I want to. It'll be my word against yours. Your little blackmail scam is over and there's not a damn thing you can do about it."

"That's not the way I see it, Hoss."

"Oh, yeah? Then try this one," Jack said, pointing down the hallway toward the bathrooms. "I'm going to walk down there and call nine-one-one and tell them I saw you at that curve that night. What are you going to do when the sheriff asks you where you were that night? Huh? What are you going to do when the sheriff checks out your story?"

"You don't want to make that call, hoss. Take my word for it, you don't want to sic the sheriff on me."

Jack turned to his tormenter and growled, "Get out of here. Leave me alone."

"Too late, hoss. We got some business outside," Bulldog said, then slammed the heel of his open hand against Jack's shoulder. The blow was so powerful Jack lost his balance and tumbled to the barroom floor in a heap, his legs entangled in the bar stool.

"Goddamn you!" Jack yelled as he kicked himself free and scrambled to his feet.

"Hey! Hey!" Junior yelled. "Take it outside, you two."

Jack looked at Junior. The big bartender was holding Black Billy and there was a look of fierce resolve on his face. Junior didn't care who won or lost the fight as long as it was done outside his bar.

Bulldog looked at Junior, then at Jack, and laughed. He slowly walked to the door, then paused and turned. With a big grin on his face, he motioned with his hand. "Come and get it, hoss. It's your turn."

Jack watched the door close, then turned back to the bar and had a drink. As he glanced at the others around him, he realized everyone was looking at him. "What the hell are you looking at me for?" he asked but didn't need to. They expected him to fight Bulldog and he knew it. "Bullshit!" Jack said, then turned back to the bar and picked up his beer. Bulldog was the last man in the bar he wanted to fight.

Jack wasn't afraid to fight. He had always been big enough and strong enough to hold his own in school yard scuffles, when he was young, and a couple of bar fights when he was in the Navy. Twice since returning from the Navy, he and a loudmouth drunk had squared off in the parking lot. Both times it had ended in a draw, with both men wrestling on the loose gravel, doing more damage to themselves than the other man when their wild swings met the sharp gravel rather than the other man's body. Tonight, it would be different. Bulldog never quit a fight and he could take any punishment another man gave him . . . and laugh.

Jack took a drink and slowly shook his head as the truth dawned on him. Sometimes a man has to do what a man has to do. He had to go out and fight Bulldog. He really didn't have any choice. He might get his neck broken, but if he stayed in here he would be called chicken . . . a coward who was afraid to face another man in a fight. He would be an outcast. Junior would still let him come in for beer if he wanted to, but he would never be part of the regular crowd of men again. Jack lifted the bottle to his lips, drained it, then set it down on the bar. He could stay or go. Either way, he would probably come out on the short end tonight. With a sneer on his face, he turned to go. He might not live until tomorrow, but with the way things were going these days, it really didn't matter that much to him, one way or the other.

"Attaboy, Jack!"

"Go get him, Jack!"

Jack paused on the small porch, relieved that Bulldog wasn't standing at the bottom of the steps waiting for him. He looked around the parking lot without seeing his antagonist anywhere. A sense of relief swept over Jack. Bulldog had gotten tired of waiting and had left. That called for another beer. As he turned to go back inside, simultaneously he heard a rifle shot and shattering glass next to his head. Someone had shot a hole in Junior's window and ruined his Budweiser sign. Jack dropped to the porch and lay there, flat on his stomach, as scared as he had ever been in his life. No one had ever shot at him before.

He slowly raised his head off the porch and stared out into the dimly lit parking lot. Then, in the semidarkness in the back of the parking lot, he saw Bulldog. The man was maybe thirty yards away, using his truck bed both as a shield and a rest for his rifle. Jack had a little .22 pistol in his truck. If he could get to it, it would take him about ten seconds to load it. It wasn't much against Bulldog's rifle, but it would be better than lying here waiting for Bulldog's aim to get better. The only problem was, Jack knew that as soon as he stood, Bulldog would take another shot at him. The next time he might get lucky.

In the next moment, Jack looked up to see Junior come out onto the porch holding a pistol down by his side. "What the hell's going on out here?" he roared in his best drill sergeant voice.

"Get back inside, Junior," a voice called from the darkness. "This ain't your business."

"I'm making it my business, Bulldog," Junior growled. "You came close to hurting some people in there. I'm not going to let you shoot up my place. Put the rifle down."

"What're you going to do if I don't? Shoot me with that little pea shooter?"

"I will if I have to."

"From up there? Bullshit. You could unload that whole damn clip at me and not get within ten feet."

"Don't bet your life on it, Bulldog."

"Go to Hell," Bulldog yelled as he fired his rifle once more. The bullet barely missed Junior's head and blasted a hole in the concrete block wall behind him. Junior flinched as the spray of exploding concrete peppered the back of his neck and head. "Next one's going to be closer, Junior. Better get back inside and stay out of this."

"Put it down, Bulldog," Junior growled. "Let's get the sheriff out here before somebody gets hurt."

"Can't let you do that, Junior. I wouldn't like that at all."

Jack was looking up at Junior when Bulldog fired once more. This time, as the bullet buried itself into the concrete block wall, Jack saw Junior stagger momentarily as his head snapped to the right. Immediately his left cheek and ear were covered by a broad stream of blood. Never moving from where he stood, Junior muttered, "You stupid fool." Holding the pistol in both hands, he slowly raised it, paused for only an instant, then fired.

With the loud roar of the pistol still ringing in his ears, Jack raised himself off the porch and looked back toward the truck. There was no one there. Either Junior had hit Bulldog, or he had ducked down. One way or the other, Junior had got Bulldog's attention.

"You stupid fool," Junior muttered again as he started down the stairs toward the parking lot with Jack following him. They found Bulldog lying on the gravel behind his truck. The right side of his skull was missing, exposing the bloody whiteness of his brain. Junior knelt down and pressed his fingers against the side of Bulldog's neck for a few seconds, confirming the obvious. "Damn," Junior muttered. "God damn it. This is all I need. Just when things were going good."

"Crazy bastard."

Junior rose, then turned and glared at Jack. "What the hell did you two get into it about?"

Jack looked up at Junior's bleeding face. The man seemed to be ignoring the small stream of blood running down his jawbone and dripping off his chin, coloring his shirt a crimson red. "Beats the hell out of me. He just came over and started giving me a bad time. I guess he was trying to start something with me tonight instead of someone else."

Junior stared at Jack. "Maybe. But I've seen men like him before. He was running from the law from somewhere because of something he did. You must have said something that made him think you were going to turn him in, so he went ape shit."

"Don't know what it was, but you saved my life. Thanks."

Junior looked at Jack, then nodded his head. "Save it for the sheriff. Don't leave until he gets here. I'm going to need you to tell him what happened out here."

"All I want right now is a beer," Jack declared as a feeling of euphoria came over him. His blackmailer had tried to kill him. Instead, the blackmailer was dead, killed by someone else. His hands were clean. Things were looking up.

Junior looked up and saw a big crowd standing outside the bar, watching from a distance now that the danger seemed to be over. "You stay right here while I call the sheriff. Don't let nobody get anywhere near Bulldog. You hear me? Nobody."

Jack wanted a beer in the worst way. His throat was dry as sand. "Sure, Junior. Whatever you say," Jack said, then looked down at the gore that was once Bulldog's head. "Are you really that good, or did you get lucky?"

Junior looked down at his weapon and shrugged his shoulders. "I used to be better."

Junior called 9-1-1, then, with a bar towel soaked with ice water pressed against the side of his face, he announced in a loud voice that the bar was closed. There were loud complaints from the men and women in the honky-tonk bar. It was much too early to go home and there was nowhere else to have some fun on a cold Saturday night in December. A dead man in the parking lot wouldn't have interfered with their partying mood if Junior had left them alone. For many, Bulldog's death would be cause for celebration, not sadness. Junior grabbed Black Billy with his free hand and slammed it down on the bar. "Last chance to walk out of here on your own two feet, folks! I mean it! I've already killed one man tonight. If I have to knock some heads to clear this bar, that's what's going to happen in one minute."

Within five minutes, the bar was empty. Within ten minutes, the parking lot was mostly empty. A few, with nothing else to do, hung around outside to see what would happen next.

Soon, a sheriff's department patrol car came roaring in, its siren screaming and light bar flashing red and blue, followed quickly by an ambulance. As the EMTs attended Bulldog, the men in the patrol car wandered slowly over to where the EMTs were working. Junior, followed by Jack, approached them.

"Howdy, Sheriff," Junior said.

"Hello, Junior," Sheriff Johns said. "What happened here tonight?"

"Bulldog took a shot at Jack. He missed but it went through my window and almost hit some people inside. When I came out, he shot at me a couple of times, then I took a shot at him."

"Looks like he got you pretty good," Sheriff Johns said, noting the bloody towel Junior was holding to the side of his head. "You all right?"

"Yeah, just a scratch," Junior said.

"Better let the EMTs take a look at it before they leave." He turned to the medical technicians. "What does it look like, Bobby?"

One of the EMTs looked up. "He was dead before he hit the ground, Sheriff."

The sheriff looked up at Junior, then at Jack. "Well, Dan's going to be here in a few minutes. He's going to want to talk to both of you. Were there any other witnesses?"

"Maybe, but I doubt it," Junior said, motioning to the small group lounging on the small porch. "Everybody inside hit the floor when Bulldog shot out my window. I don't think there was anybody outside except me and Jack."

The sheriff turned to his deputy. "J.D., why don't you go ask that crowd if anybody saw anything? If they didn't, get them out of here."

"Okay, Boss," the deputy said, then turned and walked across the parking lot to the porch. "Evening, folks."

There was a general murmur of acknowledgment by the group.

"Did anybody see what happened out here tonight? If you did, I'm going to have to ask you to stay around and answer a few questions. Then, we'll probably want to take you up to Bailey Springs and have you sign a statement about what you saw. Shouldn't take more than two or three hours. How about it? Did anybody see anything?"

There was a general disclaimer. No one had seen anything.

"Well, since none of you are witnesses, I'd appreciate it if you would all leave and let us do our job." He paused, then growled, "Do it right now, folks, and leave your glasses and beer bottles where you're standing. You wouldn't want some bad-ass deputy catching you with an open beer bottle on your way home."

There was some grumbling, but they all slowly wandered off to their vehicles. About the time the last spectator left, Dan pulled into the parking lot. Dan interviewed Junior first, then Jack. When Jack got into the car, Dan automatically extended his hand, then paused, a surprised look on his face, "Well, I'll be! Jack Constone! How're you doing, stranger?"

"I'm alive. How're you doing? It's been a long time."

"Sure has. Lord have mercy. It's been five or six years since the last time I saw you at a Thanksgiving dinner with Elaine and her folks."

"More like six. I was still in the Navy," Jack said, then frowned. Was this really happening to him? Twenty-four hours after they had found Jake's body beside a county road in Creek County, Tennessee, he was sitting in a car with a Creek County deputy sheriff who happened to be Jake's cousin.

"Well, how've you been? What've you been doing since the last time I saw you?"

"Well, I got discharged from the Navy, got married, and then came back here and got a job over in Colbert County. Been working there for five years now. How've you been? I heard some kid tried to part your hair with a bullet a few weeks ago."

With a wry grin, Dan nodded. "He sure tried."

"Sorry to hear about Jake," Jack said in a somber tone. "That's real sad."

Dan looked out the window and slowly shook his head. "It's a shame all right. He was a fine young man. It really had the family torn up, wondering what had happened to him. Finding him like we did isn't going to make it any better for anyone."

"I remember him when I was dating Elaine. He was a real character."

"Yes, he was," Dan said, then caught himself. "Now, back to what happened tonight."

"Where do you want to start?"

"Well, let's start with when you pulled into the parking lot and go from there."

Thirty minutes later, after some backtracking and rewriting, Dan had written a statement that sounded good to Jack, so he signed it. It was what had happened. All the facts were accurate. Dan had seemed to be as confused as Junior was about why Bulldog would start shooting at someone he had picked out at random in the bar, but Jack had offered no insight into their special relationship and Dan had eventually moved on.

"You can have a copy of this," Dan offered. "Just stop by the sheriff's office in Bailey Springs anytime."

"Thanks."

"Looks like you've been in another fight."

"No, not lately," Jack replied.

"You've got a new scar on your forehead, and you've got some old bruises on your face."

"Oh, that," Jack said, unconsciously touching his forehead. "I, uh, ran off the road down toward the Alabama state line on my way home from here the night before Thanksgiving. Must have split my forehead on the steering wheel. There's blood all over the cab. Totaled my pickup truck and put me in the hospital."

"Oh, yeah, I remember that. Another deputy handled it. Was anyone else involved?"

"No, just me. It was raining that night. Took that curve a little too fast. Slick tires and slick roads don't go too well together."

"That's a fact," Dan said, then extended his hand again. "Good to see you again, Jack. Thanks for sticking around. I appreciate the information."

"Is that it? That's all you need?"

"That's all for tonight," Dan said, then yawned. "I've had a long day; I've got to get out of here before I fall asleep on the job. If I need you for anything else, I'll call you, but I doubt it. Looks like Junior did what he had to do."

"I can't believe Junior got him with one shot from a pistol from that far away."

"That's a 9mm Beretta. When I was talking to Junior, he told me he shot a Beretta like that one a few thousand times when he was on a handgun competition team in the Army. I guess he was pretty good. He said he won more times than he lost until he got tired of traveling."

"Damn, I didn't know that. I'll bet Bulldog didn't know it either."

"I doubt it," Dan said, then yawned mightily. "Anyway, thanks again, Jack."

"Goodnight, Dan," Jack said, then got out of the car.

"Oh, Jack!"

"Yeah, Dan?" Jack asked, sticking his head back inside.

"What kind of vehicle were you driving when you had your accident?"

"Uh, a '93 Ford . . . F-150."

"Oh, yeah? Regular cab or extended?"

"Regular with a long bed. Why're you asking?"

"Just wondered. Goodnight, Jack," Dan said, then yawned once more.

* * * *

"Wow, look at the time," Cathy said. "I left a note for Jack that I was going to do some shopping, so I'd better get out of here since most of the stores will be closing pretty soon."

"It was wonderful, seeing you again, Cathy."

"I enjoyed it too, Pete. Are we still planning to get together again next Saturday?"

"Sounds good to me," Pete said.

At the door, they paused, gazing at one another. Cathy bit her lower lip, then asked, "I know it's none of my business. I hope you don't get mad at me, but could I ask you a personal question?"

Pete shrugged his shoulders. "Sure."

"Uh, do you like girls?"

Pete jerked his head backward and frowned. "Of course I do."

"I mean, do you like girls, you know, more than you like boys?"

"You mean, am I . . . homosexual?" Pete asked, his face crimson in embarrassment.

Cathy nodded. "It's okay if you are. I don't mind, really."

Pete silently shook his head. "No, I don't like boys. I'm a little bashful around women, that's all."

"I've noticed," she said quietly, then smiled at Pete. "I guess I should consider myself lucky. I mean, this is the third time I've been to your apartment. Lots of guys would have tried to take advantage of me to do, you know, more than talk."

"You're married, Cathy. It would be terrible for me to do something to jeopardize your marriage."

"Being here in your apartment jeopardizes my marriage," Cathy said quietly.

"I guess it does, doesn't it? I mean, we haven't done anything, but I guess some people might think we had." Pete shook his head with a forlorn look on his face. "It sure would make things a lot less complicated if you weren't married."

"We're married in name only, Pete. It isn't working. We got married for the wrong reason and after more than five years we still haven't found a good reason to stay married."

"Then, why are you still married?"

Cathy shook her head. "I guess, in a way, I'm like you. Until we started talking about California, I forgot that I don't have to put up with his crap if I don't want to. I've changed since the night I met you. Pete. My perspective on things is different now. Jack is still as mean as ever, but I don't feel so trapped anymore. I'm not as afraid of him as I was a week or so ago."

Pete gazed at the woman and slowly shook his head. "I know we shouldn't be seeing each other like this. The Good Lord will probably make us regret it one of these days," Pete said, then took a deep breath, exhaled, and said, "But I can't wait to see you again."

"I can't wait either," Cathy said, then reached out to Pete. "Can I have a little hug before I go? It won't be a big sin, will it? I promise not to get carried away." Pete smiled and held out his arms to her. She came to him and pressed her body against his. After a moment, they broke, stepped back and smiled at each other. "That wasn't so bad, was it?" Cathy asked. "I mean, we didn't get hit by a bolt of lightning or anything."

Pete shook his head, his cheeks red with embarrassment from having made full bodily contact with another man's wife. "No, we didn't."

"Can we try something else?"

"Like what?"

Cathy bit her lower lip, then said softly, "Kiss me. Please."

They came to each other once more, pressing their bodies against each other. As they embraced, their lips pressed gently together for a few seconds, then they stepped back. As they stared at each other, each knew yet another line had been crossed in their relationship.

Cathy smiled and said softly, "See you next Saturday, if I can get away."

"I'll be here," Pete promised.

"I still think you should tell Big Bad Bart to kiss your butt."

"I'm still thinking about it."

"Then do it, Pete. For God's sake, do it!"

"If I did, I'd probably go back to California to look for another job."

"Good for you. I'd go with you if I could."

"Why don't you?" Pete asked. "You know, to visit your parents."

Cathy frowned and stared at Pete, her mouth agape, at a loss for an answer. This man had asked her to leave her husband and go with him to California. She wasn't ready to do anything that serious, but maybe she could take a little vacation to visit her parents. "You know, you're right. It's been a long time since I've seen my parents."

"You really think you might come to California?"

"I might come out for a little visit. It may not be right away, but I will, just as soon as I can. That's a promise." She was sure her old Honda Civic wouldn't make it that far and she had no idea where or when she would get the airfare. She knew Jack would never give it to her. Would her parents send it to her? Maybe, if they were sure Jack wasn't coming with her.

"Then, I'll do it," Pete vowed. "I'll turn in my notice, first thing Monday morning. I really will. That's my promise to you, Cathy."

Cathy got into her car, started the engine, then looked down at her trembling hands. Dear God, what had she done? Pete had asked her to go with him to California and she hadn't turned him down, not really. Cathy smiled. There was no doubt about it, he definitely liked girls. She could feel his erection pressing against her as they kissed. It felt so wonderful! Jack never hugged her. The only time he kissed her or touched her in a loving way was to satisfy his lust without any sense or feeling for her own needs.

Would she be willing to join Pete in bed the next time? She had long since lost her virginity to other boys before the night Jack had impregnated her, and she was pretty sure Jack had not been faithful to her, so why not? Her birth control pills should work whether the man was her husband or another man. Cathy stared out the windshield and cried out, "Oh, my Lord! Jack will kill me if he finds out about this!"

15

THE FOLLOWING FRIDAY, Cathy stopped at Bart's Bargain Barn after work to get her birth control prescription refilled. While waiting for it, she wandered down the aisles. Suddenly, she looked up to see Pete walking toward her.

"Hi, Cathy," Pete said, smiling at her. "What brings you to this mad house?"

"Oh, hi, Pete. I had to get a prescription filled. I looked around when I came in, but I didn't see you."

"I was on the phone when I saw you pass by. I thought I'd come out and see how you were doing."

"I'm doing fine," Cathy said, then paused, smiling at Pete. "You're looking good."

"I feel good, too," Pete said, then grinned. "I told Big Bad Bart to kiss my rear."

Cathy's eyes grew wide, and her mouth flew open. "You did!"

Pete nodded. "I really did. First thing Monday morning. I turned in my resignation. I promised you I would, and I did. You were right. They were just using me. After I told them I was leaving, they offered me all sorts of things: a raise, shorter hours, time off . . . all the stuff they could have already given me if they really wanted me to stay."

"When are you leaving? Right away?"

Pete nodded. "I told the manager I was giving him two weeks' notice, so December the twenty-eighth is my last day. I've already told the Cross Winds manager I'm leaving before the end of the month."

135

"Oh, I'm so proud of you," Cathy said, reaching out and touching Pete's arm.

"It's all your fault. If you hadn't talked me into it, I doubt I would have done it."

"I hope you won't regret it."

"I doubt it. The only thing I regret is that I didn't do it before. Of course, if I had, then I wouldn't have met you. You're the only good thing that's happened to me in Alabama. The more I think about going back to California, the more I'm looking forward to seeing you out there. When are you thinking about coming?"

Cathy already knew the answer: probably never, certainly not for a long time. With a grim look on her face, she said, "I'll have to let you know. I'm not sure right now. Maybe we can talk about it at your place tomorrow. Are we on for tomorrow?"

"Let's don't plan on anything tomorrow. The boss is really upset that I'm leaving. I think he'd fire me now if he could come up with a good excuse, so I'd better plan on us not doing anything for a few days until he calms down a little."

Cathy paused, glaring at Pete. "You know they're confirming that you made the right decision, don't you?"

Pete nodded.

Cathy turned to go. Just as quickly, she turned back around. "Oh, do you know when they plan to have something for the guy that got killed? It's been a week now and I haven't heard anything."

"I talked to Elaine at church last Sunday. She said the county medical examiner told the family he would release the body to them this week, so they're planning to have the visitation for him this Sunday and the burial on Monday."

"Do you know where they're having the visitation? Jack took the paper with him when he went out to breakfast and didn't bring it back."

"At Greenway, I think, from six to nine."

"Do you think you can get away for that?"

"Yes, I can. He hasn't chained me to my desk yet."

"Then I'll try to make it around . . . eight? If Jack doesn't want to come with me, I'll come anyway."

"Great, maybe we'll have a few minutes to talk."

"Sure, if I come alone. If Jack comes with me, I might not have a chance."

16

Day 26
Sunday, December 20

ON SUNDAY EVENING, Jack showered, shaved, dressed in slacks and a sports coat, and joined Cathy in the long line of mourners at the funeral home to pay respects to the man he killed. The line seemed endless. It began at the main entrance, turned to the right down a long hallway and made a U-turn before entering the room where members of the Warden family formed a receiving line to greet the mourners. Neighbors and friends of Jake's parents, Elaine's co-workers, Central Methodist church members, and Jake's high school friends shook hands with the Warden family and said how sorry they were as they paid their respects to the young man in the casket. Usually, the casket was open during this period of grieving, but this time the casket was closed, and Jack knew why. He was thankful it was.

With Cathy preceding him, they eventually worked their way into the room. When Elaine first saw them, she smiled and waved. Jack smiled and made eye contact with her. Cathy, seeing Elaine waving, waved back. Most of the faces were vaguely familiar to Jack from Warden family gatherings he had attended years ago. As he introduced himself and Cathy to Jake's aunts and uncles, he discovered most remembered him from days gone by. Some seemed genuinely happy to see him again; others were more reserved.

After speaking briefly to Jake's parents, Cathy and Jack moved on to Elaine and Dan. Cathy gave Elaine a brief hug, spoke to her, then moved on to Dan. Dan remembered Cathy and thanked her again for helping with the flyers, telling her someone who had seen one of the flyers in Bailey Springs had given them some good information about what had happened to Jake.

Cathy smiled at Dan, said she was glad to help, shook his hand, glanced back at Jack, then quickly moved on. She was afraid that, if she stayed around, Dan might mention her carpool arrangements that afternoon. Jack didn't know she had spent that afternoon alone with another man, and she wanted to keep it that way. She paused briefly at the casket, crossed herself, then glanced back once more and saw Jack hugging Elaine in a tight embrace. She walked out into the hallway, looking for Pete.

When Elaine and Jack broke their embrace, they held each other at arms' length. There were new tears in Elaine's eyes as she and Jack gazed into each other's eyes.

"Hey, Jack. Didn't see you for six years, now twice in a little over a week," Dan said, extending his hand.

"How're you doing, Dan?" Jack said, shaking Dan's hand.

"Just trying to get through this. Thanks for coming."

"What've you two been up to?" Elaine asked.

"There was a little problem up at Uncle Buck's Tavern last Saturday," Dan said.

"Oh, I heard somebody talking about that," Elaine said, then knitted her brow. "The owner shot somebody, didn't he?"

Dan nodded his head. "Jack was a witness. He and I got to talk for a few minutes."

"What is this world coming to?" Elaine asked, then put her arm around Dan's waist and leaned her head against his shoulder. "Nobody is safe anywhere these days."

"I'm sorry we won't be able to attend the funeral," Jack said, looking at Elaine. "I've been off so much here lately."

Elaine gazed back at him and quickly nodded.

Jack looked into Elaine's tearful eyes and clenched his teeth as he felt tears coming to his own eyes. He wanted so badly to tell this woman how sorry he was for killing her brother, knowing he couldn't— not tonight—not ever. "I'm so sorry about Jake," Jack said, his voice rough with tears.

"I know," Elaine said, then smiled. "Thank you, Jack."

Jack walked to the casket, then paused and turned to face it. He had wanted very badly to continue walking, but Elaine and Dan would probably be watching and would wonder why he had continued past without pausing in respect. He glanced at the casket. Because of him, the desecrated body of Jacob Lee Warden was inside. Suddenly, the ghastly face he had seen that night came to him again in unusual clarity. Jack felt tremendous pressure in his gut. In a brief moment of panic, he thought he was about to vomit on the casket. He took a deep breath, forced himself to swallow, and hurried out into the hallway. As he paused, taking more deep breaths, he heard Dan calling to him.

"Hey, Jack, got a minute?"

"Sure," he said. He looked down the crowded hallway for Cathy, saw her talking to a skinny teenage boy in an ill-fitting suit, then turned back to Dan. "What can I do for you?"

"I was wondering, you said your truck was totaled. Do you know where it is now?"

"Uh, well, it's still up at Bailey Springs, at Art's Auto, as far as I know. It belongs to the insurance company now. I don't know what they're going to do with it."

"I expect they'll make a deal with Art. That was a '93 Ford F-150, right?"

Jack silently nodded.

"What color was it?"

"Red. Alabama Crimson Tide red."

Dan grinned. "You were driving a green one last night. What's the Bear's ghost going to think about that?"

"Couldn't find a red one. I got such a good deal on this '95, I couldn't turn it down. I put a big 'ROLL TIDE' sticker in the rear window, though."

"That might do. Low mileage?"

"Yeah, and this one has an airbag. Might come in handy the next time I take on an oak tree."

"It might. I'm looking for a new pickup myself," Dan said.

"Oh, yeah? A Ford?"

"No, I'm a Chevy man myself. I'm thinking of getting a Silverado."

"I thought about getting a new one, but when I found this one, I couldn't turn it down for what the man wanted for it," Jack said as Cathy rejoined them.

Dan glanced back over his shoulder at his grieving family. "Well, I'd better get back in there. Thanks again for coming."

"How's Junior doing? Is he in trouble?"

"Not with us. I expect the preachers talked about him and the devil in the same breath from the pulpit last Sunday. There's a lot of people down here in Alabama who want us to shut him down."

"He's probably paying too many taxes for you to do that."

"We did shut down his competition up the road from him, back when Uncle Buck was still running the place. We caught them selling dope on the side. Junior runs a clean operation as far as we know. There are usually fights on the weekends, but it's mostly black eyes and bloody noses."

"Bulldog wanted to put me in the grave."

Dan nodded his head. "I still can't figure that one out. We know his name and that there's an outstanding warrant for him in West Virgina, but we still don't know where he lived around here. When we find out, we might know why he decided to take a shot at you."

Jack smiled and nodded. The deputy sheriff had no idea how accurate that statement was. Hopefully, he wouldn't find out anytime soon. "Well, I guess we'd better go. Let me know if I can be of any help to you."

"I'll do that. So long, folks."

"Nice seeing you again, Dan. I hope you find the person who did this," Cathy said.

"I'm going to try my best, Mrs. Constone," Dan called out to the departing couple. Dan frowned as he watched Jack and Cathy walk away. Why hadn't Jack asked him why he had taken an interest in his wrecked truck? He sure would have if he'd been in Jack's shoes. It was just as well he hadn't asked. Dan didn't have a ready answer.

Last week, when Dan was interviewing him in Uncle Buck's parking lot, Jack had mentioned that he had wrecked his '93

Ford pickup on Greenbrier Road the night before Thanksgiving, Dan remembered that J.D. had said the mirror they found near Jake might have come from a '93 Ford pickup. So far, it was the only reason he had any official interest in Jack's truck.

Dan smiled to himself. Unofficially, the confused look he had seen on Jack's face when he had asked him about the wrecked truck had made the conversation worthwhile. Making Jack feel uncomfortable by implying that he might be under suspicion would be a little payback for his smart-ass attitude at Warden family gatherings in the past.

Dan, as well as other members of the Warden family, had silently objected to the crude way Jack had treated Elaine during the years she and Jack had dated. At Warden family gatherings, Jack seemed to get a kick out of saying something in front of other family members that he knew would embarrass or belittle Elaine. A couple of times, Jack had smacked Elaine's bottom in front of Dan and others. Dan had wanted to deck the guy for doing that, but Elaine's reaction to the abusive behavior had been so mild that Dan had kept his mouth shut, knowing if he had objected, Elaine might have gotten upset with him for interfering. He didn't want that to happen. Elaine was very special to him. He and Elaine had been much closer than cousins over the years, more like brother and sister.

When Jack had dumped her and married Cathy, Dan was the one Elaine came to with tears in her eyes. He was the one who had listened while the broken-hearted woman told how Jack had destroyed her dreams of happiness. There had to be a better way of breaking up with a woman than the way Jack did it. No love, no compassion, no feelings at all.

Later, when she married the wrong man, he was there to hear her troubles again. When she decided to divorce Russ, she told Dan before she told her husband. Dan knew Elaine's problems with Jack might not be over. He had seen the way they had looked at one another a few moments ago. There was more there than two old high school friends seeing each other again. What on earth a good-looking, intelligent woman like Elaine saw in a smart-ass redneck like Jack was beyond him.

Dan sighed as he turned to rejoin his grieving relatives beside the casket of a young man who had so much potential and had died so needlessly. He knew that, eventually, he would find the vehicle that had killed Jake and the driver who had left his body to the animals of the woods. In the meantime, he would stop by Art's before the funeral tomorrow and take a look at Jack's truck that he had wrecked the same night on the same road. It was a place to start. Until he found something better to do, doing something that was probably a waste of time was better than doing nothing at all. Then a chill crawled up Dan's neck. Unless the vehicle was somehow involved in both accidents.

17

Day 27
Monday, December 21

ON HIS WAY TO THE FUNERAL on Monday, Dan stopped at Art's Auto. Jack's truck was still there. He could see it toward the back of the small lot as he pulled in. When Dan told Art he wanted to take a look at the red Ford F-150 pickup truck, Art, with his head beneath the hood of a car said, "Help yourself."

"Is it locked?"

"What for?" Art asked without looking up from his work. "It ain't going nowhere."

As Dan approached the pickup, he slipped on a pair of latex gloves out of habit. The truck had been left unlocked in an open lot for almost a month. Anybody and everybody had been in it, on it, and around it. Even Jack had been here. If this truck had been involved in two accidents the night before Thanksgiving, there was no reason to believe any salvageable evidence remained. Still, there was no reason to contaminate it any further.

As he approached the truck from the driver's side, it still looked in fairly good shape. He could see the cracked windshield and the buckled hood, and someone, probably Art, had taped a big brown garbage bag over the broken window on the passenger's side. The outside rearview mirror on the driver's side caught his attention. It looked a lot like the mirror they had found near the body. A week ago, that bit of information might have excited him; now it was only mildly interesting to him.

144

As he walked around to the front of the truck, he examined the undamaged driver's side headlight group. Enclosed in a rectangular chrome frame that wrapped around the edge of the fender was the headlight and side light enclosed in clear rectangular plastic, and the turn signal beneath both lights in a band of yellow plastic underneath the entire lower portion of the chrome frame. He examined the corner of the turn signal, knowing he had a piece of yellow plastic in an evidence bag similar to it that was designed to fit on the passenger's side of the truck. But it was more complicated than that.

Early last week, while at the Ford dealer's parts department, he had learned that his chunk of yellow plastic could very well have been part of the turn indicator on a '93 Ford truck. He had also been told that the broken mirror he'd found was one of the mirror options on '93 Ford trucks. However, Dan also learned to his dismay that the mirror and the headlight group were common, not only to the entire F series of Ford pickups, but other Ford vehicles as well, for several years before and after 1993. Instead of leaving the dealership with a good feeling about the items he had collected at the curve, he had left knowing the parts were so common to so many Ford products for so many years that they were almost useless in his investigation.

All he knew for certain was that the parts had come from a Ford product. Once he found the right vehicle, the Tennessee Forensics Crime Lab up in Nashville might be able to use the parts to tie it to the crime scene, but the pieces wouldn't be much use in finding the vehicle. Dan sighed in frustration, then walked around to the right-hand side of the truck where he saw the massive damage that had totaled the truck. The tree had hit the right side of the truck, destroying everything from the bumper to the passenger's door and beyond.

Dan leaned over and looked closely at the damaged sheet metal. He saw nothing more than he expected to find, oak splinters and bark lodged in the sharp folds of the sheet metal. There was nothing left of the light group but mangled steel; even the chrome frame around the light group was missing. Rust had already started where sharp bends had cracked the layers of maroon paint and exposed the bare metal beneath to the damp North Alabama winter weather. The right-hand outside mirror was missing, but the mangled bracket was still partially attached to the damaged door. Dan glanced at his watch and decided that he had time to take a quick look inside the cab.

When he looked inside, he saw years of accumulated trash and dried clay mud on the dashboard, seat, and floor of an old pickup truck. He also saw the dark crimson of dried blood on the steering wheel, dashboard, and seat. He nodded. Hitting your head on the steering wheel hard enough to split your scalp would do that. As he stepped back to close the door, he noticed a wedge of yellow clay on the floor on the driver's side. He looked closer. There was an imprint on it, like someone had stepped in it with the arch of their shoe and tracked it into the truck where it had fallen off. Dan knew there was nothing unusual about that. He had tracked clay mud into his own house many times. It came with the territory. These rolling hills at the terminus of the Appalachian Mountains were covered with clay. Whenever it got wet, it stuck to anything that touched it.

Yellow clay wasn't all that unusual. Many people thought these hills were made of red clay, but red was only one of the colors. If you looked hard enough, you could probably find clay of every color in the rainbow. But it was the yellow that had caught Dan's attention. His boots and coveralls had been covered with yellow clay after climbing around on that embankment a week ago. This surely looked like it was about the same color yellow that had been on the embankment. Had Jack been down that same embankment? Dan glanced around him and once again realized how many different people could have sat in the seat over the past month and left the clay wedge behind. Even Jack could have done it when he was here.

"What do I know?" Dan murmured to himself. He knew that, according to the Report of Investigation by the County Medical Examiner that the sheriff had received, Jake had died from massive blunt force trauma consistent with the impact by a motor vehicle traveling at a high rate of speed. It also stated that, due to the condition of the body and the absence of many of the internal organs, a Toxicology Report would be delayed.

"What do I know?" Dan repeated. He knew the last person known to have seen Jake alive had dropped him off at McDonald's in Bailey Springs around sundown on Wednesday, the day before Thanksgiving, more than two weeks before he was found. Sunset was about four-thirty the day before Thanksgiving, and it would have been dark about thirty minutes later. What had happened to him then? How did he get from McDonald's to a roadside ditch over eight miles south? Did he walk that far in the rain? Someone knew the answer; that was for sure. Did the same person know how he died? Maybe.

"What do I think I know?" Dan asked himself, his brow furrowed. Jake was probably killed on Greenbrier Road, sometime after dark on the Wednesday before Thanksgiving by somebody in too big a hurry on those wet roads that night. If the toxicology report showed that Jake was high on something that night and could have been standing in the middle of the foggy road when the driver hit him, would the driver have stopped to give aid? Dan thought so, unless the driver was so drunk he knew he wouldn't pass a breathalyzer test. Knowing he was breaking the law by being behind the wheel of the vehicle, the driver probably wouldn't have stopped after hitting Jake no matter where he had been standing.

Dan looked at Jack's truck once more. Jack had been on Greenbrier Road that night, had been driving too fast in this '93 Ford pickup to keep it on the road, and was probably over the BAC limit. The problem was he lived in Helleston, and his accident had happened south of where the body was found. Dan was pretty sure Jake had died right where they had found him, a mile north of Uncle Buck's.

Whoever had hit Jake had been coming south, probably from Bailey Springs, which meant Jack wasn't involved because there was no reason for him to be north of Uncle Buck's that night. Dan frowned. Maybe, maybe not. Nothing was certain about this case right now except that Jake was dead and the driver who had killed him would go to jail when Dan found him.

Jack had wrecked this truck within two miles of where they had found Jake's body, on the same road on the same night Jake had been killed. The mirror they had found at the scene was the same type of mirror that had been installed on this pickup. They had found a piece of yellow plastic that could have been part of his right-hand turn signal, and there was yellow clay where they had found Jake, and yellow clay in Jack's truck.

Dan shook his head. He tried to keep his private life separate from his job, but in this case, they seemed to be commingled. He frowned as he posed a question to himself: personal feelings about Jack aside, if this was a stranger's truck, would I leave it here, or would I have it towed? Then he realized that, at this point in the investigation, he shouldn't be asking why, but why not?

Jake's body had been found over a week ago. Since then, Sheriff Johns had been pelted with questions about the progress of the investigation by television stations, newspapers, and family. The sheriff had, in turn, held daily meetings with Dan to find out what progress had been made. Those meetings had become less and less friendly when Dan had to admit each day that there had been no substantial progress in the case.

Dan nodded. He would have Jack's truck towed behind the fence at the sheriff's station and have the medical examiner's latent print expert check the interior for prints. There was no reason to believe Jake had ever been in this truck, but it needed to be verified. The medical examiner would get a set of Jack's fingerprints from the Navy and use them to eliminate his fingerprints from the cab of his truck. The soft tissue of Jake's fingers was mostly gone, but the medical examiner had gotten good prints from the books in the backpack that were assumed to belong to Jake.

The whole family was expecting Dan to solve this. In time, he knew he would. He looked down at the yellow clay. He would take the clay with him so that he could honestly tell them at the funeral that he already had a lead he was checking out. He wouldn't tell them how hopeless he thought it was. Telling them he was already working on something would give them some hope. That was all he could give them right now.

He went to his car, got his camera, photographed the clay where it lay, then picked it up and turned it over. The word WOLVERINE was on it in slightly raised letters of clay. Dan knew that Wolverines were a popular brand of high-top, steel-toed, work shoes. He took a photo of the bottom of the piece of clay, placed it in an evidence bag, and labeled it. Having done that, he closed the driver's door and put a sheriff's department seal on both doors. After telling Art that he had scaled the truck, Dan asked him to tow it behind the fence at the sheriff's station.

"What do you want that piece of junk for?"

"Don't know yet. I'll call and tell them to expect you."

"It's your money."

"Actually, it's the county's money."

"Whatever. As long as I get paid for the tow."

"You will . . . eventually."

* * * *

After she punched the time clock at the end of her shift at Chek Mart on Monday, Cathy hurried to Bart's Bargain Barn, grabbed a cart, and wandered up and down the aisles. On her second pass by the office area windows, she saw Pete walking toward her.

"Hi, Pete. How're you doing?"

"Hi, Cathy. I'm doing fine. I'm surprised to see you here."

"I need to buy some things," Cathy said, then smiled. "Mostly I thought I'd stop and say hello to you before I headed home. Did you go to the funeral today?"

Pete nodded his head. "The church was packed. I don't think I've ever seen so many people there."

"That's so sad. It isn't going to be a very merry Christmas for the Warden family," Cathy said. Then her face brightened. "How about you? Have you done your Christmas shopping?"

Pete nodded. "I only had to buy a few things."

"I'm done, too. Thank goodness. I had no idea what to buy Jack. I got him an insulated camouflage hunting jacket, but he'll probably take it back and exchange it, like he always does. I've never bought him anything he liked."

"Maybe I shouldn't tell you this, but I think I saw him at Elaine's house a week ago on Friday night."

"Elaine Warden? Are you sure?"

"Pretty sure. I mean, I didn't know it was your husband at the time, but when you pointed him out to me at the funeral home Sunday night, I could swear it was the same man. He's got a green pickup with a big ROLL TIDE sticker in the back window, right?"

Cathy nodded. "He sure does."

"I drove over to her house to leave some church literature. When I walked up to her house, I saw her through the glass door. She was standing there in her underwear hugging and kissing a man. I was pretty embarrassed, so I went back to my car and waited until he drove off. I waited a few minutes, you know, to give her a chance to get dressed, then I rang her doorbell. She came to the door wearing a bathrobe, so I mumbled something, gave her the literature, and left."

"A week ago Friday? That was the same night they found her brother! A half-naked woman was playing around with my husband while her brother's body was lying in a ditch in Tennessee? Oh, that's so cold! How could any decent human being do something like that?"

"I don't know, maybe she didn't know at the time, but maybe she did. She looked like she'd been crying about something."

Cathy shook her head. "I can't believe she would do something like that. When I talked to her after we got back from distributing the flyers, I got the impression that she and Jack hadn't seen each other since high school."

"I heard Elaine tell someone a while back that she almost got married right out of high school to one of her classmates. You think it might have been Jack?"

Cathy frowned. "EW? Every Woman?" Then her eyes grew wide. "EW! Elaine Warden! That lying son of a bitch!"

"What?"

"That god damned bastard!"

"What!"

"That piece of shit has been looking at her while screwing me for five years!"

Pete shook his head in confusion as he looked about, hoping no other shoppers were within listening range to this very upset woman. "I have no idea what you're talking about, Cathy, but if your husband's seeing Elaine, then I don't feel so bad about getting together with you."

"I don't feel so bad about it either, Pete. Being with you makes me feel awfully good. I'm looking forward to another nice big hug from you. When do you think we can get together again?"

"The store closes at six on Christmas Eve and all day on Christmas Day. It would be great if I could see you sometime Christmas Eve or Christmas Day."

"Oh, Pete, that would be so perfect, but I can't. I know I won't be able to get away. I wish I could, really I do, but if the stores are closed I'm not sure I can come up with a good excuse for being out of the house. I guess it'll be Saturday before we can get together. If I don't see you before then, Merry Christmas."

"Merry Christmas to you, too, Cathy."

"I'd kiss you if I didn't think it would get you fired."

"It might. Who knows what these people might do to me now that I've turned in my notice. One thing is for sure, it would embarrass me to death and you know it."

Cathy giggled. "Yes, I do. That's why I'd do it."

"Save it for Saturday. It may be the last chance we'll have to get together before I leave for California."

"Why? When are you leaving?"

"Next Monday. That's my last day at the Barn. As soon as I get done here, I'm on my way to California."

"Oh, my goodness! That's only a week away. We definitely need to get together before you leave."

* * * *

From his desk at the sheriff's station, Dan entered a long-distance number and smiled. This was going to be interesting.

"Hello?"

"Evening, Jack. This is Dan Warden."

"Oh, hello, Dan. How're things?"

"We got Jake buried. We're all pretty exhausted right now."

"Anything on the guy that hit Jake?"

"Not yet, but that's why I called."

"Oh?"

"I wanted you to know we impounded your truck."

"Uh, why would you do that?"

"We're looking for vehicles that were on Greenbrier Road the night before Thanksgiving, especially ones with damage to the right front fender. We're going to track them all down and find out when, where, and how it happened. Of course, we know how and where your accident happened; I've got a copy of the report right here in my hand. But, you understand, we've got to treat it the same way we're going to treat all the others. I don't expect to find anything."

"I appreciate that, Dan."

"As soon as your truck is behind the fence at the sheriff's office, the medical examiner is going to want to go over it, looking for fingerprints. What's your Navy serial number?"

"You want to find out if my fingerprints are in my truck? You've got to be kidding."

"Yeah, I know. I know. But it's what they do. They need yours to eliminate them from any of the others they might find."

There was a pause, then Jack rattled off his serial number. "Got that?"

Dan repeated the number, then said, "Got it. Can you think of anyone else who's been in your truck lately, other than Art?"

"Dad was up there to get everything out of it. Billy Blakeley, the guy I carpool with was in there a couple of times a week before I wrecked it. The insurance adjuster was probably up there."

"Anybody else? How about your wife?"

"Not that I recall. She drives that little Honda."

"Thanks for the information, Jack."

"Looks like you've got a big job on your hands. You don't have any idea what might have hit him, huh?"

"Not yet. That's what's making it so tough. It's going to take us some time to find the needle in this haystack."

"Well, good luck. I hope you find him . . . or her."

"We will . . . sooner or later. I thought I'd give you a call and let you know we've got your truck and why we've got it."

"I appreciate that, Dan. Thanks for calling."

"I'll be in touch. Oh, by the way, did you have a right-hand mirror on your truck the night you had your accident?"

"Uh, yeah, I did. Why?"

"It's not on the wreck and I couldn't find it at the oak tree."

"Somebody must have carried it off. It was on the truck when I left Uncle Buck's."

"Yeah, I guess you're right, somebody must have picked it up. It doesn't matter. I was just wondering."

"Anything else?"

"Uh, yeah, I almost forgot. You went straight home from Uncle Buck's that night, didn't you?"

"I tried to. Didn't get very far."

"That's right, you didn't," Dan said and chuckled. "The reason I asked is that I'm looking around for anybody who was on the road between Uncle Buck's and Bailey Springs that night. Somebody might have seen something they still remember."

"Wish I could help, Dan, but I wasn't up that way."

"I didn't think so. Well, thanks anyway, Jack. I'll be talking to you."

"Anytime, Dan."

Dan hung up the phone, then stared off into space, a frown on his face. He had called Jack to tell him his truck had been impounded, knowing it would shake Jack up a little and make him wonder what the Creek County Sheriff's Department was up to. He had certainly accomplished that! Dan could tell from Jack's voice that the information had really made him uneasy, more uneasy than it should have, Dan thought. And that was what was making him frown. Something was wrong here, and he didn't know what it was. There had been pauses on the other end of the line when they were talking about the mirror, not very long, but too long it seemed for Jack to come up with his flip answers. It was the kind of pause he had heard many times before when interviewing suspects. The pause was always there, it seemed, when he had asked them a question to which they were unwilling to answer truthfully but had been unprepared to lie about. Had Jack been lying? Or had something momentarily distracted him?

Dan shook his head. If he was going to make any real progress in this case, he would have to put his personal feelings on a back burner and start acting like a law enforcement professional. If he kept focusing on Jack, simply because he didn't like him, it would only delay and impede his search for the real killer. For now, he would give Jack the benefit of the doubt. Still, it seemed the more he tried to clear Jack, the more things he found to make him wonder about him.

"If I could find one thing," Dan said to himself. "If I could find one little thing that would show me that Jack couldn't have been involved in both accidents." Dan tilted his head to one side and frowned as an idea came to him. Maybe there was a way. It probably wouldn't prove anything, one way or another, but it was worth a shot.

18

IT WAS ALMOST QUITTING time at Chek Mart. With only three days remaining until Christmas, it seemed even the grocery shoppers were getting into a shopping frenzy. Cathy was exhausted from standing all day. Her hair was frayed, her nerves were on edge, her makeup a mess, and the woman in front of her couldn't find twenty-seven cents that she knew was somewhere in the bottom of her purse. Cathy glanced back at the long line waiting to pass through her register and saw Elaine Warden's smiling face next in line.

Elaine was dressed in an expensive business outfit and, with her workday over, her hair and makeup were still perfect. This was the woman, Cathy reminded herself, whose image on her husband's arm had invaded the privacy of her bedroom for five years during some very intimate moments. She didn't like it. With her mouth pulled tightly across her face, she nodded. Her little trysts with Pete would get a lot more serious the next time they got together.

"Hi, Cathy."

"Oh, hi, Elaine," Cathy said, glancing up, then back down to her work, quickly scanning the other woman's purchases.

"Thanks again for helping with the flyers. Dan said they were a big help."

"Oh, you're welcome."

"Busy today, huh?" Elaine asked after a moment.

Cathy looked up once more, nodded, then turned back to her work.

Elaine gave up trying to have a conversation with Cathy and took a Visa card from her wallet and handed it to her. After Cathy had scanned the card, she returned it to Elaine with the cash register tape. Elaine smiled at her and said, "If I can ever do anything for you, let me know."

"You can stay away from my husband."

Elaine tilted her head to one side, frowning. "Excuse me?"

"I'd appreciate it if you would keep your clothes on around my husband."

Elaine frowned, then raised her eyebrows. "Well, my goodness, Pete has become a nasty little spy, hasn't he? Tell me, how are things at the Cross Winds these days?"

"I don't know what you're talking about."

Elaine smiled as she gathered up her bags. "You know what they say about people who live in glass houses," she said, then turned and marched off.

Livid with rage, Cathy watched Elaine walk away, convinced that she was having sex with her husband. Cathy silently vowed to get even with her husband for being unfaithful with that woman. She turned back to the next shopper, a little gray-haired lady, and glared at her, "Two can play that game."

"What did you say, dear?" the woman asked.

Cathy ignored her and began scanning the woman's purchases.

19

WHEN JACK GOT HOME, Cathy wasn't there. It was just as well. He was going to meet Billy at Uncle Buck's for the Wednesday night pool tournament again. He didn't want to listen to any grief from her before he left. He felt good tonight. Things were looking up. Physically, most of his aches and pains were gone and he had gotten a few hours of uninterrupted sleep last night for the first time since the accident.

They had found Jake almost two weeks ago, but apparently they hadn't found the mirror. That Tennessee hillbilly sheriff's deputy didn't even know what kind of vehicle they were after. Without that mirror, it could be anything from a Volkswagen to an eighteen-wheeler. Jack grinned. With Deputy Dan on the job, his truck would be nothing but a pile of rusted metal by the time they checked all vehicles in the area with damaged right fenders.

Maybe he would give Elaine a call. She might have some news about what Dan was up to these days. Maybe she was ready for some company tonight. He grinned. Maybe she was wearing that sexy underwear and was ready to pick up where they had left off. He picked up the phone and started dialing.

"Hello?"

"Hi, Elaine. I thought I'd call and see how're you doing."

"Oh, Jack, the whole family is a wreck right now. None of us have gotten used to the idea that Jake is really gone."

"It'll take time, Elaine," Jack said, listening to the woman crying on the other end of the telephone line. "I'm sorry I

157

couldn't come to the funeral, but I've been out so much here lately, they didn't want to give me the day off."

"I understand. Thanks for coming Sunday night. That was thoughtful of you."

"Uh, has Dan found out anything yet?"

"He's trying awfully hard. He's working twenty-four hours a day, driving around southern Tennessee and northern Alabama, looking at wrecked pickups."

"Pickups?" The phone almost fell out of Jack's hand. "Dan thinks Jack was hit by a pickup truck?"

"I guess so."

"Well, I guess he has his reasons," Jack said, his hand still trembling. Why didn't Dan tell him he was looking for a pickup truck at the same time he told him they had his truck towed to the sheriff's station? Did they find his mirror? Jesus! What was that sneaky deputy up to anyway?

"We're all praying he can find out who did it. It's got the family torn apart. It's not going to be a very merry Christmas this year."

"Yeah, I can understand that," Jack said, then paused. "Well, I wanted to talk to you and tell you I'm thinking about you."

"I think about you, too. I'd like to see you again, but I won't be very good company for a few days. I'm so heartbroken about Jake right now. I can't think about anything else. I've been spending a lot of time with Mom and Dad. None of us have been able to sleep very much since they found him. We just sit around, hold each other, and cry a lot. I guess it's going to take us some time to get back to normal. I hope you understand."

"I understand. I haven't been able to get much sleep myself here lately. It's going to be tough on all of you. I'm on my way up to Uncle Buck's to shoot some pool. I'll call you again when we're done if you want me to."

"I'm going to Mom and Dad's in a few minutes."

"Oh . . . All right, I'll give you a call in a few days to see how you're doing. Maybe you'll be up to having some company by then."

"That would be great, Jack. I'd like that. Oh, by the way, I think you ought to know, someone told your wife they saw you at my house."

"So what? I don't care if you don't."

"I think she might be seeing another guy."

"She wouldn't dare. She knows I'd kick her out and file for divorce the minute I found out."

"If what you told me is true, a divorce might not be all that bad for either of you."

"You're probably right about that."

"When I talked to her at Mom and Dad's house that Sunday, I got the impression she thinks she's better than we are, just because she's from California. She's probably one of those people who think everybody in Alabama is a redneck."

"I've got news for her. I've been to California. There are more rednecks out there than there are here. They may call them something else, but they're rednecks, just like me. Besides, what's so bad about being a redneck? I sure as hell wouldn't want to live in a big city like Los Angeles, that's for damn sure."

"I wouldn't want to live in California either. All that traffic and smog. I don't see how people put up with it. Southern living is so much nicer. I like living right here in Helleston."

"I like being here, too, as long as you're around."

"I like having you around, too, Jack. I was sort of hoping we could get together again before Christmas, but with all this going on, it's not going to be a very merry Christmas for any of us, so I'll have to give you a raincheck. Give me a call in a few days if you want to. If this family can get through Christmas without falling to pieces, it will be a blessing."

"I understand. It's going to be tough on all of you. Goodnight, Elaine."

"Bye, Jack. Merry Christmas."

"Same to you."

* * * *

When Jack pulled into Uncle Buck's Tavern parking lot later that evening, he saw someone with a flashlight, its bright beam sweeping back and forth among the vehicles. It reminded him of the night, not too long ago, when he was looking down that steep slope with his flashlight. Recalling how weak the batteries had been that night, he made a mental note to buy some fresh ones. Then he frowned in puzzled wonder. Where was his flashlight? He suddenly realized he hadn't seen it since that night.

Jack checked the glove compartment, then got out and opened the lockbox in the truck bed. Junior's lights were bright enough for him to see his toolbox, jumper cables, a tow chain, and some flares, but no flashlight. He opened his toolbox and looked inside without finding the flashlight either. Unperturbed, Jack shrugged his shoulders. It was around somewhere. His dad would have found it when he cleaned out the old pickup. He had probably forgotten to give it to him along with his other stuff. Jack reminded himself to get it the next time he was out at his dad's place.

Jack locked everything and headed for the bar. As he neared the man with the flashlight, he recognized him. "Hey, Dan," Jack called out as he approached the deputy sheriff staring down at a license plate.

"Hello, Jack. What're you up to tonight?"

"Getting ready to shoot some eight ball. What're you up to?"

"Taking down a few Tennessee license plates. I'm looking for people who might have seen something between here and Bailey Springs the night Jake got killed. I know they're not going to want to talk to me in there. Maybe somebody might remember something if I talk to them when they're sober."

"Hell, Dan, I remembered something myself since the last time I talked to you."

"Oh, yeah? What's that?"

"Well, you told me you were looking for people who had been up the road that night. I wasn't up that way myself, but I saw a red Ford pickup tearing down the road, right past here as I was pulling out of the parking lot."

"Is that a fact?" Dan asked with a quizzical smile.

"That's right. I remember telling myself that it looked a lot like mine. Except it was one-eyed."

"A headlight was out?"

Jack smiled and nodded his head. "Yep."

"I'll bet it was the one on the right-hand side."

"I believe it was."

"Why didn't you mention this before, Jack?"

"You've been so busy trying to solve the case, I didn't want to start throwing stuff at you that I didn't think was important."

"Well, let me decide that next time."

"I will. I promise."

"You saw a red '93 Ford pickup, huh?"

"It was an F-150 all right, and I'm fairly sure it was red. It might not have been a '93, but it sure looked a lot like mine. Are you looking for a pickup? Last time I talked to you, you weren't sure what it was. You think a pickup hit Jake?"

"It's possible," Dan said, frowning.

"I saw it. Really, I did. I'll swear to it," Jack said over his shoulder as he walked away.

"You might have to," Dan said quietly.

Dan was pretty sure Jack was playing games with him, to make his life more difficult. Jack probably didn't like him any more than he liked Jack. Dan sighed. Personal feelings aside, he had tried something today that might have cleared Jack. It hadn't worked.

Dan had searched both accident sites, and the wreck, for pieces of yellow plastic. He had found several at the oak tree and a few very small ones that had been overlooked at the curve. He had removed the yellow turn signal cover from the left-hand side of Jack's pickup and weighed it. He had then weighed all the pieces of yellow plastic they had collected at the tree and at the site where the body was found and compared the total weight to the weight of Jack's undamaged left-turn signal. The total weight of the pieces was an ounce less than the weight of the complete unit.

If the total weight of the pieces had been more than the weight of Jack's undamaged turn signal, it would have probably meant two different trucks had been involved in the two accidents and Jack would be in the clear. Dan would have had Jack's truck towed back to Art's and got on with his search for the other red pickup Jack claimed to have seen that night.

But, since the weight of the pieces was less than the complete unit, the results were inconclusive. One vehicle might have been involved in both accidents. On the other hand, someone might have picked up some of the yellow plastic pieces and carried them away from either site. He had no way of knowing for sure. Some of the yellow plastic shards seemed to fit together, but most were too small for him to be sure. He would send all the shards from both sites to the state crime lab in Nashville and see if they could make any sense out of them.

As Jack walked away, Dan called out. "Hey, Jack. Those high-top work shoes you're wearing. What's the brand name?"

Jack stopped, turned and frowned. "Uh, Wolverine. Why?"

Dan shrugged. "I'm looking for a new pair to wear on the job."

"Couldn't do better if you're going to be on your feet all day."

"I usually am," Dan said.

"Merry Christmas, Dan."

"Same to you, Jack," Dan said, then waved and walked away.

20

Day 30
Thursday, December 24, Christmas Eve

DAN LOOKED OUT AT THE early morning gray skies as he ate his McDonald's hotcakes and sausage. The weather had been unusually warm for December for a week or so until a couple of days ago when a cold front moved in, bringing rain and much colder weather with it. Last night's temperature was down to around twenty, and it wasn't supposed to get much above freezing today. He took another sip of his coffee, looked at his watch, and smiled. It might be too early in the day to play Santa Claus for a teenager, but he would give it a shot.

About a mile north of the accident site, in his uniform and driving a county vehicle, Dan pulled over onto the shoulder of Greenbrier Road next to a gravel road. There was no sign, but according to his county map, it was Wolfe Road. He examined the mailboxes beside him. There were three, each mounted atop its own post. The first two, labeled JONES and BLACK were on sturdy posts and looked well used. The third, on an old post that was leaning to one side, had no name. The door hung open, displaying a box crammed full of soggy circulars and junk mail. Dan knew there wasn't much chance anyone up this road would tell him anything about the accident, even if they had seen something. Most people living in these hills liked to be left to themselves, either because they were involved in something illegal or because they had been taught from childhood to distrust anybody working for the government, especially law enforcement.

Dan shook his head in dismay. It was a cold Christmas Eve morning and he wanted very badly to be home with his own

163

family instead of interviewing homeowners who knew nothing and would be willing to say less. But his wife didn't want him around, and sitting alone in a furnished mobile home on Christmas Eve staring at the walls and drinking whiskey would be the first step down the slippery slope toward alcoholism. Anything was better than that.

With a wry smile, Dan nodded. He'd kill two birds with one stone today. He'd do some interviewing and play Santa for Red Black at the same time. The boy lived up Wolfe Road somewhere and Dan had a Christmas present for him. If the boy was home, today's trip would be worthwhile if he accomplished nothing else.

* * * *

The first driveway had a sign announcing it was the address of Homer and Mabel Jones. Like most people living around here, it looked like they were barely making ends meet. There was an old Chevy pickup in the dirt driveway, the body rusted and dented from many years of hard use. Dan glanced at the right headlight. It was undamaged.

Dan knocked on the door of the dilapidated single-wide mobile home and waited. Soon, an obese white-haired woman opened the door and stared at the deputy sheriff standing there, her eyes wide and her mouth open.

"Mrs. Jones?"

The old woman, without changing her expression, quickly nodded her head.

Dan displayed his badge. "I'm Sergeant Dan Warden, Creek County Sheriff's Department. Is Mr. Jones at home?"

"Homer!" the woman yelled as she turned her head to one side. "You'd better get out here. There's a deputy sheriff to see you!"

"I'll be right there," Dan heard someone call from somewhere inside the small structure. Dan heard the commode flush, then watched a haggard old man come into view, pulling the galluses of his overalls up over his flannel shirt. When the hollow-eyed old man approached the door, Dan reintroduced himself. Homer Jones glanced back into the small home, then turned back to Dan, a pained expression on his face. "Uh, do you mind if we step outside?"

"No, sir," Dan said, then held the door and stepped aside to allow the old man to pass. The old man clamped an old sweat-stained fedora on his head, grabbed an old Mackinaw coat from a peg beside the door, and walked out onto the small landing. He pulled the heavy woolen coat around him, buttoned it, then slowly ambled out into the bare front yard, his hands in his coat pockets, his eyes on the ground. Dan wondered what was going to happen next as he followed the frail old man out into the bare-dirt yard. Homer stopped, then lifted his eyes and gazed out to the sky in the west. "I figured you'd be coming for me someday."

"You did, huh?"

Still gazing off into the distance, the old man slowly nodded his head. "Ever since I saw that boy's picture in the window of the Big Bag, I knew you'd be coming for me."

Dan suddenly became keenly alert. "You mean, the young man we found down at the curve? Jake Warden?"

The old man slowly nodded his head once more. "I killed him. As sure as the earth is turning beneath us, I killed him. When I heard you folks found a body down there at the curve, I dropped down on my knees right then and there and begged God to forgive me for what I had done."

Dan knew that in the big cities, he would have to stop the man, read him his rights, handcuff him, and haul him off to jail. Instead, he put his hands in his pockets, turned and looked at the gray sky and said softly, "You want to tell me about it, Mr. Jones?"

"What did you say your name was?"

"Dan Warden."

"Are you any kin to Fred Warden?"

"Yes, sir, I'm his son. Jake was Charlie Warden's boy and my nephew."

"Lord have mercy, I sure am sorry to hear that. I've known Fred Warden most of my life. We went to school together until Dad made me quit and go to work on the farm full time. Dad's gone now . . . so's the farm. Ain't it funny how things work out that way? Your dad's got a nice insurance business down there in Helleston and I'm sacking groceries at the Big Bag to keep us from starving."

Dan didn't respond, waiting in silence for the man to start his story.

"Anyway, that's what I was doing that night, stocking shelves and sacking groceries."

"The night before Thanksgiving," Dan added.

"That's right," Homer said, then shook his head. "Damn but you'd think women wouldn't wait until the last minute to buy groceries for Thanksgiving. But they always do. That's why I was working so late. The manager decided to stay open because there were so many women buying stuff. I mean, they were cleaning out the shelves as fast as we could restock them. A couple of women were fighting over the last pan big enough to cook a turkey. They were getting ready to go at it when I saved the day by bringing more out."

Dan withdrew a small pad of paper and a pen from inside his jacket. "What time did the store close?"

"They let me go at ten. I don't know when they finally closed the doors."

"I guess you were pretty tired after a long day like that."

"Man, I tell you. I was bushed."

"What happened then, after you left the Big Bag?"

"Well, I come home."

"By yourself?"

"It started out that way, then I picked up that boy."

Dan could feel his pulse quicken. He squeezed his jaws, trying to make himself appear calmer than he was. "You picked up a hitchhiker? Where?"

"Right outside McDonald's. He was standing there in the rain, holding a cardboard sign saying he wanted to go to Helleston. I told him I couldn't take him as far as Helleston, but I'd give him a ride down to Uncle Buck's and he could hitch a ride with someone heading south from there if he didn't mind riding with some beer drinker. He said he'd take it because he'd already been there four or five hours asking folks about a ride to Helleston and no one had offered to take him down that way."

"So, you gave him a ride."

"Yeah, I did. But I made him get in the back. I used to pick up hitchhikers all the time, but these days you can't be too careful about who you pick up, so I ask them to ride in the back. I figure as long as they're back in the bed and I'm in the cab, I'm pretty safe. Lord, I sure do regret doing that to him now, knowing he's dead account of me."

Dan's mind raced ahead. Homer Jones was going to tell him how he was going around the curve too fast. Somehow, Jake had been thrown out as they rounded the curve. But, if he had, why had Homer left the body lying in the weeds and brush, like some kind of roadkill? It didn't make sense. "Tell me what happened, Homer."

"We were coming down Greenbrier Road when my hands started shaking. That's when I remembered I hadn't taken my pills. I'd forgotten about them because the boss man was making us rush around so much. I knew right then and there I might not be able to take him all the way down to Uncle Buck's and still be able to make it back home without getting sick." Homer turned and looked at Dan, a pained look on his face. "Dear Lord, I'm so sorry. I'm so sorry."

"Where did you drop him off?"

"Right down there, by the mailboxes. When I told him that was as far as I was going to be able to take him, he wasn't too happy. But, after I told him I was having medical problems and Uncle Buck's was only a couple of miles down the road, he seemed to understand. Hell, I thought it would be all right for him to walk that far at night. I walked a lot farther at night many a time when I was his age," Homer said, then shook his head. "I guess I was wrong, may God have mercy on my soul."

Dan frowned as he turned and stared at the old man. Something wasn't making sense here. He had thought he was getting a confession from a felony hit-and-run driver. Now he wasn't so sure. Dan turned and looked at Homer. "So, he got out and started walking down the road?"

Homer silently nodded his head.

"That's the last time you saw him?"

Homer nodded his head once more.

"I don't understand. What did you do to kill that young man?"

"What did I do?" the old man asked in an anguished voice. "It's not what I done. It's what I didn't do. I should have drove that old boy down to Uncle Buck's. It's not that far from here. But I didn't. Hell, I should have drove him all the way to Helleston. It would have been the Christian thing to do. It was a bad night to be out hitchhiking. I should have known something was going to happen to him, but I didn't do anything about it. Not a thing. I let him climb out and start walking down that foggy, wet road. If I had only known something like that was going to happen to him, I would have gone after him, but I didn't. I'll go to my grave knowing I killed that boy as sure as the man who run over him."

Dan reached out and put his arm around the old man's shoulders. The whole Warden family was still in shock because of what one man had done. Now, one more name could be added to the list of innocent victims: Homer Jones. His only crime was being a sick, old man trying to be a good Samaritan to a young man on a cold rainy night. Now, he would suffer, too, believing he was somehow partially responsible.

"Mr. Jones, I appreciate you telling me about this."

"You going to take me in now?"

"No, sir, I'm not. You didn't do anything wrong as far as the law is concerned."

Homer Jones stepped away from Dan. With a pained look on his face, he said, "But, what I did ain't right."

"Mr. Jones, if everything you told me is the truth, you didn't break any law I can arrest you for. If you still think you might have done something wrong, maybe you ought to talk to your preacher about it."

Homer looked at Dan, then blinked his eyes as tears welled up in them. "Me and Mabel ain't been to church for a long time. Maybe it's time we did."

Dan looked at Homer, his jaw clenched. He wanted to grab this old man and shake some sense into him. Why hadn't he called someone after recognizing Jake's picture? Those flyers were up four days before Workman called. This whole investigation would have started days earlier if

Homer had called the sheriff and told someone he had given Jake a ride from McDonald's down Greenbrier Road that night. If they had known where to start, they would have searched Greenbrier Road on foot until they found him. Instead, Jake's body had continued to be exposed to the weather and animals until Red had accidentally found him. Dan sighed and slowly shook his head. He knew the answer without asking.

This old man had been taught since childhood to distrust anyone wearing a badge. Homer had heard too many stories about the bad old days, about how crimes were solved by arresting a suspect and hounding him nonstop until he confessed, sometimes to a crime he didn't commit. Dan knew most of the stories weren't true, but from listening to his granddad tell tales about the days when he was a deputy, Dan knew some of them were. Because the old stories died hard, instead of volunteering critical information, Homer had remained silent about what he had done that night, living in fear of being arrested and dragged to some torture chamber at the sheriff's office. It was a sad situation for everyone concerned.

Dan motioned toward the highway. "I saw three mailboxes down there. How about your neighbors up the road? Do you think any of them might have seen anything?"

"Wouldn't know, don't see them much, don't talk to them. Everybody minds their own business. Mrs. Black comes by and borrows something from Mabel sometimes, other than that, we don't know anything about them."

"Does Mrs. Black have a son called Red?"

"That's them. Next trailer up the road. She and Red are up there all by themselves. Maybe we'll all have a little peace and quiet now that Bulldog's gone."

"Bulldog lived up here?"

"Sure did. Man, he was crazy. I think he stayed drunk just about all the time. He sure did like to shoot his guns. Pistols, rifles, shotguns, man, I think he's got enough to start a war up there. I swear, it sounded like some were on full automatic. He did most of his shooting during the day, but a few times he woke us up at night shooting them things. It sure did make Mabel nervous when he started doing that. Sometimes we could hear bullets whizzing over our house. I know it's not the Christian thing to say about the dead, but me and Mabel sure are glad he's gone."

"Have you ever seen his place?"

"Nope, never been up that far, not even when Catfish was there."

"Catfish?"

"Yeah, that's what everybody called him. He owned the place up there, used to tinker with wrecked cars. He'd haul wrecks up there, take an engine from one and a transmission from another and put them into something that still had good sheet metal and tires, then he would bring it down and sell it. Cranky old bastard. Some years ago, right after we moved in here, I decided to go up and see him but when I ran into that NO TRESPASSING sign I turned around. Don't know what happened to him. Some say he died; others say he's in jail," Homer said, paused and shook his head. "Then Bulldog moved in up there a while back. Out of the frying pan, into the fire."

Dan nodded his head. "Okay, thanks, let me give you my card. It's got my phone number on it. I'd appreciate it if you'd give me a call if you think of anything else about that night."

"I sure will, Dan, and say hello to your dad for me. Tell him I still remember the time me and him stole them watermelons and wound up dodging buckshot."

Dan grinned. "I don't believe I've heard that one."

Homer cackled out loud. "Get him to tell it to you sometime."

"I'll do that, sir," Dan said with a wave of his hand. "Nice meeting you, Mr. Jones."

"Nice meeting you, Dan," Homer called as he walked toward his mobile home.

Suddenly, Dan turned and called out. "Oh, uh, Mr. Jones!"

"Yeah!"

"Do you remember any other traffic on the road that night?"

"Hell fire, yes!"

Dan frowned and gritted his teeth, wondering how long he would have to work at this job before he remembered to ask all the questions. "What was it?" he asked as he walked back toward Homer, pulling out his pad once more.

"It was some drunk coming from Uncle Buck's."

"Drunk, huh?"

"Hell, yes. He was driving like a bat out of hell on that slick, foggy, road."

"He was heading north? Toward Bailey Springs?"

"Sure was, on the wrong side of the road at that. A lot of them old Bailey Springs boys get tanked up down there at Uncle Buck's, then they come ripping up the road, especially on Friday and Saturday night."

"Did you get a look at it? Do you remember what kind of vehicle it was?"

"It was a pickup, that's all I can tell you."

"Full size or one of those little Japanese things?"

"It was regular size."

"Could you tell what color it was?"

"No, like I said, it was awfully foggy and wet out that night. Dark color. It was too dark to see anything."

"Couldn't tell whether it had an Alabama or Tennessee plate on it, I guess?"

Homer shrugged his shoulders. "No, but I would guess it would be a Tennessee plate. Why would a drunk from Alabama be driving up this way that time of the night?"

"When I know the answer to that one, I'm going to know the answers to some other questions, too. Thank you, Mr. Jones. You've been a big help to me."

"I wish I could have been more help to that boy."

"Oh, do you remember what time you dropped him off?"

"Well, sir," Homer said as he unconsciously stroked the stubble on his chin. "Let me see now. I left the store right after ten. I remember Mabel was still up because she gave me heck for staying out so late. If she was still up, that would make it sometime before ten-thirty because she likes to watch the weather forecast on the Huntsville station's ten o'clock news just before she turns in. Is that any help?"

"Yes, sir, it is. Thanks again. I appreciate it."

"You're welcome, Dan. Merry Christmas."

"Merry Christmas to you, sir."

* * * *

Dan backed out onto the gravel road again and headed up the hill toward the Black's mobile home. The roadway was about the width of one and a half vehicles. If two full-size vehicles were on the road at the same time, they would get awfully close to the ditches on either side when they passed.

Dan pulled into the dirt driveway behind an old Chevy Caprice, maybe a 1990, that had seen better days, then looked at the old mobile home he knew a woman and a teenage boy called home. However, unlike Homer's mobile home that barely had enough space cleared for it, this one had about a half-acre of unmown weeds and wild grass around the sides and back. Toward the back left was an old open shed with some firewood in it. Dan wondered why they would need firewood since mobile homes don't have fireplaces. When he saw no lights in any of the windows, he glanced at his watch. Nine o'clock. Someone was home but apparently everyone was still in bed on Christmas Eve morning. He decided to knock on the door anyway.

After Dan knocked on the door several times, a tall slender woman eventually appeared in the doorway wearing a housecoat. She might have been in her thirties, but the tired, despondent look on her gaunt face made her look much older. "Mrs. Black?" he asked. "Mrs. Lena Black?"

"Why do you want to know?" she demanded.

"I'm Sergeant Dan Warden," Dan said, displaying his badge. "I'm a deputy with the Creek County Sheriff's Office. I talked with your boy the day he found the body of the young man down at the curve." As soon as he showed his badge, Dan saw the look on the woman's face change to abject fear.

"Oh, my god! You're going to arrest him! You're going to take my boy away!"

"No ma'am," Dan said patiently as he watched Red approach the door from the dark interior and stand beside his mother. As the strong stench of body odor assaulted his nostrils, Dan resisted an urge to take a step backward. "He didn't do anything wrong. He did something good. That's why I'm here."

"I don't understand," Mrs. Black said.

Dan looked past the woman and asked, "Red? Did you know there was a five-hundred-dollar reward for information about that young man you found?"

"I seen the posters, but I didn't know that was who it was. I didn't call nobody."

"Doesn't matter. You found him, that's all that counts. You get the reward," Dan said, offering a folded stack of twenty-dollar bills to the boy. "That's five hundred dollars, Red. It's all yours."

Red Black took the money, silently gazed at it for a moment, then handed it to his mother. With wide-eyed wonder, Lena Black looked at the money in her hand, then looked at Dan, her eyes wet with tears. "Oh, my God. I don't believe this," she said softly, looking down at the money in her hand. Then she looked up and added, "Thank you."

"You're welcome. Merry Christmas."

"It will be now," Mrs. Black said, paused, then looking into Dan's eyes, said, "They shut off our electricity, and our propane tank ran dry last night. This is the best Christmas present I could have asked for. Thank you."

"You're welcome," Dan said. "And thank you, Red. If you hadn't gone down there after that backpack, that boy might still be down there for who knows how long."

Lena wrapped her arm around her son. "He's the best thing that ever happened to me."

"Have a good day, folks," Dan said, turned to go, then turned back. "Did you know the man who used to live up the road, the one they called Bulldog?"

Lena paused for a moment, holding the money in a death grip, then slowly shook her head. "No, not really. I saw him driving by a few times, but I never met him."

"I'm glad he got shot," Red declared loudly. "He kept shooting at our house. I could hear the bullets whizzing when they went over. I told Mama, if he ever shot at our house again, I was going to shoot at him the next time he drove down the road," Red declared.

"Now, Red. You don't really mean that," Lena said.

Red frowned, "I ain't going to let nobody hurt you, Mama."

Dan smiled and nodded as he stared at the tall, angular woman. When she was younger, she was probably a pretty woman. She still might be if she was wearing a nice dress, put on some makeup, took a bath, and had her hair fixed. Dan watched as she slowly put her arm around her son's shoulders. Her eyes were sad and misty.

Dan looked at the distraught woman for a moment, then said, "Mrs. Black, could I see you out here, please?"

Lena Black slowly walked out onto the small porch, holding the money so tightly the knuckles of her hand were white.

Dan knew he should leave this family alone. He was a deputy sheriff, not a social worker. There were other people in the area as bad off as these two were. Creek County, Tennessee, was what the politicians referred to as an economically depressed area. What that meant was, most of the population was either on welfare, or working at minimum wage jobs. This time, he decided to make an exception. He glanced at Red looking at them from the doorway, then back to the woman. "Is there a Mr. Black?"

A cynical smile formed on Lena's face as she paused for a moment. "Not for a while. Lloyd's down in Kilby."

Dan gazed dispassionately at the woman. She had confirmed what he already knew. Her husband was in a maximum-security prison outside Montgomery, Alabama. "How much longer is he going to be down there?"

"I don't know. They gave him thirty years for robbing that convenience store down in Greenbrier. He's been in for five years already. I ain't seen him since they took him away. This car of mine wouldn't make it across the Alabama state line, much less all the way down there, even if I could afford the gas."

In a low voice, Dan said, "Mrs. Black, there are some pretty nice people working down at the county courthouse who would be willing to give you and Red a hand for a while, until you can get back on your feet. Why don't you go talk to them."

"I'd like to have a job. I don't mind working. I've worked most of the time Lloyd's been gone, but here lately I can't find nobody who wants to hire me. I'd like to get on with Bailey Springs Hardware if I could."

"They seemed pretty busy when I was in there a few days ago. You might want to go up there and apply."

"I did apply! Six months ago. I filled out a form and talked to somebody, but I ain't heard nothing since."

"Don't give up. There has got to be folks somewhere in Creek County that will give a hard worker a chance."

Mrs. Black held up the money. "This will get us through the rest of the year. I'll see what's out there in January."

Dan nodded. "Merry Christmas again."

"Merry Christmas to you," Lena said with a smile.

* * * *

Dan backed his truck out and drove along the washed-out, one-lane gravel road that seemed to more-or-less follow the ridge that ran parallel to the east side of Greenbrier Road. With both electric and telephone wires attached to utility poles along the left-hand side of the road, he assumed that some sort of human habitation was ahead of him. As he continued up the gently rising road, the terrain on either side of the road flattened until he could see several yards into the bare trees on either side. When he reached an old rusted NO TRESPASSING sign with several bullet holes in it, he thought he was getting close to Bulldog's place. When he came to a sign: WARNING: TRESPASSERS WILL BE SHOT, he could see a small building a short distance away.

The time-worn shack had a rusted tin roof with a fireplace chimney at one end. Its exterior walls had been covered with asphalt siding that looked like fake red brick and white mortar decades ago. Now there were some areas that had been patched with moldy-black plywood.

As Dan surveyed the scene, he shook his head in amazement. The small house was surrounded by two or three acres that had been cleared for farming many years ago. Now, rusted carcasses of wrecked vehicles were parked haphazardly everywhere. Native grass, weeds, brush, and sapling trees were reclaiming the land by growing in and around dozens of vehicles that had been cannibalized for their engine, transmission, or both. There was a sapling ten feet high growing out of the empty engine compartment of a nearby rusty hulk.

Dan called in and gave his location, then headed for the house, assuming Bulldog had been living in it. Until Homer mentioned him, they had been unable to find anyone in the county who knew where Bulldog lived. They had learned Bulldog's real name by matching prints from the body to FBI prints, but the only local address they had was a post office box number. The rural address Bulldog had given the post office didn't exist. The Tennessee plates on his pickup truck didn't belong to the truck and the truck's VIN number showed that it had been stolen in West Virginia. Bulldog's last known address was in West Virginia where his parole officer had been waiting to talk to him about an outstanding warrant for assault and battery. When Dan called the West Virginia family number the parole officer had given him, a man who answered identified himself as one of Bulldog's brothers. When Dan informed him that his brother was dead and then described the circumstances involved, Dan was told the family had neither the time nor the money to come for Bulldog's body or to pay to have it shipped or buried.

Dan released the leather strap over his pistol grip and knocked on the front door, then again, harder, and called out, "Sheriff's Department!"

When no one answered, he put on gloves, tried the door, and found it was unlocked. Instead of entering, however, he turned and walked around the house, stopping at the small dirty windows and peering inside. He continued circling the house until he came to the conclusion that the front half of the building was the living area and the back half was split between a kitchen and a bedroom. Satisfied that there was no one inside, he walked toward a second building.

As he approached it, it became clear that it had been Catfish's garage where he had reassembled automobiles. The doors had been left open to the elements of southern Tennessee weather for years. The rusty ramp had weeds growing around it and under it, the rusty chain hoist would no longer lift an engine, rusty tools and parts were scattered about on shelves of rotten fiberboard, and anything on the floor was being taken over by weeds and grass as well.

Then Dan frowned as he focused on a tiny building about twenty yards away from the house, near the edge of the clearing. "Is that what I think it is?" he asked. He walked over and opened the door. The odor of raw sewage assaulted his nose. "Yep." It was a fully functional two-hole outhouse and had been recently used. Dan closed the door, walked around to the back of the structure and saw how close the outhouse was to the slope of the hillside. The odor of raw sewage was even stronger. There may have been a hole underneath the outhouse at one time, but now the effluence was slowly finding its way down the back of the outhouse toward Greenbrier Road. Dan chuckled. "Like they say, it flows downhill."

The nearby hillside was littered with dozens of bottles, cans, and rusty car parts that had been discarded over the years. Cardboard, plastic, garbage, and anything else that could be burned was in a waist-high mound surrounded by charred and blackened refuse, indicating that the pile of rubbish had been set on fire from time to time in the past, but not recently.

Dan walked a few feet away from the private garbage dump, then stopped and looked down the hillside again. He could see Greenbrier Road through the leaves and limbs of the trees on the slope. From his deer hunting days, he estimated that it was about two hundred yards down to the roadway. He walked a few steps closer to the old house as he continued to look down the hillside. Suddenly, he stopped when he saw a hole, about the size of his fist, in the leaves and limbs on the hillside that allowed him to clearly see a small section of Greenbrier Road and something orange beyond it.

Suddenly, he realized he was looking at the orange tape where they had found Jake's body. Bulldog had probably watched them all day. Dan frowned, recalling that he had looked up here and seen nothing but trees. What else had Bulldog seen, Dan wondered. Had he felt the urge to visit the outhouse or to do some house cleaning the night Jake was killed and was out here when it happened? If so, what did he see? Who did he see? Dan shook his head. Not much. It was foggy that night. In any case, it was too late to ask him now.

Dan walked back to the house and through the open back door into the tiny combination kitchen and dining area. There was barely room for wall cabinets, a stove, a small refrigerator, a dining table, two chairs, and a counter with a large dishpan filled with dirty dishes. The stench of rotting food, spilled booze, mold, and something else he couldn't identify assaulted his sense of smell. Leaving the kitchen area, he came into the front room. There, a small TV set sat on a rusted stand. The TV set was surrounded by a badly worn chair and a sofa. On the sofa was a blanket, a pillow, and a rifle scope. He walked over and picked up the fourteen-inch scope. It was a good one, the same brand he had mounted on his deer rifle. Frowning, he wondered why Bulldog had left it lying on the sofa. It cost way too much to treat it like that.

Then he glanced out one of the small dingy windows toward the outhouse, then looked down at the scope, then back at the outhouse. Carrying the scope, Dan retraced his steps, found the same place near the outhouse where he had been standing to see the hole in the hillside foliage, found the hole, and put the scope to his eye. Without adjusting its focus, from two hundred yards away, the letters on the yellow tape: POLICE LINE DO NOT CROSS were in sharp focus, just as Bulldog had left it.

Dan wondered how well Bulldog would have been able to see the same section of the road on a foggy night if he had been standing here with this scope. Good enough to see the make, model, and color of a pickup truck parked down there? Maybe. Good enough to identify the driver? Probably not.

Once back inside, he replaced the rifle scope on the sofa, then looked about the room once more. Between the chair and sofa was an end table with overflowing ashtrays, empty beer cans, and a telephone. He worked his way across the room and into the bedroom. A bed with dirty rumpled sheets and blankets filled most of the room. Underneath the bed was a large metal box. Dan tried to move it, found it heavy, and decided to leave it alone. What little floor space remaining was covered with piles of soiled clothing.

Dan returned to the middle room and stared at the telephone on the small table and frowned. That didn't make sense. What was a man living in abject poverty doing with a telephone? Still wearing his gloves, he picked up the telephone and held the handset close to his ear. It was connected; he could hear a dial tone.

Then he paused once more and raised his nose in the air. Marijuana. That was the other smell. It was here in this shack somewhere. Dan looked down at the telephone and nodded his head. If Bulldog was dealing, he had to have a way for his customers to contact him. Dan looked about him at the filth the man had called home. He would have to get a warrant and some help. He was willing to bet there were illegal drugs here and, according to Homer, some illegal weapons as well.

As he replaced the receiver, he noticed a partial page of telephone listings from a telephone directory under a beer can. He carefully removed the can and looked closer. It had been torn from the Helleston directory. A name was circled: Constone, Jack. What was Bulldog calling Jack about? Was Jack into drugs? Was that what the fight at Uncle Buck's was all about? Dan looked up from the scrap of paper and stared out the dirty window to the outhouse and the hillside down to Greenbrier Road. Then, he looked back down at the phone number and shook his head. "No. Don't even think it." There was absolutely no reason for Jack to have been on this road north of Uncle Buck's that night. Dan gazed at the piece of paper. "Don't let it be Jack. For Elaine's sake, don't let it be Jack."

Passing by the Black's place on his way back down to Greenbrier Road, Dan noticed that Lena Black's car was gone. He nodded and smiled. She was probably on her way up to Bailey Springs to get her electricity turned on. Then he shook his head. It was Christmas Eve, tomorrow was Christmas Day, and then the weekend. Good luck with getting that done before next Monday.

* * * *

Back at the station, Dan put his hand on the telephone handset, then paused, organizing his thoughts. After a moment, he began dialing.

"Hello?"

"Jack? Dan. I know it's Christmas Eve. I hope I'm not interrupting anything."

"Not around here. Christmas Eve is pretty quiet around our house. We're going out to Greenbrier tomorrow and see Mama and Daddy and the rest of the family, that's about all we do."

"Well, anyway, I won't keep you long. I wanted to tell you that I was checking out the neighbors around the accident site today, you know, to see if anyone saw anything that night."

"Dan, why are you calling me on Christmas Eve to talk about your investigation? I can't help you. I didn't have anything to do with it."

"Didn't say you did, Jack. It's just that your name keeps popping up."

"Did it pop up again?"

"I'm afraid so. When I interviewed you after Junior shot Bulldog, I got the impression that you and Bulldog didn't have anything to do with each other."

"You got that right. Nobody liked that bastard."

Dan paused two seconds, then asked, in a slow, even tone, "What did he call you about?"

"What did he call me about?"

Dan smiled as he heard the panic in the man's high-pitched voice. Although Bulldog had Jack's number, Dan hadn't been sure that Bulldog had called it. Now he was. "Yeah, he called you about something, didn't he?" If Jack said no, he would check Bulldog's long distance phone bills. If Jack said, yes, he had some explaining to do.

"Uh, well, uh, yeah! He did call me. A couple of times. But, you know, like I said, we didn't do any business."

"What did he call you about?"

"It was about, uh, you know, uh, a gun he had for sale. One night in Uncle Buck's, he heard me say I was looking for a 9mm, so he called me and tried to talk me into buying his, but I told him his price was too high. He called me once or twice after that, but I told him I wasn't interested. He got mad at me for not taking him up on his offer. That might be why he took a shot at me."

"That might have done it," Dan said and sadly shook his head. The man was lying. He had interviewed enough people to tell, by listening to their voices and how they reacted to his questions, whether they were lying or not. If Jack was lying, what was the truth? Why would he lie about what he had talked to Bulldog about? After seeing what Bulldog could have seen with that rifle scope, Dan thought he knew. It made him feel sick. "Well, thanks for your time, Jack. Just tying up some loose ends here."

"Anytime, Dan. Hey, you still got my old truck up there?"

"Right now I do. Sheriff Johns has been after me to get it out of here, though. He says it's an eyesore. I guess I'll call Art in a couple of days and tell him to come and get it."

"It was a good one. Well, hang in there, Dan. Merry Christmas."

"Merry Christmas, Jack." Dan had spent many hours driving all over northern Alabama and southern Tennessee looking at wrecked Ford trucks, especially those with damage to the right front fender. With only one exception, there was no reason to believe any of them were anywhere near Greenbrier Road the night before Thanksgiving. The one exception, the only pickup he could locate with right front headlight damage and had been anywhere near Greenbrier Road that night, was

Jack's truck. But something still didn't make sense to Dan. "What would a drunk driver from Helleston be doing north of Uncle Buck's that time of night? Does he have a girlfriend up there?" Dan asked, expressing the one real problem he had with considering Jack as a suspect.

* * * *

The young woman wearing a name tag that said her name was Suzie said, "Thank you, Mrs. Black. Have a nice day . . . and a Merry Christmas.'

"So, I'm all paid up, right?"

"Yes, ma'am. You sure are."

Lena Black took a deep breath, exhaled and smiled. "So, what time today are you coming down to turn on my electricity?"

"I'm sorry, but it won't be today. It's Christmas Eve. We've already let all our installers go home for the day."

"All of them?"

"Yes, ma'am. I'm sorry."

"Tomorrow is Christmas Day. Your installers work on Christmas Day?"

"No, ma'am. They don't."

"And, after that, there's the weekend. Do they work on the weekend?"

"No, ma'am. They don't."

"So, the best you can do is have someone come out next Monday, is that right?"

"Yes, ma'am."

"That's four more days without electricity even though I've paid my bill, right?"

"Yes, ma'am. I'm afraid it is."

Lena glared at the woman. "Are you the only one here?"

"No, ma'am. Mr. Wright, the manager, is still here."

"Get him out here. I want to talk to him."

"But . . ."

"Get his lazy ass out here, right now!"

Lena watched the young woman turn and walk down a short hallway and knock on a door. She said something to the closed door, then opened it, entered, and closed the door behind her. After a couple of minutes, Lena heard the door open and soon the young lady and a middle-aged man dressed in a rumpled well-worn suit came toward her. With a fake smile pasted on his mouth, he looked at her as he approached. "Good morning, uh, Mrs. Black. Is that right?"

"Lena Black. Yes."

"Suzie tells me you've got your account up to date."

"I sure do."

"It was long overdue, as you know. So much so we were forced to discontinue service to you."

"No shit. I wouldn't have noticed if you hadn't told me."

The manager held up his hand, palm out, and smiled. "I do appreciate you bringing your account up to date, and I can understand that you would like to have your electricity turned on today, but as Suzie pointed out to you, all our installers have gone home for the day."

"What about you?"

"I'm afraid I can't."

"Why not? Have you ever been an installer?"

The manager smiled and nodded. "Many years ago."

"Then why don't you do it? It can't be all that complicated."

"I'm not allowed to. I'm not in the union anymore. They might file a grievance if I did."

Lena frowned as she looked at first the manager then at Suzie, then back at the manager. "Listen to me, both of you, very carefully," she said, took a deep breath, and exhaled. "I live in a rented trailer with my teenage son. His daddy ain't around anymore, so we're having to make do the best we can.

"Like you said, you've cut off our electricity. That means we're in the dark except for some candles and, since the well pump runs on electricity, we've been having to take jugs down to the creek for our water to cook with, drink, and flush. The stove is gas, so I've been able to fry the squirrels my boy kills along with some things from our relatives.

"But, without electricity, we don't have any heat either, so I've kept the top burners on the gas stove on at night to give us a little heat but last night the propane tank ran dry. So, we woke up this morning in the cold and dark, wondering what the hell we were going to do to get through the day when a Christmas Angel, in the form of a sheriff's deputy, showed up at our door and gave us enough money to get the propane tank filled, the electricity turned on, and maybe a few things on top of that.

"All of a sudden it was going to be a great Christmas Eve! We called the gas company and they said they'd be right out, so my boy stayed home with enough money for them while I drove up here to pay the electric bill." She paused, glaring at the manager. "But, to keep the union from getting mad at you, we're not going to have heat, light, or water for four more days. Right?"

The manager sadly shook his head. "I'm really sorry, Mrs. Black. I wish I could help you, but I can't."

"I think you can," Lena said, then walked around the edge of the counter and reached for the telephone. The manager quickly put his hand on top of Lena's, preventing her from lifting the receiver. Lena looked up at the manager and snarled, "Get your goddamn hand off me, you son of a bitch!"

The manager took his hand away, frowning. "Who are you calling?"

Lena picked up the receiver. "I'm calling the Bailey Springs cops, and if that don't work, there's a deputy sheriff by the name of Sergeant Dan Warden who might be interested in hearing you tell him why you can't turn on my electricity today."

The manager stepped back and held up both hands, palms out. "All right, all right. You win. I'll come down and turn on the electricity."

Lena slowly replaced the receiver. "When?"

"As soon as I can find the keys to one of the trucks."

"You know where I live?"

"The account is at twenty Wolfe Road."

"That's it. It's a gravel road on the left going south on Greenbrier, just short of that curve where they found that kid's body. It's the second trailer you come to. My name is on the middle mailbox down on Greenbrier."

"I'll find it."

"Good for you," Lena said, paused, then added, "My son was the one who found the boy down at the curve. A deputy sheriff showed up this morning to give him the reward for finding it, that's why I've got money to get our power turned on." She paused again, looking into the manager's eyes. "Because a boy got killed, Mr. Wright, I've got money to get my power turned on and you're acting like a jackass rather than a human being on Christmas Eve."

The manager silently glared at Lena, then turned to Suzie. "You can lock up and go home after she leaves."

"Thank you, sir. Merry Christmas."

"Merry Christmas," Lena called out to his back.

The manager silently waved his hand as he disappeared into the back.

Lena picked up the receiver again.

"Wait, you're not supposed to use that."

"It's Christmas Eve, Suzie. Get into the spirit of the season."

"You're not calling the police, are you?"

"No, it's a local call, so relax for a couple of minutes and I'll be out of your hair," Lena said, then entered a number muttering, "At least the damn phone still works, I hope."

"Red, it's Mom. Have you heard from the gas company? . . . They have! Wonderful. I'm getting ready to leave here. Scrooge is coming down there in a few minutes to turn on the power . . .. What? . . . No, that's not his name. I'll tell you about it later, meanwhile I'm on my way home, but I thought I'd stop at the Big Bag and buy a few things for dinner tonight. I'm not much for turkey, but I was thinking about a ham with all the trimmings. I might even buy a pumpkin pie since I know that's your favorite . . .. Bye. See you in a little while. If Scrooge gets there before I do, wish him a Merry Christmas. He'll love that."

21

Day 31
Friday, December 25, Christmas Day

LATE CHRISTMAS MORNING, Dan drove to his house in Bailey Springs, picked up May and the kids, and drove down to Helleston to join the other members of the Warden family for a Christmas Day gathering at his uncle's house. Usually a festive occasion, today it was very somber. Every adult he greeted asked him the same question, "Is there any news?" Time after time, he would have to put them off with, "No, nothing new, but we're working on some things we already know."

Later, after everyone had eaten their fill of turkey, ham, vegetables, and a wide selection of home-made desserts, Uncle Charlie was telling a story about the days when he was a deputy here in Chickasaw County, Alabama. Dan was tired from long days and nights with little sleep and was about to doze off when he heard his uncle declare "Man alive! That old boy was so drunk he didn't know if he was coming or going!"

Dan, suddenly alert, looked at his uncle and asked. "What did you say?"

"I said, he was so drunk he didn't know if he was coming or going."

"That's what I thought you said."

Uncle Charlie frowned at him, then continued his story without further interruption.

When Uncle Charlie was done with the story, Dan excused himself, found May and led her into a vacant bedroom. "I'm going to have to leave for a little while. Are you and the kids going to be all right here?"

May nodded. "We'll be fine. Something happening at work?"

Dan nodded. "There's something I need to check. I should be back in a couple of hours."

May looked up at her estranged husband, then nodded.

"If you need to leave before I get back, Dad can run you home."

"We can wait until you get back," May said, then looked into Dan's eyes. "You look awfully tired. Have you been getting any sleep lately?"

"Some. Not enough, I guess."

May sadly shook her head. "You're working too hard."

Dan shrugged his shoulders. "It's all I've got going these days."

"Some of us would care more for you if you cared less for that job."

"I know," Dan said, looking at May. He took a deep breath, exhaled and sadly shook his head. "I know."

May bit her lower lip, then said, "We'll wait for you. If you've got time, maybe you could stay for a little while after you bring us home. I'd like to talk to you about, you know, letting you move back in again."

Dan looked at his wife, smiled and said, "I'd like that a lot, but I got to tell you, until I get Jake's killer behind bars, that's about all I can think about. Lord knows I miss you and the kids, but this thing is eating me up. I feel like I'm so close, but I don't have anything right now. Not a thing. That's why I've got to leave. I've got to check on something."

May smiled and said, "I understand."

Dan frowned as he looked into his wife's face. "Do you?"

The smile on May's face disappeared. "To be honest, I'm not sure. But I'm trying to."

Dan smiled. "Maybe we can talk about that, huh?"

May smiled once more, then nodded her head.

"See you in a little while," Dan said as he turned to go.

"Drive carefully," May called out to him.

Dan drove to the sheriff's office in Bailey Springs in his Chevy pickup, checked out a Chevy Caprice patrol car, then drove to the Bailey Springs Big Bag Market. He checked his watch and jotted the time on a note pad beside him and pulled out into traffic. "Okay, Homer, let's stop at McDonald's, pick up Jake, and head south."

At McDonald's, he pulled in, parked and noted the time once more as he gazed at the fast-food restaurant, mildly surprised that it was open on Christmas Day, even more surprised that there were customers inside.

He shook his head. Sometimes, it's the little things in life that make the biggest difference. For example, he usually came here for breakfast because he liked their hotcakes, sausage, and coffee. But if he wanted a hamburger, he would go a few blocks farther down the street and eat at Burger King. He knew he had gone to Burger King the night before Thanksgiving because he remembered walking around eating a Whopper while they searched the Square Deal pawnshop for stolen property and marijuana. They found both.

If he had chosen to buy his hamburger here that night, instead of at Burger King, he would have seen Jake trying to hitch a ride and his cousin would still be alive today. "Oh, Jake, why couldn't you have borrowed a quarter? All you had to do was call collect. Somebody would have come for you."

Dan noted the time once more, then pulled back out into traffic. He thought Homer would have maintained a safe speed, probably well below the speed limit in the fog, so he did the same.

He turned into the gravel road at the three mailboxes, stopped and noted the time. He looked at the elapsed time, then added five minutes for Homer to get to his truck after he clocked out that night. Twenty-two minutes. Dan had called the TV station and was told their weather forecast came on at twenty past the hour. Homer said he was home before ten-thirty, so he must have gotten home around ten-twenty-five. Close enough. So far, so good.

"Okay, Homer, you're heading home on Wolfe Road. Meanwhile, Jake is walking south on Greenbrier Road, and a crazy drunk in a pickup truck is heading north on

Greenbrier toward Bailey Springs." Dan turned on the car's roof-mounted emergency lights, looked both ways, and backed out into the two-lane county road.

As he shifted into Drive, he said, "Okay, Jack, you're so drunk you don't know you've turned north instead of south after leaving Uncle Buck's. Let's see how fast you can drive drunk on a foggy night on a slick highway and still keep it between the ditches." Dan stepped on the accelerator and listened to the roar of the big engine as the needle of the speedometer quickly passed the speed limit and continued turning. When he reached sixty, he eased up on the accelerator.

The south end of Greenbrier Road near the Alabama state line was too hilly for a tractor to plow, but northward toward Bailey Springs both sides of the road had small farms with homes of various sizes and ages interspersed with mobile homes of various ages in an area of the county where there were no building codes. There was also Central High School, about halfway to Bailey Springs. Dan knew the school was closed today, but he still concentrated on the road as he approached it, praying an innocent citizen wouldn't get in the way of his dangerous experiment.

When he saw the stop sign at the intersection with Boone Parkway, he slowed, then stopped. Was this as far as Jack had come? He wasn't sure, but he was willing to bet that when Jack saw the big stop sign and the sign beneath it indicating he was only a mile from Bailey Springs, he realized what he had done, and turned around. Dan did the same, noted the time once more, then pressed the accelerator and headed south.

Knowing how sharp the curve was at the accident site, he slowed to safely negotiate it in his lane. After passing the orange tape, he pulled over until his right side tires were on the narrow shoulder, then stopped. He glanced at his watch. About sixteen miles in seventeen minutes on a twisting, hilly, two-lane road in daylight. He didn't think Jack could have done better driving drunk on a foggy night, probably worse. He frowned. Could Jake have walked from the mailboxes to the curve in seventeen minutes? He knew a fit person could easily walk three miles an hour. From the curve to the mailboxes was a little over a mile. Dan nodded. Jake had enough time to get here while Jack was driving to Boone Parkway and back.

Dan sat in the car for a moment, staring straight ahead, looking at nothing, trying to imagine what would have gone through Jack's mind that night, knowing he had hit a man. Would he have stopped to find out how badly the man was hurt, or would he have kept driving? Dan thought Jack would probably have kept going, knowing the law didn't look too kindly on drunk drivers who hit pedestrians. Then he recalled the yellow clay in Jack's truck from the bottom of a Wolverine work shoe. Maybe he did decide to take a look at what he had done.

Leaving his flashing lights on, Dan slowly walked back to the tape. As he walked, Dan reminded himself that it was a dark, foggy night. Jack wouldn't have walked down this road without a flashlight. Did Jack have a flashlight? If he went looking for the body, he would have needed one to see anything on a foggy night. Art had told him he had let Jack's dad take all Jack's tools and papers from the truck a day or so after the accident. Art would have no idea what had been taken from the truck and Dan wasn't sure how he could go about asking Jack or his dad about a flashlight without stirring up a hornet's nest of questions he wasn't ready to answer.

Standing on the shoulder, Dan looked down at the crime scene tape. Did Jack go down there? Frowning, Dan slowly shook his head. As drunk as Jack was, even if he had a flashlight, he wouldn't have gone down that muddy bank. "I know that boy. One look at what he'd done and he was out of here." Dan looked down at the shoulder of the road. There was yellow clay beneath the fallen oak leaves. Dan nodded. "He was probably standing right here when he got that clay on his Wolverine safety shoes."

Dan returned to his car, noted the time, and drove away. This time he stayed within the speed limit. "He's just killed a man. He's scared . . . confused now. He'd be driving slower, trying to decide what to do."

When Dan reached Uncle Buck's Tavern, he pulled into the empty parking lot and paused. Jack might have stopped here. Maybe he went in and had a beer. No, a man who had just killed another man would need some time by himself to think. Whatever he thought, he didn't go inside to call 9-1-1, so he probably didn't stay too long. Dan noted the time and headed south.

When Dan passed by the big oak tree, he pulled over onto the shoulder, noted the time once more, then did some calculations. Homer saw the pickup truck around ten-twenty-five speeding past him heading north. Add another seventeen minutes for Jack to turn around and get back to the accident site after passing Homer, spend five minutes there, then give him five minutes to get to Uncle Buck's, spend five minutes there, then another five minutes to drive south and hit the oak tree. Add another five minutes for the farmer to call 9-1-1 and you get seven minutes after eleven o'clock.

"How about that?" Dan said, then repeated it. He had confirmed earlier that the 9-1-1 call had come in at eleven-seventeen that Wednesday night. It could have been Jack in the truck heading north past Homer. Even if he had been driving a lot slower in the fog and rain; even if he'd gone down the embankment for a few minutes; even if he had spent more time at Uncle Buck's; there was still enough time after Homer saw the truck for Jack to drive north, turn around, hit Jake, then plow into the oak tree before eleven-seventeen.

Dan frowned. But when did Jack leave Uncle Buck's? If he didn't leave until eleven or later, it couldn't have been him that Homer saw. If he had left around ten-twenty or earlier, it could have been him. Dan shook his head. It would be a big help if he knew when Jack had left Uncle Buck's the Wednesday night before Thanksgiving. Dan sadly shook his head, knowing how hopeless it would be, trying to pin down when some drunk had left a rowdy bar a month ago.

Suddenly, he jerked his head up. With a surprised look on his face, he gazed off into the distance. "Maybe not," he murmured to himself, then grabbed the file beside him and leafed through it until he found the statement Jack had signed the night Bulldog had been killed. He quickly scanned it until he found the section he was looking for " . . . I usually shoot pool on Wednesdays with Billy Blakeley, but I come up here by myself on the weekends. Billy's wife has him on a short leash."

Dan called the dispatcher on his radio, who found Billy Blakely's number in the Helleston phone directory. She tried calling it, waited until the recorder answered, ended the connection, and informed Dan. Dan nodded. Billy and his family were probably spending Christmas Day with other members of his family. He would have to wait until tomorrow to pursue his brainstorming.

Dan sighed, started the engine and headed back to the station, now convinced there was a good possibility that Jack's red '93 Ford truck had been the vehicle that had killed Jake. The only problem was proving it. The only possible eyewitness was dead, and a jury would laugh him out of the courtroom with the flimsy circumstantial evidence he had. Just because Jack's truck could have been the one Homer had seen didn't mean it was him and Dan knew it. It was possible the truck Homer had seen heading north was not the one which had hit Jake later coming south. It was even possible Jack was telling the truth about seeing the other red Ford truck.

Junior had his parking lot pretty well lit by some big pole lights, and the roadway would have been well lit as well, light enough for Jack to see the make, model and color of a passing truck. At the moment, however, Dan didn't believe it. Still, until he had something to refute the story, something that would tie Jack and his truck to the accident, there wasn't much use in even thinking about arresting him.

"Ah, man! What am I going to do?" Dan muttered as he pondered the contradiction he faced in seeking justice for his cousin. He was now convinced that Jack Constone was a possible suspect in the death of Jake Warden. On the other hand, he knew that if Jack really was the offender, his close relationship with Elaine would never be the same.

* * * *

192

When Dan returned to his uncle's home, he found a place to park around back. As he got out, his uncle came out to meet him.

"Well, welcome back. I didn't know you were leaving until you were gone."

"I had to check on something."

"Did you find out anything?"

Dan nodded his head. "I believe I did."

"Is it going to help?"

"It might."

"Good, good," the older man said and squeezed Dan's shoulders hard before he released him and stepped away. "Come on in. The women have been waiting for you to get back. They want to take some pictures."

22

Day 32
Saturday, December 26

IT WAS EARLY SATURDAY morning, the day after Christmas. Dan and the dispatcher were the only ones in the office. Dan stared out the window for a while, going over his conversation with May after he had brought her and the kids home from the family gathering yesterday. The conversation had been civil and, he thought, they had made some headway toward a possible reconciliation.

After an hour or so, however, it was obvious they weren't going to resolve everything all at once. She was upset at him for not calling to tell her about the kid taking a shot at him, among other things. She hated his job and wanted him to give it up because worrying about him was driving her crazy. On the other hand, he loved his job almost as much as he loved his wife and kids and didn't have the slightest idea what he would do if he wasn't a deputy sheriff.

His dad had a successful insurance business in Helleston and had wanted Dan to come to work for him for a long time. Dan had never told his dad, but selling insurance was somewhere below cotton farming on his list of desirable life vocations. Dan sighed, picked up the phone, and entered a long-distance number.

"Hello?"

Dan smiled at the sound of the high-pitched child's voice. "Let me talk to your daddy."

"Just a minute. Daddy! Telephone!"

Dan listened to the din of noise for a minute or so, then someone picked up the phone.

"Hello?"

"Billy? This is Sergeant Dan Warden. I'm a deputy sheriff in Creek County, Tennessee. I'd like to talk to you for a minute."

"Wait a minute, let me take this thing into a bedroom so I can hear you."

Dan heard Billy having a brief conversation with someone, probably his wife, then a door closed, and the noise subsided.

"Okay, now I can hear you. What's up?"

"Sounds like your kids had a good Christmas."

"Oh, it's not too bad this morning. Most of the batteries are already dead. Yesterday was a madhouse at my brother's place, though, with his three and my two going at it full speed most of the day."

"Yeah, I know what you mean," Dan said. No, he didn't. Not really. Not this year. This year he had awakened alone in an old, rented mobile home on Christmas morning. He had dropped off his gifts for May and the kids at the house earlier in the week but May had not allowed him to be there at the crack of dawn to see his kids opening their gifts from Santa. It was one of the lowest points of his life.

"So, what can I do for you, uh, Dan, right?"

"Right. Deputy Dan Warden," Dan said, then paused. "The reason I'm calling is that I'd like to ask you a couple of questions about the night before Thanksgiving. Do you remember whether or not you were up at Uncle Buck's that night?"

"Sure was. That's the night me and Jack won the big pot. I'm not sure if I should admit this to a deputy sheriff, but after we won the tournament, we got into a beer drinking contest with the guys we beat at eight ball. All four of us got pretty plastered."

"Sounds like you had a lot of fun."

"We did until Jack stumbled into a couple on the dance floor and got into a shoving match with the man. When Junior got his billy club, I grabbed Jack and got him outside before anybody started swinging. It was for his own good. He wasn't in any shape to take on anybody."

"Once you got him outside, did he leave?"

"As far as I know he did. The last time I saw him, he was walking toward his truck with a beer in his hand, cussing me out. I didn't wait around to see if he left, it was too cold and wet to hang around outside."

"How long did you stay after Jack left?"

"Not too long. Jack and some of the others stay around until Junior closes the place sometimes, but I've got a deal with my wife."

"What's that?"

"She lets me go up to the line and have a few beers sometimes on Wednesdays, but I have to be back home in time to help put the kids in bed."

"What time is that?"

"Well, it's supposed to be nine, but, like I said, we were celebrating a little and I sort of lost track of time, if you know what I mean. When I looked at that clock and saw it was ten-thirty, I knew I was in trouble. Man! She let me have it with both barrels when I got home."

"So, Jack left before ten-thirty?"

"Far as I know, he did. Why? What's so important about how long I stayed after Jack left?"

Dan smiled. Billy hadn't figured out where the conversation was heading. He was about to, though. "You drove back down to Helleston after you left Uncle Buck's, right?"

"Sure did."

"Down Greenbrier Road?"

"Every time."

Dan paused, then asked, "On your way home, did you see Jack's truck wrapped around that oak tree?"

"No, I didn't. Wait a minute! That don't make no sense. He left Uncle Buck's before I did."

"You sure about that?"

"Yeah, pretty sure. I mean, I didn't actually see him drive off, but I saw him walking out to his truck and I know he didn't come back inside."

"Did you see his truck in the parking lot when you left?"

"I don't remember seeing it, but the parking lot was still pretty full when I left."

"And you didn't see his truck at the tree, right?"

"Hey, I admit to having a few beers that night, but I sure as hell would have noticed that red pickup wrapped around that oak tree if it had been there."

"Well, I guess he must have wrecked it after you passed by."

"I guess he did, but that don't make sense either, does it?"

"No, it doesn't," Dan agreed.

"Well, I'll be damned. I never thought about it that way before. I'm going to ask him where he went the next time I see him."

"Yeah, I'd be interested in knowing that myself."

"If I find out, I'll let you know."

"I'd appreciate that," Dan said.

"Anything else?"

"Not today."

"Well, I hear a kid crying. I'd better get in there and find out which one tried to kill the other this time."

"Thanks again, Billy."

"Anytime, Dan."

Dan hung up the phone, then paused, smiling. Now, he would call Jack and get his version of the story before he had a chance to talk to Billy. From talking to him before, he had gotten the impression that Jack had left the parking lot immediately after leaving the building. If he did, where did he go? Dan thought he knew. He picked up the phone and entered a number.

"Hello?"

"This is Dan Warden. Is Jack Constone there?"

"Oh, hi, Dan. This is Cathy. No, Jack isn't here."

"Do you expect him back anytime soon?"

"I don't know. He left a while ago to return a jacket he got for Christmas."

"Oh," Dan said, obviously disappointed.

"Would you like me to give him a message?"

"No, that's all right. I'll try to call him later."

"Have you found out who ran over Jake Warden yet?"

"No, not yet," Dan said quietly.

"Oh! That was so awful, leaving him in that ditch like that. What kind of person would do something like that to another human being?"

"I wonder about that myself."

"I sure hope you find out who did it."

"I'm going to do my best."

"Nice talking to you, Dan. I'll tell Jack you called."

"Nice talking to you again, Cathy," Dan said, then slowly replaced the receiver. With his lips drawn tightly across his face, he shook his head in frustration. "Well, shoot," he said, then got up to leave. Bradley Hancock at Bailey Springs Hardware was on his agenda this morning. "I hope he still remembers me," Dan said as he headed out the door.

* * * *

Cathy scribbled a note to Jack about the call from Dan, then picked up the phone and called Pete's home number. After it rang four times, she heard the recorder beep. She tried his cell phone number and got the same recorded message. "Hi, Pete. This is You-Know-Who. Sorry I missed you. If you get back this morning, give me a call at home. The phone number is in the book. I'm here all by myself. See you later."

Ten minutes later the phone rang. "Hello?"

"Cathy?"

"Oh, hi, Pete," Cathy said, relieved that he had called. "Merry Christmas . . . plus one."

"Merry Christmas to you, Cathy. I was in the shower when you called. I wasn't sure if I should be calling you at home."

"That's all right. We can talk. Jack's gone to swap the hunting jacket I gave him for something else, as usual. What's up?"

"They hired a new guy to take my place. He's going to be working some days and some evenings until he gets trained. They want me to be there with him and show him how to do my job. I'm sorry."

"Oh," Cathy said, clearly disappointed. "That's too bad. I was really looking forward to another hug today."

"I know, I was, too. My boss is really upset with me for leaving. He told me if the new guy wasn't trained by the time I left, he wouldn't give me a good recommendation. He knows that no matter what job I apply for next, my new employer will check back here to see what kind of record I left. So, I've got to grab something to eat and go right back. The whole place is a zoo with the after Christmas sales and exchanges. Is there any way we could get together sometime later today for a few minutes?"

"How much later?"

"I'll be here most of the day. I told the boss I needed to leave by four and he agreed. The new guy is really sharp, so they're going to let him try it solo tonight. I'm so exhausted. I may pass out on you, but I really want to see you this evening if I can. Is there any way you can get away this afternoon or this evening? I really want to see you before I leave for California."

"I'll try," Cathy said, noting a sense of urgency in his voice. "I want to see you, too. Maybe I'll check out the after Christmas sales around four."

"That would be great."

* * * *

Dan found a place to park his old brown and tan Chevy pickup in the crowded Bailey Springs Hardware parking lot. It was his own vehicle, but it had in-the-grill emergency lights and a two-way radio he could use to contact the sheriff's dispatcher if he needed her. On the other hand, it was over five years old. The gas mileage wasn't as good as it had been, the transmission was beginning to worry him when he shifted, and he was getting tired of the brown and tan color. It was time to trade up.

The new 1999 Chevy Silverados looked nice at the Bailey Springs Chevy dealer, but they didn't have one on the lot with the color and options he wanted. On the other hand, the Chevy dealer down in Helleston had a black one that appealed to him.

Even more appealing was learning they offered their law enforcement discount to a Tennessee deputy sheriff.

Dan took a deep breath and exhaled as he considered what he was doing here this morning. He knew Sheriff Johns frowned on his deputies using their job for personal gain or favors. At the same time, Dan knew that the side of their county vehicles declared that they served and protected. As he grabbed the door handle, he decided that what he had in mind wasn't really doing himself a personal favor, but he might be doing a service to one of Sheriff Johns' constituents. Close enough.

Wearing jeans, a flannel shirt, and a jacket to protect him from the bitter cold and to hide his holstered weapon, Dan hurried into the big building. Once inside he paused, looking at the huge racks filled with just about anything anyone would want to find in a hardware and building supply store. It wasn't as big as the Home Depot down in Helleston, but it was close.

As the number of vehicles in the parking lot indicated, the place was mobbed with customers. Some of them were checking out the after Christmas sales, the rest were standing in long lines at the Customer Service desk with Christmas presents they wanted to exchange or return for a refund.

Dan continued to look around, hoping to find the manager, Bradley Hancock, with no success. He had about decided to leave the crowded store and come back another day when it might not be so mobbed when he heard a voice call out to him.

"Dan Warden! Son of a gun! How're you doing?"

Dan turned and smiled. "Hey, Brad," he said, extending his hand. "I'm fine. How're you doing?"

Brad grinned as he shook Dan's hand, then waved his arm at the mob around Customer Service. "It's a madhouse, like it is every year the day after Christmas," he said, paused, then added, "So, how're you doing, stranger? I almost didn't recognize you in your civvies. What's up with you these days? You don't have a box to return, so you must be here to check out the sales we have on power tools. Don't blame you. Some of them are seriously discounted."

"Got all the tools I need for now, Brad. What I'd really like is five minutes of your time, when you've got time, but I can see that this is not a good time."

"I've always got time for you, Dan. Follow me."

Dan followed the store manager as he walked over to the Customer Service area, then walked behind the counter and spoke a few words to the first person working there. Then, working his way around and through the stacks of returned goods, he continued on toward the back where there was a wall of glass panels with a glass door in the middle. "In here, Dan," he called out as he opened the door.

Dan followed the manager into the small room, barely big enough for a couple of visitors' chairs and a desk with a computer, phone, and an in-and-out basket. There was a clock, a calendar, and several plaques on the walls, commending him or his store for doing something outstanding during past years.

Brad made himself comfortable behind the desk. "Have a seat, Dan," he said indicating the visitors' chairs. When Dan was seated, Brad grinned. "Man, I sure do appreciate what you did for my boy. Sixteen-year-old kids don't realize they can ruin their whole life doing something stupid like that."

Dan nodded. "Sometimes jail isn't the right thing to do with a sixteen-year-old boy. How is he doing these days?"

"He's doing great. He's a freshman at Vandy. He's home for the holidays, so I put him to work," Brad said, then pointed to the tall, skinny kid in the back of the Customer Service area. "That's him there. I figured he needed the money, and I need the help, so I got his butt out of the house this morning and put him to work restocking the returns that haven't been opened."

"If you're looking for more help, I'd like to talk to you about that."

Brad frowned. "You interested in moonlighting, Dan?"

Dan laughed out loud. "No. God, no. I've got more to do than I've got time to do as it is," he said, paused, then said, "On the other hand, I ran into a situation a couple of days ago that I'd like to talk to you about."

Brad frowned, clearly uncomfortable with the new line of conversation, then leaned back in his chair, interlocked his fingers across his gut and said, "Sure, tell me about it."

Dan briefly described Red Black and his role in finding the body, then talked about his experience with both Red and his mother on Christmas Eve and how destitute they seemed to be. "Anyway, on my way out the door, she said she wanted to work and thought she would like to work for you. I've only met her that one time, but I think she might do a good job for you."

"Sure, tell her to come in and fill out an application. We'll take a look."

"She said she filled out an application, and was interviewed six months ago, but never heard back from you."

Brad frowned as he reached out for his keyboard and began typing. "What did you say her name was?"

"Lena Black."

After hitting a few keys, Brad said, "Twenty Wolfe Road?"

"That's her."

"Hmmm . . . age . . . thirty-one . . . son . . . Myron . . . husband . . . Lloyd . . . education level . . . tenth grade," Brad said, paused as he read more, then said, "No work experience until five years ago. Spent about three years working for Landers Landscaping down in Helleston . . . must have got tired of the commute because she started working for Bailey Landscaping right after leaving Landers, then got laid off back in July of this year," Brad said, then looked up at Dan. "At which point she came in here and applied for a job."

"What happened? Do you know?"

Brad frowned as he read more. "The comment by the person who interviewed her is "Possible conflict of interest.""

"What does that mean?"

Brad shrugged his shoulders. "Could mean any one of several things, Dan. It's sort of a catchall phrase we use when the person interviewing the prospective employee detects something the person said, or wrote on the application, that led him or her to believe that the person wouldn't fit in with the rest of the team here. For example, having a work background of only five years for a woman her age might be a red flag. What had she been up to since she dropped out of high school until she hired on at Landers?"

Dan stared at the man for several seconds. He was pretty sure he knew what the interviewer's problem was with Lena. At some point in the interview, Lena had told the interviewer that her husband was in prison. Some people might assume that a family member of an incarcerated inmate might be capable of doing the same thing. Prejudice. The world was full of it.

Brad glanced up at the clock, then looked at Dan. "Anything else?"

"How well do you know the person who did the interview?"

"I know her very well."

"Then, tell me this," Dan said. "If Lena had explained her brief work history by telling her that she was a fulltime housewife until her husband was arrested and convicted of armed robbery and is now in prison for thirty years . . . do you think the interviewer might have written that note on Lena's application because she would feel uncomfortable working with the wife of a convicted felon?"

Brad looked past Dan, through the glass to the Customer Service area beyond, without responding.

Finally, after several seconds of silence, Dan said, "I'm not asking you to hire her. Sheriff Johns wouldn't like it if I did. What I am asking is that you take another look at her. If you don't like what you see, it's fine with me."

Brad pointed to the screen. "Is that phone number still good?"

"As far as I know, it is. She said the only thing working when I was there was the phone."

Brad picked up the phone and entered the number. "Hello? Is this Lena Black? . . . This is Brad Handcock at Bailey Springs Hardware. How are you today? . . . That's good to hear, Mrs. Black. The reason I'm calling is that we have several openings at the moment, so we're looking at applications we received earlier this year for possible candidates to reinterview. Are you currently employed? . . . Oh, I'm sorry to hear that. I wasn't aware of that. I'd like for you to come in and talk to us again. Would nine o'clock Monday work for you? . . . Great. Come to the Customer Service desk and tell them you have an appointment with me. If I'm not there, I will be shortly. All right? . . . Great! Talk to you on Monday, Mrs. Black." Brad hung up the phone and looked at Dan. "Okay?"

Dan stood and extended his hand. "You're a good man, Brad."

Brad stood and shook Dan's hand. "So are you, Dan. Happy New Year."

"Happy New Year, Brad."

* * * *

It was after four and a college football bowl game was on when the phone started ringing. For an instant Jack tensed, thinking it might be Bulldog, then he smiled and relaxed. Bulldog was dead. "Hey, the phone's ringing!" Jack yelled out, then scowled as he heard the sound of water running in the shower. He picked up the phone and growled, "Yeah?"

"Jack? Billy."

"Hey, Billy, what's happening, man?"

"Not much. Still full of all that food I ate yesterday."

"Know what you mean. We were out at my folks yesterday. Lot of good food out there, too."

"Well, to tell you the truth, the reason I called is to let you know a Tennessee deputy sheriff called me this morning. Has he called you?"

"Cathy said he called while I was out, but he didn't say what he wanted. Why? What'd he want?"

"I'm not sure. He asked me a lot of questions about the night you got kicked out of Uncle Buck's. Remember?"

A cold chill crawled down the back of Jack's head and across his shoulders. "Yeah, how can I forget? What sort of questions was he asking you?"

"Well, mainly, he wanted to know if I saw your truck wrapped around that oak tree on my way home."

"Why would he ask you that?"

"I told him you left Uncle Buck's before I did. When I told him I didn't remember seeing your truck there at the tree, I guess he thought I had been too drunk to notice it. The thing is, Jack, I don't think I was that drunk. I would have seen your truck if it had been there. Where did you go after you left the bar?"

Jack clenched his teeth. Yeah, right. Why don't I come right out and admit that I had been so drunk that I drove north instead of south and wound up killing somebody on the way back? That would make everyone happy, especially one sneaky deputy sheriff.

"Jack?"

"Yeah, Billy?"

"I didn't know if you were still there."

"I'm still here," Jack said, then smiled as an idea came to him. "And that's why you didn't see my truck against the tree that night. I didn't leave Uncle Buck's right away."

"You didn't?"

"Nope. Once I got to my truck and got it warmed up, I took a little nap."

"You passed out, that's what you mean."

"No, man, I didn't pass out. I decided to take a little rest before heading back to Helleston."

"I don't remember seeing your truck when I left."

"I don't remember seeing yours when I left."

"I know I didn't see your truck at the tree, so you must have left after I did."

"I guess so."

"I'm glad that's cleared up. That deputy had me wondering there for a while. I didn't like the way he insinuated that I was too drunk to see my friend's truck wrapped around a tree."

"Don't let him get to you. I've dealt with him before. He's a sneaky bastard."

"I can believe that."

"Thanks for calling, Billy."

"See you bright and early Monday. Same time, same place."

"Your turn to drive," Jack reminded him.

"I heard they're going to announce some more layoffs Monday."

"I heard the same. I don't think they'll lay off anybody this time of year."

"I wouldn't put it past them."

"I guess we'll find out."

"I guess so. See you Monday," Jack said.

"Oh, hey! Wait! What about New Year's Eve. You folks coming?"

"Wouldn't miss it."

"Looks like we're going to have about a dozen couples from our old Double Head days again. That should make a good party. Oh, I saw Elaine Warden the other day when I was up at the office for a few minutes. I invited her and her husband to join us. She said she was divorced but might come by for a while anyway. That would be great, wouldn't it?"

"Yeah, it would."

"I don't know her all that well anymore. I didn't even know she was divorced, but she still looks like one of the finest pieces of ass to come out of that school." Billy laughed. "But you would know that, wouldn't you?"

"I might," Jack admitted.

"Anyway, we've already arranged for the kids to spend the night with Mama and Dad, and Doris is getting some of the other women lined up to make the food. All I have left to do it make a liquor run to Huntsville."

"Too bad you can't just buy your stuff from Junior."

"Yeah, but I've heard that Chickasaw County deputies will go easy on you if they stop you and find booze with an Alabama tax stamp on it in your trunk, but they'll impound your car for bootlegging if it's got a Tennessee tax stamp on it."

"Yeah, I've heard that, too. That's why I always make sure any booze I cross the state line with is in my gut."

"I hear that! See you Monday."

"Later."

* * * *

With the noise of the college football game on, Cathy stood before a full-length mirror in underwear she usually reserved to wear underneath a party dress, trying to decide what else to wear. She wanted it to be something special. Tonight might be the last time she would see Pete before he left for California. It might even be the last time she would ever see him. She liked Pete a lot, maybe enough to want to go to bed with him. Could she? Would she? Cathy was convinced Jack was having an affair with Elaine Warden. Still, she wasn't sure she wanted to take that giant step herself. "Oh, hell," Cathy muttered in frustration at her predicament. Less than a half-hour before she was to meet Pete, she still wasn't sure what she wanted to happen once she got there. That bothered her a lot.

How far she had come in such a short time. Four weeks? Was that all? It seemed an eternity since the first night she had met Pete. There had been something special about that night. She had felt a sense of freedom and self-determination she had never felt before. Even now, she was amazed that she had been so bold as to initiate a friendly relationship with a man that night. Where had she found the nerve to even think of doing something like that, she wondered? She smiled. "You've always had it. You just didn't know it," she whispered to her reflection. She went to her closet, chose a white sweater and red slacks and hurriedly dressed. She checked her makeup once more, then put on her long coat and sneakers, grabbed her purse, dropped a pair of red leather flats in it, and hurried down the hallway.

"Bye. I'm going out for a few minutes to check on the after-Christmas sales," Cathy called out as she reached the front door, anxious to leave before he discovered she was dressed much too nicely to go shopping.

With his eyes and mind on the television, Jack gave a half-hearted wave to her. "Just remember, we eat at six o'clock around here," he growled. As soon as the door closed, he picked up the phone and called Elaine. Spending a couple of hours with her would be a lot more fun than watching football. After four rings, her answering machine came on. He hung up the phone and went back to watching the game.

* * * *

When Cathy arrived at the Cross Winds, she removed her sneakers, put on her shoes, then adjusted the rearview mirror to check her hair and makeup once more. Satisfied, she paused momentarily to gaze at her reflection. A month ago, if someone had told her she was going to a man's apartment tonight expecting to get laid, she would have thought them to be insane. Cathy stared intently at her reflection. Maybe she was the one who was insane. If Jack knew where she was tonight, he might really do serious harm to her. She knew he was capable of it.

"Let me take your coat," Pete said as she stepped inside his apartment. Cathy turned her back to Pete and allowed him to help her with her coat. Pete draped her coat on the back of one of the bar stools, then turned back to her. "Wow, you really look great tonight, Cathy."

"Thanks," she said, then added, "I've got a little Christmas hug saved up for you." Pete came to her and wrapped his arms around her. They stood with their bodies pressed against one another for a moment, then Cathy pulled her head off Pete's shoulder, turned her head up to him and gazed into his eyes. "Oh, Pete, you feel so good to me," she murmured as Pete's lips met hers.

When they broke, Pete said, "I didn't mean to do that. It just came over me."

"That's all right. I don't mind. We can pretend there's some mistletoe hanging from the ceiling."

"Oh!" Pete said with a start. "I've got a Christmas present for you."

"Oh, Pete, you shouldn't have. I don't have one for you."

"Just being here is all the present I want from you," he said, then released her. "Here, let me get it." Pete walked over to the counter, picked up a small green box wrapped with red ribbon, and handed it to her. "Merry Christmas, Cathy."

"Oh, thank you, Pete." She took the small box and opened it. It was a small golden heart with diamond chips around the edges on a thin gold chain.

"Oh, Pete, it's precious. Thank you."

"I've never given my heart to anyone before," he said solemnly.

Tears welled up in Cathy eyes. "I hope you never give it to anyone else."

"I doubt it."

"Put it on me," she said. When he had fastened the clasp around her neck, Cathy looked down at the small gold heart resting on her sweater for a moment, then she gathered up the small piece of jewelry and, pulling open the neck of her sweater, dropped it inside. "There. Now your heart is next to mine. Here, feel," she said, taking his hand and pressing it against the side of her left breast. "Can you feel my heart beating against yours?" she asked as she gazed up at him.

Pete's face turned red as he nodded, his hand still pressed against the married woman's breast.

After a moment, when it became clear to her that he wasn't going to voluntarily remove his hand anytime soon, Cathy slowly removed Pete's hand from her breast and smiled. "It's beautiful, Pete. Thank you. It's the most wonderful Christmas present I have ever gotten from anyone." Her eyes filled with tears. "It's hard to believe you're leaving for California. This may be the last time we will ever see each other for a long time."

"Not too long, I hope. I think I'm going to leave my heart in Alabama when I go back to California," Pete said morosely.

"I think you might be taking a little piece of my heart back with you when you go to California," Cathy said, smiling happily at the man.

Suddenly, with a pained look on his face, he blurted out, "I swear to God, Cathy, I'm crazy about you. I don't know, maybe I'm just crazy. Never in my life did I ever think I would feel this way about another man's wife. I know it's wrong, but I want you so badly, I can't sleep at night, thinking about you."

Cathy paused for a moment, gazing at Pete, then smiled. The man was in love with her! He really was! For the first time in her life a man had fallen in love with her. It felt wonderful. "Oh, Pete, you're so sweet."

"I want you, Cathy, more than I've ever wanted anything in my life, from the first minute I saw you that night sitting across from me in the other booth. Then I saw your wedding band and I knew it would never happen."

"Would it make a difference to you if I wasn't wearing my wedding band?"

Pete cocked his head to one side and said, "If you ever take that little gold band off, it will change a lot of things."

Cathy looked into Pete's eyes and saw the love for her she had never seen in the eyes of her husband. Maybe it would be a sin to have sex with this man, she decided, but it would be a greater sin to allow him to pass from her life without ever sharing his body. A quiet calm came over her as she asked, "Would you like me to take my ring off . . . right now?"

With his lips pressed tightly together, Pete shook his head. "Oh, Cathy, we can't. We just can't," Pete said earnestly, a pained look on his face.

Cathy wrinkled her brow. She had just offered to have sex with this man and he had turned her down. Was he really homosexual after all? "Why? I don't understand."

"I want you so badly, Cathy, really I do. But I want a lot more. I want to spend the rest of my life with you," Pete said, then paused. "Don't you see? I don't want it to start this way. I'd feel really awful, doing anything with you tonight, knowing your husband is waiting for you at home. I want it to be something wonderful when it happens between us, Cathy. I don't want you to have to confess it to your priest. I don't want to hang my head when I hear my minister talking about man's sins against God and other men. I know we're sinning a little, just because we get together to talk, but we've never done anything really bad in the eyes of God. I'm afraid something terrible might happen if we give in to temptation tonight."

Cathy frowned as she gazed at Pete, trying to understand him. For the first time in her married life, she had offered to have sex with another man, only to have him refuse her because it was morally wrong. Of course it was morally wrong! That was part of the excitement, didn't he see that? She closed her eyes and shook her head. He was right, of course. If she had given herself to him tonight, in the years to come, she would look back on it as a one-night stand with a man she barely knew. She knew she should be grateful that this man's moral fiber was stronger than hers. She opened her eyes and gazed up at Pete. "I've never met a man like you," Cathy said quietly.

"I've never met a woman like you, Cathy."

"Well, if some good loving is not on the evening's agenda, what else do you have in mind to pass the time?"

"You like eggnog? I've got some I could heat up in the microwave."

"Hot eggnog is nice, especially with cinnamon. It's even better with a little rum in it."

"I have cinnamon. I've also got a little rum."

"You do!"

Pete grinned and nodded his head.

"How long have you had that?"

"I bought it when I was still living in Huntsville."

"A born-again Christian, with rum in his apartment? Pete! I am shocked! I am absolutely, totally shocked!"

Pete laughed at her feigned tirade. "We all have our little sins, I guess. There's only been one perfect man on earth. They crucified Him," Pete said as he walked back into the kitchen area. "How much rum do you want in yours?"

"How much do you have? The only alcohol we have at home is Jack's beer. I hate the taste of beer. I don't see how he can drink as much as he does."

"I think there's enough to last the evening," Pete said, holding up the half-full bottle for Cathy to see.

Cathy giggled. "If it isn't, I'm going to be in a lot of trouble."

When Pete had the drinks ready, he brought them to the living area and set them on the coffee table. They sat at opposite ends of the couch and sipped the hot liquid.

"So, I hear you're thinking about taking a little vacation out to California?" he said.

Cathy gazed at Pete, smiled and nodded her head. "Could be." They began to talk about what they might do and the places they might visit together in California. When they finished their first drink, Pete rose to prepare another. Cathy heard an old favorite song begin to play. Smiling, she rose from the couch and immediately realized she was a little light-headed. "My goodness," she said as she tried to steady herself. "I think I'm feeling the rum already. How much did you put in my drink anyway?"

"Just enough for flavor. I've got to get rid of it before I leave. Do you want me to make this one lighter?"

"No, thanks, the first one was fine," she said, then began to hum the familiar tune as she slowly turned about the floor, holding her arms about herself. "Hurry up. I want to dance with you."

Pete set the two glasses on the coffee table and came into her arms. They danced slowly, their bodies pressed together, until the song ended. When it was over, they remained standing, their arms locked around each other. Cathy turned her eyes up to Pete and asked, "Do you think that mistletoe is still up there?" Pete responded by kissing her once more. The kiss lasted until the next song began to play, another old favorite.

"Oh, gosh, this one brings back memories," Cathy murmured, her head resting on Pete's shoulder.

" . . . California . . . the beach . . . " Pete said.

"I was at a party when I was fifteen. There was this older boy there who asked me to dance with him. He was so tall and good-looking. This was the song they were playing. We sneaked out and got into his van. That was a very special night for me. Oh, that was so long ago."

They returned to the couch and sat close to one another as they sipped their drinks. The conversation about the fond memories of their childhood in California continued, interrupted occasionally by another dance to an old song intermingled with hugs and kisses. As Cathy finished her second eggnog, she casually asked, "What time is it?"

"Oh . . . almost six," Pete said casually as he glanced at his watch.

Cathy screamed, "My god! I'm going to be late. I've got to get out of here! He's either going to kill me or make me wish I was dead!" She jumped up, grabbed her purse, and sweater and hurried into the bathroom. In less than five minutes she was out and at the door. Pete helped her with her coat, then she turned, grabbed his shoulders, and kissed him quickly. "Oh, god, I've got to get out of here. Bye," she said frantically, then quickly exited the apartment and hurried to her car.

Pete closed the door, then murmured, "I love you, Cathy."

* * * *

Jack had fallen asleep in his recliner while watching the Saturday football bowl game. He looked up at the clock and frowned. It was after six o'clock. Cathy was late. That meant his supper would be late and his stomach was already growling. The ballgame had been too one-sided to keep him from falling asleep; now he was awake again, and hungry for something more substantial than chips and beer. "Goddamn her lazy ass! Where the hell is she?"

The phone rang. Jack nodded, expecting it to be his wife, calling to say she had put her car in a ditch or wrapped it around a telephone pole somewhere. He picked up the receiver and growled, "Hello!"

"Yeah, Jack. This is Dan Warden again."

Jack paused. He was in no mood to talk to this Tennessee hillbilly deputy sheriff right now. Instead, he wanted very badly to curse and scream at him. Dan had gotten Billy to tell him he hadn't seen the wreck on his way home, forcing Jack to change his story. Now, he had to remember that he was passed out in his truck in Uncle Buck's parking lot for a while. Would that work? It would have to for now. "Yeah, Dan. What can I do for you today?"

"I'd like to talk to you about a couple of things. You got a minute?"

"Yeah, sure. What's on your mind?" Jack asked, knowing very well what was on the deputy's mind.

"Do you remember you told me you saw a one-eyed red Ford pickup coming south past Uncle Buck's the night Jake got killed?"

"That's right. Just like mine."

"Well, to make a long story short, I need to find that pickup in the worst way and I think the driver might have been at Uncle Buck's that evening. So, what I'm asking is, do you know of anyone else at Uncle Buck's that was driving a red truck that night?"

"No, Dan, I don't. That doesn't mean there wasn't one there. His parking lot gets full on busy nights."

"Yeah, I know. I've already talked to Junior. He said he doesn't know any regulars who drive red Ford pickups except the one you had. He said that didn't mean someone couldn't have been there with one."

"That's right. There's a bunch of us that show up pretty regularly, but I always see some strangers in there every time I go."

"I've made a few phone calls to the owners of those plates numbers I copied down in Uncle Buck's parking lot. So far, nobody remembers another red Ford pickup on the road that night. I guess I'll have to keep calling."

"I'm glad it's your job and not mine."

"I'm going to have to start with what I have and go from there. Just to refresh my memory, you saw the pickup right after you left the bar, right?"

Jack smiled, silently thanking Billy for his call. "Well, no, Dan, that's not exactly the way it happened."

"Oh?"

"I didn't want to tell you this, but I left the bar almost an hour before I left the parking lot."

"What were you doing out in the parking lot all that time?"

"Well, that's why I didn't want to say anything to you about it. I was afraid you might get the wrong idea. You see, I'd put in a long day at work, then Billy and I had been shooting pool and drinking beer for a few hours, so when I got out to my truck, I felt really tired. So, I decided to take a little nap."

"You went to sleep? Out in the parking lot?"

"I sure did. But, you know, I didn't want to tell you because I was afraid you might think I had got drunk and passed out, but I was just tired. When I woke up I felt better, so I drove straight home. At least, that's what I tried to do. I didn't get very far."

"Did you wake up by yourself, or did someone wake you?"

"I woke up by myself. Why? Is that important?"

"Right now, the only thing that's important to me is finding that red Ford truck."

"I wish I could be of more help, Dan."

"There is one thing you could do for me. I've talked to the sheriff about you seeing that red truck. He said I should have you come up here to Bailey Springs so we can sit down and talk about what happened that night."

"You mean . . . officially? As a suspect?"

"Well, as far as being a suspect, I don't know about that, more like a person of interest because of your red truck. I might read you your rights, but that's pretty standard these days any time we talk to anybody about anything. All these nitpicking lawyers are driving us crazy. Anyway, the thing is, I've called your buddy, Billy, and I talked to Junior, too. Neither of them know exactly when you left Uncle Buck's. I'd like to try and pin that down."

"There's nothing to pin down, Dan. I left the bar around ten, got into my truck, uh, took a little nap, woke up around eleven, drove south, hit a tree, and wound up in the hospital."

"I have no problem with that, Jack. Like I said, you're not a suspect. It's just that the sheriff would like an official interview with you for the record. It's looking more and more like that red pickup you saw is the one we're after and, so far, you're the only person who saw it good enough to identify it."

"I didn't see it all that good, Dan. It was moving fast. I remember it looked a lot like mine, that's all."

"Except it had a broken headlight."

"That's right. On the right-hand side."

" . . . and both your headlights were fine until you hit that tree, right?"

"Uh, right."

215

"Anyway, you'd be doing me a favor if you'd come up to Bailey Springs and sit down with me. All I need is a short statement for the record about that one-eyed, red pickup you saw that night. Shouldn't take more than thirty minutes or so."

"I'll think about it."

"I'd appreciate that, Jack. In the meantime, if you see anyone driving a one-eyed red Ford pickup, let me know."

"I'll do that, Dan."

When Jack heard the hum of the dial tone, he held the receiver out at arm's length and stared at it. "Damn you!" he screamed at the phone. "Damn you, Dan Warden!" he yelled once more and threw the phone onto the floor. As he stood there, looking down at the tiny inanimate object, his body began to tremble as pent-up rage rose within him with no suitable object available on which to unleash it. "He knows! Damn it, he knows! He just can't prove it." Jack looked up to see Cathy's car coming into the driveway. "About goddamn time, you little California bitch," he muttered through clenched teeth, redirecting his frustration toward a more controllable target.

* * * *

The drive across town had been an unusual experience for Cathy. She was a little drunk and knew it. Now, she tried to hurry into the house on legs that didn't always respond as she expected. She stumbled through the front door and hurried down the hallway to the bedroom.

"Where've you been?"

"Shopping. I told you that when I left."

"You're doing too damn much shopping here lately. I told you we don't have money to throw away these days."

"I didn't buy anything. I just looked at the sales."

"Don't you have anything better to do than walk up and down store aisles? Where's my supper?"

"Give me five minutes to change clothes, for god's sake. If you're in such a big hurry to eat, fix it yourself," she called back as she continued down the hallway.

"What the hell's got into you? Take that damn coat off, get in the kitchen, and fix the damn supper. Right now!"

Cathy paused at the bedroom doorway. She sighed and her shoulders slumped. It wasn't fair. She had just spent a couple of hours with a wonderful, loving man. Now that she was home, she had to deal with a man who treated her like dirt. It was time for things to start changing in this house. "Jack, do me a favor? Go to Hell."

"What did you say to me?"

"I said . . . go to Hell. I'm getting tired of you ordering me around."

"You little bitch. Get your smart ass back here."

"Go to Hell!" Cathy hurried into the bedroom and slammed the door behind her.

Jack glared down the hallway. "God damn you! Get your goddamn ass back here!" He paused, waiting for the recalcitrant woman to answer. When there was no answer, he walked back to the living room, picked up his beer, and took a long drink. As the rage within him continued, he glared toward the hallway once more. What was the world coming to? His foreman was a young kid, just out of college, with whom he shared a mutual dislike. He had truck payments he couldn't afford, and a deputy sheriff who was getting damn close to putting him in jail.

Now he had to put up with a woman who wouldn't stop long enough to give him a civil answer to a simple question. "By damn, I can sure as hell do something about that!" He took another swallow of beer, banged it down on the table and stormed down the hallway. He flung open the bedroom door, allowed it to crash loudly against the bedroom wall, then glared at his wife in her underwear.

Cathy yelled, "Jesus Christ! What the hell is the matter with you?"

"I think it's time you started giving me a civil answer when I ask you a question."

"I think it's time you went to Hell."

"You little bitch! I've put up with you long enough. You act like a kid, you're going to get treated like a kid," Jack yelled, his face livid. He unbuckled his broad leather belt, jerked it out of the loops, folded it, grasped the ends in his right hand, and pointed to the bed. "I'm going to whip your ass so hard you won't be able to sit for a week."

With her arms down by her side and her hands clenched tightly, Cathy walked close to Jack and glared up at him. "No, you're not. Not now. Not ever again."

Jack was momentarily startled by her defiance. "You think I won't?" Jack challenged as he glared down at her.

"If you do, I'll cut your dick off and flush it down the john," Cathy declared, then watched as her husband's face turned beet red as he clinched his jaws tightly together. His mouth was a tight line across his face as his eyes opened wider. She heard him draw a noisy breath through his nostrils. As she looked up at the raging man, out of the corner of her eye she sensed a blurred motion but wasn't quick enough to react to it. Jack's left fist met the side of Cathy's jaw full force. The blow was so hard it snapped the woman's head to one side as she stumbled backwards. She fell against the side of the bed, then slid down to the floor, momentarily unconscious.

Sitting on the floor, the confused woman felt the stinging pain on her face and loud ringing in her ear as tiny points of light swirled about in front of her eyes. He had never hit her this hard before. No one had hit her this hard before. It hurt like hell.

As tears filled her eyes, Cathy clenched her teeth, forcing herself not to cry. She wouldn't give him the satisfaction. Then she saw the small gold heart Pete had given her resting against her breast and a rage against this man rose within her. She didn't have to put up with this! No man had a right to do this to her! Slowly lifting her head, she looked up at him. "You bastard! I swear to God, if you ever hit me again, I'll make you regret it to the day you die." Her eyes grew wide as she watched her husband raise the belt high. She lowered her head and wrapped her arms about her face, hoping to protect it from the rain of painful blows she knew was coming.

Jack looked down at the woman cringing in fear at his feet. "You little piece of California dog shit! You're not worth the effort," he said, then turned to leave.

"Goddamn you! I hate you! I hate you!" Cathy screamed as Jack left the room.

Jack put his belt back into his pants, then grabbed his jacket and keys and slammed the door behind him. He climbed into his truck and sat for a moment, grasping the steering wheel hard, trying to control himself. "I don't believe it! I don't believe I was getting ready to beat the living daylights out of my own wife. I was that close to putting her in the hospital."

Jack shook his head. He didn't want to put her in the hospital. He didn't want to put anybody in the hospital. He had been there himself. It was painful. What he wanted was a woman he could talk to; someone he could tell that he was about to go out of his mind. It would be so wonderful to have a woman like Elaine for a wife. He could tell her his troubles and, somehow, things would work themselves out. But Elaine wasn't his wife, Cathy was. He couldn't tell Elaine his problems and Cathy wasn't in any mood to listen. "Lord have mercy on my soul! How did I get into this mess?" Jack started the engine. Turning on the wipers, he headed toward Tennessee. A few more beers might keep him from asking questions that he was afraid to answer.

Cathy stared at the empty bedroom doorway, gently massaging her painful jaw. She now knew Jack was capable of doing real harm to her. Somehow, she had to escape while she still could. If Pete could make a permanent move to California, so could she. She could leave this redneck state and her abusive husband and never look back.

With a grim look on her face, she nodded. Pete had shown her the way. She could say she was going to visit her mom and dad. That would be fine with Jack; he hated his in-laws. Once she was out in California, she would mail him the divorce papers. Cathy wiped her eyes, blew her nose, then crawled over and picked up the phone and entered a long-distance number. When her first call was complete, she called Pete and told him she needed to see him again right away.

* * * *

The noise of a Saturday night crowd welcomed Jack as he entered Uncle Buck's again. He walked through the couples on the dance floor, speaking to those he knew, and found his favorite barstool unoccupied. Junior's face was a mess. There was a two-inch line of black surgical stitches on his left cheek and still more holding together what was left of his left ear lobe. By the time Jack was seated, Junior had a cold bottle of beer in front of him. Jack tossed a twenty on the bar. When Junior returned the change, Jack left the money on the bar. It would be gone before he left tonight. Jack took a long drink and stared at his reflection in the mirror behind the bar.

What was the answer? If he really hadn't wanted to do it, why had he even thought it? One thing was for sure. If there had been a gun in his hand, he would have shot her. She had really gotten to him. She was a woman, almost half his size. Yet, she had caused him to totally lose control. He had slapped her around a few times before, but only when she needed it. Tonight, he knew he had come very close to putting his own wife in the hospital. That he might be capable of doing that worried him.

On top of everything else, apparently he had one more thing to worry about. When he was out at his dad's farm on Christmas Day, they had looked everywhere for his flashlight without success. His dad assured him he had taken everything from inside the truck and from the lockbox in the bed as well. The only thing he left was the trash on the floor. Jack remembered that when he had gone up to take a look at the wreck, he had checked it for anything his dad might have left and found nothing worth taking. "Where in hell is that thing?" Jack wondered out loud as he took another long drink.

After a couple of minutes, Junior removed the empty bottle, returned with a full one, and helped himself to some of the money on the bar without saying a word to the man across from him. Jack appreciated that. It was one reason why he enjoyed coming here. If you wanted to talk and it wasn't too busy, Junior had some great stories to tell and was willing to listen to yours. But when a man wanted to do some serious drinking, Junior kept the beer coming, but otherwise left you alone. Jack stared at the tiny bubbles rising through the golden liquid as he slowly turned the bottle round and round in his fingers. If only he had stopped long enough to make some plans somewhere along the way, things might have turned out differently.

Why didn't he reenlist in the Navy? The work was interesting, and he was good enough at it to make second-class petty officer in less than four years. By now he could have been a first-class petty officer, on his way to chief. Once you got to be a chief petty officer in the Navy, your working days were over, sitting around drinking coffee and giving orders until you put in your twenty is all you did.

Shortly after arriving in San Diego, he had learned which bars in the sailor's part of town were popular with WestPac widows, the lonely wives of sailors deployed to the western Pacific for months at a time. After buying one of the women a couple of drinks, it wasn't unusual for her to take him home for the night. If only he had stayed with those women instead of dating a naive teenage girl he had met at the zoo, everything would be fine. He could have had a wonderful life with Elaine as his wife and mother of his children. Jake would be alive, and he and Dan would be beer-drinking buddies. It could have happened. Instead, he was almost twenty-eight, coming up on thirty fast, and had done nothing worthwhile in his entire life. Nothing he had tried had worked out for him.

* * * *

Back in his apartment for the second time that day, Cathy allowed Pete to examine her bruised and swollen jaw. "What happened?"

"He hit me with his fist, Pete. He hit me harder than he's ever hit me before."

"No one should be allowed to hit a woman, especially you."

"Usually, he kicks my butt when he comes home drunk and mad about something or someone else and decides to take it out on me. But this time it was worse for some reason. I thought he was really going to hurt me."

"Jesus," Pete whispered.

"The only times he really hurts me is when he comes home drunk. But, tonight, he was already in a foul mood about something when I got home late. He pulled his belt out of his pants and said he was going to beat me with it. I told him I would cut his dick off if he did, so he hit me with his fist instead."

"God damn him! God damn him to Hell! No one should hit you like that. I'll kill him. I swear to God, I'll kill him."

Cathy was amazed at the transformation that had come over the mild-mannered man she had known for the past four weeks. There was fire in his eyes. "No, Pete, no," she said, suddenly afraid of what she might have instigated. "It's okay, really it is. Let it go. Please?"

"No one's ever going to do that to you again, not as long as I'm around."

"Thanks, but all I want right now is for someone to hold me for a few minutes. I need to go back pretty soon, but I had to see you for a little bit."

Pete looked at Cathy and nodded. "Let me make an ice pack to put on that. It'll sting a little, but it'll make the swelling go down."

Cathy nodded and tried to smile. It was going to be all right. She had someone who would take care of her, at least for a few minutes. She sighed. "Pete?"

"Yes, Cathy?"

"I want to follow you to California."

"I thought that was the plan."

"No, I mean, I want to drive to California, in my little car, right behind you."

Pete's eyes lit up. "Really? You want to go to California with me?"

Cathy smiled and nodded her head.

"Oh, Cathy, that would be so great!"

"My little car has lots of miles on it. I'm not sure it will make it all the way, but if it does, I'll have something to drive when I get out there."

"I'll take you anywhere you want to go after we get there."

"I called my parents tonight before I called you. I asked them if I could come home for a little visit. They said I was welcome anytime, for as long as I wanted to stay, as long as I didn't bring Jack with me. They told me my old room is still waiting for me anytime I want to move back." Cathy paused, took a deep breath, exhaled, and said, "So, I've decided to make it a permanent move. But, once I get out there, I don't want to have to depend on you or my parents or anyone else for very long. Besides, I'm going to be taking an awful lot of stuff."

"Uh, when would you like to leave?"

"As soon as we can. My marriage is over. All I want right now is to get back to California."

"I was planning to leave Monday after the manager checks the apartment and returns my deposit. It's about two thousand miles to San Diego. If you really want to drive your car, we'd better plan on at least four days to get there. That will get us to California by the end of the year."

"That would be nice, wouldn't it?"

"Maybe we could celebrate New Year's Eve together."

Cathy grinned and nodded her head. "That would be a perfect way to start a new year. I just hope you don't mind letting me follow you. I might not be able to drive as fast as you can."

"That's all right. We'll take our time."

"Great! I don't have much money. It'll save on motel bills if we could share a room," Cathy said. When she realized what her suggestion implied, she quickly added, "That is, if you'd like to do that. I'll be officially separated by then. But we could get a room with two beds if you want to. It's up to you."

Pete's cheeks turned a rosy red as he grinned. "Once we're on the road, one bed would be fine with me."

Biting her lower lip, Cathy smiled at him as a warm, peaceful feeling came over her. "As far as I'm concerned, we're already on the road," she said as she removed her wedding ring. She placed it on the counter, then grabbed the bottom of her sweater and pulled it over her head and off, displaying her bra. "My underwear is a matching set. Let me show you," she said as she kicked her shoes off and quickly pushed her pants down and stepped out of them. See?"

Pete stared at the woman, then slowly nodded his head.

"Now, uh, let's check out your bed," she said, then grabbed his hand and led him into the bedroom.

* * * *

A few minutes later, both were lying on the bed, each gently stroking the bare skin of the other's body and smiling at one another in the aftermath of their lovemaking. Cathy glanced at her watch. "I'd better get back."

"Stay here, Cathy. Please? I don't want you to get hurt again tonight."

"Oh, I'll be all right. Whenever he hits me, he always regrets it and acts nice to me afterwards, until he gets crazy drunk again. He's up at Uncle Buck's Tavern right now. As long as I'm back before he gets back, everything will be fine. Really it will. Tomorrow morning, he will act like nothing happened."

"Why do you put up with a man who does things like that?"

Cathy shrugged her shoulders. "I didn't think I had much choice, not knowing anyone here in Alabama but his family and his friends. Besides, after listening to the other women at work talking about what their husbands do to them, I considered myself lucky. I guess I came to believe that getting knocked around by my husband came with the territory. Then I met you."

"I would never hit you, Cathy."

"I know," Cathy said, and smiled. "Anyway, I think I'll be all right tonight. Besides, I've got to go back and start thinking about what I want to take. I know I don't have enough room in my little car to take everything. Good lord! I can't believe I'm really leaving this place."

"Do me one favor, please? Call me tomorrow on my cell phone when you have the chance. I need to know you're all right."

Cathy nodded her head. It felt good to have someone who cared about her. "I will. I promise," she said as she moved her hand down to his crotch. She smiled at him, then positioned herself over his thighs. "I don't have to leave just yet."

* * * *

The Saturday night crowd was still going strong as Jack tried to focus on the fuzzy image staring back at him from the mirror behind the bar. He decided that this wasn't going to solve anything. A man couldn't stay drunk for the rest of his life. He grabbed the money off the bar in front of him, then pushed himself off the bar stool and wandered across the dance floor to the front door. Outside, he stopped on the small porch for a moment, talking in big gulps of the cold, damp air as he looked about the parking lot for his red truck; then he remembered it wasn't red anymore and why. Holding on to the handrail, he stumbled down the short flight of steps, then headed in the general direction where he thought he had left his green pickup.

After he crossed the state line back into Alabama it began to rain. A few miles later, the small white frame building of the old Greenbrier Methodist Church came into view. As he drove past, he abruptly stepped on the brakes, much too hard. The pickup slid on the wet pavement and eventually came to a stop, still on the highway but blocking both lanes. He quickly backed up and pulled into the church parking lot, no more than a gravel area to one side of the small building. Jack turned off the engine but allowed the lights to continue to shine on the church, the only building nearby. He stared thoughtfully at the church, listening to the rain pelt down on the top of the cab.

Except for weddings and funerals, it had been a long time since he had been to church, here or anywhere else. He had been a member here once, maybe he still was. There had been a revival meeting one hot summer night when he was eleven, maybe twelve. As the congregation sang and the minister summoned unrepentant sinners to come forward, Jack felt the power lift him from his seat and carry him down the aisle. After he was baptized, he attended church a few times with his mother, but he quickly decided that sitting on a hard bench while listening to a boring sermon wasn't worth the effort to get up before noon on Sunday. The last time he could remember coming to Sunday services in this church was sometime before he joined the Navy. It had been a long, long time ago.

Jack slowly shook his head as he stared at the old church in the glare of his headlights. He had to get some help from somebody somewhere, that was for sure. He was going to go out of his mind if he didn't. As he continued to stare at the old building, he shook his head and snorted. "Hell, I don't even know the damn preacher's name."

23

Day 33
Sunday, December 27

CATHY LOOKED ACROSS the breakfast table the following morning and said quietly, "I've been thinking about visiting my parents."

Jack raised his head and looked at the bruise on his wife's jaw. "Oh, yeah? When do you think this is going to happen?"

"I'd like to leave in the next few days. Tomorrow, maybe."

"Tomorrow?" Jack asked, a surprised look on his face. Then he frowned. "Our little squabble last night didn't have anything to do with this, did it?"

"Maybe, a little bit. But I've been thinking about it for two or three weeks now."

Jack shrugged his shoulders. While looking down at his plate, he said, "I got a little carried away last night. I've got a lot of things on my mind these days."

Cathy silently nodded while looking down at her plate. The comment was as close to an apology that she had ever gotten from this man. "I know. You haven't been the same since you wrecked your truck. You're still having nightmares that wake me up. Something's bothering you, that's for sure."

Jack cocked his head and stared at Cathy for a moment, then shook his head. "We can't afford for you to fly out to California, and that little piece of shit you drive won't make it that far."

"I called my parents last night; they'll pay for my plane ticket if I come by myself."

"Is that a fact?"

"That's a fact."

"How long are you planning on staying?"

Cathy stared into her husband's eyes. "I don't know. A couple of weeks maybe."

Jack frowned. "What are you trying to tell me?"

"I'm trying to tell you that I'm going to visit Mom and Dad. I haven't seen them since the day I left there."

There was a long pause as each stared into the other's eyes.

"I don't give a damn what you do. Leave today if you want to. Stay as long as you want to."

"I will. Besides, from what I've heard, you're not going to be lonely while I'm gone."

"What the hell is that supposed to mean?"

"I've heard rumors about you and Elaine Warden."

"There's no more truth to those rumors than the one I've heard about you."

Cathy smiled at him, then said sweetly, "I believe that."

Jack stared at his wife in silence, frowning. Then he rose and looked down at the stranger across the table from him. "I'm going out to Greenbrier. I don't need a damn airplane ticket to go see my mama and daddy. You coming?"

"No, thanks. I need to wash some clothes and do some housecleaning," she said. "Besides, I want to visit Tommy's grave. Today's his birthday, in case you've forgotten."

"Jesus, I did forget," Jack said, a pained look on his face.

"I thought we agreed we would visit his grave together on his birthday."

"I know."

"Do you want to go with me or not?"

"No, you go ahead. I might stop by next week sometime."

As tears welled up in Cathy's eyes, she said, "We can't do anything together, can we?"

"Not today, that's for sure."

"Sometimes I think he's better off where he is than he would have been with us," Cathy said quietly.

With his lips pulled tight across his face, Jack stared at his wife. "I don't doubt that for one damn minute," he said, then grabbed his coat and stormed out the door. He backed out of the driveway and roared away, more angry about forgetting his son's birthday than he was at Cathy, but he wasn't going to let her know that.

Maybe he would stop by tomorrow on his way home from work. He had never mentioned it to her, but he had made several trips to visit his son's grave by himself over the years. He didn't like to go to the cemetery with Cathy because he usually got a little misty-eyed when he was there. It would have been embarrassing for her to see him with tears in his eyes. His dad had always told him, "Real men don't cry. They gut it out and get on with their business."

As far as Jack knew, the only time Cathy ever went to the cemetery was when they went together on their son's birthday. It was pretty obvious she had no real feelings for the small boy down in that deep, dark hole in the ground. She wouldn't understand that there were times when a man needed to be alone with his boy, even if he was dead. Anytime Jack felt low because of something that hadn't gone his way, he would stop at the grave for a few minutes and stand there. While looking down at the ground, he would think about all the wonderful things he could be doing with his boy if he were still alive.

He still remembered the day his son was born, like it was yesterday. After waiting outside while she was in labor, he had walked into her hospital room and saw Cathy, her face still shiny with sweat from her long and difficult delivery. With a Kodak Fun Saver disposable camera he had bought in the gift shop, he took a picture of her as she managed a weak smile for him with their son in her arms. In that moment, he thought Cathy was the most beautiful woman in the world. Then she had offered his son to him to hold. As he took the small bundle in his trembling hands, fearing he would drop it, he knew he could never send Cathy and his son away. Then someone took a picture of the three of them. The same day they brought the baby home, Jack, with the exuberance of a new father, went to Bart's Bargain Barn and bought a football, and a baseball glove, bat, and ball.

Then, one night, a couple of weeks later, the baby died. The doctor said it was sudden infant death syndrome, SIDS, but both parents later accused the other of being responsible for their son's death.

After his son's funeral, Jack opened a pint of whiskey. When he had drunk the entire contents, he went into the nursery, picked up the baseball bat, and destroyed everything in the room. When he had finished, he took the pieces of the crib out into the backyard and used them to start a small bonfire. Then, he returned to the house and grabbed anything that might remind him of his dead son and hauled it out to the fire as well. At one point, when Cathy tried to reason with him, begging him to save the things for their next child, he turned to her and snarled, "If you ever get pregnant again, so help me God, I'll rip it out with my bare hand!"

With Cathy crying and pleading with him to stop, he added the child's toys and clothing to the flames, then anything else he could find, including all the photos of him. When he found the package of negatives, he added that to the flames as well. Jack later regretted burning the boy's pictures. The one he remembered most was the one someone had taken of the three of them. He wished he had saved that one. He'd give a lot of money to see it one more time.

Jack sighed as he pulled into his dad's driveway. What a mess he had made out of everything in his life. He had regretted that afternoon's drunken rage ever since. There had been a moment, while he was still smashing the crib, when Cathy had come into the room, screaming for him to stop. He had turned and, for an instant, redirected his rage. When he had threatened her with the bat, she had turned and run screaming from the room. He had come awfully close to beating his wife senseless with a baseball bat that day. He hadn't told Cathy, but it scared him, knowing he was capable of doing something like that when he was drunk. He had never apologized for that day, and he hadn't apologized for knocking her on her ass last night either. He knew he probably should say something, to let her know he wished he hadn't done it, but he remembered what his dad had always told him, "Never apologize to anybody for anything. It's a sign of weakness in a man."

Jack sighed. Maybe he should have given her a good whipping instead of decking her with his fist. His dad had whipped him with his belt while he was growing up. The belt had raised a few welts on his butt and legs at the time, but he had gotten over it.

* * * *

After passing through the ornamental iron gate of the cemetery later that morning, Cathy drove along a familiar one-lane access road toward a small knoll in the back and parked in her usual spot, near a large evergreen tree. She got out, zipped up her jacket against the bitter cold, then opened the hatch and retrieved her purse, a small plastic stool, and a plastic bag containing some items she would need.

The cemetery was relatively new with many plots still vacant. To facilitate mowing, no monuments were allowed to be erected above ground, only small ground-level granite markers were allowed. The cemetery was so large, first-time visitors needed a map to find the burial plot of a friend or loved one. Cathy knew the way to her son's grave without a map.

For several weeks after he had died, she had visited the grave often. After a few months, her visits became less frequent, but took on a different meaning. In the beginning, her visits were lonely vigils to honor the dead child, but as the months passed, she became comfortable speaking to her son's grave, relating her problems and anxieties to him when no one else would listen.

Jack had never shown any interest in trying to understand her or her feelings toward him. She hadn't developed any close friendships with other women, and her mother was a long distance call away on the other side of the continent. When her world seemed to be too much of a burden to her, when no one else seemed to understand her or care about her, Cathy would come here and find solace by relating her problems to her son. He always listened, always understood, and never argued. Her little talks with her son usually improved her outlook on life.

"Happy Birthday, Tommy," Cathy said softly as she approached his grave. Then she stood and looked down at the engraved words she had long since memorized. "You're five years old today. You must be a big boy up in Heaven now." Cathy paused, sniffed, then said, "I wish I could see you up there, just for a minute. It would be so wonderful."

Cathy set the plastic stool near the marker, sat on it, and opened the plastic bag. She brushed away the grass clippings, then squirted a liberal amount of household cleaner on the stone. After scrubbing the dirt and bird droppings with a small brush, she wiped the stone dry with paper towels. Satisfied that the marker was sparking clean once more, she stowed everything back in the plastic bag.

She stuffed her cold hands into the pockets of her jacket, hunched her shoulders, and gazed down at the brown dormant grass covering the grave of her son. She sniffed as tears welled up in her eyes. "Tommy? I'm going to California tomorrow. I don't know when I'll be back. This may be the last time I can come and see you for a long, long time. Don't think I don't love you just because I can't come to visit you, and don't worry about me. I'll be fine.

"I've met a man, Tommy. He's really sweet. I think he loves me. He's given me the strength to leave Jack and start my life over. You'll be so proud of me. I'm going to college and then get a good job. After that, maybe I can find a very special someone to love as much as they love me. Wouldn't that be great? You'd like to have some brothers and sisters, wouldn't you? I'll make sure they learn to love you as much as I do." As her chin began to tremble and tears began to run down her face, she reached into her purse, found her packet of tissue, wiped her eyes, blew her nose, then continued. "I'll always love you from the bottom of my heart, Tommy. I wish I could take you with me, but I can't. Oh, I'm going to miss you so much."

With fingers trembling from the cold, she dug out her wallet from her purse, opened it, pulled out an old snapshot, and silently gazed at it. The picture was the one taken of the three of them in the delivery room. She sniffed back her tears as she carefully reinserted the snapshot inside wallet. It was the only picture anyone had of her son. She had rescued it from the edge of the fire that awful day while Jack was in the house looking for more to destroy. Fearing Jack might still burn it if he knew it existed, she had kept it a secret from him ever since.

Cathy stood, gathered her things, then gazed down at the small granite block once more. "I'll try to come and say good-bye to you before I leave tomorrow. But, if I can't, I want you to know that you're the most precious thing in my life, and always will be. Bye, Tommy. I love you."

* * * *

"Hello?"

"Hi, Elaine, Jack. I called you yesterday, but you weren't there."

"Oh, Jack, hi. Yeah, I was over at Mom's house again. She's really feeling low. Burying Jake right before the Christmas holidays has really got her down. Me, too, I guess. The whole family had a hard time getting through Christmas Day."

"I'm here all by myself and the football game is too lopsided to be interesting. I thought I'd come over and see you for a while if you're going to be home."

"I'm going to be home, but you'd better not come over. I wouldn't mind some company, but I think I'm getting a cold. My head's all stuffy and I'm running a fever."

"Yeah, your voice does sound a little different."

"If I feel any worse tomorrow, I may not go to work."

"I hope it's not the flu. Some of the men at work have it."

"It's probably a cold. I usually have one about this time of year. Some of the kids were hacking and coughing at my parents' place when I was out there Christmas Day, I think I might have caught it from them."

"Well, I'll talk to you in a day or so to see how you're doing. Cathy's going to California to visit her parents, so I'll be rattling around the house by myself while she's gone."

"How long is she going to be gone?"

"I don't know. A couple of weeks, maybe longer."

"I might have you over for dinner while she's gone, to keep you from starving."

"I'd really appreciate that. With both you and Mom feeding me, I might survive."

"You're going to need a lot of nourishment before I'm done with you. Bye."

Jack stared down at the phone, listening to the hum of the dial tone, and grinned.

* * * *

"Hi, Pete, this is You-Know-Who. I wanted to check in and let you know everything is fine and on schedule for tomorrow. I still can't believe I'm doing this, but I am. I'm really going to do it! Bye."

* * * *

With Jack watching a Sunday professional football game, Cathy rearranged her closet, sorting and dividing her clothes between what she absolutely needed to take with her, what she would like to take with her if she had room in her car, and what she wouldn't be seen dead wearing in California.

She took her shower early and was in bed with the lights out, pretending to be asleep, when Jack came to bed. With her back turned to him, she clenched her hands in tight balls, desperately hoping he wouldn't demand to have sex with her. Mentally, she was no longer a partner in this marriage. Submitting to him would be tantamount to rape. After a few minutes, she heard Jack's slow breathing. Soon afterwards, she was asleep as well.

24

STILL WEARING HER nightgown and bathrobe, Cathy sat alone at her kitchen table. With soft music from a CD player filling the quietness of the room, she sipped her coffee and stared out at the cold December morning. Jack had left the house before she had gotten up, leaving early enough to join other men at a fast-food restaurant where they ate breakfast, drank coffee, and formed their carpools for the ride to work. Cathy tried to remember the last words she had spoken to Jack last night. She recalled going into the living room and asking him about something before she took her shower and went to bed, but couldn't remember now what it had been about. It hadn't occurred to her then that the brief conversation might be the last words she would ever speak to her husband.

Was that how it would end? After five years of arguing and screaming hateful words, would the last words spoken between them be some innocuous words of civil conversation neither could remember? Cathy sadly shook her head, then glanced at the kitchen clock for the tenth time in the last five minutes. It was time to dress and go to work if she was going to work. She had planned to leave today and was mentally committed to it. Still, she hadn't done anything yet that couldn't be undone. She could dress, go to work, then come home and prepare supper for her husband tonight, and he would never know how close she had been to leaving him.

Cathy glanced down at her wedding band as she absentmindedly turned it about her ring finger with the thumb and forefinger of her right hand. She didn't have an

235

engagement ring. This little gold band was all Jack could afford when they got married. She slipped the gold band off her finger, placed it on the table and gazed down at it, recalling all the pain and heartaches it represented. A sudden feeling of sorrow swept over her. There was a tiny grave with a tiny casket in it on a hillside cemetery in Helleston. She would never see it again after today. It made tears come to her eyes. Her son had never had a chance at life. Maybe it was just as well.

She glanced up at the clock once more. She had to make up her mind, one way or the other, in a few minutes. Then she looked back down at the wedding band and realized she had already decided. Her wedding band was off and would stay off. It was time to get busy.

The ringing of the phone startled her. "Hello?"

"Cathy?"

"Oh, Pete!" In an instant of panic, she had imagined it might be Jack, calling to tell her he was taking the day off for some reason and was on his way back home.

"I just wanted to call, you know, to see if you're still going with me today."

Cathy took a deep breath. "Yes! I'm coming with you, just as soon as I get packed."

"Great. I called the Barn. The store manager isn't in yet, so my letter of recommendation isn't signed. As soon as he gets in, I'll go down, get the letter, and we'll be on our way. With any luck, we'll be in Texas before we stop tonight."

"Oh, that's so great! I'm going to throw my stuff in my car, then I'll go to the bank as soon as it opens at nine and get some money. I don't know how much is in the account, but when I find out, I'm going to write a check for all of it. Maybe it will be enough to get me to California."

"I should have the letter by then and we'll be on our way."

"California, here we come!"

"Absolutely! See you in a little while. Oh, I almost forgot. I'm calling you on my cell phone. My apartment phone is already disconnected, so you'll have to call me on my cell phone after this."

"Will do. See you soon."

* * * *

With a cup of hot McDonald's coffee in his hand, a stomach full of their hotcakes and sausage, and a search warrant in his back pocket, Dan walked outside the sheriff's station to Jack's wrecked pickup truck. He stopped a few yards from it and gazed at it, wondering what else he could do to bring this investigation to a close. For four days now, he had been convinced that Jack Constone had been driving this pickup when he killed Jake Warden, but it was all circumstantial. He couldn't prove in a court of law that this was the vehicle, nor that Jack was driving it when it had hit Jake. He hadn't been able to find anything that tied this vehicle to the crime.

Dan was convinced that the mirror they found in the weeds near the body came off this truck, but there was no way to prove it. The state crime lab had tried to match the scratches and abrasions in the bracket hole to the broken mirror post, but it was inconclusive. The oak tree had folded the bracket for the mirror mounting post.

He believed Jack had tracked the yellow clay from the accident site into this truck that night. But it would be tough to convince a jury it was a viable piece of evidence after it had been lying on the floor of an unlocked vehicle in an open parking area for almost four weeks. When he took the piece of clay to the site, he found one area on the roadside where the clay seemed to match, but areas on either side clearly did not.

The yellow and clear plastic shards had been identified as belonging to the headlight, side light, and turn signal light of a series of Ford vehicles over several years, one of which was the 1993 F-150. The state crime lab had used its microscopic wizardry to find probable matches between shards found at the crime scene with other shards he had picked up at the oak tree. But Jack had done too good of a job covering up his crime. There was nothing left on this truck with which they could make a specific match with the evidence they had found at the crime scene. A good lawyer would waste no time pointing out that the source of the shards at either location was suspect because both locations had been open to the public after the hit-and-run accident.

Dan was convinced Jack was driving the truck Homer Jones had seen speeding north that night, but Homer hadn't been able to positively identify the truck as this one. When Dan had checked the timeline for Homer and Jack that night, he had come close. Very close. Too close for it not to represent what could have happened. Yet, Jack could testify that he had seen another red truck that night. If he did, it would be tough to disprove.

The only possible eyewitness was dead. Dan was convinced Bulldog had seen Jack's truck at the accident scene that night, recognized it from Uncle Buck's, and had chosen to blackmail him rather than report what he had seen. Dan was now sure blackmail, not the purchase of a 9mm pistol, was the issue between Jack and Bulldog the night Junior had shot Bulldog. According to his telephone bill, Bulldog had made several long-distance calls to Jack's number after Jake had been killed, never before. Most of the calls lasted less than a minute, but the ones on the first, fifth, and twelfth of December were longer. In addition to thirty kilos of marijuana in the ceiling of Bulldog's shack, they had found an arsenal of weapons in a locked box under the bed, including two 9mm pistols. If Jack wanted to claim the calls were about a potential gun sale instead of blackmail, it would be tough to disprove without Bulldog around to testify against him. Even if he could, a parole violator who'd spent most of his adult life in prison and had an outstanding warrant in West Virginia might not be a reliable witness.

Dan walked over to Jack's truck, leaned over, and rested his arms on the edge of the bed. He took a deep breath and sighed. It was frustrating. He knew who did it, how, when, and where. He just couldn't prove it. It was all good stuff, but it was all circumstantial. If he could find one thing . . . just one thing . . . that would put Jack in this truck when it hit Jake, then all the other stuff could be used to strengthen the case. Without it, he was awfully afraid a good lawyer might be able to get a jury to return a not guilty verdict. If that happened, Dan would quit law enforcement for good. His family would never forgive him either.

There had to be something somewhere. There just had to be. But, where? The medical examiner had said that Jake had died instantly due to massive impact trauma. The accident site had been thoroughly searched, the only possible eyewitness was dead, and the prime suspect had an alibi. The only thing Dan had left was the truck. He walked over and opened the driver's side door.

Although Dan was now convinced that this was the hit-and-run truck, he hadn't bothered searching through all the trash on the dashboard, seat, and floor of the truck, believing hamburger wrappers, clay dirt, and the other trash couldn't possibly have anything to do with his case. But now, the only thing left to do was to clean out all the trash inside the cab, send it to the state crime lab and hope someone there would be able to find the needle in the haystack he needed to make his case.

Dan got a large evidence bag, put on a pair of latex gloves, and gathered every piece of trash and dirt that was large enough to pick up with his fingers. After labeling the bag, he got a vacuum cleaner, installed a fresh bag and began to vacuum the interior of the truck as well. After he had vacuumed the floor, he switched to a long thin attachment and inserted it into the narrow gaps on top, around and under the dashboard, then behind, around, and under the seat. When he jabbed it under the seat on the passenger's side he felt something move. He shut off the vacuum, put his head down close to the floor and looked underneath the seat. At first, it looked like a black tube, then he recognized it for what it was. A flashlight.

Dan called the Ford dealer and the county medical examiner. In a few minutes, two Ford technicians arrived. When the medical examiner arrived, the technicians spent a few minutes removing the rusty bolts from the seat tracks while Dan and the medical examiner took pictures. With the seat out of the way, Dan and the examiner looked closely at the black plastic flashlight and saw smears of yellow and deep maroon coloring on its smooth surface. The yellow seemed to match the color of the clay on that slope and the maroon looked like dried blood. Dan's eyes grew wide. If the maroon coloring was Jake's blood, and if prints could still be recovered from that flashlight and they belonged to Jack, he had his case.

It would be even tighter if he could find more of Jake's blood somewhere else inside the truck. The steering wheel? The seat? They would check the entire interior with a microscope. The medical examiner would know Jake's blood type and they would also know Jack's blood type from his Navy records. Dan knew they would find Jack's blood from his head wound all over the interior, but if Jake's blood was a different type and they found a smudge of it anywhere in that truck, and he was now willing to bet they would, Jack would go to jail for a very long time. Dan felt an overwhelming sense of frustration. He had assumed that Jack hadn't gone down that steep, muddy embankment. Apparently, he had and had gotten Jake's blood on his flashlight while he was down there. "Lord have mercy! How long is it going to take me to learn how to do this job?"

* * * *

After spending an hour trying to decide what to take and then filling the large grocery bags with shoes, underwear, and personal items from the bathroom, she opened the hatch of her car and began hauling armloads of clothes out to it. Soon, the rear of the little car was filled with a huge pile of clothes surrounded by grocery bags filled with items from the bathroom, closet, and drawers of the dresser. There were more bags on the front seat and floorboard on the passenger's side. Trembling with nervous energy, Cathy returned to the house once more and walked through each room, looking into the closets and drawers once more, wondering if she had forgotten something important, wondering where she would put it if she had.

Satisfied that there was nothing more she wanted enough to try to fit it in her car, she took a deep breath, found a notepad and wrote a note, telling Jack to send the divorce papers to her in care of her parents. She put her wedding ring on top of the note. As she walked into the living room, she paused to turn off the portable CD player. Jack had bought it and considered it his. Most of the CDs were his as well. Impulsively, she decided to take it with her. It would be a nice break from listening to radio DJ chatter on the trip. She got a bag and started going through the discs, trying to choose which ones to take and which ones to leave. "To hell with it," she muttered, and tossed all the CDs into the bag, picked up the player, and left.

Shortly after nine, Cathy stopped at the bank and, after showing them her checkbook and her driver's license, learned that there were over nine hundred dollars in the joint checking account. She wrote a check for the full amount. Her hand trembled when she wrote the check, knowing she would be in deep trouble if she wasn't halfway to California before Jack found out.

* * * *

Before moving it, the medical examiner took several pictures of the flashlight using the close-up lens on his camera, then he carefully placed the flashlight in an evidence bag. Before the Ford servicemen left, Dan had them remove the steering wheel and the seat cover as well. Since they already had Jack's prints and blood type from his Navy file, the medical examiner thought they might get a comparison done today. DNA tests would take several weeks to confirm that the blood on the flashlight belonged to Jake. If they did, and Jack's fingerprints were on the blood, he would need a very good lawyer. If Jake's blood was on the steering wheel or seat as well, Jack would spend a long time in jail.

* * * *

Cathy parked at the Cross Winds, hurried up to Pete's door and knocked. When Pete opened the door, there was a gloomy look on his face. "What's the matter?" she asked.

"I don't have it yet."

"The letter?"

Pete nodded his head. "The last time I called, the secretary said the manager was in Huntsville and wouldn't be back until sometime this afternoon."

"This afternoon? When?"

"I don't know."

"Oh, no. Are you really sure you have to have it? Can't we leave now and let them mail it to you?"

Pete shook his head. "They're playing games with me. They're still mad that I'm leaving. If I leave without the letter, I won't ever get it. I know these guys. They would do something like that, just to get even with me for not being their slave anymore."

"Oh, I can't believe this is happening."

"We'll have to wait a little longer. I'm sorry. There's nothing I can do about it."

"Well, is there anything we can do in the meantime? Are you all packed?"

"Almost. The furniture belongs in the apartment. I sold my TV to a guy that lives downstairs. I'm going to leave the kitchen stuff. Everything I haven't already thrown out is in these boxes."

"Well, let's take them down. It'll give us something to do and then we'll be ready to go when you get that damn letter."

On the last trip down, Pete walked over and looked at Cathy's car. "This tire is low. It doesn't have much tread left on it either."

"Oh?" Cathy said, inspecting her tire for the first time.

"Yeah, and the others don't look any better," Pete said as he walked around the car.

"What do you think we should do?"

"If we're going to be stuck here for a while, we'd better replace your tires."

"Do tires cost a lot?"

"Not if we get some off brands. Anyway, I really think you'd be better off getting some good tires before we start, rather than waiting until we get out in the middle of nowhere and have one go flat."

At the tire store, the service man showed Pete that the front brakes were badly worn. The service man estimated it would be two o'clock before he could have the brakes refurbished and repaired. Pete told him to go ahead with the brake job and to change the oil as well. He gave the service manager his cell phone number and left.

On their way back to the apartment, they stopped and bought orders of barbecue, fries, and soft drinks. Pete found his portable radio in a box in his car's trunk and brought it up as well. Time passed slowly, mostly in silence. Both were subdued and disappointed with the morning's events. They both were anxious to be gone. After they had finished eating, they sat on the couch and engaged in small talk, both of them wanting very badly to be on their way.

"I noticed you're not wearing your wedding band."

Cathy, glanced down at the band of white skin on her ring finger, then looked up at him and smiled. "It feels nice, like I took a big load off my shoulders when I took the little band of gold off my finger." She fingered the tiny gold chain around her neck. "I still have your heart next to mine, though."

"That means it's really over. Your marriage, I mean," Pete stammered.

"Uh-huh, it's really over," she said. She smiled as an erotic idea came to her. She turned and looked into the bedroom. When she saw the bare mattress on the bed, her smile disappeared.

They talked about their life's dreams. Pete told Cathy how he was looking forward to getting back into aerospace engineering. His lifelong dream had been to be on the design team for the spaceship that would carry men to Mars. Cathy told Pete about her dream of being a television reporter.

* * * *

Carrying the paper sack containing his lunch from Burger King, Dan hurried into the sheriff's station, hoping he could eat it before meeting with Sheriff Johns to update him on his investigation.

As if he didn't have enough to do today, he had bought a new truck and had planned to go down to Helleston and swap his old Chevy pickup truck for his new 1999 Chevy Silverado 1500 sometime today. He was looking forward to getting a new vehicle, but they would need a couple of hours to switch his equipment over to his new truck.

As he passed by the dispatcher, she called out to him, waving a small piece of paper.

"Lena Black called! Wants to talk to you," she said and handed him a note.

Dan carried the note and his lunch to his desk. He pulled his cheese Whopper, Coke, and fries out of the bag, grabbed a few fries and stuffed them in his mouth as he jammed the straw into the top of the Coke. He took a sip of the Coke, then unwrapped the Whopper, opened it, tore two tomato ketchup packets open, and squeezed the contents onto the meat. He reassembled the Whopper and took a big bite out of it. Five minutes later, having finished his lunch, he glanced at the note, then at the clock, then entered the phone number.

"Hello."

"This is Sergeant Warden, Mrs. Black. I'm returning your call."

"Oh, yes! I just wanted you to know I've got a job!"

"Good for you."

"I told him I'd like to work outside if I could. He said he'd keep that in mind but about all that's out in the Garden Shop these days is some frozen plants and Christmas trees that didn't get sold. So, I'm going to be working inside for a while, restocking the shelves, which is fine with me when it's as cold as it has been here lately. When spring comes, I hope I'll get outside."

"I think you'd enjoy that."

"I will. In the meantime, I'd really like to do something to show you how much I appreciate what you did for me."

"I didn't do much."

"Maybe you don't think so, but I know better. So, I was thinking about asking you to have supper with me and Red sometime."

"I'm married."

"Well . . . bring her, too."

"We're separated."

"Well . . . that makes two of us, don't it?"

"Thanks for the invitation, Mrs. Black."

"You're more than welcome. If you ever get a chance, drop by and see us sometime. I ain't much of a cook, but I know how to make a cup of coffee."

"I might take you up on that."

"Great!"

"Happy New Year, Mrs. Black."

"It will be, thanks to you. Happy New Year to you, too."

* * * *

It was almost one o'clock when the medical examiner called. There was a tentative match on two partial prints in the dried blood with the forefinger and middle finger on Jack Constone's right hand. There was also a good match on the smeared clay to Jack's left thumb. The blood on the flashlight was 'B' negative, the same as Jake's blood type. Less than two percent of the population had that blood type. Jack's military records listed his blood type as 'O' positive, the most common blood type. They would submit the dried blood on the flashlight for a DNA comparison but that might take several weeks.

After discussing the report with Dan, Sheriff Johns agreed with Dan that they now had probable cause to believe Jack Constone was responsible for the death of Jake Warden and should be charged with first-degree vehicular homicide and felony hit-and-run. Dan wanted to get a warrant issued for Jack's arrest that afternoon. Instead, the sheriff suggested that Dan try to get Jack to come up to Bailey Springs on his own. They would arrest him in Tennessee, avoiding the time and paperwork that would be required to extradite him if he was arrested in Alabama.

After the two men agreed on the plan, Dan told Sheriff Johns he needed to go down to the Helleston Chevy dealer and get his new truck. While he was down there, he wanted to stop and tell Jake's sister what they knew and what they planned to do. The sheriff agreed.

Dan had to tell Elaine. She had to hear it from him before she heard it from anyone else. Dan knew how close she and Jack had been in high school, and apparently still were. It was going to be hard on her to find out that Jack was going to be arrested for killing her brother. Dan shook his head. She had been so proud of him when he had been promoted to sergeant. Now, the job was going to tear them apart. It seemed that the damage and destruction to other human lives because of one stupid, unconscionable act by a drunken driver would never end.

On his way out of the station, Dan told the dispatcher he would probably be down in Helleston for the rest of the afternoon. He also told her that, while he was picking up a new truck, she wouldn't be able to contact him while they were transferring his radio and some other things from his old truck to his new one, but she could try calling him at the Helleston Chevrolet dealer or at Elaine Warden's number.

"You should get one of those little cell phones and carry it around with you."

"Maybe someday. Right now, I hear they're not much good except in big cities and on major highways. That eliminates Creek County, Tennessee, for now."

* * * *

Shortly after two o'clock, the electronic beeping of Pete's cell phone disrupted his conversation with Cathy. They quickly returned to the tire store where Cathy's car was waiting for her. After she paid the bill in cash, Pete gave Cathy his cell phone and told her he was going to the Barn and would stay there until he got his letter. She said she would return to his apartment and wait for him there. "It'll be a few minutes before I get there," she said. "I'm going to make a quick stop at the cemetery and say goodbye to Tommy."

Pete gazed at her in silence, then nodded, understanding. "Take your time. Stay as long as you like. Just keep the phone with you."

"I will."

"Say goodbye to him for me, too."

Cathy smiled and nodded.

* * * *

Dan looked up at the clock at the Chevy dealer. Three-thirty. He thought he would have been out of here by now. When he asked if he could use a phone to make a local call, the salesman readily agreed and pointed to an empty desk with a phone. "Help yourself. They've already moved your lockbox to your new truck's bed, they've got your behind-the-grill lights working, and they were about done with your two-way radio the last time I checked. It should be about ready. I'll go check again." Dan waited until the salesman walked away, then picked up the phone and entered a number.

"Hello?"

"Oh, hi, Elaine, this is Dan. I was going to leave you a message to call me. I didn't expect you to be home."

"I left at noon. My cold was making me feel so tired, I came home, made me some hot soup, and climbed into bed."

"I hope I didn't wake you."

"No, I was already up. I'm beginning to feel a little better. What's up with you?"

"I'm at the Helleston Chevy dealer, waiting to pick up my new truck."

"Oh, what did you get?"

"It's another Chevy."

"What color?"

"This one's black."

"Oh, I like that."

"Anyway, while I'm down this way, I'd like to come by and see you for a few minutes, if you feel up to it."

"You got some news about Jake?"

"Yes, I do."

"Does it have anything to do with Jack?"

"I'm afraid so."

"Oh, Dan, why can't you find somebody else to pick on? He got laid off today. He doesn't need anybody else giving him a bad time right now."

"Just let me talk to you for a few minutes, that's all I ask," Dan said, then waited, listening to the silence on the other end for several seconds.

"I guess so. You won't change my mind, though."

"That's all right, Elaine, I understand," Dan said then looked at the clock. "I should be done here in a few minutes. How about four? Would that be all right?"

"That'll be fine. Bye."

Dan hung up the phone, then reached into his pocket for his phone listing. He found the number he wanted as he saw the salesman looking at him from a distance with his thumb up. Dan nodded, held up two fingers, and entered a number. When he got a busy signal, he hung up, glanced at his watch, and decided to wait a couple of minutes and try again.

* * * *

"Hello?"

"Cathy? Pete. I'm calling to let you know I still don't have the letter. The manager still isn't here. The assistant manager said that if he's not here by four, he'll sign it himself."

"Four!"

"That's what he said."

"I can't believe this! Jack might be home by then. God knows what he'll do when he reads the note I left him. We've got to get out of here! He'll kill me if he finds out I took all the money out of the bank account. Can't the assistant manager sign it now?"

"I asked him to. He said he didn't want to unless he had to. They're squeezing every drop of blood out of me they can."

"I don't believe this. I just don't believe this is happening to me."

"Hang on, Cathy. We'll be on our way in a few minutes. I promise you."

"Oh, god, I don't believe this."

* * * *

"Hello?"

"Hi, Elaine. How's your cold?"

"Oh, Jack. My cold's doing just great. I don't feel good though. I went in for a half-day and then came home. How're you doing?"

"I've got some bad news and I've got some good news."

"I think I know the bad news."

"Oh, yeah?"

"I saw your name on today's layoff list."

"Oh, yeah, I guess it did come down from mahogany row."

"I'm sorry, Jack."

"That's all right. I'll survive. Billy got his walking papers, too. We've been discussing our future at his house over a beer or three."

"What's the good news?"

"When I got home, I found a note from Cathy. She's on her way back to California. She packed her car with everything she could and left me."

"I'm sorry to hear that, Jack."

"No, you're not, and neither am I. I should have kicked her ass out a long time ago. The only thing that bothers me is that she took my CD player and all my CDs with her. I don't mind her leaving, but it really irritates me that she took all my CDs."

"If you want to get them back, I think I know where she is, if she hasn't left town yet."

"Oh, yeah?"

"A guy I know at church lives over at the Cross Winds apartments. I happen to know he and Cathy are close. He told me at church yesterday that he was leaving for California today. Sounds like too much of a coincidence to me. I certainly have changed my opinion of those two here lately. If you want your CDs back, you might find her over there."

"Nah, to hell with her. I was getting ready to kick her out anyway. You're all I want, Elaine. As long as I've got you, I don't care what else life hands me. I can take it."

"Oh, Jack, you're so sweet."

"I'd like to come over for a few minutes."

"You can if you don't mind sharing my germs, but Dan just called and wants to stop by and talk to me about Jake. I don't think it would be a good idea for you to be here. You're not his favorite person these days."

"I know."

"He's trying awfully hard to find out who killed Jake. He keeps hinting that maybe you might have had something to do with it, but I can't believe that. He's just taking his frustrations out on you."

"I think you're right. I can live with it if you don't start thinking the same way."

"I don't think that's likely. It would be the end of the world for me. I simply refuse to believe you had anything to do with it."

"Thanks. With things going like they are for me, it's nice to know there's at least one person who still believes in me."

"He'll be here around four. Wait until about four-fifteen. He should be gone by then."

"Sure, see you then."

Jack put the phone down, raised his arms over his head and yelled, "All right!" Suddenly, the phone rang. Frowning, he picked up the receiver once more. "Hello."

"Jack? Dan. How're you doing?"

"I'm in kind of a rush right now, Dan. What do you want?"

"I'm sitting here at the Chevy dealer, waiting for them to finish doing whatever it is that they're doing to my new truck, so I thought I'd give you a call while I'm waiting. You remember I asked you the other day to come up and talk with us? I wonder if you'd given it any thought?"

"Not really."

"Elaine told me you got laid off today."

"Bad news travels fast."

"I'm sorry about that, but if you don't have anything else to do tomorrow, I thought you might like to come up to Bailey Springs and sit down with us."

"I'll think about it."

"How's nine o'clock sound?"

"Like I said, I'll think about it."

"Don't think about it too long, Jack. Time's running out to do any thinking."

* * * *

In the quietness of the vacant apartment, the shrill sound of the cell phone startled Cathy. "Pete?"

"Yeah, Cathy. I wanted to tell you I'm still here. The manager still hasn't shown up and the assistant manager still refuses to sign the letter."

"For crying out loud! What is it with those people?"

"I'll be there as soon as I can. I promise."

"I'm going out of my mind, but I'll be here."

* * * *

"Hi, Elaine. I'm a little early."

"Hello, Dan. Come on in," Elaine said without enthusiasm. When he entered, she shut the door, then looked up at him. "Jack is on his way over. Just tell me what you have to say and then please leave."

Dan looked at his cousin, knowing their relationship would never be the same after today. When all else fails, blame the messenger. Still, he had to be the one to tell her. It would be worse if she got the information from anyone else. "All right. Can we sit down?"

She shook her head. "I really want you out of my house before he gets here. Just tell me what you want to tell me."

Dan took a deep breath and exhaled. "All right," he said, paused, then began to tell her the same things in the same way that a prosecutor would tell a jury in his opening statement to a jury. As he talked, he could see the pain form on her face, then her eyes closed as tears leaked out of them and down her cheeks. He ended it by saying, "We found Jack's flashlight under the seat of his truck with dried blood and mud on it. We're sure it's Jake's blood on the flashlight. We found Jack's fingerprints in the mud and the blood. We believe Jack hit Jake with his pickup, got his hands bloody when he went to see if he was alive, then left him down there like some kind of roadkill," Dan paused, then said softly, "I'm sorry, Elaine. I'm truly sorry for your sake that it was Jack, but he has to pay for what he did to Jake."

Elaine raised her head, tears streaming down her face. "You'd better go."

"You sure you don't want me to stay until Jack gets here?"

She closed her eyes and shook her head. "Please go. Oh, my god! Please, just go."

* * * *

As Dan drove away from Elaine's house, a green pickup truck with a big ROLL TIDE sticker in the rear window passed him, then pulled into Elaine's driveway. It had to be Jack.

Dan's gut began to ache, knowing he was allowing the killer of Elaine's brother to go into her house. What would happen once he got inside? Had he convinced her that Jack had killed Jake? He wasn't sure. What would Jack do now? He wasn't sure of that either, but he was going to stick around to find out. He was very sure of that.

Dan drove through the intersection, then, halfway down the next block, he turned around in someone's driveway and parked on the street facing Elaine's house. With the engine idling and the heater blowing hot air to keep the truck cab warm, he waited, and watched. He looked about the interior of his black '99 Chevy pickup, admiring the new features it offered. The new truck was both good and bad news. On one hand, as long as he didn't let Jack see his face, he was certain Jack wouldn't know he was being followed by a Tennessee deputy sheriff. On the other hand, if he needed help, he was probably out of range for his radio.

He was determined to follow Jack wherever he went from here. If Jack went home, Dan would wait for him in Bailey Springs tomorrow morning. If he drove up to Uncle Buck's Tavern, he would try to get a warrant for him tonight. If he decided to run, Dan would follow him to Hell if necessary.

* * * *

"Hi, good-looking, how's your cold?" Jack asked as Elaine opened the door to him. Then he wrinkled his brow when he saw the tears flowing down her face. "What's the matter?"

"Did you do it, Jack? Did you kill my brother?"

Jack paused for a split second, then shook his head. "No."

"Oh, my god! You did! You killed Jake. You killed my brother!"

"No, no, I swear, I didn't have anything to do with it."

"I can see it in your eyes, Jack. Oh, my god, I don't believe this is happening to me."

"Elaine . . . "

"Don't . . . just go . . . please go," she said, then walked into her bedroom and closed the door. Jack could hear her crying through the closed door. The sound tore at his soul.

Jack walked to the front door, then turned around and looked about him, knowing it was the last time he would ever be in this house. His chance for happiness in this life was gone. As he opened the front door, he heard Elaine's bedroom door open.

"Jack, wait."

Jack turned and saw Elaine standing in her bedroom doorway, tears streaming down her face. "He asked me not to tell you, but Dan is going to arrest you tomorrow."

"Thanks for telling me."

"What are you going to do?"

"I don't know. I've never been wanted by the law before. I don't know what I'm supposed to do," Jack said, then paused, a look of resignation on his face. "What do you want me to do, Elaine? You want me to give myself up?"

Elaine gazed at Jack for a moment, then burst into tears. "I don't want you to go to jail," she wailed.

"I will if I give myself up. I'll be a gray-haired old man before I get out. What I did was wrong. I know that."

Elaine sniffed. "I can't believe this. If it had to happen, why couldn't it have been anyone but you?"

Jack paused. "Elaine, if I found someplace where I could start all over again . . . could I call you? Would you come?"

Elaine slowly shook her head as tears traced down her cheeks.

"Then I might as well give myself up. My life is over anyway."

"Do whatever you have to do, Jack, just don't ask me to come visit you in jail. I couldn't stand that."

Jack stood in the doorway and looked back at Elaine for a long time. Finally, he took a deep breath, exhaled and said, "Goodbye, Elaine. I swear to God, I'm so sorry for everything I've done. Please forgive me."

"Oh, God!" Elaine wailed as she walked into her bedroom and closed the door.

Jack stood for a moment, staring at the closed bedroom door, then walked out and quietly closed the door behind him.

* * * *

Dan had expected to be sitting in the cold for some time, but he had barely gotten comfortable when he saw Jack's green pickup come toward him, turn at the intersection in front of him, and disappear. Dan quickly pulled out and, upon reaching the intersection, saw Jack almost a block away. Dan turned and followed. In all the years he had been a deputy, he had never tried to follow someone covertly. He quickly decided it wasn't as easy as they made it seem in the movies. Several blocks later, Dan was two vehicles behind Jack as he turned onto a four-lane road that had been built years ago to allow traffic to bypass the congestion of downtown Helleston. Like many bypass roads, over the years it had attracted big malls and superstores and was now more congested than the downtown streets.

When Jack turned into a bank parking lot, Dan pulled into a small strip mall parking area next door and watched him approach the ATM machine. He stood there for several minutes, punching buttons, waiting, then punching more buttons and waiting again. Finally, he raised his fists, slammed them down onto the machine, then hurried back to his truck and sped off. As Dan pulled out into traffic behind Jack, he shook his head. "He's mad about something now."

* * * *

"Hello?"

"I've got it, Cathy. I'm leaving right now. We'll be on our way to California as soon as I get there."

"Oh, thank God! Hurry! Oh, please, hurry!"

* * * *

Once they were back on the four-lane bypass, Dan had difficulty keeping up with Jack amid the heavy traffic. With several vehicles between them, he had to sneak through a red light on the tail end of a stream of traffic at a busy intersection to keep from losing him. It would have been embarrassing to have been pulled over by the Helleston police for running a red light. He had no authority in Alabama and very few friends.

In the midst of thousands of people on their way home for the day, he almost lost Jack. He had lost him, in fact, until he noticed a green pickup with a big ROLL TIDE sticker on the rear window turning into the Cross Winds apartments. Dan turned into the apartment complex driveway, drove slowly around the side of the first building, then quickly stopped when he saw Jack, about twenty yards away, stopped in the traffic lane between the parking spaces. Dan watched as Jack stared out of his side window at the small gray Honda Civic hatchback next to him. After a moment, Jack continued down the traffic lane and pulled into a parking space at the far end. Dan backed into a vacant space across from the gray hatchback and waited. As far as he could tell, there was no back way out of the parking area. When Jack decided to leave, he would have to pass his way. Dan watched Jack's truck, wondering what he was doing here; whom had he come to see?

When he was still sitting in his truck five minutes later, Dan realized Jack was waiting for someone, too. "This might get interesting," Dan muttered to himself as he looked at the long shadows at the end of the day. It was close to sunset; it would be dark soon afterwards. He nodded. "This might get very interesting once it gets dark."

* * * *

Pete showed Cathy the letter. It was nothing more than a standard form filled in with his name, address, employee number, social security number and period of employment followed by the terse statement, "Employee is subject to rehire."

Cathy was livid when she saw the form had been signed by the assistant store manager, who had been there all day.

"What does, 'subject to rehire' mean?"

"It means they didn't fire me."

"That's it? This is what we've been hanging around for all day? For this?" she screamed.

Pete nodded. "It's not what I thought I was going to get. But I guess I'm not surprised."

"Jesus Christ! We ought to go down there and burn the place down or something."

Pete shook his head. "I just want to get out of this state, once and for all."

"I'm with you."

"I'm so glad," Pete said, then added, "I love you, Cathy."

"Oh, Pete, you're so sweet," Cathy said, then paused. "We can still make it to Memphis tonight. Let's find a motel room with a great big king-size bed and I'll let you show me exactly what you mean when you say that."

Pete grinned and nodded his head. "I've got a better idea. It's about to get dark. I would feel better if we drove during the day so I can see you behind me better. Let's stop in Florence for the night. We'll get something to eat and start out again early tomorrow morning."

Cathy beamed. "Sounds wonderful," she said. "Oh, here. You'd better take your cell phone. I'm not sure I know how to use all those buttons."

Pete took the phone and nodded. "It's too bad both of us don't have cell phones. We could talk to each other while we're driving."

"That would be neat. Maybe I'll get one when I get to California."

* * * *

Out in the parking lot, they stopped beside Cathy's car. Pete glanced up at the dying light in the late afternoon sky. "It's going to be dark before we get to Florence, but I'll keep an eye out for you."

"I just hope I'll be able to keep up with you. My little car starts shaking when I go over sixty."

"Could have been those bad tires, or it could be your front end is out of alignment. We should have had them do that, too, but it's all right. Just go as fast as you're comfortable. I won't leave you."

"Thanks."

"If traffic gets in between us, or if you get stopped by a red light, don't worry, I'll wait for you to catch up. And, if you want me to stop for some reason, flash your headlights at me a couple of times."

"Thanks, I will."

"Ready?"

"Ready!" Cathy said, then suddenly lunged toward Pete and kissed him. She quickly got into her car, started the engine and rolled down the window. "I just know this is going to be so great!"

"See you in Florence," Pete said, knowing his face was turning red in the twilight.

"I can hardly wait."

"Neither can I," Pete said, then pointing his finger at her chest, "Better buckle up. There are some crazy drivers out there."

"Oh, yeah," Cathy said, then grabbed her shoulder strap. "I usually do because my little car doesn't have an airbag. I'm so nervous right now, I forgot."

"Goodbye, Alabama," Pete called out as he walked to his car.

"Hello, California!" Cathy yelled after him.

* * * *

It was Cathy Constone, Jack's wife! Dan was sure of it. He had met her the day they had posted the flyers about Jake and then again, the night they had the visitation for Jake. Dan watched as she kissed the other man on his mouth, then got into the gray hatchback. As the other man approached him, Dan realized he knew him, too. Pete . . . Somebody, one of Elaine's friends. Dan smiled and nodded his head. Apparently, Pete was a better friend of Cathy Constone.

Dan watched as Cathy backed out, then waited as Pete backed a blue Mustang out of his parking space. As he drove away, Cathy followed closely behind. Dan turned and looked down toward the rear of the parking area in time to see Jack's green pickup approaching. Dan ducked his head down below the dashboard as Jack drove past, then quickly followed. "Now what is he up to?"

The strange caravan of a blue Mustang, a gray Honda hatchback, a green Ford pickup truck, and a black Chevy pickup truck worked its way through heavy traffic and a series of traffic signals on the bypass to get to US 72 where they turned west toward Florence. The road between Helleston and Florence was mostly a five-lane highway, with two travel lanes in each direction and a turn lane in the middle. Except when the road passed through Rogersville, Killen, or one of the other small towns on the way, the speed limit was sixty-five, with most traffic doing at least seventy. In the fading light of a winter's day, the five-lane highway was not as busy as it would be soon when many of the westbound Huntsville area workers would be passing through Helleston on their way to their homes in Lauderdale County.

It was after sunset, but not yet totally dark. It was that time of day when some drivers had already turned on their headlights while others chose to drive with their parking lights on. There were others who continued to drive without any lights at all. Jack was one of those. Pete and Cathy had already turned on their headlights. At the moment, there were two cars between Dan and Jack, and one between Jack and Cathy, but Dan wasn't worried about losing any of them. Pete and Jack's wife were going somewhere together, and Jack was following them. All he had to do was follow Jack.

Fifteen minutes later, all the eastbound traffic had passed them heading toward Athens and Huntsville, and there was a break in the westbound traffic. At the moment, the four vehicles were the only traffic on this section of the five-lane highway. Pete was in the outside travel lane doing a sedate sixty with Cathy no more than a few car lengths behind him, Jack was about fifty yards behind the two, and Dan was another fifty yards behind Jack. Dan glanced at his new truck's gas gauge. Full. He had no idea where they were going, or how long it would take to get there. One thing was for sure . . . long before the tank ran dry, he would find a way to stop this silly game.

As Dan came over the crest of a low hill, he could see a long stretch of the five-lane road ahead of him, sloping gently downward, then slowly rising up to the next hill crest about a half-mile away. There were several homes on either side with a red clay bank several feet high on the left side of the roadway. Suddenly, Dan sensed that Jack was accelerating away from him. Dan quickly accelerated as well, closing in on the other vehicles. Whatever Jack was up to, was about to happen now.

* * * *

With his headlights off in the semidarkness, Jack approached Cathy's car. "You piece of California dog shit!" he snarled. "You think you're going to get away with taking all my money and running off with another man? Huh? Is that what you think?" Within a few feet of Cathy's bumper, he turned on his bright headlights, pressed his hand on the horn, and kept it there.

Inexplicably, in response to the sudden bright lights and the sound of the horn right behind her, the confused woman stepped on her brakes.

"God damn you!" Jack cried out. He hit his brakes in response to the other vehicle's brake lights, but he was much too close to prevent the grill of his newly acquired truck from hitting the hatchback's bumper. When she pulled over into the inside travel lane and accelerated away from him. Jack pulled over into the lane behind her, then continued left into the center passing lane and accelerated until the front of his truck was even with the rear of her hatchback. "Now it's my turn. Let's see how you like this," he said.

* * * *

Dan had seen Jack hit the rear of Cathy's vehicle when she applied her brakes. Then, apparently attempting to get out of the way of the road rage vehicle behind her, she pulled over into the left-hand lane only to see Jack cross over into the passing lane and pull up beside her. "Oh, my God," Dan said as he watched Jack cut sharply to his right, driving his truck's grill at an angle into the left rear of the smaller vehicle.

Pursuing law enforcement officers know it as a PIT maneuver - precision immobilization technique – hitting the rear corner of a pursued vehicle at an angle causes the vehicle's rear tires to lose traction. The vehicle spins out of control, resulting in possible damage to the vehicle and injury or death to the pursued.

Dan watched Cathy's vehicle spin counterclockwise with the hatch up, ejecting grocery bags and clothing onto the highway. It continued to spin until it was moving backwards as it crossed the eastbound travel lanes. With no breakdown lane, the vehicle continued backwards off the low shoulder until it slammed into a six-foot high clay bank.

It bounced off the bank with so much recoil energy that it rolled back onto the travel lanes directly toward Jack.

* * * *

Jack tried to avoid the Honda Civic coming toward him by turning left but it was too little too late. The passenger's side of her vehicle slammed into the front of his truck, causing both vehicles to spin. When the noise died, the wreckage that once was Cathy's vehicle was partially blocking the passing lane and the inside westbound lane and Jack's damaged truck was sideways in the eastbound lanes.

Jack looked down at the deflated airbag in his lap. Cathy had hit the front of his pickup hard enough for it to deploy. "How about that?" he said. "It worked. It really worked." Suddenly, there was a bright glare of headlights shining into his side window from above the crest of the hill. When he turned to look, an eighteen-wheeler appeared over the hill. "Oh, my god," he whispered softly.

* * * *

Dan stopped in the outside westbound lane with his window down and listened to the silence. Neither Jack's truck nor the Honda were running, and he couldn't see either driver. He was about to get out and check on the condition of the drivers when he saw the headlights of an eastbound vehicle coming over the brow of the hill. "Oh, no," he said softly as he saw a trailer truck moving at a high rate of speed approaching the wreckage.

All five lanes were partially blocked by the two vehicles, and the clay bank near the road prevented the driver from taking evasive action. At seventy miles an hour, he slammed on his brakes. The tires briefly caught fire, then melting rubber comingling with melting asphalt created acrid black smoke that boiled away from the truck as it continued to slide along the roadway.

Dan watched in awe as the big eighteen-wheel rig smashed into the driver's side of Jack's pickup so hard that the smaller truck, impaled against the front of the road behemoth, became airborne for a brief moment as glass, chrome, and sheet metal exploded in every direction. Dan watched helplessly as the vehicles approached him in the eastbound lanes. When the noise of bending metal, breaking glass, and melting rubber ended, the nose of the tractor-trailer was still buried in the cab of the smaller pickup truck. Jack's bloody head was hanging outside the driver's broken window from an extended neck.

Dan reached for his two-way radio microphone, hoping to reach his dispatcher in Bailey Springs, Tennessee, from close to forty miles away. After a couple of attempts with nothing but static in response, he hung up. He saw several houses nearby. They would have telephones. It was the only option he had. As he got out and hurried toward the trailer truck, he saw Pete running toward the gray hatchback.

Dan heard a groan and looked up to see the dazed truck driver with his deflated airbag in his lap. "You all right up there?"

"Oh, man, what happened?"

"Are you all right?"

"Yeah, yeah, I think so."

"Get on CB Channel 19 and tell everybody to be ready to stop on US 72 west of Helleston. Got it?" Dan watched the dazed man slowly nod his head. "Stay where you are, sir. Help will be here soon."

With a grim look on his face, Dan walked over to the small car. What remained of it was right-side up, but the hatch and hood were up and both doors were open. There was no airbag. Cathy Constone was still in the driver's seat, slumped against her shoulder belt. As he approached it, he could hear Pete's voice.

"Cathy? Can you hear me? Please say something."

"How is she?" Dan asked.

Pete turned and looked at Dan. There were tears streaming down his face. "I don't know. I just don't know. She hasn't said anything. She hasn't moved."

"Let me see," Dan said. As Pete moved aside, Dan reached in and carefully placed his fingertips on the side of the woman's neck. There was a pulse. He looked at the other man and nodded. "She's alive," Dan said, then noticed that the other man was carrying a cell phone. "Are you Pete?" Dan asked.

The frail young man turned to Dan. There were tears in his eyes. "Yes."

"I'm a deputy sheriff. Will that cell phone work out here on US 72?"

"Maybe."

"Check and see," Dan said, then watched the young man turn it on and push a couple of buttons.

"I've got two bars."

"Dial nine-one-one and let me have it," Dan said and waited until the man handed him the cell phone.

"Nine-one-one. What is your emergency?"

"This is Sergeant Daniel Warden of the Creek County Tennessee Sheriff's Department. I'm reporting a multiple vehicle accident with multiple injuries on US 72, approximately fifteen miles west of Helleston, Alabama. All lanes are blocked by a sedan, a pickup truck and a tractor trailer. I am requesting traffic control, fire, and medical assistance."

"Thank you, sir. Stay on the line, please."

"Ma'am, I'd like to, but it's getting dark out here and there's an eighteen-wheeler blocking both eastbound lanes below the top of a hill. If I don't get up there and put out some flares, it's going to get a lot worse than it already is. I'm going to give this to someone else. If you have more questions, ask him."

"Fine. Alabama State Troopers will be there in approximately five minutes. Fire and medical equipment are on the way."

"Thank you, ma'am," Dan said, then offered the cell phone to Pete. "Help is on the way. Stay on the line if she has any more questions. I've got to put out some flares."

Dan ran to his pickup, turned on his behind-the-grill lights, then drove over the clothing, pieces of chrome and broken glass strewn over the highway as he threaded his way around the wrecked vehicles to the top of the rise. As he looked back, he could see two westbound cars stopping short of the wreckage. Good. Westbound traffic should be no problem, they could see what had happened in plenty of time to make a safe stop. It was eastbound that had to be warned.

With his emergency lights pulsing red and blue from inside his truck's grill, Dan parked in the outside travel lane at the top of the hill. Opening the toolbox in the back of his truck, he grabbed a handful of flares, put his flashlight in his armpit, and started trotting westbound, lighting flares and throwing them into the eastbound lanes. He had lit four before he saw another eighteen-wheeler rapidly approaching. Dan grabbed his flashlight in one hand and, with a lighted flare in the other, waved his arms at the truck. With his tires complaining, the driver slowed as he approached the crest of the hill. When he saw the wreckage below him, he stopped and turned on his flashers. The sight of the trailer's brake lights and flashers was enough warning for two cars approaching from the west to stop in time as well.

As the sound of multiple sirens became louder, Dan got back into his truck and drove back down to the hatchback. "I believe we've met. I'm Dan Warden," Dan said, extending his hand.

"I'm Pete Torrey," Pete said, shaking Dan's hand. "She's Cathy Constone."

Dan nodded. "Did you know her husband was following you?"

Pete shook his head. "Not until he ran up behind her like that. I knew it had to be him to do something like that."

"Where were you two heading?"

"California," Pete said, then paused. "She was going to visit her parents in San Diego. My parents live nearby. We were going to travel together."

Dan looked at the mounds of clothing and sacks of personal items that had been ejected from the open hatch of the Honda and nodded. It was going to be a very long visit, that was for sure.

"Shouldn't we get her out of there before the car explodes?" Pete asked.

Dan smiled. In the movies and on television, cars always exploded in a big ball of fire after a wreck. In real life, usually they didn't unless the fuel tank had been ruptured. He closed his eyes and inhaled slowly. He could smell the pungent odor of burning rubber, with a little antifreeze and hot motor oil added to the mix, but there was barely a whiff of gasoline. She was very lucky. Her hatchback's gas tank was very vulnerable in rear-end collisions. He turned and looked down at Pete. "I think she'll be all right here. It's important that we don't move her until the EMTs get here. Why don't you stay here with her until they get here?"

Pete looked up and nodded. "You think she'll be all right?"

"I don't know, Pete. You'll have to let the EMTs take a look."

"Pete," Cathy whimpered softly.

"I'm here, Cathy. I'm right here."

Dan looked up to see an ambulance approaching from Helleston. "What do I know?" Dan asked himself as he watched traffic continue to back up in both directions as curious onlookers gawked at the death and destruction. "I know the man who killed Jake is dead." As Dan watched the emergency vehicles work their way around and through the wreckage, he clenched his jaws tightly and shook his head. "You got away with it, didn't you, Jack? You'll never have to suffer the way you have caused others to suffer. May you spend eternity in Hell for all the pain you have caused."

Dan pulled his badge out of his belt and held it high in the palm of his hand as he walked toward an Alabama State Trooper. It was going to be a long, cold, miserable, winter night for Southern law enforcement.

THE END

THANK YOU FOR YOUR SUPPORT

If you enjoyed ROADKILL, I would appreciate it if you would spread the word about the Dan Warden Series of novels on social media and emails to friends and family since I don't do any advertising otherwise. Leaving a review on Amazon would be a big help, too. Exposure is everything for a self-published author, and reviews help so much.

COMING NEXT

THE TOMATO PATCH

ANOTHER
DAN WARDEN STORY

A preview of

THE TOMATO PATCH
By
Larry Quillen

Chapter 1

Friday, May 9, 2003

THREE HOURS AGO, Lloyd Black had been behind the walls and electrified fences of Kilby Correctional Facility, a maximum-security prison, near Montgomery, Alabama. Now, for the first time in ten years, he gazed at the old single-wide mobile home where he had once lived. There were lights on in most of the windows. Someone was home. The bedroom he had shared with his wife was on the left end; his boy's smaller bedroom was on the right end. In between was a bathroom, a utility closet, a kitchen area with a small dining table, and a living area. Many times during the past ten years he had wondered if he would ever see it again.

He looked at the unfamiliar Ford Escort hatchback parked next to him. It had a few years on it, but not as many as his old Chevy Caprice would have on it now. She had probably traded it in on the Ford. Too bad. He'd had some good times in it.

The little Ford looked like it could get him wherever he wanted to go from here. If his ex-wife didn't live here anymore, he would have to get the keys to it any way he could from

1

whoever was inside. Without a weapon, he wasn't sure how he was going to do it, but he didn't have much choice.

He wouldn't kill anybody unless he absolutely had to, but he would do whatever he had to do to keep moving. There would be no parole if the law ever caught him this time. He would spend the rest of his life in prison. If they didn't strap him in the chair down at Atmore, he would die in prison anyway, as an old man. He slowly shook his head. "I couldn't take it," he said softly.

As Lloyd walked toward the mobile home, he realized his walk was unsteady. With a wry grin on his face, he recalled how, back in the old days, drinking three beers was just enough to make him feel good. Now, after ten years without one, he was just about drunk. Lloyd snorted as he grabbed the handrail to the steps leading up to a small porch and looked up. What the hell? He'd walked up these steps before, a lot drunker than he was now.

Holding the railing for support, Lloyd climbed the short flight of stairs to the small wooden porch and paused. The front door was open to allow the evening breeze to help cool off the interior, but the screen door was closed to keep the mosquitoes and other bugs outside. He paused, listening for any sound beyond the screen door. He could hear the hum of a motor from inside somewhere. Other than that, he heard nothing.

Through the rusty screen, he looked into the mobile home's ten-by-twelve living area and saw no one. Lloyd tried the screen door. It was unlocked. The rusted hinges squealed as he slowly pulled it open and stepped into the living area. The humming noise had stopped. He slowly closed the screen door and looked around. It looked like the same furniture, in the same arrangement he had lived with ten years ago. To his left just inside the door was a bookcase, a small couch with end tables, and a coffee table with a bowl of candy on it. There was a lamp on one end table and a telephone on the other. Toward the back of the small living area was his old club chair and footstool facing the television in the corner. Lloyd nodded. The mobile home and its furniture were rented. Just because he recognized the furniture didn't mean anyone he knew still lived here. He didn't recognize the Ford, that was for sure.

The door to the darkened bedroom to his right was ajar. He walked over, gently pushed it open, and took a quick look inside. There was an unmade bed, but no one was in the room at the moment. It used to be his son's room. Maybe it still was. Lloyd had named him Myron, after his granddaddy, but everyone called him Red.

Lloyd paused again. When he heard no one, he hurried past the couch and around the room divider to the kitchen area and opened the drawer where the knives once were. They were still there. He picked up an old steak knife with a five-inch serrated blade and plastic handle. He palmed it upside down, cradling the plastic handle in his curled fingers with the blade up inside the sleeve of his coveralls. It wasn't much, but it was a weapon. He might need it to get what he wanted before he left here.

There was a small dining table with a couple of chairs against the back wall of the tiled kitchen area. Pepper, salt, mustard, and a bottle of ketchup were on the table. Lloyd walked out of the kitchen and positioned himself near the dining table where he could see down the hallway. To his right was the back door, down the hallway to his left was the open door to the bathroom. Across the hallway from the bathroom were folding doors hiding the clothes washer and dryer. At the end of the hallway was the open door to the master bedroom. If anyone was home, they had to be in the bathroom or the master bedroom. "Anybody home?" he called out.

"Who's there?" a female voice called out from the master bedroom.

"Lena? Is that you?"

"Yeah. Who's out there?"

"It's me. Lloyd."

"Lloyd?" Lena called out, and then came into view from the master bedroom, tying the sash around her bathrobe. She stared wide-eyed at her ex-husband. He looked much bigger and older than she remembered. "Oh, my god! It really is you!"

With a sloppy grin on his face, Lloyd nodded as he appraised his ex-wife. Even with a shapeless bathrobe on, she looked good to him.

Lena walked down the short hallway and stood near him. "Jesus Christ, Lloyd! You'd better get out of here before that deputy comes back."

"They've already been here?"

"About thirty minutes ago. He said you'd escaped, and they thought you might be coming up this way. Is it true? You broke out?"

"Yeah. Me and a couple of others went under the fence."

"Oh, my god!"

Lloyd looked about the familiar place. "Where's my boy?"

"He's working at McDonald's."

"Damn. I'd sure like to see that redheaded boy, but I've got to get out of here before that deputy shows up again." Lloyd paused, and then said, "I need your car, Lena. I need all your money, too."

"I can't let you have my car, Lloyd. It's all I've got to get to work."

Lloyd slowly approached Lena, shaking his head. "I need it, Lena. I've got to have it. I've got to get out of here before they come back. If they catch me, I'll spend the rest of my life behind bars. I couldn't take that."

Lena stared at the big man. There was a time when she cared enough about this man to marry him. Now something in his eyes, in the way he looked at her, made her feel uncomfortable being alone with him. "My purse is in the bedroom," she said quietly.

"Go get it. Hurry up!"

Lloyd watched Lena walk back down the hallway toward the bedroom, then he turned and hurried back to the end table next to the couch, grabbed the thin telephone cable into a loop and cut it with the serrated-blade knife. He looked down at the knife and decided he would no longer need it to get what he needed from this woman. He looked about for a moment, then stepped over to his old club chair, lifted the front edge of the cushion, and slipped the knife under it.

He was back at the dining table when Lena returned. She slammed her large purse down on the small table so hard it knocked over the ketchup. Ignoring the bottle, she

4

rummaged through the contents until she found her keys. She threw them down on the table beside her purse and glared at her former husband. "There, you happy now? I don't have a way to get to work. I'll be out of a job again."

"Everybody's got problems, Lena," Lloyd said as he grabbed the keys. "How much money do you have?"

Lena found her wallet, opened it, and threw the bills on the counter. "There! Take it all! Now, I can't eat until payday."

Lloyd picked up the bills, then looked up at Lena, frowning. "Twenty-seven dollars? That's all you've got?"

"I'm not rich, Lloyd. Me and Red barely get by."

"Where're my guns?"

"They're gone."

"Gone?"

"Me and Red have had it pretty rough since you've been gone. For a time, we didn't have money to buy food or anything. I hocked your guns so we could eat."

"Jesus Christ!"

Lena opened her wallet again and pulled out a credit card. "You want this, too? I owe so much on it; you might as well take it."

"It wouldn't do me any good. Every time I used it, they would know where I was. I need cash, Lena. It's got to be cash, but I need more than this," he said, holding up the money.

"Go see your daddy. He'll give you some."

Lloyd shook his head. "If they've already been here, they'll be waiting for me over there."

"You've got all I have. It's the best I can do."

"Where's your ATM card?"

Lena pulled it out of her wallet and offered it to him. "Here take it, but it won't do you any good. This close to payday, there won't be more than ten or fifteen dollars in my account."

"Damn!" Lloyd said, glaring at his ex-wife, focusing his rage on her. If Denzil had let him keep some of the money, he would be on his way to Canada now. If his ex-wife had a few more dollars in her purse, he could still be in Canada by this time tomorrow. If he had one of his old pistols, he could find a little mom-and-pop gas station somewhere along the way and get all the gas he needed and a few dollars in his pocket as well. Instead, he was running out of time and options fast.

Lloyd stuffed the keys and money in his coveralls. As he turned to go, he paused. Something had been boiling inside him for three years. Now was the time to vent his anger. He turned back to face her. "It really pissed me off when you divorced me."

"What did you expect me to do? I thought you were going to be in there for another twenty years."

Lloyd stared at Lena. She didn't understand what she had done to him, and he didn't have the time or patience to explain it to her. She didn't know the day she divorced him was one of the darkest days of his life. The one hope he had held onto all those years inside was believing someday he would get out and she would be standing outside the prison gate waiting for him. There had to be a way to punish her for what she had done to him. He pointed at his ex-wife in her bathrobe. "Open it up. I want to take a look."

Lena stared in silence at the man in front of her as she slowly backed away from him until she was at the back door. "You'd better get out of here, Lloyd," she said as she put her hand on the doorknob.

Lloyd pointed his finger at her. "Don't try it," he warned. "You won't get far barefoot. When I catch you, you'll wish you hadn't."

Lena stared at the man as he slowly approached her. It was hard for her to believe she had once been married to him. He was a stranger to her now, much older, a lot bigger, and with a mean look in his eyes that disturbed her. She released the doorknob and walked past him into the kitchen area. The idea of disrobing in front of this man made her feel uncomfortable. She turned and glared at him. "Why don't you just get out of here and leave me alone?"

"You'd better do what I tell you to do, woman. You know what happens when you get smart with me."

"I'm not going to let you hit me again. You're not my husband no more."

"Oh, yeah?" The big man reached out and grabbed a handful of her robe between her breasts.

"Damn it, Lloyd! Let me go and get the hell out of here," Lena cried out as she tried to pry his hands away from her robe. "You're drunk! I can smell it on your breath. You always liked to hit me when you were drunk, didn't you? Not anymore, you hear? You ain't got no right."

"The hell I don't," Lloyd said. While holding on to her robe with one hand, he slapped her hard with the other, then he flung her down onto the tile floor like a rag doll.

Stunned, Lena shook her head, trying to clear the cobwebs. It had been a long time since anyone had treated her like this, not since the last time this same man had done the same thing to her. Rage began to boil within her.

Lloyd looked down at the woman at his feet. "I've got the right to do anything I want to do to you, you got that?" Lloyd said, glaring at the woman. "Just because you got some piece of paper saying we not married don't mean shit to me. I'll decide what I've got the right to do, not you! You want some more? I used to give it to you pretty good when you needed it. I still can. It's up to you."

Using the table for support, Lena pulled herself up from the tile floor, her ear ringing and her face stinging. She stared at the man who was once her husband and slowly shook her head. She was taller than most women, but she knew she was no match for a man as big as Lloyd. She glanced at the back door behind the man, knowing the exit was now closed to her. She turned and walked quickly toward the living area.

"Hey, come back here," Lloyd called out. He followed her into the living area where he saw her standing beside the couch, the telephone handset against her face. Smiling, he walked over to his old club chair, sat on the arm facing her, and watched her frowning. He pulled the zipper of his coveralls all the way down to his crotch, then pushed the garment over his shoulders and pulled his arms out of it. When he saw her dial a three-digit number again, he called out, "What's the matter? Nobody home?"

Lena looked up at him, then grabbed the telephone base, lifted it, and saw the severed cable. "Damn you to hell!"

"Most likely," Lloyd said. He stood, pushed his shorts and coveralls down to his ankles, then sat on the arm of the club chair in his undershirt and spread his legs. "Now, you drop that robe and come over here and show me what you're good at. I've about run out of patience with you."

"No!" Lena cried out and unconsciously pulled the top of her robe closer together as she looked at her ex-husband's genitals. "Take what you've got and get out of here! I ain't interested!"

Lloyd leaned back, slipped his hand underneath the seat cushion, grabbed the knife, and showed it to her. "I don't give a damn whether you're interested or not. I haven't had a woman in ten years. I'd say I was due. Now, take the damn robe off and get over here and do what you're told. I'll use this to make you wish you had if you don't."

"You've changed, Lloyd," Lena said as she opened the sash on her robe and pull the edges of the garment aside. As the man stared at her nakedness, she looked at the screen door across the room, trying to decide if she could get to it before he got to her with his knife.

Lloyd stared at the woman and nodded his head. "You look good, Lena. You look damn good. Gravity is starting to work on you, but for an old broad, you still look good. Now, come here and show me what you're good at before I have to use this knife on you."

"God damn you!" Lena yelled as she turned and bolted for the front door. At the same time, Lloyd, his feet restricted by the clothing around his ankles, lunged toward her. As he landed hard on the thin carpet, he grabbed the hem of Lena's robe which caused her to stumble and fall as well. As he struggled to pull the woman back to him by pulling on her robe, Lena tried to extract her arms from the robe.

"God damn it! Stop fighting me," Lloyd yelled.

"No!" Lena yelled as she kicked the robe away and hurried to the open door of her son's bedroom. "Get away from me!" the naked woman screamed as she slammed the door shut and locked it.

"You'd better come out of there! Don't make me bust down the door," Lloyd growled as he pushed himself off the floor. "No man is going to want you when I get done with you if I do."

Lena turned on the light and looked about the small bedroom. Then, in one corner of the room, she saw the old .22 rifle her son used for squirrel hunting. He had been shooting at cardboard targets out behind their mobile home one day when she had joined him out of curiosity and had shot the rifle a few times. She walked over and picked it up. It was her only hope. As she looked at it, she remembered the ammunition tube could hold several bullets, but the bolt was closed so she couldn't see if there were any in it or not. She hoped she wouldn't need to find out.

"Hey! Get out here before I bust down the door," Lloyd called. He pulled his clothes back up to his waist, picked up the knife, then shuffled over to the small couch near the front door. He noticed a bowl on the coffee table with individually wrapped pieces of butterscotch candy in it. Candy had been hard to come by in prison. Butterscotch was his favorite. He missed it. He reached out, grabbed a handful, and stuffed them in a pocket.

Lena opened the bedroom door and pointed the rifle at her ex-husband. "Get out of here, Lloyd."

"What the hell?" Lloyd said in bewilderment as he looked at the rifle pointed at him in the hands of a naked woman. For ten years, he'd fantasized about seeing this woman naked again, but never like this, not while she was pointing a gun at him. His sense of self-preservation urged him to put some distance between him and the gun. He slowly rose from the couch and, with the knife in one hand and holding up his coveralls with the other, he slowly moved away from the woman toward the rear of the living area. "I thought you said you hocked all my guns!" he accused.

"This is Red's squirrel rifle."

"That's not Red's gun. That's my old Marlin 60. It's good for squirrels, but all it's going to do is piss me off if you shoot me with it. I've got a better idea. Why don't you give me the gun before you hurt somebody with it?" he asked, then took a step forward.

Lena pointed the rifle in the general direction of her ex-husband. "Get out of here, Lloyd. You've got my money. You've got the keys to my car. Just go. Leave me alone. I swear I'll pull the trigger if you don't."

Lloyd grinned as he took another step. "I don't think you will. I don't think you've got the guts."

Lena squeezed the trigger. The gun didn't fire, but it did make Lloyd stop in his tracks. She tried again, and then again, becoming so frustrated with it, she was jerking the whole gun, trying to get the trigger to move.

Lloyd laughed out loud. "You stupid broad. You've got the safety on!"

Lena looked down at the rifle, frowning, and then recalled Red showing her the button behind the trigger. In her panic, she had forgotten about it.

"Bring it here. I'll show you how to shoot it," Lloyd said.

Lena quickly pushed the button, then pointed the rifle in Lloyd's general direction and pulled the trigger once more. The noise of the rifle shot was loud in the confined space of the mobile home.

The impact of the .22 Long Rifle bullet striking Lloyd's stomach caused the surprised man to stagger backwards until he hit the back wall. With his coveralls down around his ankles again, Lloyd looked down at his white undershirt and saw pink fluid oozing out of a small hole near his belly button. He looked up at Lena. "You shot me," he said, a look of confused amazement on his face.

"I told you I would," Lena said, tears in her eyes. "You just wouldn't listen to me."

"Say your prayers bitch. You're about to meet your maker," Lloyd said as he took a slow, unsteady shuffling step toward Lena while holding his stomach with one hand and the knife in the other.

With tears in her eyes, Lena pointed the rifle at her ex-husband. Without aiming, she fired again, and then continued shooting in the general direction of the man while spent cartridge shells ricocheted off the nearby wall.

In the quiet aftermath, after the rifle no longer responded when she pulled the trigger, she watched the big man stare down at the pink and red fluid oozing out of several holes in his white undershirt. Then he looked up at her, a look of pain and confusion on his face as he dropped to his knees, and then fell face-forward onto the carpet.

With her ears ringing, the acrid smell of gunpowder in the air, and spent .22 cartridge shells scattered about the room, Lena watched and waited for any sound or movement from the man.

After several minutes of silence, it occurred to her to check and see if the man was still alive but doing so would require her to touch him. The thought was revolting. When she saw no movement nor heard any sound from the man for several more minutes, she dropped the rifle on the couch and picked up her robe. After wrapping the garment tightly about her trembling body she picked up the rifle and returned it to her son's bedroom, having no idea where more ammunition might be or how to load it if she found any.

She returned to the living area and stared silently at the man's body, intent on running out into the night barefoot if he suddenly rose from the floor. There was no movement for as long as she watched.

She needed to get dressed, but to do that, she had walk past the man to get to her bedroom. She still wasn't sure if he was still alive or not. If he was playing possum, he would grab her as soon as she got anywhere near him. She slowly approached the man, ready to turn and run at the first hint of movement. Once around his body, she hurried into her bedroom where she dressed and put on shoes. On her way out of her bedroom, she stopped at the nightstand next to her bed and found a partial pack of stale cigarettes.

Once again, she slowly approached Lloyd, watching for movement. When she saw none, she hurried past him and out of the house onto the small front porch. Her hands were shaking so badly, she had to hold the match with both hands to light the cigarette.

As she drew the smoke deep into her lungs and slowly exhaled, she turned and looked back through the screen door at the man's body lying in the living area. The right thing for her to do would be to walk down the hill to Homer Jones and ask him to let her make a call. What would she tell the sheriff if she did call? She shook her head in dismay. They might believe she had been forced to shoot him if she told them he had threatened her with a knife, but would they believe she needed to shoot him a whole bunch of times?

How many times had she shot him? She had no idea. It was all sort of a blur in her mind. She was just trying to stop him from coming after her with the knife. Would the sheriff accept the explanation when he found out how many times she had shot him? She wasn't sure.

Maybe the sheriff would take the man's side. He might tell her that, if she'd gone along with Lloyd and done what he wanted her to do, he'd still be alive and long gone by now. She nodded her head. If she had to do it over again, she probably would, knowing how it would end otherwise.

She didn't know of anyone, family or friends, who had killed someone. Her daddy and her brothers had spent some time in the Creek County jail for doing things they shouldn't have, but none of them had killed anybody. She had. A cold chill crawled up her spine. After she told the sheriff what she had done, she might spend the rest of this night in jail, and a lot more nights after that. It bothered her that she had shot her ex-husband. It might bother the sheriff, too.

She took another drag from the cigarette, and then sat in one of the chairs on the small porch. She slowly nodded, making a decision. She wouldn't walk down the road just yet. Red would be home soon. Between the two of them they could decide what to tell the sheriff.

Chapter 2

AFTER FINISHING HIS shift at McDonald's, Red pulled into the bare dirt front yard in his old 1990 Chevy Caprice and saw his mama sitting on the small front porch, smoking a cigarette. "I thought you said you'd quit smoking," he called out.

"I had. This is the first one in almost four months," Lena said. As Red reached for the screen door, she added, "Wait a minute, Red. Don't go in there."

"Why not?"

Lena took a deep drag and exhaled. "Lloyd came home a while ago."

"Dad's home? They let him out?"

"He broke out. A deputy came by looking for him. No sooner had he left than Lloyd showed up."

Red looked into the living room through the screen door and saw a man lying on the floor in the back of the room near the television set. "What's he doing on the floor? Is he asleep?"

"Lloyd's dead, honey. I killed him."

"You killed him? You killed Daddy?" the confused teenager asked as he stepped closer to the screen door.

"I guess so. He ain't moved since I shot him."

"Why?" Red asked with look of anguish. "Why'd you do that for?"

"I had to, honey. He didn't give me no choice. I gave him the keys to my car and all the money I had, but he came after me with a knife, so I got your gun and shot him. I don't know how many times, but I kept shooting until the gun wouldn't shoot anymore. He hasn't moved since."

"The tube was full, Mama. There were fourteen shells in it!"

"Fourteen? Oh, my God! I don't remember shooting him that many times."

"Oh, Jesus, Mama! Have you called the sheriff?"

"He cut the telephone cord. I thought I'd just sit out here and wait for a deputy to show up again." Lena turned her head up and looked into her son's eyes. "The thing is, if a deputy comes back tonight and finds him in there, he might put me in jail."

"They wouldn't do that, would they?" Red asked, believing it was a real possibility. It suddenly occurred to him that he might never see either of his parents after tonight. "Can't you tell them you had to because he had a knife?"

"I guess I could. They're going to wonder why I shot him so many times, though. How many bullets did you say were in that gun? Fourteen?"

"That's what it's supposed to hold, but I can put fifteen in it if I want to," Red said, paused, then added, "I don't see why they won't believe you had to shoot him to keep him from hurting you. It would be called self-defense, wouldn't it?"

"It might if I hadn't shot him so many times. They might think shooting a man once or twice would be enough. From the way our folks talk, you can't trust the law around here to do right for people like us. You've got to be a rich man to stay out of jail these days."

"I know. That's what everybody says," Red said, then slowly shook his head in confusion and frustration. Ten minutes ago he was feeling great. Now, his daddy was dead and his mama might go to jail for killing him. It couldn't get much worse. "What are we going to do, Mama?"

Lena looked up at her son, tears in her eyes. "It's up to you, honey. You can go down the road and tell Homer Jones you need to call the sheriff if you want to. I don't have the heart to do it myself. Or we can just sit here and wait for a deputy to show up again. I know they're going to lock me up when they see what I done."

With his lips drawn tightly, Red shook his head. He felt sad about his daddy, but vague ten-year-old memories of the man couldn't match the closeness he felt for his mama. They had always been close through the bad times they had shared since his daddy left. "I'm not going to let anybody lock you up, Mama."

"They might as soon as they find Lloyd in there. If I try to tell them I did it just because he came at me with a knife, they're going to wonder why I shot him so many times."

"Maybe we can take Daddy down the road somewhere and then call the sheriff and tell them where he is."

"As soon as they find him, they'll come knocking on our door, asking us questions. They'll know for sure we had something to do with it."

"He's my daddy! I'm not going to throw him in the woods and let the animals eat on him! That's what happened to the body I found down at the curve. I had nightmares about it for a long time after. I don't want my daddy looking like that when somebody finds him."

Lena nodded her head, remembering the troubled sleep her son had experienced several years ago after finding a body that had been exposed to the elements and animals. "I don't want it either, Red. It wouldn't be the Christian thing to do to anybody," Lena said, then paused. "I guess we might as well leave him where he is, wait for the deputy, and let me take my medicine."

Frowning, desperately looking for a solution, Red asked, "Couldn't we bury him somewhere around here and not tell anybody? I sure don't want Daddy laying out there in the woods where the animals can get at him. They might come after me someday for burying my own daddy, but if we bury him deep enough, maybe they never will find him."

Lena gazed at Red. "It's up to you, honey. The Lord knows my family and Lloyd's family haven't had much luck with Tennessee judges and juries, so I'm willing to bury him around here somewhere, if you are. But, if we're going to bury him, we need to do it now. They might come back anytime."

Red took a deep breath. "There's a shovel and a pickaxe out in the old shed. I'll get them and get started digging."

"Maybe we ought to get Lloyd out of the house first, in case a deputy does come back tonight," she said as she rose from the chair.

Red silently nodded and walked inside. The first thing he noticed was the spent .22 cartridges scattered about on the floor. "We'd better pick these up before that deputy shows up again."

Lena followed him inside. "I'll do it, but let's get Lloyd out of here first. Get that old blanket from over the washing machine. We're going to need it."

Red paused at the body of his daddy as conflicting emotions washed over him. He sniffed as tears welled up in his eyes, then turned and walked away down the hallway.

Lena picked up the knife, put it in the kitchen sink, then checked her ex-husband's pockets. In one pocket she found her keys and money. In the other, she found butterscotch candy. She took the keys and money. She left the candy. With Red's help, she wrapped the body in an old blanket, and then they struggled to drag their cumbersome burden out the back door and down the back stairs.

While Lena returned to the house to clean up, Red found a flashlight and headed for the old woodshed to search for tools to dig a grave.

For many years, there had been a small two-bedroom house with a fireplace where the mobile home now stood. Fifteen years ago, the old house had burned to the ground and the landowner had replaced it with a used single-wide mobile home. An open woodshed in the back of the clearing had escaped the fire. It still had a small pile of fireplace logs and a few hand tools in it.

With his flashlight, Red swept away spider webs, and then pulled aside long-discarded junk until he found a shovel, a pickaxe, and a chopping axe. All the tools were rusty and the old handles were weathered gray, but they would have to do.

There was an ache in Red's chest as he looked at the blanket-shrouded body of his daddy lying in the moonlight. He wished he could have seen him alive tonight long enough to talk to him for a few minutes. He couldn't remember what his daddy's voice sounded like. Now, he would never hear it again. It made him sad.

In the light of the moon, Red made three attempts to dig a hole in the clay soil behind the mobile home. Each time, after digging only a few inches down, he struck huge rocks, too big to move. In desperation, he moved to the right side of the property and found a small area of soil near the trees that would give to his shovel and pickaxe. For the first few inches, he had to cut through roots with the dull chopping ax. After that, he used the pickaxe to break up a few inches of the clay soil before switching to the shovel to clear the loosened dirt out of the hole before going back to the pickaxe again.

Lena came out to check on Red's progress and to bring him a glass of water. When he stopped to drink, Lena picked up the shovel and scooped out the loose dirt in the shallow hole. When she was done, she stepped away and let her son back into the hole with the pickaxe.

They continued to alternate between digging and shoveling until well past midnight. From time to time, when the teenage boy had become exhausted, Lena allowed him to rest for a few minutes while she took the pickaxe and dug into the clay earth herself. After hours of adrenaline-fed digging and shoveling, a lot of water, a lot of sweat, and a couple of blisters, they had dug a hole almost three feet wide, about five feet long and almost five feet deep. Large rocks prevented them from making it any deeper, wider, or longer.

While they were digging the hole, both had looked toward the front yard many times, fearing the headlights of a Creek County Sheriff's vehicle might appear out of the darkness. When the hole was dug, the two struggled mightily with the heavy bulk in the blanket as they pulled it across the backyard. Pulling that much weight across the backyard after the exhausting effort of digging the hole was too much. Both collapsed on the ground, gasping for breath. After several minutes, they forced themselves to rise.

They rolled the body into the hole, and then Red got down into the hole with the body and twisted and turned it, trying to make it fit. By turning the body on its side and pulling the knees up in a fetal position, Red was able to fit the body around the rocks in the hole. When his mother handed him the bloody blanket, he tucked it around the body and climbed out of the hole.

"There, that ought to do fine," Lena said gazing down at the man's body in the shallow grave.

"Don't you think we should say a prayer or something?"

Lena tilted her head to one side. She was surprised at her son's request. She and Red hadn't been to church in a long time. "That would be nice. Would you like to say a prayer?"

"The only one I know is the Lord's Prayer."

"Well, then, why don't we say that one?" They bowed their heads, clasped their hands, and intoned the prayer together. Then they lifted their heads, looked at each other, and smiled. "I think that was a nice thing to do, Red."

Red shrugged and looked down at the man in the hole. "He was my daddy. I don't remember much about him, but he's the only daddy I'll ever have." Red turned, looked at his mother, and sniffed. "What was he like, Mama?"

"Lloyd was an old country boy, honey. He was a hard worker, but he never found anything he liked doing enough to work at it long enough to get good at it." Lena gazed down at the grave, sadly shaking her head. "Lord knows he was a hard man to live with sometimes."

"I remember he took me hunting and fishing sometimes."

"Hunting, fishing, working on old cars, and drinking beer with his friends was about all he was good at."

A cold chill coursed down Red's back as he realized his mother was describing his own life up to this point. Was this where he was going to end as well? "I'm going to find a way to make some good money," Red vowed. "I ain't going to waste my life living on the crumbs the people around here throw me."

"Well, honey, I hope you find something you like. It's awfully hard to find a good job around here."

"I'll figure out something," Red said, then tossed a shovelful of dirt into the hole. Both Red and Lena heard the soft thump as the dirt landed on Lloyd's body. The sound sent chills through them. Red sniffed again. "I'm not going to let somebody bury me like this," Red said, then started shoveling again.

Lena watched her son at work in the pale moonlight and felt sad for him. She had never told him, and she knew this was neither the time nor place to tell him, but she was fairly sure Lloyd wasn't his daddy.

She had been a wild girl when she was a teenager. She was sixteen and a high school sophomore when she crashed a party for high school seniors. A combination of beer and marijuana made her memory of the night hazy, but she was pretty sure she'd had sex with at least two of the seniors, maybe more. A few weeks later, when she discovered she was pregnant, she told one of the boys he might be the father. He told her it wasn't his, for her to pick on one of the others who had screwed her that night, and to leave him out of it. When she told Lloyd she was pregnant with his child, he shook his head and said, "I ain't ready to get married, but Daddy will horsewhip me if he finds out he has a bastard for a grandchild."

After Red was born, his red hair was startling to everyone in both families. Thankfully, they found a second cousin of Lloyd's father with red hair. It seemed to satisfy most of the curious relatives. Lena was the only one who knew the other boy had red hair himself. That boy had gone to college and now lived with his wife and two redheaded girls in a big home in the nicest part of Bailey Springs. It had worried Lena over the years that Red might someday unknowingly date one of his half-sisters, but the young girls were attending Bailey Springs High School in town and Red had graduated from Central High School, a county school south of Bailey Springs. As far as she knew, Red had never met his real father or either of his half-sisters.

Lena walked over to her son, wrapped her arms around him, and held him close to her. It had been years since she had hugged her son, but this seemed like a good time to show her only child how much she loved him. "It'll be all right, Red. Really it will," she assured him, having no idea if it would or not. "We'd better hurry up and finish before they come back," she said, then picked up the pickaxe and began to rake the dirt into the hole with the broad end of it while her son used the shovel.

When the hole was filled, there was still a considerable amount of loose dirt scattered about the hole. "I'll go finish cleaning up the living room and take a shower. I couldn't get the blood out of that damn carpet. I took a bathmat and put over it for now," Lena said. "You'd better come in and take a bath yourself. If anybody sees how dirty and sweaty you are, they're going to wonder what we've been up to for sure." In the dim light from the mobile home, she had also seen blood on her son's clothes and arms, but she chose not to mention it.

"Mama?"

"Yeah, honey?"

"What about the grave? Anybody can see it when they drive up. If the sheriff comes looking for Daddy, they're going to wonder what we've been doing back here."

Lena looked at the freshly dug clay soil piled around the gravesite. Unconsciously, she stuck a finger in her mouth and began to chew on the nail, something she hadn't done since she was a teenager. "Well, I guess we'll have to find something to plant there so it won't look like a grave." Suddenly, Lena's face brightened. "I know. The store got a batch of tomato plants yesterday. If we spread the dirt around the hole a little, making it a little wider and longer, we could have us a little tomato patch there. How does that sound?"

Red silently nodded. "Yeah, Mama, tomatoes would be fine. There's a hoe and a rake in the shed. I'll go get them."

Using the garden tools, they spread the loose clay dirt around until they had a rectangle about six by eight feet. "There," Lena said. "That looks fine. I'll get some tomato plants first thing tomorrow morning."

"I've already told Bobby Ray I'd come over and help him work on his car tomorrow."

"That's all right. I can plant a few tomatoes by myself," she said, then frowned. "How many bullets did you say were in that gun of yours?"

"It's supposed to take fourteen to fill the tube, but sometimes I stick one more in there . . . so, fourteen, maybe fifteen. I don't know for sure."

"I could only find thirteen of those little shells."

"There should be one or two more around somewhere."

"Well, I hope we find all of them. Some deputy might wonder what a rifle shell was doing in our living room if he found one."

"Then, keep them out of there!"

"I'll try," Lena said. "Whether it was fourteen or fifteen, I guess I didn't hit him with all of them. There are some little splintered holes in the wall and window screen. It's a good thing we had the window up. There would have been hell to pay if I'd shot out the window."

"You need to find some way to cover up those holes, Mama."

"I'll think of something," she said then suddenly gasped. "Oh, Jesus! I've got to get a new telephone cord."

"Get one that's long enough so I can take the telephone into my room."

"I'll see if the store has one that long. Hurry up! Put those tools away and get inside. There'll be hell to pay if the sheriff shows up and sees you out here this time of night," Lena called out as she walked away from her ex-husband's grave. "I'll plant those tomatoes first thing tomorrow morning. If the sheriff doesn't send a deputy out again tonight, he sure as hell will send one out sometime tomorrow."

Chapter 3

LIEUTENANT DAN WARDEN of the Creek County, Tennessee, sheriff's department grabbed his keys and was on his way out the door of his rented mobile home in Bailey Springs, Tennessee, when the phone rang. He paused, letting it ring twice more while trying to decide if he wanted anything or anyone to interfere with his usual Saturday morning routine. He walked over and picked up the receiver. "Hello?"

"Dan? This is Elaine."

"Oh, good morning, Elaine. How've you been?" Dan asked, truly glad to hear her voice. He had enjoyed a close relationship with his first cousin, more like brothers and sisters, for many years. Then, a few years ago, her high school boyfriend had killed her brother in a drunken hit-and-run accident and hadn't reported it, leaving the body exposed to the animals and elements, like roadkill. When Dan's investigation confirmed that her old boyfriend had killed her brother, Dan had been the one to tell Elaine. Their relationship had been cool and distant ever since.

"I called to let you know I talked to May yesterday. She said she was planning to bring Bobby and Bart down to the family gathering at Dad's house tomorrow. It's Mother's Day, in case you've forgotten."

"I haven't forgotten, Elaine. I plan to be there," Dan said slowly, trying to keep his cool. Bobby and Bart were his kids. It would be nice for everyone to see them, including himself.

"There's one more thing."

"What's that?"

"I don't want you upsetting May by giving her the third degree about her boyfriend."

"May's got a boyfriend?"

"You know very well she does. I'm asking you, for the benefit of the rest of the family, not to make an ass of yourself while she's here."

Dan clenched his teeth. The trial separation May had insisted on five years ago had become permanent when she had filed for divorce a couple of years ago. It occurred to him that his ex-wife had more clout with his family than he did. How did that happen? "Yeah, Elaine, I promise to behave myself."

"Well, good for you. Thank you very much." Click.

Dan slowly replaced the receiver and shook his head. "Good Lord have mercy. What next?" he wondered out loud as he grabbed his keys and headed out the door. There were two vehicles parked out front. One was the unmarked Ford Crown Victoria assigned to him by the sheriff after he had been promoted to lieutenant. The other was his personal vehicle, a black Chevy Silverado 1500 pickup truck. It was Saturday, so he headed for the pickup.

* * * *

Dan had been a deputy for the Creek County, Tennessee, Sheriff's Department for many years after having served as an officer in the Army military police corps. A couple of years ago, Sheriff Johns had promoted him from Sergeant to Lieutenant and placed him in charge of the department's newly organized Crime Investigation Department.

The understaffed Creek County Sheriff's Department found itself stretched to the limit to provide coverage twenty-four hours a day, seven days a week, for the entire unincorporated area of Creek County, Tennessee. Late-night coverage usually consisted of two deputies in separate vehicles, each patrolling several square miles. If either needed backup from the other, sometimes it was a very long wait.

The day shift was Dan's usual shift, but because he was in charge of the department's crime scene unit, he was sometimes called out in the evening or late at night. Dan loved his work, but it had cost him the only thing he loved more: his wife and kids.

Usually, the job didn't require Dan to work on Saturday morning, but since his divorce, he had settled into a Saturday routine that began with breakfast and a newspaper at McDonald's. When he was done with both, he would refill his coffee cup and take it to the Sheriff's Department to see if anything interesting had happened during the night.

On this Saturday morning, he walked into the station with his coffee and called out to the weekend dispatcher, "Morning, Doris." He smiled at the matronly woman who had been a fixture in the department for longer than he had been a deputy, maybe longer than he had been alive. "Anything new?"

"Morning, Dan. Lloyd Black was on the ten o'clock news last night. Did you see it?"

"Nope. Last I heard, he was still down in Kilby. What did he do to make the news?" Dan asked as he pulled the lid off his coffee cup and took a sip.

"Lloyd and two others escaped yesterday."

"Have they caught them yet?"

"Caught one. He and his girlfriend were in a motel outside Atlanta. The desk clerk recognized his picture on the local news and made the call. Haven't got a thing on Lloyd and the other one since we got this last night," Doris said, offering Dan a sheet of paper. "There's a chance Lloyd might be heading this way since his wife and kid still live around here. We sent Earl down there last night to talk to them. Mrs. Black said she hadn't seen him."

"Let me see what you've got," Dan said to the dispatcher. He took the information and, between sips of hot coffee, scanned it. Three inmates from the Kilby Correctional Facility east of Montgomery, Alabama, had been found missing at the eight o'clock count last night. Apparently, they had used broomsticks to hold up the bottom of a five-thousand-volt electric fence for each other. They had then climbed a razor wire fence that wasn't electrified and fled into the dense woods beyond. The authorities suspected transportation had been waiting for them on a two-lane road beyond the trees because the dogs had followed their scent to the road, and then lost it. The sheriff and state troopers had established roadblocks, and state helicopters had been used, but, so far, only one had been found. Dan scanned the information on each man. Lloyd Black was serving a long sentence for the armed robbery of a convenience store a few miles south of the Tennessee state line. The other two were serving life sentences for murder.

Dan glanced up at the clock. It was now nine o'clock Saturday morning. That meant Lloyd and the other one had already been missing for more than twelve hours. Not good. The longer it took to find them, the wider the net would have to be cast.

"Has Sheriff Johns seen this?"

"He was notified last night. I called him again a few minutes ago and told him there was nothing new. He knows Earl went down and talked to Mrs. Black last night. She let him look around, but he didn't find anything. Sheriff Johns said he'd be in later if anything came up."

"Has anybody checked with Mrs. Black this morning? Does she have a phone?"

Doris opened the phone book. "Black, L., 20 Wolfe Road, right?"

"That's probably her. Last time I saw her about four years ago, she and her boy were living in a mobile home on a gravel road just off Greenbrier Road."

"You want to call her?"

Dan looked up from the information sheet. "No, I'll go down there. I don't have anything to do this morning. Anything else?"

"Nothing yet. It must have been really quiet down at Uncle Buck's. We didn't get a single call."

Dan returned the information sheets to Doris, put the cover back on his coffee, and then grinned at the dispatcher. "Well, there's always hope for tonight."

"That's for sure. Saturday night is usually good for at least one call from that honky-tonk beer joint."

Dan turned to go. "I'll be down at Mrs. Black's place. Give me a call if you get anything new on Lloyd."

"Turn your cell phone on and I will," Doris said.

"The battery keeps going dead if I leave it on."

"Nobody can call you if you don't."

"That's the whole idea," Dan said, smiled, and turned to go. "Call me at Mrs. Black's number if you need me." He waved as he turned and walked away.

* * * *

The Creek County Sheriff's Department and county jail were on Pulaski Road, just east of Bailey Springs. Dan soon turned off Pulaski Road onto Boone Parkway to avoid downtown Bailey Springs. At the intersection with Greenbrier Road, he turned south onto it and headed toward the Alabama state line. After driving for almost ten miles on the winding two-lane county road, past cotton, corn, and soybean fields intermixed with small well-maintained brick homes, older mobile homes, a county high school, and a couple of mom-and-pop stores, he encountered a stretch of highway with woods on either side because the hills were too steep to cultivate. Soon he slowed at a cluster of three mailboxes on the left side of the road, and then turned onto the narrow gravel road just beyond. Roads like this were common in Creek County, Tennessee, where low-income people lived in run-down houses and decaying mobile homes.

It had been four years since Dan had reason to be on this road, but he still remembered that Lena Black and her son, Red, lived in the second mobile home off Greenbrier Road. He also remembered the abject poverty he had seen when he was here that Christmas Eve. He had gone to the Blacks' home to give Red the five-hundred-dollar reward for finding a hitchhiker's body.

Dan pulled his black 1999 Chevy Silverado 1500 pickup truck onto the bare dirt in front of the older single-wide mobile home. The one he lived in was a two-bedroom unit, about twelve feet wide and forty-eight feet long with about six hundred square feet of floor space. He thought this one was about the same size.

Things had changed for the Blacks since he had been here four years ago, and for the better. He remembered an old Chevy Caprice parked on the dirt out front. A much newer Ford Escort was now parked nearby and there were landscaping plants in the front yard and around the trees. He recognized azaleas and monkey grass. Several other shrubs and flowers looked familiar, but he didn't know their names. It looked like they were getting ready to plant something else, too. He could see a small area of fresh dirt in back of the mobile home. As he watched, a tall woman, dressed in blue shorts and an orange University of Tennessee T-shirt, appeared from behind the house, a shovel in her hand. She was slender from the waist up, but from the waist down, she appeared to have powerful thighs and legs. When she turned and saw an unfamiliar pickup truck in her front yard, she stopped and stared.

Dan glanced down at himself. He was driving his own truck, dressed in his usual Saturday morning blue jeans and golf shirt. Except for the badge clipped on his belt, and his pistol in his holster, she had no reason to believe he was a deputy sheriff on an official call. Dan reached for his black baseball-type cap with the sheriff's department logo, put it on, and dismounted from his truck. "Mrs. Black?" he called out. "Mrs. Lena Black?"

"That's me!" she called out. "What can I do for you?"

As he walked toward her, he said, "My name is Dan Warden. I'm a deputy with the Creek County Sheriff's Department. It's been a while since I've seen you. You probably don't remember me." As he came close to her, he smiled and extended his hand.

"Sure, I remember you. How're you doing, Mr. Warden?" Lena asked with a smile as she took Dan's hand in hers. Dan was surprised at how hard her small hand squeezed his.

"I'm doing fine, Mrs. Black," Dan said.

"What can I do for you this morning?" Lena asked.

"Well, I thought I'd stop by and see how you were doing," Dan said. He paused, and then said, "I believe a deputy came out last night and told you Lloyd had escaped from prison."

"Yeah, he did. I thanked him for coming by and letting me know," she said, then shook her head. "We ain't seen him."

Dan nodded and smiled. "I'm glad. I'm off duty this morning, but I thought I'd stop by anyway and see how you and Red were doing these days."

"We're doing just fine, thanks to you."

"I didn't do much."

"You got me the job at the store, and don't say you didn't, because I know you did. The manager told me the only reason he took a chance on me was because you asked him to. I sure do thank you for that."

"I was glad to help. How's it working out?"

"Well, the first job I had, restocking shelves, didn't work out too well, but then he let me work outside where all the plants and garden things are. I've been there ever since. I really like it."

"I saw some new plants around the front."

"Oh, yeah, those were all throwaways. Sometimes I'll bring something home we're going to throw out anyway. Sometimes it lives; usually it dies. I'm trying to get some roses to grow there beside the house, but they ain't doing too good. Every time I look at them, bugs are all over them, eating the leaves and buds. I wish I could grow rose bushes. If I had my way, I'd have this whole place covered with red roses."

Dan smiled. He had never met a woman who didn't like roses. "Looks like you're getting ready to plant something else," Dan said, pointing to the shovel she was holding.

"Oh!" Lena said with a start as she glanced down at the shovel. "Uh, yeah! I am. I was getting ready to plant some tomatoes back there," she said, pointing to the small plot of fresh-turned earth behind her.

"Need some help?"

"No, thanks. I only have ten plants. It won't take me too long. Red already dug it up for me," Lena said. "You remember my boy, don't you?"

"I sure do. His red hair is hard to forget."

Lena grinned. "It's red all right. He's grown some since the last time you saw him, though."

"I'll bet he has," Dan said with a wry grin on his face.

"Anyway, he's already dug up the ground so all I have to do is stick the plants in. It won't be too much trouble. Besides, I wouldn't want you to get all dirty just to help me plant a few tomatoes."

"I've been dirty before, Mrs. Black. I'd like to help if I could. I'm off duty."

Lena tilted her head to one side and silently gazed at the deputy sheriff. "Well, all right. Come on then . . . and call me Lena."

"My name is Daniel, but everybody calls me Dan to my face. Lord knows what they call me behind my back."

Lena laughed. "Well, Dan, you've got yourself a job," she said, offering the shovel to Dan. "I'll get the tomato plants out of the car." She paused, frowning as she looked at the pistol strapped on Dan's belt. "You think you're going to need a gun while you're planting tomatoes?"

Dan glanced down at his Glock 19 pistol, and then glanced back up at Lena. She was right. Ordinarily, a man didn't need a weapon to plant tomatoes. But this time it was different. A couple of escaped prisoners could show up at any time. Without a weapon, he would feel like a fool, and might wind up dead. Stranger things had happened to lawmen. He smiled and said, "You never know about tomatoes. I remember they made a movie once about tomatoes going on a rampage and killing everybody in town."

"Oh, yeah! I saw that one. Well, if you're going to protect me from these tomato plants, I guess you'd better keep your gun handy."

"It doesn't bother you, does it?"

"Well, maybe a little bit."

"I'll take it off if it really bothers you."

"That's all right. It doesn't bother me much. Besides, I like the idea of a big, strong man protecting me from my tomato plants."

Dan grinned, then burst out laughing. "Yes, ma'am. That's what I'm here for."

With Dan carrying the shovel and Lena carrying the plastic tray of tomato plants, they walked back to the newly dug soil that covered an area about six feet wide and eight feet long.

They spent a few minutes deciding exactly where to place the tomato plants. After marking the locations for the plants with small twigs, Dan began digging shallow holes and soon discovered the soil toward the center was much easier to penetrate than the soil around the edges. With so few plants, he suggested she plant all of them closer to the center and she agreed.

"Make sure it's buried deeper than it was," Dan suggested as he watched Lena lift one of the root-bound plants from its plastic containers.

"Oh, why?"

"I don't know why, but my mama always buries part of the stem in the ground when she plants tomatoes. She leaves a hole around it too, so when you water it, the water stays around the plant. Tomatoes need lots of water."

"Oh, I didn't know that. You're handy to have around. I might think up some more jobs for you when we're done here."

Dan focused on Lena's sparkling eyes as she looked back at him, her gaze unswerving. "Bring'em on," Dan said.

"I'd like to have a little bigger spot, so I could plant some other things. It's so rocky around here, though, I guess I'll have to be satisfied with my little tomato patch."

"I'm going down to Helleston for a family get-together tomorrow. If Dad isn't using his rototiller, I'll throw it in the back of my truck and bring it over next Saturday. It should do a pretty good job on this red clay dirt around here."

"Oh, I couldn't ask you to do that."

"I'm volunteering."

Lena smiled up at Dan. "Well, if you're sure you wouldn't mind."

"I live in a mobile home pretty much like yours, Lena. I get bored, not having anything to do on my days off," Dan said. Then he added, "I'm divorced. Have been for a while now."

"Oh, yeah?" Lena said, a hint of interest in her voice. Immediately, she changed her tone and added, "Oh, that's too bad." After a pause, she said, "I divorced Lloyd about three years ago."

"Oh, I didn't know," Dan said as he suddenly looked at Lena in a new light. He had noticed soon after he arrived that her breasts moved freely and independently beneath her T-shirt, suggesting she wasn't wearing a bra. He had tried to avoid looking at her chest, but now he made a point of appraising Lena's figure. He decided Lloyd Black's loss might be his gain, if he went about it the right way.

"Once I started getting regular paychecks, I got enough money together to pay a lawyer to do the job. Being married to a man who was going to be gone for thirty years didn't make much sense to me."

Dan nodded his head. "We thought you were still married to him. That's why we sent a deputy down last night when we found out Lloyd and two other inmates had escaped."

Lena concentrated on putting another tomato plant in the soft ground, then she looked up at Dan. "You really think he might show up here?"

"It's possible. They caught one last night over in Georgia, but nobody has heard from Lloyd or the other one. If all three stuck together, we'll find Lloyd and the other one in Georgia. If they've split up, there's no telling where Lloyd and the other one might be now." Dan paused for an instant and added, "That's why I thought it would be a good idea for me to keep my weapon handy, in case he showed up while I'm here."

Lena looked at Dan, smiled, and nodded her head. "What should I do if he shows up when you're not here?"

Dan thrust the shovel into the soft ground and said, "Keep your doors locked, and call nine-one-one. Do you have a gun in the house?"

"Red has Lloyd's old rifle he uses to hunt squirrels."

Dan nodded. He recalled Red waving at him with a rifle after he found the body in the ditch. While Dan was interviewing Red, he had taken a closer look at the rifle. It was an old Marlin 60, just like the one he'd had as a teenager. It was a fun gun to shoot. May made him get rid of it. He wished he still had it. "A twenty-two is good for shooting squirrels without destroying a lot of the meat, but it's not a very good defensive weapon. You can shoot a man in a lot of places with a twenty-two and all you're going to do is make him mad."

Lena nodded. "I can believe that."

"You can?" Dan asked.

"Uh, yeah. I've seen those little bullets. They're awfully small."

Dan looked at Lena, smiled, then took a card from his wallet and offered it to her. "Here. If you need to call me, my home number and my cell phone number are there. You might not get me on my cell phone, though. I usually keep it turned off."

"How long do you think it will take to catch him?"

"Most are caught within forty-eight hours, at a friend's or relative's home. They're usually looking for a place to hide, or transportation and money so they can keep moving."

"What happens if you don't catch Lloyd within forty-eight hours?"

"Then he'll be a lot tougher to find. Some go for weeks, months, sometimes years before they're caught."

"Well, I appreciate you looking out for me and Red."

"It's my job, ma'am," Dan said in a slow drawl.

Lena laughed at his bad imitation of a Texan.

When the tomatoes were planted, Lena thanked Dan for his help. Dan promised to return the following Saturday with a rototiller. As he backed his truck out onto the gravel road, Dan looked at the tall, good-looking woman waving to him. He smiled and waved back. He knew she was a high school dropout, living in a dilapidated mobile home, working at a low-paying job, raising a son on her own, with the stigma of being a convict's ex-wife hanging over her head. Yet, in the few minutes they had been together this morning, he sensed she had more self-confidence than any other woman he knew. From what he'd seen this morning, and from a couple of brief conversations he'd had with her boss at the store, Dan had gotten the impression she had the grit and determination to take anything life handed her without complaining or apologizing to anyone. He liked that in a woman.

As he drove off, Dan nodded and smiled. Maybe she was a little rough around the edges; that was all right with him.

He was, too. Then he remembered she had been divorced for three years. He wondered if she was as lonely for a little company at night as he was.

As Dan drove down the narrow gravel road toward Greenbrier Road, he saw an old Chevy Caprice coming toward him. As Dan approached the other vehicle, both drivers slowed and carefully guided their right-side tires onto the dormant grass and weeds on the shoulder while trying to stay out of the ditch a few inches farther away. When the contractor built the roadbed, he didn't anticipate that a full-size Chevy sedan and a full-size Chevy pickup might want to pass on it someday. The two vehicles were able to keep all wheels on the road surface without scraping paint or banging rearview mirrors, but just barely.

As they passed, Dan glanced at the other driver and saw a shock of brick-red hair. As he turned onto Greenbrier Road and headed back toward Bailey Springs, he smiled. He had just missed Red Black again. It was about par for the course. Red was as slippery as a greased snake. Whenever the sheriff's department caught Randy's gang up to no good, Red was never anywhere around. Dan nodded. One day they would catch him doing something. None of them got away with everything all the time.

DON'T WANT TO WAIT? HERE ARE MY BOOKS THAT HAVE ALREADY BEEN PUBLISHED.

JENNY CAY

A former Tennessee deputy sheriff and a woman in the DEA witness protection program try to outrun Bahamian drug smugglers.

EXCERPT FROM JENNY CAY

RICK WALKED OVER to the dying man, looked down at him, spat on him, and snarled, "*¡Pedazo de mierda!* You let a woman get the best of you!" Rick continued to look down at the man for a moment, then kicked him hard in the ribs. When he saw no reaction, he turned and looked at Dan and Jenny. "Now, what should I do with you two?"

Dan's mind had trouble processing what he had just seen. He had never seen a man kill another man in cold blood. He had killed a couple of men when he was a deputy sheriff, but that had been in a running gun battle, and they were trying to kill him at the same time. Not like this. The heavyset man simply pointed his weapon and fired, as though he were shooting at a paper target. Dan shook his head. There was no doubt about it. This was the end of the line.

A peaceful feeling came over Dan. It hadn't been a bad life. He hadn't done everything he had wanted to do, and he hadn't accomplished as much as he had wanted to do, and there had been a few things he might have done differently if he had a chance to do it all over again, but, all in all, it had been a good life. "Go ahead, you bastard," Dan said bitterly. "Whatever you're going to do . . .do it and get it over with."

Click here to download this book from my webpage:
http://larry.booklocker.com/

DIGGER

Deputy Dan Warden hunts for an elusive serial killer who leaves baffling clues. A woman who may be clairvoyant offers to help interpret the clues, but Dan's task becomes more difficult when a raunchy, homicidal ex-con shows up with his mentally challenged half brother. A personal agenda to reunite with his ex-wife and children adds to the pressure as Dan tries to close the case before the killer strikes again.

EXCERPT FROM DIGGER

THE KILLER PULLED OUT of the parking area and turned north. Ten minutes later, he turned his headlights off as he approached the farmer's pasture; then he found the well-used dirt road and drove the short distance to the illegal dump by moonlight. He parked near the edge of the big ditch, looked about for lights, then dropped the tailgate and opened the big black plastic bag enough to expose the dead woman's lower body. He removed her panties, wrote his number on her torso, then pulled the bag down and retied it.

After checking the area for lights once more, he picked up the bag and carried it to the edge of the big ditch. The killer paused for a moment with the weight of the woman's body in his arms, then dropped the bag. He watched it roll down the bank and come to rest on the refuse already there.

The killer gazed down at the big trash bag for a moment, trying to decide how he felt about the woman's death. He felt nothing. It was very disappointing. He had put a lot of time and effort into planning this one.

Click here to download this book from my webpage:
http://larry.booklocker.com/

THE ROGUE

Dan is asked to return to the Bahamas to help identify a rogue DEA agent. As a covert agent, Dan learns his life depends on his skills in identifying who's his friend, who's willing to sacrifice him for personal gain, and who wants him dead to avenge old grievances.

EXCERPT FROM THE ROGUE

CALLAS PAUSED, THEN SAID, "You will be asked to make no contact with anyone associated with the DEA in the Bahamas, or with the Royal Bahamas Police Force, or to identify yourself as a DEA representative to anyone there."

Dan frowned and his eyebrows went up. "You've got a rogue cop down there? One of your people is on the take?"

"We're not sure. We need a knowledgeable outsider for a week or two to assess the situation."

Dan chuckled. "Your timing is perfect, Callas. I had already cleared my schedule for some time off next week. I was planning to go to Alaska, but those plans got scrubbed."

"What's in Alaska?"

"Jenny Smart is, or was when I talked to her on Monday. I was thinking about going up to see her next week, but she said she was leaving town and didn't know when she would be back." Dan paused, frowning at Callas. "She's in your witness protection program. Do you know where she is?"

"No, I don't," Callas said honestly. "I wish I did."

"I'm giving odds on the Bahamas."

"It would be dangerous if she were there," Callas said.

"I agree, but danger has never stopped that woman from doing something."

Click here to download this book from my webpage:
http://larry.booklocker.com/

THE RAMPART ALERT

A woman kidnaps a baby from a shopping cart. In the weeks that follow, Dan Warden remains convinced that the child is alive. He joins in the hunt, while innocent lives for hundreds of miles around are devastated by the woman's action.

EXCERPT FROM THE RAMPART ALERT

Lieutenant Jason Rampart, a deputy for the Chickasaw County, Alabama, Sheriff's Department, heard his cell phone chime, saw that it was a call from his wife, and answered it. "Hi, Patsy. What's up?"

"He's gone!"

Jason frowned at the frantic voice. "Who's gone?"

"My baby!"

"Johnny? Johnny's gone? Gone where?"

"I don't know."

"Where are you?" Jason asked as he ran to his vehicle.

"At The Big Bag! He was in my shopping cart. Now he's gone!"

"Have you told the manager?" Jason asked as he started the engine and turned on his behind-the-grill emergency lights.

"He's right here. I guess he heard me screaming."

"Have you called nine-one-one?" Jason asked as he turned on his siren and pulled out into traffic.

"You're my nine-one-one!"

Click here to download this book from my webpage:
http://larry.booklocker.com/

SNOWBOUND

In 1952, David Hobbs is a wealthy charismatic psychopath. He's also a self-proclaimed hypnotherapist for friends and coworkers. While under hypnosis during therapy sessions, Hobbs' guests reveal misdeeds from their past that have caused someone's death. Hobbs intends to dispense justice himself by killing them and burying their bodies in the abandoned ice pit in the old farmhouse cellar.

EXCERPT FROM SNOWBOUND

Holding his protected left arm in front of his neck, Kyle looked up at his adversary, knowing Hobbs was about to kill him. He felt no fear, only regret that he had failed to save Debbie's life. If what Hobbs said was true, if they had met in a former life, then surely they would meet again in another life. If there was a God in heaven, when they met again, he would destroy this devil for all time.

Hobbs smiled as he looked down at his adversary. "So, this is the way it is to end between us this time. *Bon.*"

Kyle's eyes momentarily widened when he saw Debbie appear in the stable doorway less than ten feet behind Hobbs with a gun in her hands.

"Le coup de grace, mon ennemi," Hobbs said as he held his sword high with both hands while smiling down at Kyle, enjoying the moment of victory.

Kyle watched as Debbie raised the gun in both hands. Both men heard the metallic clicking sound as she cocked the hammer of the single-action revolver. Looking puzzled, Hobbs paused. The gunshot rang out in the quietness of the barn hallway.

Click here to download this book from my webpage:
http://larry.booklocker.com/

THE LOST PEOPLE

The sequel to SNOWBOUND is a slice-of-life story that spans many years before Kyle Lancer learns he must confront supernatural forces for the woman he loves.

EXCERPT FROM SNOWBOUND

As Kyle contemplated the emptiness of the high school football stadium around him, he recalled the night of the snowstorm when David Hobbs claimed the ghosts of the colonial farmhouse were lost souls because they had become lost on the way to their final destination.

Kyle nodded. Like those lost souls, there were lost people wandering through life not knowing where they were going or how they were going to get there. He knew he was one of them.

Click here to download this book from my webpage:
http://larry.booklocker.com/

Ingram Content Group UK Ltd.
Milton Keynes UK
UKHW010627050623
422889UK00001B/438